Mistaken

D0048213

Mistaken

First Impressions Are Never What They Seem

Karen Barnett

Abingdon fiction

a novel approach to faith

Nashville, Tennessee

Mistaken

ISBN-13: 978-1-4267-7449-2

Published by Abingdon Press, P.O. Box 801, Nashville, TN 37202
www.abingdonpress.com

The persons and events portrayed in this work of fiction are the
creations of the author, and any resemblance to persons
living or dead is purely coincidental.

Library of Congress Cataloging-in-Publication Data

Barnett, Karen, 1969-
Mistaken : first impressions are never what they seem / Karen
Barnett.
    pages cm
    ISBN 978-1-4267-7449-2 (binding: pbk., trade pbk. : alk. paper)
    I. Title.
    PS3602.A77584M57 2013
    813'.6—dc23

2013014893

Scripture quotations from The Authorized (King James) Version.
Rights in the Authorized Version in the United Kingdom are vested
in the Crown. Reproduced by permission of the Crown's patentee,
Cambridge University Press.

Printed in the United States of America
1 2 3 4 5 6 7 8 9 10 / 18 17 16 15 14 13

*To my parents, Ken and Janette Dunmire,
for teaching me to say, "Yes, I can."*

Acknowledgments

It takes a special person to be married to a writer. My husband, Steve Barnett, has taken on far more than his share of the load . . . of everything. Steve, I will never be able to write a hero that can hold a candle to you.

I am thankful for my kids, who have graciously allowed me to drag them to museums, car shows, historical societies, and antique stores. They have been wonderfully patient with their mom even when it means vacating the house so I can write.

Many wonderful writing friends have offered both critique and encouragement on this project, especially Connie Brzowski, Heidi Gaul, Marilyn Rhoads, Patricia Lee, and Tamera Bowers. Thank you for sharing your knowledge with me!

I am grateful for the many writing instructors and mentors from the American Christian Fiction Writers, Oregon Christian Writers and the amazing Mount Hermon Christian Writers Conference, especially Randy Ingermanson, Brandilyn Collins, Mary DeMuth, Tricia Goyer, and Lauraine Snelling.

I owe a huge debt of gratitude to the kind people of Port Angeles, particularly Kathy Monds and the staff of the Clallam County Historical Society, the Historic Joyce Depot

Museum, and Don Perry of the Port Angeles Underground Heritage Tour. (I apologize for my characters referring to Port Angeles as a "dirty mill town"—today it is a sparkling gem in the shadow of the Olympics.)

Thank you to my dear friend Sarah Sundin for her guidance with the pharmacy scenes and to Dr. Aaron David for helping me refine the medical scenes. As always, any errors are mine alone.

I could not have done this without the prayers and encouragement of my church family at Willamette Community. Thank you!

To my agent extraordinaire, Rachel Kent of Books & Such Literary Agency: your calming spirit has seen me through many anxious moments. I can't imagine walking this road without your wise guidance. And to my fellow Bookies—I love you all.

And finally, I will be forever grateful for Abingdon Press and their willingness to take a chance on a new writer in a tough market. I particularly want to thank Ramona Richards, Cat Hoort, Jenny Youngman, Susan Cornell, the fantastic art department, and everyone else who has worked behind the scenes to make this project a success. It's been a blessing working with you.

1

Port Angeles, Washington. 1926

LAURIE BURKE CLUTCHED THE STEERING WHEEL OF HER FATHER'S MODEL T as the car lurched down the deserted road toward the beach, the headlights barely denting the dark night. Rain spilled over the edges of the canvas top and soaked her coat, wetting her to the skin. The automobile plowed through a low bog, tires casting up a spray of muddy water.

If it weren't for her brother, Laurie would be asleep in her bed. She tapped her fingernails against the wheel and breathed a quick prayer. *One honorable man in my life—is that too much to ask, God?*

As the road veered to the west, tracing the coastline, Laurie slowed the automobile to a crawl, scanning the murky shadows for signs of life. A darkened vehicle waited on the side of the road. Perched near the edge of the bluff, the car's front wheels pointed in the direction of the Straits, not that one could see the water on a night like this.

Carefully, she guided the Ford in beside the other automobile. Empty. She hadn't expected to spot lovers necking in the front seat, but only fools would be out on a storm-swept beach in the dark of night.

Laurie twisted a long strand of beads as her stomach churned. She took a deep breath and closed her eyes. *Please God, don't let my brother be one of those fools.*

Hands shaking, she retrieved the flashlight, one of her father's prized possessions from his time in the Great War. In his current state, she couldn't imagine he'd notice it missing.

Before lifting the hood over her hair, she ran fingers through the short locks, still adjusting to the sensation of the cropped edges curling around her ears. She'd long admired the girls at work with their stylish bobs, so when Amelia had offered, Laurie jumped at the opportunity, even against her father's wishes. Now, with the cold air rushing down her neck, she felt like a freshly shorn lamb turned out to an icy pasture.

The wind pressed against the door as Laurie rattled the handle. With a mighty heave, she flung it open, her shoes squelching in the mud as she stepped to the ground. The gale sent her hood flying, chilly droplets pelting her face. The flashlight tumbled from Laurie's fingers as she turned her back to the wind.

Laurie wrestled the hood into place before scanning the ground at her feet. She crouched, feeling around in the muck until her fingers brushed the cold metal. With a push of the button, the light clicked on. Standing, she swung the beam in a wide arc, searching for the path that wound down the bluff to the beach. Images of long-ago summer picnics flooded her mind, the memory of mother's hand warm around hers, Johnny running ahead to be the first to the water's edge. The plan seemed sound earlier, but now her knees trembled. The tree branches above her head thrashed like a thousand arms waving her away. Laurie steeled herself. If her brother was on that beach, she wanted to know.

Movement near the other automobile drew her eyes and lifted the hair on her arms. She aimed the beam at the car— empty. She swung the flashlight in a protective circle, pausing at each suspicious shadow.

Just pretend it's a lovely summer afternoon. Laurie squared her shoulders and stepped away from the relative safety of her father's car. Her confidence lasted for all of six steps before she caught her toe on a tangled root and pitched forward, landing on her hands and knees in the mud. Tears stung at her eyes.

Johnny, I'm going to wring your neck when I catch up with you.

Laurie wrinkled her nose at the muck and pushed herself up to her knees. The flashlight created a comforting bubble of light around her.

It also helped her see the unexpected hand as it clamped onto her arm.

Laurie shrieked. Swinging the flashlight, she brought it down on the strange wrist with a loud crack.

The arm recoiled as a yelp rang through the dark night.

Heart pounding, she swung a second time, the glow illuminating the man's face just before the hard metal impacted it, the flashlight ricocheting from her fingers. Laurie scrambled backward, dragging her new coat through the mud.

"Wait, wait," a voice panted.

Laurie swallowed the urge to scream, her throat clenching. Could she find the car in the dark? And what good would it do? She'd never get it cranked in time.

The light blazed in her direction. She struggled to her feet, determined to put a safe distance between herself and this stranger.

"No, stop! I'm not going to hurt you!"

Laurie darted for the trees and threw herself into the ferns surrounding their bases, heart pounding.

"I was just trying to help. I'm sorry I frightened you." He pointed the flashlight under his chin, the light illuminating his features and pooling under the brim of his hat. "Please, come out."

The glowing face did little to reassure her. Laurie shivered in the brush. Which terrified her more—the strange man or the pitch-black forest? She cleared her throat. "Who are you?"

The light swung back toward her, glaring in her eyes. Laurie pressed lower into the dripping plants.

"My name is Daniel Shepherd. And I—well, as ridiculous as it sounds on a night like tonight—I was delivering something. I thought I saw lights out on the beach, so I stopped."

Laurie lifted her head. "Let me see your face again."

The stranger obliged. Not one of Johnny's mill buddies—a point in his favor.

Laurie struggled to her feet, her coat slimed with a combination of mud and pine needles.

The man remained motionless, pointing the light at her feet as if to guide her steps. "I *am* sorry."

She stopped a few feet away and stretched out her hand. "I'll need my light."

"Of course." He held it out, handle first. "I hope you won't be using it as a weapon this time."

She snatched it and scuttled backward.

He touched the red welt below his eye and winced. "Can I ask a question now?"

Laurie swallowed, willing her shaking knees to still. "Yes."

"Who are you—and do you know why those people are out on the beach during a rainstorm?"

"That's two questions." She scrutinized him in the flashlight's dull glow. The man's nice coat and hat set him apart from the typical Port Angeles mill-rats. Perhaps a banker or a doctor? He didn't look like trouble. *Sometimes a handsome face equals trouble.*

She held the light with one hand and jammed the other into her coat pocket for warmth. "Th-they're oyster picking."

The man's eyes narrowed. "Oysters?" His cheek twitched as if he fought a smile. "Of course." Rain dripped from the edge of his hat, the corner of his mouth curving upward. "Is this a good beach for . . . oysters?"

"The best." Laurie tipped the beam higher so she could get a clearer view of the dimple in his cheek. "Do you like oysters, Mr. Shepherd?"

"Well, I haven't had them in years, but I believe it's practically a staple around here, isn't it?" He lifted a hand to shield his eyes.

Laurie lowered her arm so the light puddled on the man's chest, illuminating the tie and jacket and the chiseled edge of his chin. "Yes. We love our oysters."

The rain pattered down around them, the silence growing awkward. She shook her head at the absurdity of the moment. "Does it strike you odd we're discussing seafood in the middle of the night?"

"In a rainstorm, yes." The dimple reappeared, accompanying a brief smile. "Perhaps we could discuss it another time?"

A flutter rose in her belly. "What do you mean?"

He took a step closer. "I mean to say, I hope we can speak again, sometime. In the daylight, of course." He tipped his hat back, providing a clear view of his face.

Nice face. Laurie shook herself. She needed to remember why she was here. Flirting with strangers wasn't on the agenda. "I should go. My friends might need help with their"—she cleared her throat—"their oysters."

"Would you like me to walk you down there?"

Laurie pulled her mud-splattered coat close. "I'm familiar with the trail, thank you." She took a step backward, hesitant to leave the warmth of their brief conversation.

"You didn't tell me your name." His soft voice crossed the space between them

"Laurie—Laurie Burke."

His eyebrows rose. "Burke? It's a pleasure to meet you, Miss Burke. I think I know some of your family."

Her hope faded like a candle snuffed by the rain.

"My name is Shepherd, I—"

"Yes, so you said. Now, if you'll please excuse me…" She spun on her heel, leaving him standing in the rain. The last thing she wanted to do was discuss her family.

"Good night, Miss Burke." His voice trailed after her.

The rain eased, but her shoes slipped along the leaf-strewn ground. Laurie chose her steps with care. She risked a quick glance over her shoulder, but Mr. Shepherd had been swallowed by the shadows. A twinge tugged at her heart. *It's for the best.* Still, meeting a handsome and mysterious stranger on the bluff brought a flicker of excitement to this otherwise discouraging night.

She picked her way down the steep trail. The sky cleared, a gusty wind driving the clouds from their places and the moon casting a dim radiance over the beach. Switching off her light, she allowed her eyes to adjust to the gloom.

In the distance, a lantern rested on the sand, illuminating the feet and legs of a small group of people gathered around two boats. The men hefted bulky, burlap sacks, stacking them on the ground. Crude voices and laughter rang clear in the damp air.

Laurie pushed her fingers deep into the pockets of her wool coat, all traces of warmth vanishing. She stalked toward the figures, the sand shifting with every step. Pausing a few feet away, she flicked on the flashlight, its beam slicing through the darkness. The men shouted, arms flying to shield their faces. Two dove over the side of the boat into the shallow surf. The burst of activity reminded her of kicking over rocks to watch crabs scuttle across the sand.

She directed the light at each individual in turn, recognizing several—from church, of all places. Her brother stood stock-still at the water's edge, a bag balanced on his shoulder, his hat pushed low on his head.

"Johnny." Her stomach twisted.

Squinting against the glare, he lowered the burlap sack onto the shore. "Laurie? Blast it all, girl—what are you doing here?"

A couple of heads popped up from the waves like sea lions.

Johnny strode to where she stood and wrenched the light from her as he swung his own in a wide arc around the beach. He turned on Laurie, eyes bulging. "Are you crazy? What were you thinking? You could get us all locked up."

Laurie folded her arms. "I was thinking my brother had more sense than to fall in with rumrunners. But I guess I was wrong."

Johnny grabbed Laurie's elbow and yanked her away from the boats. "How did you know?"

"I heard you on the telephone. I'd hoped you'd taken a real delivery job, not this sort of nonsense." She spit the words in his face. "What about Dad? Are you the one bringing him liquor?"

"Just shut up about it, will you? You know we need the money." He glanced up at the bluff. "How did you get out here?"

Laurie set her jaw. "I drove the Ford."

"Our lookout just let you waltz onto the beach? What is he doing, sleeping?"

Laurie's heart fell. *Daniel Shepherd—it figures.*

Johnny kicked at the ground, sending up a spray of wet sand. "Worthless piece of dung." He pushed his hands against his eyes. "Shoot, if you'd been a G-man you could have busted this whole operation wide open."

Laurie grabbed his arm. "That's what I mean. It's not worth the risk."

He shook her loose. "Go home, Laurie." Johnny turned and trudged away.

She stumbled and fought to regain her balance on the slippery rocks. "Maybe I should call those federal agents." Her voice rose over the roar of the wind.

When her brother rounded on her, Laurie gasped and darted toward the path. He caught her three steps later, his arm locked around her midsection, pinning her arms to her sides.

She shrieked as he spun her around, the icy gleam in his eye reminding her of their father. "Johnny, I'm sorry."

He grunted in response, hauling her to the grass at the bottom of the bluff. "Go home. And keep your trap shut."

Laurie wound her way up the path, swallowing hard against the lump in her throat.

Mr. Shepherd waited at the top. He reached out a hand as if to assist her in the final climb. "So, how are those oysters?"

A sour taste crawled up her throat. She brushed aside his hand. "I just remembered, there's a law against gathering oysters under the cover of darkness."

He glanced toward the pinpricks of lights on the beach. "Well, if it's the middle of the night, who's going to know?"

Laurie examined the man's rugged jaw and wide smile in the moonlight. If she'd met him on the streets of Port Angeles, she'd never have guessed he was a common criminal. "Doesn't make it right." She headed back toward the automobiles.

"I suppose there's a few men down there who might get hurt if somebody were to find out."

A prickle climbed Laurie's back. *A threat?* She pulled her coat close. "Then we'd better make sure nobody says anything."

Mr. Shepherd reached for the Ford's crank. "They won't be hearing it from me. I'd hate to see harm come to anyone." The engine rattled to life.

Laurie slipped into the driver's seat. "I think we understand each other."

He leaned against the automobile. "I actually don't like oysters, much, myself." His voice softened.

She stared at his hands, resting on the top rim of the door. *If only.* "Me, either."

The tires slithered through the mire as she backed out into the night. She wanted to get as much distance between her and her brother's mistakes as she could before dawn.

As the taillights disappeared into the night, Daniel shook himself. Johnny's kid sister had sure grown into a beautiful young woman. A shame she'd fallen in with rumrunners. Johnny, too, most likely.

He reached into his pocket and touched the coin he kept as a reminder of his past. He certainly couldn't cast any stones at the Burke family.

Welcome home, Daniel.

Blowing on his hands to warm them, Daniel turned toward his own automobile. He didn't relish getting back on that rutted, twisty road. Late night deliveries from the drugstore had never been a problem in Seattle, but out here in the sticks, it was a different story. Next time, he'd take Granddad's advice and tell them to wait until morning.

Daniel shook the moisture from his coat before climbing in the driver's seat. The rain had finally stopped and the sky lightened toward dawn. He stretched his arms up over his head. The long night had not been a complete waste. He closed his eyes for a moment, remembering the all-too-brief smile on Laurie Burke's face. *Oysters.* No one went to Crescent Beach for oysters. But, it definitely had natural beauty—even in the dark of night.

Johnny Burke's little sister. Maybe there's some hope for this old town, after all.

He reached down and switched on the ignition. The engine rumbled in response. Throwing one arm across the back of the seat, he eased the car backward onto the highway. When he turned forward once more, he paused. The headlamps cut a path through the dark night, exposing a car hidden in the brush, a shadowy figure reclining behind the wheel.

Daniel shook his head as he drove away. Apparently he and Miss Burke had not been alone, after all.

2

"LAURIE! YOU DID IT—YOU GOT YOUR HAIR BOBBED!" ANNE-MARIE'S shrill voice cut through the bright office.

Laurie stood on tiptoes as she tucked her bag up on the shelf above the coat rack, wincing as the stiff muscles in her neck complained. The headache had started behind her eyes during the long drive from the beach, but now it seemed to have spread throughout her body. Maybe she'd stop at Larson's Drugs after work and pick up some headache powders.

Anne-Marie and Susan swept into the coatroom, rushing at Laurie with wide smiles.

"Let me look at you." Anne-Marie reached out to touch Laurie's finger waves. "Don't you just love it? Oh, wait—let me see it with the hat." She pulled Laurie's cloche off the hook and plopped it on her head.

Laurie dug her toes into her shoes and waited while the young women fluttered around her.

"It's perfect, Laurie. Did Amelia cut it for you?" Susan glanced back at the workstations.

"Do you think she'd do mine, too?" Anne-Marie fingered a wisp of her strawberry blonde hair. "My mother will simply kill me." Her laugh bounced off the walls of the small room. "But I am an adult, after all."

The mention of mothers jabbed at Laurie's heart. She removed the hat, gripping the narrow, turned-down brim. "Well, at least I don't have to ask anyone's permission."

Anne-Marie's eyes widened. "What did your father say?"

Laurie ran her hand over her hair, checking the waves. "He thought it looked very smart." She hung the hat back on the hook. *More like, "Watch your smart mouth."* Laurie strode to her workstation.

Susan hurried to catch up with her. "Your hair looks adorable, Laurie, but the rest of you?" She clucked her tongue. "What's going on? Is your father ill again?"

How often had Laurie used that excuse? People were going to think her father was an invalid. "No, I've just had trouble sleeping. Headaches, mostly."

"Perhaps you should see Dr. Pierce."

Doctor Pierce dosed most of his patients with a generous serving of brandy. His bulbous red nose suggested he wasn't opposed to self-medicating. Laurie squeezed Susan's hand. "It's just a little headache, I'll be fine."

Sinking into her chair at the end of the long row of switchboards, Laurie settled the headset over her ears. She took a moment to press cool fingers against her temples, hoping to push the pain aside. Every time she closed her eyes, she pictured Johnny down at the beach, a load of whiskey at his feet, or her father when she arrived home—passed out on the sofa, an empty bottle clutched to his chest.

Six years had passed since the country went dry. How come everyone around her was sopping wet?

Her earpiece buzzed. Laurie cleared her throat. "Number please?" She grasped the cord, prepared to make the switch. Less than four seconds, like her boss always said.

"PA-1477. Mrs. Harold Murdock calling for Mrs. James Smith."

"Yes, Mrs. Murdock, I will connect you directly. Thank you." Laurie pushed the cord into the appropriate outlet with a click.

The rest of the day passed in a mind-numbing blur of voices, cords, and switches. At least it prevented her from fantasizing about a certain handsome stranger. Naturally, he turned out to be a low-life scoundrel—she drew them like mosquitoes. But it didn't mean she had to push up her sleeves and invite them to take a bite.

By quitting time, her head throbbed, eyelids dry as sand paper. Laurie shoved her arms into her coat sleeves. After a quick stop at Larson's drugstore, she'd head home to start dinner. She'd poured two cups of coffee down her father this morning to get him off to the mill before the whistle blew. By dinnertime, he'd be exhausted and hungry as a bear.

Laurie buttoned her coat, the fraying edges a reminder that her newer one was in need of a good sponging. She waved to the girls and stepped out onto Main Street, taking a deep breath of the fresh spring air. Thankfully the breeze blew the stench of the pulp mill out over the water and not into the streets.

She tucked her hands into her pockets and window-shopped down the street. The mercantile had beautiful spring hats on display, if only she could squirrel away a few more dollars from her paycheck. The blue one would likely do for another season. Maybe she could add a few silk flowers.

"Laurie!"

Laurie's spirits lifted as Amelia hurried down the street, a shopping bag perched on one hip, a pink sweater matching the blush in her cheeks. "I'm so glad to see you. I was hoping we could stop by Larson's and then walk home together. I have been craving a soda for days and your brother never seems to have time to take me anymore." Amelia shifted the bag to her other side.

"Another soda? We just went two days ago." Laurie steered the conversation away from her brother.

Her friend laughed as she caught her breath. "What can I say? I've got a sweet tooth."

"I only have a few minutes. I need to get supper on."

The women linked arms and walked down the street together. Amelia, at barely five feet tall, had to tilt her head to look up at Laurie's hair. "How did you do this morning? Did you style it like I showed you?"

Laurie touched her hat. "I was pretty busy getting Daddy ready, but I managed a few waves. Of course, this hat crushed most of my hard work. It's a little too snug."

Amelia's hand tightened on her arm. "How's Johnny?"

Laurie's heart ached. "He's—he's working a lot. I haven't seen much of him."

Amelia sighed and stared at the ground as they walked. "Me, either."

Planters loaded with sunny yellow daffodils lined the walk outside Larson's store. The door's cheery jingle never failed to inspire a flood of childhood memories. Laurie could almost taste the penny candy.

Old Mr. Larson added the soda fountain to the drugstore last summer, creating an immediate sensation in the small community. Even the grizzled old loggers from the lumber camps came dragging out of the woods to perch on Larson's cherry-red stools and sip the bubbly concoctions.

"Well, if it isn't Miss Burke and Miss White." Miles Larson ran a washcloth down the long marble counter. "Peas in a pod, you two are!"

Laurie smiled. "It's good to see you, Mr. Larson."

The older man adjusted his glasses. "It's always a treat when you young ladies stop by. Have you come to pick up your father's prescription, Laurie?"

Laurie bit her lip. That was the last thing her father needed. "No, sir. Amelia and I just thought we'd stop in for a soda."

"Well, you look like you could use a little pick-me-up with those dark circles under your eyes. You aren't coming down with something, are you?"

She settled herself onto a stool. "No, I'm fine—just a little headache."

"Well, they say that soda is the best thing for that. The bubbles help to ease the tension and the sugar gives your spirits a lift at the same time." He pulled two tall glasses from the shelf. "How about a cherry cola?"

"That sounds perfect, Mr. Larson."

He added syrup to the glass as he looked over the top of his wire-framed glasses at Amelia. "And a cherry phosphate for you, like usual, young lady?"

A bright smile crossed Amelia's face. "No, not today. A green river, I think."

Mr. Larson topped Laurie's drink with seltzer water. "Trying to keep me guessing, are you?" He wiped the edge of the glass with a napkin and added a straw before setting it on the counter.

Amelia's giggle bubbled over like the soda. "I thought I'd try something new."

As Mr. Larson reached for the lime syrup, he glanced up at Laurie. "That's a new haircut, isn't it?"

Laurie tucked a wave behind her ear. "Yes. Just yesterday, in fact."

"I cut it for her, Mr. Larson." Amelia beamed. "Doesn't she just look divine?"

The pharmacist grinned. "It looks just fine, ladies. It might just take some getting used to for an old fellow like me. The fashions these days . . . women trying to look like men with their short hair, men wearing trousers so baggy they look like skirts. I don't understand it, but I guess I don't have to, do I?" Mr. Larson placed Amelia's drink in front of her.

Laurie touched her hair and glanced at her reflection in the mirrored back of the soda fountain. She hoped she didn't look like a man. Movement drew her attention. Speaking of men—a dark-haired one with broad shoulders was approaching from the back of the store.

Mr. Larson leaned forward. "Ladies, I don't know if you would remember my grandson . . ."

Laurie stared at the mirror, a flush creeping up her neck. The man's smile was unmistakable—even in the daylight.

When her intense blue eyes locked on him, every intelligent word disappeared from Daniel's mind. He'd been trying to forget the woman all day and now she sat, just three feet away, golden-brown hair glinting in the low-angled rays of sunshine drifting through the large front windows. She sat with her back straight, shapely legs curved around the side of the stool's center post.

If only he'd inherited his grandfather's gift for small talk. After fifty years behind the drugstore counter, Granddad knew everyone in town and the fastest way to put them at ease. The skill kept customers flocking to his business and ignoring his competitor on Third Avenue.

A bell-shaped hat cupped around Miss Burke's face, framing her cropped hair and intensifying her gaze. Her lips parted ever-so-slightly and a pink blush spread across her cheeks.

Her companion spun the stool around to face him. "You're Mr. Larson's grandson?" A pair of warm brown eyes sparkled as she grinned at him, a spray of freckles dancing across a heart-shaped face.

Granddad stepped out from behind the counter and clasped Daniel on the shoulder. "Yes, this is my grandson, Daniel Shepherd. He grew up here, but ran off to the University of Washington as soon as he was of age."

The young woman held out her hand. "I'm Amelia White."

Daniel cleared his throat and took her hand. "It's a pleasure."

Miss Burke swiveled on her stool, the blue of her eyes stealing the air from his lungs.

Miss White, apparently unaware of Daniel's predicament, slid off her seat still grasping his hand. "Mr. Shepherd, this is my friend, Laurie Burke."

Daniel managed a nod. His throat had gathered cobwebs. He coughed once before speaking. "I think Miss Burke and I have already met."

Miss Burke's eyes widened, the blush on her cheeks darkening. "No, I don't believe we have, Mr. Shepherd."

Obviously she wouldn't admit to meeting him. He reached into his pants pocket and took hold of the coin inside, running it between his fingers as he thought. "I'm sorry. You looked familiar to me, but I must be mistaken."

She fidgeted and shook her head, causing her wavy hair to bounce against her pink cheeks.

Daniel searched for the perfect mixture of words to neutralize the awkward moment. "I know—you're related to Johnny Burke, right? He and I went to high school together."

Miss Burke lips pulled back from her teeth. Apparently he'd just stepped from one viper's nest to another.

Miss White's features, on the other hand, lit up like a light bulb. "You know Johnny? Why, that's Laurie's brother!" She turned to Miss Burke, bouncing on her toes. "Laurie, he's a friend of Johnny's. We should get them together. Maybe we could all meet somewhere for dinner or something."

Laurie Burke turned to her friend. "Amelia, I think I've had enough soda." She stood, reaching for her pocketbook.

Her friend caught her sleeve, a pout springing to her lips. "No, Laurie, please stay longer. What about your headache?"

"I feel much better now and I really should get home." She slid a nickel onto the counter for her drink.

Daniel leapt on a new tactic. "I could mix you up something—for your headache, I mean."

She glanced at him, eyes narrowed. "No, thank you. I'm fine."

Granddad wiped the counter with a damp cloth. "Before you go, Miss Burke, let Daniel fetch your father's prescription. I'm sure Ray would appreciate it if you brought it with you."

Finally, a way to get back into the lady's good graces. Daniel hurried across the store and slipped behind the druggist counter, checking under the counter for packages. Bottles stood in a neat line, names handwritten on the labels. He crouched down, balancing on his heels. "Burke, Burke . . ." He pushed several containers aside before spotting one marked with a government seal. Amber-colored liquid washed against the glass walls as he pulled it closer.

WHISKEY, PROOF 100. For Medical Purposes only. Sale or use for other purposes will cause heavy penalties to be inflicted. Patient: Raymond Burke. Physician: Dr. Philip Pierce.

His throat clenched. His grandfather dispensed alcohol? Daniel shook his head. *So does every drugstore from here to Florida.* His fingers curled around the neck of the bottle, the smooth glass warm and familiar in his grasp. Too familiar. Sweat broke out across his palm as his hand trembled. Gripping the bottle, he straightened.

Miss Burke had followed him across the store. He plunked the bottle down on the pharmacy counter, the sound echoing through the quiet store. The young woman flinched.

A chill descended on Daniel, as if he'd stepped into a cold rainstorm. *I thought I left this all behind in Seattle.* He released the bottle's curves, pushing his hand into his pocket and pressing the smooth-edged coin into his palm. *Give me strength, Lord.* "Raymond Burke? Is that your father's name?"

A tiny crease puckered between her brows. "Yes."

The woman he had spent so much time thinking about today not only associated with bootleggers, but also bought alcohol at the drugstore. Daniel frowned. "I'll slip it in a bag for you."

⊙━━◆━━⊙

Laurie snatched the package from Mr. Shepherd's hand, her eyes stinging.

Mr. Shepherd leaned across the counter and lowered his voice. "I'm glad to see you got home all right."

Laurie drew in a quick breath. "I can take care of myself."

"I see that."

Her heart thudded in her chest. He already knew about Johnny—now he knew about her father, too.

"Tell Johnny I said hello."

Mr. Shepherd's gray eyes reminded Laurie of darkening storm clouds just before a lightning strike. She could still hear his words from last night: *I wouldn't want anyone to get hurt.*

Mr. Larson was such a sweet old man. Didn't he realize his grandson was a scheming rumrunner and gangster?

As she stared into the handsome face masking the heart of a scoundrel, Laurie straightened her shoulders. If Daniel Shepherd believed she would be easily intimidated, he was dead wrong. She'd lived with her father long enough to learn a thing or two. She set the bag down, placed both palms against the counter and leaned forward. "Does your grandfather know what you are?"

The color washed from his face. "What do you mean?"

It was too late to play innocent. She recognized a crook when she saw one, and she wasn't going to let him bully her into submission. "You know exactly what I'm talking about, you and your midnight deliveries."

His brow furrowed, which only made his gray eyes more startling.

Laurie snatched the bag and turned away, stashing the bottle under her coat.

3

THE BACON HISSED AND BUBBLED, ITS RICH SCENT WAFTING UP INTO Laurie's face as she leaned over the stove. She turned it carefully with a fork, pulling back just as a splatter of grease popped free of the pan. A golden stack of pancakes waited in the oven.

Laurie swept her drawing papers into a neat stack at the end of the kitchen table, out of the reach of accidental spills and smears. Her mouth dried as she stared at the top sketch. The unsettling image had demanded to be recorded, not releasing her until she'd put pencil to paper. A shadowy stranger in the foreground gazed out over the windswept bluff and down to the straits, where two boats floated on the waves.

Heavy footsteps clomped on the back porch. Laurie dropped the paper on top of the sketchbook, scurrying back to the stove.

The back door window framed her father's weary face, bushy brows squeezed together and low over his granite-colored eyes. Her heart skipped as he wrestled with the knob.

She sped across the shabby yellow floor and yanked the door open.

Father's hunched shoulders straightened as he stepped over the threshold. "Why did you lock the door, girl? You knew I was on my way home."

Laurie bit her lip. The door hadn't been locked, but she knew better than to say so. "Dinner's ready. You hungry?"

He grunted. "I'm so hungry that I could eat the plate and silverware along with whatever's on them." He sucked in a deep whiff through his nose. "Is that bacon?"

Laurie nodded. "And coffee, too."

He set his tin lunch bucket down on the counter with a clatter and sank down in the kitchen chair. He lifted a cup. "Fill 'er up."

Laurie relaxed. The one thing that could get her father in decent spirits was dinner—especially if she served breakfast foods. He could be in the foulest of moods and a geyser of complaints, but he rarely grumbled about hot food. Assuming she had it ready when he walked in the door, she could count on him being good-tempered—at least as long as the food lasted.

She tipped the coffeepot, sending a stream of the dark brown liquid into his cup. "How was your day?"

He pulled the cup to his lips and blew gently across the surface of the earthy-smelling brew. A grunt followed. "Don't ask." His grizzled brows pulled low over his eyes.

Laurie gripped the warm platter of hotcakes with a towel and set it down in front of him, adding the pile of bacon to the side of the plate. She pulled a lump of butter from the icebox and placed it on the table next to the molasses and applesauce. Stopping for a moment to lean on the back of one of the chairs, she studied her father's face. Lines crossed his brow and circles darkened his eyes. His late night couldn't have helped his outlook at work.

"Your brother was late, again." He scooped up a spoonful of applesauce and slathered it on his stack of pancakes.

Laurie fetched the cinnamon from the spice rack, placing it at her father's elbow before he thought to ask for it. Her shoulders tensed at the mention of Johnny. Did Dad know what her brother was doing?

Dad's fingers closed around the bottle and he slid the cap off, adding a dusting to his applesauce. He set the bottle down without bothering to replace the cover. "He'd better be more careful. The big man don't take kindly to the boys turning up late and hung over." The edges of his eyelids were rimmed with red from his own late-night pursuits.

Her stomach leapt. "Johnny was hung over?" She dropped into the nearest chair. Even at the worst of times, Johnny rarely drank. She'd assumed he'd gotten into rumrunning for the money, not the booze.

"Most of the boys were, anyway. Don't rightly know about him." Her father ran a big hand through his thinning hair. "But he was late."

Laurie leaned back, releasing the breath she held trapped in her chest. She didn't need another drunk in her life. As long as Johnny still had some good sense in his head, maybe she could talk him out of this rumrunning business.

"That a new picture?" Dad nodded at her stack of drawings as he shoved a forkful of pancake into his mouth. "Let me see."

She picked up the drawing and held it out.

A flash of recognition crossed his face. "Crescent Beach, ain't it? We used to go out there for picnics, back . . ." His voice faded and his eyes clouded.

Laurie slid the drawing back into the notebook and closed the cover. *Back when Mama was alive.*

She stood and walked to the stove, her eyes glazing as she stared at the grease-filled frying pan waiting to be washed. The odor of scorched bacon fat filled the air.

The squeak of the chair legs sliding across the kitchen floor sounded behind her. Father's voice cracked. "We should go out there again . . . sometime." He walked from the room, leaving her in silence.

Laurie turned and faced the dishes, still half-filled with pancakes and applesauce.

It was going to be a long night.

❦

Daniel sorted through stacks of boxes in the cluttered storeroom while his grandfather locked up. Daniel picked up one miniature glass bottle, the label so faded he couldn't even read it. Blowing gently, he sent a puff of dust into the air. He placed it back on the shelf, making a note to talk to Granddad about some of the junk back here.

He still hadn't broached the topic of dispensing alcohol. Daniel ran his hand through his dark hair, his throat tightening.

He closed his eyes, remembering Laurie Burke's pursed cherry-red lips as he handed her that bag—as if she'd rather touch a dead snake. That woman was a puzzle with a few pieces missing. Her words echoed in his ear. *Does your grandfather know what you are?* Daniel shook his head. There's no way she could know about the life he'd left behind.

He gazed at the gleaming line of bottles along the bottom shelf. His stomach churned. Perhaps it wasn't a good idea to be alone back here.

The sound of shuffling footsteps raised Daniel out of his thoughts. His grandfather swayed unsteadily under the crate of glasses.

32

"Here, let me get that." Daniel rushed over to rescue the crate.

"Thank you. Those get heavier every day." Granddad released his hold on the box, letting it sink into Daniel's waiting arms. He squeezed his fingers into a fist and shook them loose. "My hands are aching a bit. I think I'll grab a few aspirin."

Daniel set the crate on an empty shelf in the storeroom. "Things were busy at the fountain today. How do you keep up with that and with the prescriptions?"

"I had a high school gal helping out for a few months, but she got behind in her studies and had to quit." He opened a drawer filled with pain remedies and pulled out a few aspirin tablets. "Business really picked up after we added the fountain. I had my doubts when you first suggested it, but the place has been buzzing like a beehive ever since."

Daniel stretched his back, aching after the long day of compounding prescriptions at the pharmacy counter. "You need to hire a soda jerk or two, Granddad. There's far too much work for you to do by yourself. There's too much for *two* of us to do. The store's not a one-man operation anymore."

"I know, I know. I've got a few young folks coming in tomorrow. Why don't you talk to them?"

"All right." Daniel paused, watching as his grandfather slipped the aspirin into his mouth. "How many of those are you taking a day?"

The older man frowned. "Don't start."

"Would you rather I ask how many bottles of liquor do you sell a week?"

"I wondered how long it would take for you to ask about that." He leaned against the row of shelves. "Just about every drugstore in America is selling medicinal liquor, Daniel. Some are making a killing off it. I'm not fond of the idea and I don't encourage folks to buy it. But if we refuse to sell alcohol, it will just give folks another reason to go to our competition."

Daniel ran a dusting cloth along the newly organized shelf. "What about people who don't have a medical reason for buying it?"

Granddad shook his head. "That's not our place to say. Take it up with their doctors. We just fill the prescriptions, we don't write them. Not everyone who tips the bottle has a problem with it."

Daniel looked away, a sudden weight crushing his chest.

"Come on, son. Tell me you didn't sell alcohol in that big fancy drugstore in Seattle."

"Of course we did, but I still didn't like it. And that wasn't my store."

His grandfather's eyebrows rose. "And neither is this."

"I didn't mean—"

The older man flapped his knobby fingers like he was brushing away an annoying mosquito. "I know what you meant. But, it's still my store and I make the decisions. I'm the responsible party—I'll even take care of all the liquor prescriptions if it will make you sleep easier." He crossed his arms. "And when it's your store, you can run it into the ground with your morality if you choose. Just remember, it's God's place to judge. Not ours."

Daniel went back to straightening the shelves as his grandfather left. He clenched the damp cloth and scrubbed at a dark stain on one of the back shelves.

⌖

"Laurie!" Her father's slurred shout echoed off her bedroom walls.

Laurie shook her head, trying to clear the sleep from her mind. She'd been dreaming of walking along the beach in the dark. A man had been waiting just ahead in the moonlight.

Now a very different figure stood silhouetted in the light pouring in her bedroom door. Laurie blinked and sat up, clutching at her sheet. "Dad? What's wrong?"

He staggered a few steps into the room. "Where's my bottle?" His ragged voice suggested he'd already finished one.

She slid out from under the covers and snatched her robe off the end of the bed, the floorboards icy under her bare feet. "It's late. Why don't you get some sleep?"

He gripped the doorframe. "Don't treat me like a child. I'm the father here and I'll have your respect, girl. Now, where'd you hide it?"

Her thoughts raced. She'd stashed the pharmacy bottle on the back porch, hating the idea of bringing it into the house.

When she didn't answer, he slammed his hand against the wall making Laurie jump. "I'm not asking you again!"

"I'll go look for it."

He stumbled backward leaving a path for her.

Laurie slipped past him and out into the bright hallway. Rather than heading for the stashed booze, she walked into the kitchen and dug through the cupboard, rattling the dishes as she stalled.

Her father sank down onto the sofa with a grunt. "Why don't you get me a sandwich while you're at it?"

"Sure." She pulled out a plate. "How about a glass of milk to help you sleep?"

He yawned in response.

Quietly, she eased the mustard and leftover ham from the icebox. A little food wouldn't hurt his mood. He'd barely touched his supper. She pushed the hair out of her face and fought the urge to yawn, herself.

Taking a quick nibble of the ham, she spread a thick layer of mustard on the brown bread and glanced over at her dad. His eyelids listed. She slowed her hands, using the knife to draw patterns in the mustard. After a few minutes, soft snores signaled her success.

Laurie set down the knife and braced her hands against the counter. *Thank you, Lord.* She finished preparing the sandwich and tucked it in the icebox next to the milk bottle, ready for the morning. Laurie turned and faced her father, licking the mustard from the tip of her finger as she gazed at him, slumped against the cushion.

Mama's picture sat on the end table, her blue eyes smiling through the shadowy room. For a brief moment Laurie was a little girl, clutching Johnny's hand at the funeral and listening to the hushed whispers floating above their heads.

Her father had run from his grief—straight to the Great War.

Laurie wiped her hands on the dishtowel and tiptoed across the room to pick up the tinted photograph. *So beautiful.* She ran her fingers through her own short locks with a jolt of regret.

She placed the photo back on the table and lifted Mama's crocheted afghan from the rocking chair. Laurie unfolded the heavy blanket and draped it over her father. She crept over to the lamp and clicked it off.

A voice slurred through the darkness. "Where's my sandwich?"

Laurie's shoulders fell. "I thought you were asleep."

"You're so slow, it's no wonder I dozed off."

She turned to see him rising from the sofa. His fingers wove through the afghan, lifting it to his face before tossing it to the floor. His eyes darkened.

"Forget the sandwich. Just get my bottle."

"No." As soon as the word slipped past her lips, she regretted it. A cold sweat broke out across her skin

"What did you just say to me?" Father's fingers curled into a fist as he swayed on his feet.

"You don't need more to drink. You've got to work in the morning. If you miss another day, they're going to fire you and what's going to happen to us?"

He pointed a finger her direction. "You shut your trap, girl. I won't have you backtalking me."

Her eyelids burned from the held-back tears. She braced a hand against the wall. She knew better than to throw fuel on flames, but exhaustion muddied her thoughts. "And I won't be giving you that bottle."

His hand closed over the framed picture on the table and flung it.

Laurie flinched as it exploded against the wall above her head, shards of glass raining onto her hair. Mama's face fluttered to the floorboards. Laurie reached for the picture, as her father's hand closed around her shoulder and forced her back against the wall.

"You won't be talking to me that way. Now, get me that bottle." Her father shoved her down the hall toward the kitchen.

Laurie closed her eyes, just long enough to take a breath. She strode to the back door and flung it open, the cold night air blasting against her face. Walking to the bench, she lifted the faded cushion and retrieved the brown drugstore bag.

Her father loomed in the doorway.

"Here." She thrust it toward him. "Take it."

He glowered a moment before ripping the bag from her hands, stepping inside, and slamming the door in her face.

She touched the wooden door as moths fluttered around the porch light. A loud click sounded as the lock turned.

A lump rose in her throat. "Dad . . ." She pounded her fists against the door, rattling the hinges.

The window went dark.

Laurie woke to her brother's hand shaking her shoulder. She lifted her head from the wicker bench, her back complaining at the sudden movement. Her robe and hair were damp with morning dew.

"Laurie, what are you doing out here?" Johnny crouched and slid a hand under her elbow, helping her unfold her limbs and rise to a sitting position.

Her head swam. What was she doing? The night flooded back.

Johnny sat on his heels, eyes stormy. "Dad?" When she nodded, he sprang up and strode to the back door. The pounding tore through the quiet morning air.

"Johnny, stop! Everyone will hear you."

His hand rattled the locked knob. "Oh, like they don't know?" He scowled and rapped on the door a second time. "You can't keep covering for him. I'm getting you out of here. Come live with me."

"I will not." Her throat tightened. "What makes you any better? You're sneaking off at night with your rumrunning cronies. Do you expect me to believe that you're not drinking, too?"

Johnny kicked the door. "I'm nothing like him."

"Besides, you live with a bunch of guys from work."

"I'll get my own place." He turned away and struck the door a last time.

The curtains pulled back from the window and Dad's face grimaced. The door swung open. "Why are you making such an unholy racket? My head feels like I got hit with a sledge already."

Johnny pushed past him. "Yeah, and why is that, Dad? Why did I find Laurie sleeping on the back porch?"

Laurie stood shivering in the morning breeze as the two faced off. Her father turned to her with a blank look.

"You lock yourself out?" He reached out a hand. "Get in here, girl. Why didn't you wake me? I've gotta' scoot or I'm going to be late."

"Dad," Johnny glared at his father. "You did this. You locked her out here when you were drunk."

Her father's face paled in the morning light. "You don't know what you're talking about." He set his jaw. "Laurie, get in here before you catch your death."

Laurie slipped past them, putting her hand on Johnny's arm to stop further argument. "It's not worth it."

She hurried through the house, stopping in the hall at the sight of the broken frame lying on the floor. She bent down and lifted the photograph, shaking loose the jagged pieces of glass. She carried the picture to her room and hid it in her dresser drawer. A quick glance at the clock confirmed she only had twenty minutes to clean up the mess and get ready for work. Pulling on a dress and a warm sweater, she rubbed her arms to stop the shivering.

Her father appeared in the doorway, shoulders stooped.

She unpinned the wave combs from her hair, keeping her eyes down. *Here it comes.*

He took a hesitant step inside. "I'm—I'm sorry about last night. I didn't know you were out there."

Laurie jabbed a bobby pin into a curl, securing it so it curved seductively over her eyebrow. She glared at him in the mirror as she watched him turn away. *Of course you didn't.*

4

DANIEL HEFTED THE TEARDROP-SHAPED SHOW GLOBE INTO PLACE BY THE drugstore window, suspending it from the silver chains connected to a bracket on the wall. The brilliant blue liquid sloshed gently in the glass casing, the morning sunlight setting it sparkling like a deep tropical sea. Tropical seas sounded pretty good about now. Anywhere but Port Angeles sounded pretty good, in fact. His eyes watered from the mill stench drifting in the early morning air.

He wiped the glass with a damp cloth and stood back to admire the look.

The owner of the pharmacy in Seattle had scoffed at such old-fashioned symbols. Now, seeing it hanging in his Granddad's window, a swell of pride rose in Daniel's chest. He still remembered leaning against the counter as a small child watching as his grandfather mixed the chemicals, magically turning the liquid into a dark blood red or a dazzling emerald green. He loved guessing which mixtures of chemicals would create each hue. By his twelfth birthday, he'd mastered all the recipes.

A flash of blue outside drew Daniel's eye. His pulse quickened as he recognized Laurie Burke, her blue dress a perfect complement to the freshly mixed globe.

Does your grandfather know what you are? Her words haunted him. He deserved an explanation. Daniel rapped on the window, catching her attention. He gave the show globe one final wipe with the polishing cloth before stepping down from the window display and hurrying through the front door.

Laurie Burke's cool gaze sent goose bumps climbing his arms. He gestured to the window. "What do you think?"

She darted a look at the blue globe. "It's lovely. My favorite color."

He couldn't help staring as her eyes mirrored the exact shade of sapphire he'd spent the morning concocting. "It looks good on you." The words slipped out before Daniel could stop them.

The young woman took a quick breath, her hand fluttering to her chest.

Daniel scrambled for words. "Your dress—and, and . . ." he swallowed, " . . . and your eyes."

She glanced down as if she had forgotten what she was wearing. "Oh, yes." A pink glow touched her cheeks. "Well, thank you . . . Mr. Shepherd."

Change the subject, you idiot. "I mixed it myself—the show globe. It's copper sulphate, water, and ammonia." *Chemicals, really? Is that going to impress the lady?*

She gazed back at the window. "It's perfect—like the straits on a warm summer day."

"It's been a while since I've seen it during the summer. My grandfather has a boat and he used to take me sailing when I was a boy. And my mother and I would picnic at Crescent Beach . . ." His voice trailed off, the recent memory of standing on the bluff with a mysterious young woman scattering his childhood recollections. He cleared his throat. "Yes, well. Maybe sometime we can—"

She broke in. "Excuse me, Mr. Shepherd, but I really must get to work."

His heart sank as she walked away. "All right, have a nice day." He lifted a hand in farewell and stood and watched until she disappeared into the switchboard office, two blocks away.

The sudden realization hit him like a rock between the eyes. He'd meant to confront her about her callous accusation the other day. Instead he'd complimented her dress and her eyes and nearly asked her out on a date. He pressed his fingers against his eyelids. This woman had a strange effect on him.

Granddad's smiling face appeared in the window. He pulled the door open. "Well, well—pretty little thing, isn't she?"

Daniel straightened his tie. "I suppose."

"Bright blue eyes."

"Uh-huh." Daniel stepped past him, into the store.

"Seems like you've taken a fancy to that color." Granddad nodded toward the show globe.

Daniel ignored the teasing as he made his way over to the coffeepot and filled a mug for himself. "You want some?"

His grandfather smirked as he removed his glasses from his shirt pocket and slipped them on, hooking them behind his ears. "There are a lot of pretty girls in this town. Aren't you glad you took my offer?"

Daniel lifted the steaming cup. "There were plenty of women in Seattle. I came here for you, remember? I'm just here to help out until you hire a manager. I'm not looking for any long-term entanglements."

The older man chuckled. "You say that. But I think small town life might agree with you." He leaned back against the counter. "And you know it's my dream that you take over the shop. I agreed to the short-term deal to get you up here. Now

I'm counting on Port Angeles's charms to make you want to stay."

Daniel took a sip of the coffee, grimacing as the liquid scalded his throat. "And what kinds of charms could an old mill town like this one offer?"

"I've noticed quite a few lovely ladies coming by lately, and I imagine the number will be growing over the next few weeks."

"And why is that?"

His grandfather laughed, well-worn lines forming around his eyes and mouth. "I don't think they are coming to see me." He lifted his cup.

The door jingled and two rosy-faced teenage girls sauntered in, busy with whispers and giggles.

Daniel gulped down his coffee, attempting to ignore his grandfather's chuckle.

"Yes sir, Port Angeles has many charms, Daniel. Many charms."

❦

Laurie tucked a loose wisp of hair behind her ear. She closed the door behind her, taking a deep breath of the stuffy air in the switchboard office.

She must be mistaken. That man couldn't have been preparing to ask her out on a date. She shivered. As if she would go anywhere with a rotten rumrunner, even if his dimpled smile made her knees melt. There had to be someone out there who was decent, trustworthy, and not connected with booze in any way. *Of course it wouldn't hurt if that someone looked like Daniel Shepherd.*

She buttoned her sweater up to her neck. Even though the office was warm, Laurie's arms and legs ached with the cold. Little wonder after spending the night on the back porch. If only she could keep her father from drinking. Maybe she should have a conversation with Dr. Pierce and convince him to stop writing those prescriptions for her father.

Laurie pasted a smile on her face as she waved at the women lined up along the switchboard stations. She hurried to the coatroom to deposit her hat and pocketbook.

But talking to Dr. Pierce would mean admitting her father's problem to the world.

5

Laurie smoothed her hair in the church lavatory as her friend fidgeted, passing a small Bible from hand to hand.

"Come on, Laurie. I want to get a good seat."

Laurie gave her bob one last pat and pinched her cheeks before turning to Amelia. "All done." She frowned at her friend's hair. "I wish I had your natural curl."

Amelia pushed open the bathroom door. "I want to save a spot for Johnny, just in case. He told me he's been working double shifts at the mill. " She sighed. "I can't remember the last time he made it to church, the scamp."

"Yes, well, I wouldn't count on him being here today, either." Laurie hurried to keep up with Amelia as she maneuvered through the crowd like a salmon heading upstream.

A stranger among the familiar crowd drew Laurie's attention. She lost track of her feet, nearly treading on Amelia's heels as she studied the man's square jaw and olive-green eyes. He slipped off his gray fedora, exposing a head of wavy blond hair, and leaned forward to shake hands with Pastor Yoder, his smile brightening the room.

45

She touched Amelia's back without a word. Her friend turned, her smile fading into a questioning glance as she followed Laurie's gaze.

"Ooh, who is that?" Amelia rose on tiptoes. "I've never seen him before. I'd remember a face like that. He's almost as handsome as Johnny and definitely better dressed."

Laurie pressed her pocketbook to her chest. "He seems to know Pastor Yoder."

"He must be new in town. Let's go introduce ourselves." Amelia snatched Laurie's hand and pulled her toward the men.

Laurie dragged her feet, preferring to study him from afar. The man was like a fine work of art, best appreciated at a comfortable distance. Besides, it wouldn't do to look too eager.

Amelia yanked her along, and within moments she was gazing into eyes that were greener than the thick blankets of moss that grew in the nearby forest. Every word in her vocabulary melted from her mind. As usual, however, Amelia had enough for both of them.

Pastor Yoder, a twinkle in his eye, introduced them. "Samuel Brown, may I introduce Miss Amelia White and Miss Laurie Burke?" He turned to address the women. "Mr. Brown just arrived in Port Angeles last week. In fact, I believe he's living just a few blocks down the street from you young ladies."

Amelia shook his hand. "You're living in the Cherry Hill neighborhood, Mr. Brown? That's simply delightful! I live on Oak and my friend Laurie lives on Laurel."

"Laurie on Laurel? Sounds like a great title for a song." Mr. Brown smiled. "I am renting a house on Laurel, also. I had no idea I had such lovely neighbors."

Laurie's mind buzzed. "Um, yes. Laurel." *No more sleeping on the back porch.*

Amelia pressed her hands together. "Oh, the old Smythe place, right? I noticed someone had leased it."

As Pastor Yoder excused himself, Amelia stepped to the other side of Mr. Brown to close the circle. "What brings you to Port Angeles, Mr. Brown?"

"I work for the Department of Revenue."

Amelia's brows rose. "Revenue? As in money?"

"No." He chuckled. "I'm in the Bureau of Prohibition. There's not much money there. Not clean money, anyway."

Laurie's mouth went dry. *A revenuer.* "You mean like bootleggers and moonshiners?"

Amelia laughed. "If only we had that much excitement around here, Mr. Brown. I think you'll be sadly disappointed. Port Angeles is a rather dreary little town. No one around here would be wrapped up in that sort of business."

"That may be true"—Mr. Brown flashed them a smile—"but I'd appreciate it if you ladies kept your ears open. I know I can trust good church-going people like you to help keep our area free of such nonsense." He gestured with his hat toward the church pews. "It looks like things are about to begin. Will you join me?"

Laurie and Amelia started down the aisle, Mr. Brown trailing behind. Amelia whispered into her ear, "As if we'd have gangsters here in Port Angeles. But I almost wish we did, if it brings good-looking federal agents to town. Isn't it exciting?"

Laurie swallowed, following Amelia into the back row and settling herself on the bench. She tugged at the hemline of her dress as Mr. Brown slid in next to her. Now that she knew he was after men like her brother, he seemed much less attractive. *First impressions aren't always what they seem.* She struggled to breathe, too conscious of the man at her side.

The organ played a familiar hymn, but Laurie's mind kept wandering back to her brother. Surely this would convince Johnny to give up rumrunning for good.

She closed her eyes for a heartbeat. *This isn't what I meant by a man of honor, God.*

As she reached for the hymnal rack, her hand collided with Mr. Brown's.

He sat back with a smile. "You go ahead. I know the words to this one."

Her stomach fluttered. A government man who knew his hymns? "No, I can share with . . . " she glanced over at her friend, but Amelia was already sharing her book with an elderly woman to her left. Amelia raised her brows and nudged Laurie's elbow with her own.

Laurie turned back to Mr. Brown. "What I meant to say is, I would be pleased if you would share the hymnal with me." She opened the cover, rifling through the pages.

A light danced in his face, "It would be an honor, Miss Burke. How gracious of you." Mr. Brown stepped closer, his shoulder brushing hers. He slid his hand under the book's cover, his fingertips caressing their way up her wrist.

A quiver shot up her arm and she yanked her hand away.

The man smiled, the book balanced in his palm. He directed his eyes to the front, raising his voice to join the congregation in singing "Be Still My Soul."

Laurie's cheeks burned. She stared down at the page, the notes and words swimming in time to the lilting music of the organ. She'd imagined it, certainly—and yet, her skin tingled from his touch.

Her gaze darted about the room. How many of these men had she spotted on the beach? Pastor Yoder had mentioned he'd be speaking on God's mercy and forgiveness. If he knew what his congregation did under the cover of night, he might choose to preach on sin.

As if on cue, Daniel Shepherd turned and glanced back at her, a slight frown darkening his face.

Laurie straightened her shoulders, focusing her attention on the page. *Let him watch. It must make a rumrunner nervous to know there's a federal agent in town.*

Her concentration slid right past the music. Instead, her eyes lingered on the sparkles of light bouncing off Mr. Brown's gold watch. After two more stanzas, she stole another glance at Mr. Shepherd, eyeing his strong shoulders and dark hair. He might be handsome, but there was no way she would let her heart get trampled by another dishonorable man.

As Mr. Brown's rich voice picked up the harmony on the next hymn, Laurie's uneasiness about the man faded. She'd overreacted to his touch, assuming the worst. Gripping the pew in front for balance, Laurie's heart rose with the beautiful music, the warmth of his arm against hers no longer so objectionable.

Even better, Mr. Brown knew nothing of her family.

❦

Daniel hooked his thumb in his coat pocket, balancing the hymnbook in his other palm. Who was the man with Laurie Burke? And why did he care? Daniel turned his eyes back to the front, but his voice trailed off. His grandfather's tenor rang out steady beside him as the congregation belted out the final strains.

Not much had changed in this church since he had left eight years ago. Pastor Yoder's fringe of hair sported a bit more gray and the choir had new robes, but the same wobbly-looking old man banged away on the rickety pump organ.

One difference haunted him as the pastor rose to speak. Daniel's grandmother no longer sat at his side. She hadn't lived to see the legacy of her faith—that when Daniel plummeted over a cliff of his own making, the memory of her love and faith gave him the ability to fall straight into God's arms.

Daniel's collar rubbed at his throat, as if it tightened with every word of the sermon. So far he'd managed to keep his secret from his family and hometown. He glanced about the room, spotting familiar faces among the congregation. Teachers, family friends, Sunday school instructors. How would they feel if they knew? His gaze paused once more on Laurie Burke. *Perhaps everyone has secrets.*

The pastor leaned forward on the pulpit, driving home a point. "God isn't up in heaven making lists of your deeds, counting up your good works to see if they outweigh the bad. If you've sought His forgiveness, He's washed you clean. 'Therefore if any man be in Christ, he in a new creature: old things are passed away; behold, all things are become new.' The prophet Micah says God will toss our sins into the depths of the seas. So who are we to question His forgiveness? Why do we continue to live with the millstone of sin and guilt around our necks?"

Daniel swallowed, acid burning in the back of his throat.

I can be that new creature, as long as no one discovers the truth.

⟡

Laurie and Amelia walked home, Amelia buzzing like a bee about Samuel Brown and his sudden appearance.

"Didn't he have just the most delicious smile you've ever seen?" Amelia fiddled with her pearl necklace, knotting the long strand in the center of her chest

Laurie hugged her pink cardigan tight as her thin cotton skirt fluttered in the breeze. "I'm not sure I would call it delicious." She wrinkled her nose at her friend's odd choice of words.

"Well, how would you describe it?"

Laurie caressed her elbow—the same one that had been brushing against Mr. Brown's only fifteen minutes ago. She dropped her hand, tucking it into her pocket. "I don't know—it was a nice smile."

Her friend's jaw dropped. "Nice? Those flowers are *nice*." She gestured to a nearby flowering rhododendron. "His smile was heart-stopping."

Laurie tucked her pocketbook under one arm. "You used to say that about Johnny's smile."

Amelia shot her a dirty look. "Laurie, you know I've never had eyes for any man other than your brother and I never will. But, if I did . . . that Samuel Brown might just steal the top spot on my list."

Laurie laughed. "Amelia, you've had 'eyes' for lots of men."

The tiny blonde stopped in her tracks. "Laurie Burke, don't say such a thing."

Laurie paused, surprised by the hurt in her friend's face. She touched Amelia's arm. "I'm just teasing. Everyone knows your heart belongs to Johnny."

Her friend's eyes glistened as she dropped her gaze to her shoes. "I wish he felt the same."

Laurie groaned. "Johnny's an idiot. He adores you. He's just being stubborn. He probably won't propose until he can buy you a house and a ring."

"That will be years with what he makes at the mill." She looked up at Laurie, her lips turned down in a pout. "We could live in a tree for all I care, he knows that. We could even move in with you and your father. Wouldn't that be fun? We'd be like sisters."

Laurie stifled a shudder. She tucked an arm around her friend's waist, nudging her toward home. "I think it's romantic. He wants to give you the best. That's worth something." Her heart skipped. That must be why Johnny was rumrunning—for Amelia's sake. She'd be furious if she knew.

Laurie steered the conversation to happier ground. "You said Mr. Brown would steal the top spot on your list . . . that means you have one—a list, I mean."

Amelia's eyebrows pinched. "Johnny's at the top of my list, I told you that."

"Yes, yes, I got that." Laurie smoothed her skirt. "I mean, who else? Just for fun."

"Well, now that you mention it, Mr. Larson's grandson is a regular Rudolph Valentino."

Laurie bit her lip. She didn't want to be reminded about Daniel Shepherd.

Her friend prattled on. "Did you notice Mr. Shepherd staring at you during church? Speaking of delicious smiles."

"No, I didn't." Laurie twisted her silver bangle bracelet. "Besides, he's not on my list at all."

"So you do have a list! Who's at the top?"

Laurie reached for names and came up blank. Daniel Shepherd's face in the shadows on the bluff filled her mind.

"It's Mr. Brown, right?" Amelia clapped her hands together. "I knew it! I could tell you liked him, right off. I've been praying for you to meet the perfect man and he shows up at church of all places."

Laurie gave her friend a half-smile, content to let Amelia believe what she would. It was certainly safer than the other option. She pushed Mr. Shepherd from her mind and let her thoughts wander back to Samuel Brown.

A quiver ran through her. *A federal agent? Johnny would kill me.* She blew on her hands to warm them. *But, I suppose a federal agent is better than a rumrunner.*

6

AFTER SAYING GOODBYE TO AMELIA, LAURIE HURRIED TO JOHNNY'S boarding house. She wrinkled her nose at the belching smoke-stacks along the waterfront. A yellowish haze tainted the spring air with the fumes of rotting wood pulp and sulfur.

Johnny and two other men sat on the front porch steps, deep in conversation. Laurie slowed her pace, ducking behind a neighboring hedge.

"We can't go tonight." A small man with brown hair hanging far past the edges of his tweed cap gestured with grimy hands. "I'm on early shift. If I show up at work one more time with whiskey on my breath, they'll send me packing."

Johnny scoffed. "There's nothing saying you have to drink the stuff, Lew."

"Stay out of my business, kid. Just 'cuz you're hauling your stash back to your old man don't mean the rest of us can't enjoy the spoils." He jammed a lit cigarette between his lips and took a long drag.

Laurie held her breath, palms damp.

"Well, if not tonight, when?" A third man spoke.

"Let's make it Thursday, if the weather's not too bad. I'm sick of this rowing in the rain business. We could swim there and back and get less wet." Lew's whining voice carried clearly on the breeze.

Her brother spoke up. "You sat in the car during the last drop. We were the ones getting soaked. But, the weather doesn't get much better than this. I think we should go tonight."

Lew exhaled, smoke curling around his head. "Who made you boss?"

Laurie caught a glimpse of the third man—a burly fellow with a round, red face. He pushed to his feet with a grunt. The others fell silent.

The heavy-set man dangled an unlit cigar from the tips of his meaty fingers. "We don't want 'fine.' You boys think this is some pleasure cruise? You want to go boating, do it on your own time. The rain hides us better—unless you want to be sitting in the county jail come morning."

His gravelly voice made the hairs on the back of Laurie's neck rise.

Lew rubbed both hands on his stained overalls. "Who's going to be looking? Nobody cares what we're doing. I don't think we need all this cloak and dagger business."

Johnny leaned back against the steps; his hands wrapped around one knee. "I think Jerry's right. We shouldn't be taking any chances. I don't want to meet any G-men on the beach."

"There ain't gonna' be no G-men. You've read too many newspapers. If we was in Seattle or Tacoma, maybe; but no one cares about that stuff up here."

Laurie took a deep breath and stepped into the open. "You're wrong."

The three men swung their faces toward her, Johnny and Lew jumping to their feet. The smaller man lost hold of his cigarette, juggling to prevent the butt from dropping into the weeds.

Johnny took a step toward her. "Girl, you got to stop sneaking up on me like that."

She placed her hands on her hips. "Someone needs to, before you get yourself locked up or killed."

Jerry shoved his hat back on his head and stared. "If it ain't the girl from the beach. You said she wasn't gonna be no trouble, Johnny."

Johnny pushed past the two men and grabbed Laurie's elbow. "She's not." He yanked her down the walk toward the road.

"Hold it." The big man strode forward until his shadow fell over Laurie. "What were you trying to say?"

Laurie stuck out her chin and wrenched her elbow from her brother's vise grip. "There's a revenuer in town looking for you."

Jerry pulled off his hat, his round head topped only by a few long hairs pulled from one ear to the other. His light-colored brows were drawn down into a scowl.

Johnny latched on a second time, digging his fingers into her arm. "She's just saying that because she wants me to quit."

"Let her go, Johnny. Let's hear her out." The man's voice softened.

Johnny released his grip, but hovered like a dog with raised hackles.

Lew closed the circle, a grin on his face. "She's a peach, Johnny. I never figured you came from such good-lookin' stock. How about an introduction?"

"Shut up." Johnny growled as he curled his fingers into fists.

Laurie ignored them, turning instead to the balding man, hoping he had an ounce of sense in his skull. "I met a man at church today . . ."

Lew snorted.

Jerry gestured for the man to be silent. "And?"

She glanced at her brother. "He said he worked for the treasury department—"

"That don't mean nothing." Lew crossed his arms across his barrel-shaped chest. "He's probably just some pencil-pusher who stopped through to do something at city hall."

She took a deep breath. "He told me they'd had reports of boats running Canadian whiskey into Port Angeles. He's here to put a stop to it."

Johnny rubbed his hands over his face while Jerry jammed his cigar between his teeth. Even Lew looked taken aback.

The crushing weight lifted from Laurie's chest. "Now you can give up this ridiculous venture. There's no way you can keep making trips to Canada when you've got federal agents on your doorstep."

Lew flicked ashes from the end of his cigarette. "What are we gonna do, Jerry? We can't shut down now, I got orders coming in."

Jerry swung his hat back onto his round head. "No one's quitting. We've just got to watch our backs. Someone must have squealed to the feds." He turned and glared at Laurie.

Johnny stepped closer. "No way, Jerry. It wasn't her."

The big man crossed his arms over his chest and curled his lip. "That true, sweetheart?"

Laurie nodded. *As if I would get my own brother in trouble.*

"We can trust you?"

Laurie glanced toward Johnny, her pulse quickening. "Yes, of course." She ran fingers over her arms, trying to chase off the sudden chill.

"Good. Here's what we're going to do." He pointed a finger at Laurie's nose. "You're going to be our eyes and ears. You keep track of that fellow and see if you can find out what he knows."

Johnny's face reddened. "No way. My sister is not a part of this."

Jerry tossed his cigar butt on the ground and smashed it flat with his work boot. He glared at Johnny with close-set eyes. "Seems to me she already made herself part of this. I didn't ask her to show up on the beach or to come to this meeting. Maybe you're the one with the loose jaw in this operation. How did she know about the shipment? The meeting?"

Laurie grasped Johnny's sleeve. "He didn't tell me anything."

Johnny growled. "Stay out of this, Laurie."

She elbowed her way between them. "I work at the switchboard—that's how I figured out about the beach. And I didn't even know about this meeting, I just wanted to tell Johnny about the agent."

Johnny grabbed her wrist and dragged her to the gate. "Laurie, I told you to stay out of it. I don't want you here." He gave her a shove that sent her staggering out into the road.

"Hold it." Jerry strode over to the ramshackle fence. "You're an operator?"

Laurie nodded.

He ran his hands along the top of the fence rail. "You listen in on conversations?"

A flush climbed her neck. "We're not supposed to, of course. But I'd been wondering why Johnny had been acting so peculiar."

The heavyset man paced the yard. "Take her on home, Johnny." He slid another cigar from his breast pocket, rolling it between his fingers. "Then head back here. We need to have a little chat."

Her brother walked out of the yard in silence, his jaw grinding.

Laurie hurried to keep pace, mapping out the upcoming argument in her mind. Johnny had to give up this ridiculous activity and focus on his relationship with Amelia. Maybe they could all get their lives straightened out for once.

Once they reached the corner, out of earshot of the house, Johnny rounded on her. "What do you mean showing up like that? Didn't I warn you to stay away?" His eyes flashed.

Laurie recoiled, shocked by the intensity of his words. The hairs along her arms stood at attention. "I thought you might want to know."

He kicked at a stone sending it skidding across the road. "Laurie, you don't have any sense in that brain. These people are dangerous. I don't want you anywhere near them." His brows pinched. "If you got something to say, talk to me."

She clamped her hands on her waist. "And when am I supposed to do that? When you're at work? When you're hauling bottles of whiskey around the beach? When you're yelling at Dad for drinking or for making you late?" She twisted the corner of her sweater. "No, let me see—I'll talk to you when you're taking Amelia to the soda fountain. Oh, wait—you never do that anymore."

His shoulders slumped. "Laurie . . ."

The burning in her throat refused to be extinguished. "Amelia comes crying to me because she thinks you don't care. What am I supposed to tell her? That you're running whiskey so you can afford to buy her a ring?"

He started off down the street. "You don't understand anything."

She trailed after. "Amelia loves you. She doesn't want a fancy house or ring. If she knew you were doing this, she'd be heart-broken."

He stopped. "Don't you breathe a word of this to her."

Laurie dug her fingernails into her palm. "Quit running whiskey and maybe I'll keep your little secret."

Johnny threw his head back and stared up at the sky. Laurie could see his Adam's apple working in his throat as he swallowed. "I can't."

Her stomach clenched. "Why not?"

"I owe some people money."

Laurie pressed her lips together. "If you're in trouble, I could help."

His face twisted. "Why'd you have to go and tell Big Jerry that you work for the switchboard? That's the last thing I need."

"Why?"

Johnny grabbed her shoulders. "Just promise me you'll stay away from him. No matter what he asks."

She frowned. "But if it could help you—"

"I've just got to make a few more shipments and I'm getting out."

Her heart rose. "Really? You'll quit?"

He nodded. "So, promise me. Stay away from Jerry. And stay away from that G-man, too. I don't want you mixed up in any of this nonsense."

Laurie nodded. "As long as you promise me you're quitting."

His lip turned up in a half-smile. "I can't wait to be done. I never want to row those waters again." He gave her a gentle shove. "Now get on home. I'm going to see what I can do to smooth things over with Jerry."

"All right." She moistened her lips. "And Johnny—"

"Yeah?"

"Come by and see Amelia, soon. Won't you?"

He smiled. "I'd like nothing better, Sis. I'll swing by this evening and take her for a stroll."

"Perfect." Laurie hurried off, leaving her brother at the corner. Two blocks passed before she remembered about Daniel Shepherd. She glanced back, but Johnny had already disappeared.

He said to stay away from both the revenuer and the rum-runners. Obviously, that must include Shepherd, too.

7

Ediz Hook wrapped around the Port Angeles harbor like a protective arm. Daniel strolled the rocky strip of land, the soft spring sunshine warming his shoulders even as the gusty wind off the Strait tugged at his sleeves. The breeze couldn't budge his dark mood, his thoughts consumed by the image of a beautiful young woman and the vain peacock in the pinstriped suit who'd wasted no time cozying up to her. Daniel lifted his collar, leaning into the wind. He had no claim on Laurie's attentions and she'd made it perfectly clear that she had zero interest in his.

Scooping up a smooth stone, he cocked his arm and sent it skimming across the surface of the waves. *God, give me wisdom. Show me what to do.* He stared past the water to the hazy shore of Canada less than twenty miles away. As a boy, he'd chucked many a rock as hard as he could with the fantasy of hitting the distant beach.

During the night he'd woken with Miss Burke's words running through his mind. *"Does your grandfather know what you are?"* Daniel shivered as the breeze whipped the perspiration from his face. If Granddad knew, he'd never have asked him to work at the pharmacy. And inherit the place? Not a chance.

He scooped up a handful of pebbles and tossed them, one by one, into the water. Pastor Yoder said God casts sins into the depths of the sea. *So why do they still haunt me?* Daniel hurled the last pebble as hard as he could. It splashed into the harbor, sinking beneath the waves.

Daniel buttoned his coat and continued down the path, gulls spinning lazy circles over his head. He adjusted his hat to block the sun's glare. He needed to confront Laurie Burke and find out what exactly she knew.

Daniel reached the far end of the spit where the lighthouse warned boats of the nearby rocks. He sat down on a bench and stared out over the foaming surf. Looking into the deep blue of Laurie Burke's eyes could mean risking some equally dangerous waters.

⌒══✦══⌒

The silvery-haired widow drummed her fingernails against the marble counter, the lines on her brow deepening with each passing minute.

Many charms, indeed. Daniel counted to ten. "Mrs. McAllister, I've wrapped up your rheumatism pills just the way you requested. Is there something else?"

She peered over the rims of her tiny gold-rimmed glasses. "Mr. Larson always fills my prescriptions. He understands how I like things. Perhaps he should check before I take them home."

Daniel slid the packet across the counter. "Granddad is out of the store today. He's going to be taking Mondays off. If you'd like, I could hold your prescription and have him inspect it in the morning."

She huffed. "I always pick my pills up on Monday afternoons. How could he be so insensitive as to leave a youngster like you in charge on the day he knows I'm coming?

Daniel straightened to his full six-foot height. At twenty-six, he could hardly be called a youngster. "Mrs. McAllister, Granddad left detailed instructions about your pills." *Not that I needed them.* "I followed them to the letter. He even wrote that you liked your strawberry soda topped with fresh strawberry ice cream, not vanilla." He pressed both palms against the marble countertop.

Mrs. McAllister fiddled with the clasp on her purse. "Well, we'll see if you get *that* right, now, won't we?"

Daniel sighed as he followed the gray-haired matron to the soda fountain. It had been a slow day, but a few people sat at the counter enjoying their drinks. A cherub-faced little girl bounced on one of the stools while her mother steadied it with a free hand.

As Daniel mixed Mrs. McAllister's strawberry soda, the bell over the door jingled. He opened the door to the icebox and retrieved a scoop of ice cream before glancing toward the front.

Daniel saw a tall man looming in the doorway, decked out in a charcoal-gray suit and matching fedora.

Daniel swallowed, a sour taste springing to his tongue. The man didn't look so much like a choirboy without a hymnbook in his hand.

Daniel finished preparing the soda and wiped the edge of the glass with a napkin before plunking it on the counter in front of Mrs. McAllister. "Your soda, ma'am. I hope you enjoy it."

He didn't bother plastering the usual greet-the-customer smile on his face as he stepped out from behind the fountain. "Can I be of some assistance?" Daniel held out his hand, still chilled from the freezer.

The man returned the handshake, his eyes flickering at the icy touch. He released his grip and rubbed his palms together, a gold ring glinting on his pinky finger. "Shepherd, isn't it?"

A prickle wandered across the back of Daniel's neck. "Have we been introduced?"

The corners of the man's lips twisted upward in a half-smile. "Not exactly. I am Agent Samuel Brown, a Prohibition officer with the U.S. Treasury Department." His gaze wandered the store. "I'd like to speak to the owner. That would be your grandfather, correct?"

Daniel's throat clenched. A revenuer? "Yes. Miles Larson. I'm afraid he's not in on Mondays. Would you like to make an appointment to see him or is there anything I can do for you?"

The bell jingled again as a freckle-faced teenager scurried in, out of breath. "I'm sorry I'm late, Mr. Shepherd. My teacher kept me after class. It won't happen again, sir."

Daniel nodded. "That's fine, Marcie. School is important."

Marcie raised her fingers to her lips. "Oh, I'm sorry for interrupting." She fled from the two men and ducked behind the fountain counter, reaching for an apron.

Daniel turned back to Mr. Brown. "As I was saying—"

"Just how many kids do you have working here, Mr. Shepherd?" Brown's eyes narrowed as he withdrew a notepad from an inner pocket of his suit coat.

"Marcie is the first. Business has picked up since we added the fountain. We may hire another in a few weeks. My grandfather has enough work to do just keeping up with the pharmacy without scooping ice cream, too."

Mr. Brown took off his hat and held it to his chest. "Do employees have access to the alcohol that you keep on site?"

Daniel folded both arms across his chest. "Suppose you tell me what your business is here, Mr. Brown, and perhaps I should ask to see your identification as well."

Samuel Brown drew out a gold US Prohibition Service badge. He raised his voice, its sound carrying across the small store. "I understand this pharmacy was issued a license to dispense alcohol via prescription. I need to examine your stock and your storage methods."

Several of the customers turned in their seats, eyes wide.

"When did the Bureau of Prohibition begin to care about small family drugstores? Of course, I'd be more than happy to show you our supplies, if it would make you feel better." Striding to the rear of the store, Daniel opened the storage room and switched on the lights. He drew a key from the breast pocket of his lab coat and unlocked the low cabinet that housed the spirits.

Samuel Brown crouched, examining the bottles. "Is this all of it?"

"That's everything we have in at the moment. We never keep large amounts—just what we need to fill prescriptions and mix tonics."

Mr. Brown balanced on his heels, one eyebrow raised. "Tonics?"

"You want to see our permits?"

Mr. Brown stood, brushing off his pant legs. "No, that's not necessary. I just needed to observe that your alcohol was properly secure and that you are ordering from legal suppliers, which is evident from the seals on your bottles."

Daniel stepped to the side to let the agent pass before he locked the cabinets. Something about Samuel Brown made Daniel's skin crawl.

Brown shoved his fedora back along the crown of his head. "Inform your grandfather we'll be doing routine inspections." He raised his chin and offered Daniel a tight-lipped smile. "And make sure none of your soda jerks has access to those cabinets. Drinking is a big problem with the young people these days. I'd hate to see them pilfering away your profits."

Daniel, gritting his teeth, escorted Mr. Brown to the door only to have it swing open with a merry jingle.

Laurie Burke hovered on the threshold, her blue cup-shaped hat framing a pale owl-like face. Her gaze flicked from the soda fountain to the pharmacy counter.

Samuel Brown stepped forward with a wide smile. "Miss Burke, what a pleasure to see you again."

Her mouth dropped open. "Mr. Brown, I'm surprised to see you. I was just coming in to . . ." Miss Burke's gaze skirted the room a second time.

Daniel stepped close. "For those headache powders?"

Her face brightened. "Yes, that's right—headache powders." She followed Daniel to the pharmacy counter, casting furtive glances at the agent as she slipped off her gloves and tucked them into her purse.

Mr. Brown trailed behind. "I hope everything is all right."

Her lips parted as she sucked in a quick breath. "Yes, fine. I've just been struggling with some headaches the past few days. I haven't been sleeping well, I'm afraid."

Daniel laid several containers out on the back counter. *I'd bet my last dollar that she came here for another bottle of whiskey.* Even so, Daniel felt no compulsion to share her secret with the likes of Samuel Brown. He measured the ingredients into a granite mortar.

Brown, leaning against the counter, tipped his hat back. "While you're waiting, Miss Burke, perhaps you would allow me to buy you a soda?"

Her hand gripped the edges of her coat. "I suppose . . . yes, that would be nice, Mr. Brown. Thank you." She leaned across the counter. "I'll be back for those powders later, Mr. Shepherd."

Daniel reached for the pestle, his shoulders tightening. "They'll be waiting." He brought the tool down with more force than necessary, missing his thumb by only a fraction of an inch.

A woman rumrunner and a rude Prohibition agent—a match made in heaven.

⌒═══╪═══⌒

Laurie settled herself on the padded stool, conscious of Mr. Brown lurking only a step behind. She'd promised Johnny to stay clear of him, but when it was a choice between Daniel Shepherd and Samuel Brown, she figured spending time with the federal agent would be the wiser decision.

Mr. Brown perched on his stool and leaned toward her, as if sharing a secret. "I quite enjoyed singing with you in church yesterday. You have a lovely voice."

Laurie smiled. "Thank you. But I'm afraid you must have been hearing Amelia. Out of mercy for those sitting around me, I try to limit my volume. Singing is not one of my talents."

He cocked his head. "Perhaps I was mistaken. Well, then— I look forward to learning your many other talents."

Laurie turned to examine the menu hanging above the counter.

"So if music isn't your passion, what do you enjoy, Miss Burke?"

She studied the swirls of color in the marble counter. "I like to draw, but I'm not sure I would say I'm talented." She glanced at him, noting the firm line of his jaw, a tiny cleft in the center of his chin. His face would be a joy to sketch—much easier than the shadowy image of Mr. Shepherd she had just completed.

"Oh?" His eyebrows rose. "What types of things do you draw?"

"Nature scenes, mostly. The water, the mountains, wildlife . . . that sort of thing. And sometimes people, too. I rarely show them to anyone, however."

He smiled. "I'd love to see them, someday. If you would consider me one of those rare 'anybodies' that you speak of. I'm quite partial to nature scenes. It's one of the reasons I took this assignment. I wanted to see the mountains I'd read so much about."

"The Olympics are breathtaking. You should hike up to Hurricane Ridge. There's no place in the world more beautiful." She fought to keep the wistful tone out of her voice. Years had passed since she'd walked those trails.

"Port Angeles does seem to have more than its share of beauty." His gaze didn't waver. "Maybe you could show me some of its lovelier spots."

Laurie's mouth went dry, but thankfully, Marcie Connor arrived to take their order. "Marcie, when did you start working here? Your sister didn't say anything about you taking a job."

The girl grinned, revealing a mouthful of crooked teeth. "I just started two days ago. Anne-Marie is green with envy. She even talked about quitting the exchange to work here." She cupped a hand around her lips, dropping her voice to a loud whisper. "She thinks Mr. Larson's grandson is the bee's knees, if you know what I mean."

Laurie smiled. "I'm not sure I do know." She glanced over her shoulder to where Mr. Shepherd still worked at the pharmacy counter, his back to them. "But, Anne-Marie always understood these things better than me."

Mr. Brown cleared his throat. "I believe I'd like a root beer float. How does that sound to you, Miss Burke?"

Laurie kept her expression neutral. "Root beer sounds fine, but I'd prefer a chocolate egg cream."

"A woman who knows her own mind. I like that." Mr. Brown smiled.

Laurie noticed Marcie staring at her companion with round eyes, a touch of pink showing beneath her freckles. "Marcie, have you met Mr. Samuel Brown?"

Marcie shook her head, her dark curls bouncing. She wiped her hand on her apron and held it out.

As Mr. Brown shook the girl's hand, Laurie continued. "Mr. Brown, may I introduce Marcie Connor? I work with Marcie's sister at the telephone exchange."

When the agent released her hand, Marcie scurried off to fill their order, her fingers fluttering to her chest. Laurie smiled. One would think the girl had never seen a handsome man before. Of course, had her reaction at church been any different?

Mr. Brown swiveled toward her again, his knee brushing hers. Laurie pulled her legs back and crossed them on the far side of the stool.

He gazed at her without saying a word, making Laurie feel like an insect under a microscope. "You work at the exchange?"

"Yes." Laurie dug a handkerchief from her purse, overcome by a sudden need to have something in her hands.

"That must be interesting work." He rested his chin on his hand.

"Not really. You sit on a stool, flip switches, and move cords from one hole to another."

He laughed, sitting back and running a hand through his blond hair. "Well, if you put it that way. But I've always heard that the operators in these small towns know everybody and everybody's business."

She glanced over her shoulder, distracted by the banging of the mortar. How much grinding did headache powders need? "Not really. We're not allowed to listen in, you know. But I do know certain folks' habits pretty well."

"Like what?"

Laurie folded the handkerchief into a neat square. "I know Mrs. Simon plays cards at Mrs. Grant's house most days after lunch. So, if her son calls during that time, I'll ring her there. And Mr. Johansson has been helping his neighbor with some automobile repairs, so if I don't find him at home, I might check next door."

He chuckled as Marcie arrived with the drinks. "There you go—knowing folks' business. That's not a bad thing, now, is it?"

Laurie pulled her soda close and picked up a long spoon. "No. I just don't like the thought that we're collecting gossip or any such nonsense."

"Of course. Gossiping would be rude, but what if you overheard information that someone was in trouble?"

Laurie frowned. "What sort of trouble?"

"Let's say an emergency or . . ." he paused, "or a matter for the police, perhaps?"

"I suppose we would contact the authorities. We called the hospital for old Mrs. Jenkins last year when she was feeling ill." Laurie rolled the straw between her fingers.

"What about something illegal?"

Laurie dropped her hand back to her lap. "If someone asked, I could connect them to the police department."

Mr. Brown pushed his drink back. "Let me lay it on the table for you, Miss Burke. What if you overheard someone discussing illegal behavior? Would you contact the police?"

The sweet drink turned sour in Laurie's mouth. "Mr. Brown, as I said, we do not listen in on conversations. I don't see any way that I would 'overhear' something like that."

His green eyes darkened, like dusk creeping over the forest. "I informed you and Miss White that I was in town on business, seeking information on possible rumrunning operations. I hope you are aware that if you have knowledge of such illegal activities, you're obligated to share that with me or you could be considered guilty of aiding the criminals."

Laurie's heart jumped into her chest. "I don't know what you mean." She pushed the drink away and slid off of the stool. "And I don't think I will be of any use to you, sir."

Mr. Shepherd appeared at her side with a small bag. "Your headache powders, Miss Burke." He stepped in front of Mr. Brown and lowered his voice. "I thought you might want them sooner, rather than later."

"That's very kind." Laurie swallowed hard, gazing up into Mr. Shepherd's gray eyes. "What do I owe you?"

"This one's on me."

Mr. Brown appeared at the pharmacist's side, his fingers curling into a fist as he glared at the man.

Anxious to be away from both of them, she nodded. "Thank you, Mr. Shepherd. I'm grateful. And thank you for the soda, Mr. Brown."

The agent slipped on his hat and tipped it to her. "I hope we can do it again sometime, Miss Burke. I'd like to talk to you more."

She clenched the paper bag in her fingers. *I bet you do.*

8

LAURIE DUG THROUGH HER PURSE AS SHE HURRIED HOME. THE BOOTLEGGER-pharmacist and the Prohibition agent—it figured that the two best-looking men in town were both off limits. She felt like a kitten being teased with a piece of string. She pulled out a pocket mirror and checked her reflection, cheeks blotchy and pink.

Mr. Brown's no better than that Big Jerry.

A figure in the park across the street caught Laurie's eye. Johnny strode toward the waterfront, his hands jammed into his trouser pockets, shoulders hunched.

She jammed the mirror into her pocket and hurried after him, catching Johnny as he arrived at the dock. "Going fishing?"

Dark circles surrounded his eyes, dull in the late afternoon shadows. "I wish I had time."

Laurie pushed up the sleeves on her sweater. "So, where are you heading? Are you going out on a"—she glanced around the deserted dock—"a run?"

Lines scored Johnny's forehead. "When did you turn into such a snoop?"

His words jabbed at her. "I'm the little sister. It's my job. Remember?" She followed him along the dock to where his longboat bobbed in the water.

He gripped the rope, perching on the edge of the dock. "I'm not a kid anymore, Laurie. I'm entitled to a little privacy."

She crossed her arms. "I'm not a kid, either. And yet you keep treating me like one—like I can't handle the truth."

He tossed the rope onto the boat and stepped in. "Sometimes you can't. That ain't my fault."

Heat crawled up Laurie's back. "I'm tougher than you give me credit for."

He used the oar to push away from the edge. "And sometimes you're too tough." The splash of the oars increased as the boat drifted away, Johnny pulling harder strokes as he entered open water.

The breeze plastered her skirt back against her legs. She turned and walked back up the length of the dock. A burly figure stepped out from one of the larger boats. "Well, if it ain't sweet lil' Laurie." Big Jerry blocked her path, solid as the dock's wooden pilings.

Laurie's throat tightened. "What do you want?"

"You and your brother exchanging information again?" He crossed his arms across his wide chest before leaning over to spit into the waves.

"He didn't tell me anything."

"Course not. He never says nothing to you, does he? But somehow you seem to keep turning up, like a bad penny." He took a step toward her, his shadow crossing her path. "I saw you talking to that G-man. You looked mighty cozy in there, sipping sodas like lovers." The man's lip curled.

"We're not—"

"Oh, no. You're an unsullied little flower, aren't you?" A booming laugh burst from his chest. "I know how you girls work. You've probably got a flask hidden in your garter." He reached for her leg.

Laurie knocked his hand away. "Get away from me."

A second laugh followed the first. "You're the motherless daughter of a drunkard. Your brother is embracing his destiny. What makes you think you're any better?"

Laurie reddened as she tried to push past him, the reek of the mill heavy on his clothes.

He grabbed her arm, lowering his voice to a hoarse whisper. "Listen here, kitten. Your brother is going to be the first to go to jail if that fed gets wind of what's going down here. You need to think about where your loyalty lies."

She wrenched her arm free, but he still blocked her path.

"You keep making pretty with that Brown fellow. Watch him. But you keep your mouth shut—got it?"

"Why should I?"

His dark eyes glinted. "Cause I'd hate to see your brother fall off the boat one of these nights. Halfway to foreign shores, if you know what I mean."

Her stomach sank to her knees.

"Do we understand each other?" He placed a dirty finger under her chin.

Laurie spoke through clenched teeth. "Perfectly."

9

Laurie stormed down the spit, kicking rocks as she walked. *Fetch my bottle. Mind your own business. Keep your mouth shut. Listen in on the bootleggers. Spy on the G-man.*

She grabbed a handful of rocks and flung them out into the water. The lapping of the waves against the rocks soothed her nerves, but did little for the ache in her heart. Remembering Big Jerry's threats, she reached for more stones.

A nearby bench beckoned. Laurie dragged herself over and flopped down. Was it wrong to reach for a better future? A bootlegger's sister? A drunk's daughter? She stared out at the waves as the sun dropped low on the far horizon.

To keep Johnny safe, she needed to convince both Jerry and the agent she would cooperate.

She tugged at a long stem of beach grass, pulling it loose and rolling it between her fingers. A massive cargo ship inched past, far out in the channel, sending waves crashing against the rocks. Laurie's fingers itched to sketch the scene. If only she could direct every aspect of her life the way she controlled a pencil.

She pushed up to her feet, turning back toward town before she lost the last of the evening's light.

If I'm to convince Samuel Brown, I'll need to meet with him away from the soda fountain. She stopped mid-stride. Big Jerry knew she had met with Samuel Brown. The information must have come from Mr. Shepherd. *An eye on the agent; an ear on the bootleggers.* A smile tugged at the corners of her mouth. *Maybe I can do both.*

⚬══╪══⚬

Daniel finished cleaning the icebox and lined it with a fresh supply of sawdust. Blowing on his fingers to thaw them, he walked to the front of the store and checked that the closed sign was visible in the window. Glancing out the window, he caught sight of Laurie Burke walking through town, her face practically glowing in the setting sun. The tension in his shoulders eased. She had seemed quite disturbed after her meeting with Samuel Brown.

Something about that man raised the hairs on the back of Daniel's neck. Brown's attitude was smug, like everyone in this town was beneath him.

Now, as he watched Laurie walk down the street, Daniel noticed a spring in her step and a glow to her lovely face. A peculiar sensation ran along his arms, like ants crawling across his skin. He shook himself, irritated by the surge of protectiveness that flooded through him, all for a woman that he barely knew. And what he did know about her was troubling. She was obviously strong enough to take care of herself. In fact, she had told him that once already.

Daniel turned away, making a last visual survey of the drugstore before he locked up for the night. He caught his reflection in the soda fountain mirror. Remembering those blue eyes gazing up at him in the mirror made his heart pitch in his chest.

He couldn't warn her about Brown. But, maybe he could look up an old high school friend.

⌒—▲—⌒

Daniel walked down through the older part of town, pressing the back of his hand against his nose to block the reek of the mill. Dilapidated old shacks and boardinghouses clung to the bluff overlooking Hollywood Beach like the residents clung to their meager life. While so much of the country rode the soaring wave of stocks and bonds, the people in this neighborhood still scrambled to pull together enough pennies to feed their families.

Weeds grew knee high between the shacks, except where they were smothered by piles of refuse. A rat skittered through one of the piles, turning a bold eye toward Daniel as he passed.

Daniel pulled the scrap of paper from his pocket, double-checking the address he'd recorded. Johnny evidently lived on the edge of this morass. *With a steady job and a lucrative rum-running business, he should be able to afford better accommodations.*

The address matched the last house on the street, its front walk littered with cigarette butts. Daniel shoved the paper in his pocket and took a deep breath before knocking.

Moments later, a short man yanked open the door about six inches and glared from the threshold, eyes red and watery. His sweat-stained shirt hung cockeyed on his thin frame, buttoned off-kilter. "Yeah?"

Daniel cleared his throat. "I'm looking for Johnny Burke."

The door didn't budge. "What do you want with him?" The rancid smell of his breath floated out onto the doorstep. "Who are you?"

Daniel took a step back, surveying the small man from the dooryard. Was this one of the rumrunners or just one of the recipients of their bounty? "My name is Shepherd. Johnny and

I went to school together. I just thought I'd stop in and see him."

The door opened a crack further, the man's hand clamped along the edge. "He ain't here. Try the docks."

"Thank you." Daniel tipped his hat, but the small man only grunted in reply, wiping the back of his hand under his bulging nose.

Daniel hurried away, convinced the defiant stare tracked him down the street. The air felt fresher and lighter by the water, though the smell of the pulp mill reached through every corner of town today—rich or poor. As he approached the boathouse, he noticed a long boat rowing into the bay. Daniel shoved his hands in his pockets and waited as the boat approached the dock, gliding in to a waiting slip.

Like everything else in this town, Johnny Burke appeared to be stuck in time, his lean, muscled frame changing little since high school, shoulders curved like a dog kicked once too often. As Daniel approached, Johnny tipped his head back, his light blue eyes missing the mischievous glint that had made their female classmates swoon and the teachers hot under the collar. "Help you?"

"Johnny—it's Daniel. Daniel Shepherd."

His friend cupped a hand over his brow to block the sun's glare. "Daniel?" It took a moment for a smile to spread across his face—as if the muscles lacked practice.

Johnny sprang out onto the dock, his long legs unfolding. He tied the boat before grabbing Daniel's hand and shaking it with vigor. "What are you doing in Port Angeles? You couldn't wait to shake off the dust of this town." He shook his head, his brows pulling down. "No one ever comes back."

"Yes, well, my granddad is getting older and he needed some help with the store." Daniel's throat tickled as he watched the years tumble back down onto his friend's shoulders.

"That place has been hopping for months—ever since Mr. Larson added the soda fountain. It sure brought some new life to this little town." He retrieved his things from the boat and the pair made their way up the dock toward the shore. "My girl likes to spend every minute she can there."

Daniel grinned. "I think I met your girl. Amelia White?"

The corners of Johnny's lips lifted. "Yep. Don't go getting any ideas." He jabbed a finger at Daniel's chest. "She's mine."

"I wouldn't dream of it. Besides, you were always the one stealing girls from me back in school."

"Yeah, well. I was the big man back then and you were the book worm." He shrugged. "Now I'm just another mill rat and you're the druggist with the celluloid collar."

Daniel shifted uncomfortably. "She was in the drugstore just the other day, with your sister."

Johnny hefted the bag over his arm. "Those two are thick as thieves, always have been." He smiled again, reaching his hand out for Daniel's shoulder. "It is good to see you. We should go fishing or something. You can catch me up on all the news of Seattle. I bet the parties are wild down there. You got a girl in the city?"

Daniel's chest tightened. He didn't want to think about Seattle. "No girl," he said. "But fishing sounds great. I haven't been since I left town."

"We can fix that. I work late tonight, but I'm off tomorrow. Sound good?"

Daniel ran a hand through his hair. "You're working a shift at the mill tonight?"

A shadow crossed his friend's face. "Not exactly. I'm just helping some friends with a little job they got. You know, making some extra dough on the side."

Just as I thought. "Tomorrow would be fine." He eyed Johnny's longboat. "I'm not too handy with the oars. How about we take my granddad's boat?"

Johnny's eyes brightened as he glanced down the row to where the larger boats were moored. "He wouldn't mind?"

Daniel shook his head. "He told me he rarely takes it out anymore. I can't wait to hear all the Port Angeles news."

Johnny laughed. "Well, that would take all of two minutes. You know nothing ever happens here."

Daniel smiled. "Yeah, sure. Nothing."

10

THE RISING SUN CAPPED THE FOOTHILLS, LIGHT SPILLING DOWN OVER THE sleeping town, the dawn air as fresh as a drink from a mountain spring. Thankful for his warm coat, Daniel hunched his shoulders as he walked down to the docks. Spring in the Northwest was always a varied concoction as the winter rains grudgingly gave way to summer sun.

He and Johnny hadn't been the best of friends in high school, but their brief encounter yesterday suggested Johnny longed for simpler times. Daniel looked forward to reminiscing, as long as it remained restricted to childhood. And especially if it gave him the opportunity to find out how Johnny and his sister got mixed up in the booze-smuggling business.

Daniel hurried down the street as the bay came into view. The blue of the water in the early morning light nearly stole the breath from his chest. What was that Laurie had said about the show globe in the store window? *Like the straits on a warm summer day.*

Johnny reclined in his own boat, his feet kicked up on one of the bench seats. "You're early. Missed the fishing that much, did you?"

Daniel laughed, adjusting his fishing gear on his shoulder. "I didn't miss fishing, but I missed being out on the water."

"I know what you mean." Johnny picked up a chest of supplies. "It's the most relaxing thing in the world. Assuming of course, that you're out there for fun and the weather's cooperating."

As the pair walked to the far edge of the marina, Daniel spotted his grandfather's boat bobbing in the gentle waves, the peeling paint on its aft wheelhouse crying out for attention. Granddad had bought the aged fishing boat thirty years ago and remodeled the craft inside and out, making it into his refuge from city life. Countless weekend expeditions along the hidden inlets and waterways around the Olympic Peninsula had given Daniel a deep and profound love for the water. Now the old boat sat lonely and forgotten.

"It's glorious," Johnny breathed. "My favorite boat in the harbor."

Daniel hopped aboard, glancing around in surprise. "You're joking. Granddad warned me the engine might not even start."

Johnny rubbed his hands together. "I can take care of that. Motors are my specialty. Just wish I had one of my own."

Daniel stood on the deck and gazed out at the horizon. The sky was clear enough to see all the way across to Canada. "Weather looks good today."

"Yeah, it should hold out for us." Johnny climbed aboard and stretched, a few audible pops coming from his spine.

"Sure you're up for this? You look exhausted. How late did you work?"

Johnny straightened. "I just got done a couple hours ago." The circles around his eyes confirmed his words.

"You haven't slept yet?" Daniel frowned.

"No, I'll catnap this afternoon. I don't have to be to the mill until tonight. I'm on late shift this week. Besides, I've always got energy for fishing."

Daniel shook his head. "I don't know how you do it. You work a full shift at the mill and work all night . . ."

"It's no big deal. I ain't got a family to worry about. When I do, I'll cut back. But for now, I like to keep busy." Johnny untied the mooring lines.

Daniel pulled his hat lower over his forehead as the morning breeze tugged at the brim. "What about your sister and your father?"

"Laurie's all grown up now, and she takes care of things at home. My father still works at the mill, so I see him there when our shifts overlap." Johnny curled his lip, running a hand across the stubble on his chin. "He and I don't see eye-to-eye on most things, so that's about as much togetherness as we can stand."

It only took Johnny a few minutes to get the old motor going. The men fell silent as they motored out around the spit and into the larger waves of the Strait, the wooden wheelhouse protecting them from the rushing wind and spray.

Looking back toward the city, Daniel's heart swelled. As much as he hadn't wanted to return to Port Angeles, he'd never grown tired of this view of it. The industrial town clung to the shoreline, ribbons of smoke driven inland by the onshore breezes. The jagged peaks created a background of staggering beauty, as if God had painted a stunning portrait only to have humans drop an ugly town right smack in the middle.

Johnny caught his eye and nodded back at the view. "Not as pretty as Seattle, eh?"

Daniel made a face and shrugged. Mount Rainier dominated Seattle's skyline, but as Daniel stared out at the scene, he decided that he preferred the rugged Olympic Mountains, after all. "You get out here very often?"

Johnny licked his lips, staring out at the waves. "Not for fishing, but I get out on the water quite a bit. A buddy of mine has a little delivery business."

Daniel gripped the controls. "What type of deliveries?"

Johnny ignored the question and pointed at a nearby shore. "Freshwater Cove sound like a good spot?"

Slowing their speed, Daniel guided the boat into the secluded bay. "I hear your sister's working at the switchboard." He cut the boat's engine and let it drift.

For about a year now, I think. Not much else for girls to do in this town until they're married." Johnny readied the fishing gear.

"She's a little young to be thinking marriage, isn't she?"

His friend snorted. "She's twenty-one. You've been gone a while, Daniel. She's not the knobby-kneed kid she was when you left."

Daniel baited a hook, his insides squirming like the night crawler. "She got her eye on any of the local boys?"

Johnny raised his eyebrows, a smirk tugging at the corner of his mouth. "Tell me this isn't going where it sounds like it's going."

"What do you mean?"

Johnny bumped his elbow, chuckling. "She ain't got a fellow. Leastways, not that I know of. But I think she's a little young for you, old man."

Daniel reddened. He tossed his line over the side. "And I'm no older than you and you're seeing her best friend, right?" Suddenly realizing his oversight, Daniel backpedaled. "Not that I'm looking. I mean . . . I wasn't saying—"

Johnny cast his own line. "I don't know whether to be relieved or insulted. She is my little sister, you know. It's my duty to watch out for her. But I'd hate to have you thinking she ain't good enough for you."

"That's not what I meant at all. She's a beautiful looking young woman—quite stunning, in fact. It's just that—"

Johnny's laugh cut him off mid-sentence. "No wonder you've been so fidgety. Well, you watch out, she's a handful. Got a mind of her own, that girl."

Daniel's pulse quickened. "Will you let me finish a statement? I was just going to say that I've seen her around town with that Samuel Brown fellow. I thought maybe they were an item."

The color drained from Johnny's face. "Samuel Brown—the federal agent?" He gazed out at the horizon, his jaw working like he was chewing on his thoughts. "Not possible."

Daniel tugged at his line. "He bought her a drink at the soda fountain just yesterday."

Johnny set his pole down, his face dark. "If you're joshing me, I'll toss you out of this boat right here."

Daniel touched a hand to his chest. "It might be perfectly innocent, but . . ." he leaned closer, determined to deliver the message he'd planned. "I don't know him very well, but just between us—I don't trust the man. Something seems off about him."

Johnny picked up his pole, his knuckles white. He shook his head. "I haven't met him." He yanked his line. "But I don't like it."

Daniel let his line drift, his mind wandering along with it.

❧

Laurie perched on the bench outside the Clallam County courthouse; her legs crossed and toe bouncing as she kept her gaze locked on the double doors. Samuel's automobile sat in the parking lot. He must be in there, but she had no way of knowing when he might emerge.

Her insides twisted into an impossible knot as she glanced up at the giant clock tower. Only a few minutes before it clanged the hour. She'd dawdled for twenty-five minutes already. *This is a bad idea.* Laurie pushed to her feet and headed down the sidewalk, when the door creaked behind her. She paused, crouching to fiddle with the strap on her shoe.

"Hello there, Laurie!" Mrs. McAllister's voice warbled out behind her. "Isn't it a lovely day today? My lands—what have you done to your hair?" She clucked her tongue. "How is your dear father doing?"

Laurie cringed. Mrs. McAllister had been a long-time friend of her mother's and one of Laurie's Sunday school teachers when she was little. She turned to face the diminutive woman. "Hello, Mrs. McAllister. Father is doing well. And how are you?"

Laurie's stomach sank as an eager smile spread over the woman's wizened face.

"Laurie, I can't begin to tell you the difficulties that have plagued me this month." She gripped a hand onto Laurie's wrist like an iron shackle, her voice droning like a mosquito on a hot summer evening.

Laurie tried to focus on Mrs. McAllister's words, but her gaze wandered back to the doorway, the sidewalks, and out into the parking lot. His car still rested in its spot, the sunshine glinting off of the nickel plating and gleaming ivory paint.

As Mrs. McAllister's tirade moved from the county land assessor's mistakes with her property taxes to her myriad of medical complaints the door swung open a second time. Samuel Brown stepped outside, settling his hat onto his head, his face severe.

As the clock began to toll, Laurie's breath caught in her chest, her wrist still locked in the woman's claw-like grip. She couldn't let the last thirty minutes be a complete waste.

Mr. Brown drew closer, his eyes remained fixed on the sidewalk as if he were deep in thought.

Laurie patted Mrs. McAllister's hand, hoping she would understand the subtle hint. "Mrs. McAllister, I hate to interrupt you, but I am concerned that you might not have met the newest visitor to our town."

Mrs. McAllister paused mid-sentence, her eyes lighting up behind the tiny spectacles. "Oh?"

As Mr. Brown glanced up, his somber expression vanished, a smile rushing to fill its place. "Miss Burke, what a pleasure to see you again."

The dramatic change in his countenance kicked off a flutter in Laurie's stomach and she took the moment to introduce Mrs. McAllister.

The tiny woman peered up at the man through her thick glasses. "Brown, is it? Welcome to Port Angeles, Mr. Brown. Are you just visiting with us or are you planning to stay?"

The agent pushed his hat back on his head and squinted up at the sun. "Well, the weather is surprisingly nice up in this corner of the state and there's so much natural beauty." He lifted his hands to gesture at the mountains, but trained his eyes on Laurie. "It certainly makes a man want to stay. But, I'm afraid I'm on temporary assignment."

Mrs. McAllister finally released her grip. "Such a shame. We need more young folk around here. Particularly young men, I believe. Right, Laurie?"

A flash of heat climbed Laurie's neck.

The older woman patted Laurie's arm, aiming one last disapproving look at her bobbed hair. "Well, it was nice talking with you Laurie. Give your father my best, now, will you?"

She turned to Mr. Brown. "And it was nice meeting you, Mr. Brown. I hope Laurie can convince you to stay." She sauntered away, leaving Laurie grasping for words.

Samuel came to her rescue. "She seems like a nice woman."

Laurie massaged her wrist. "She is nice—a little forward, perhaps, but nice." She'd been planning this moment all afternoon and now she couldn't remember what she'd intended to say.

Samuel gestured back at the courthouse. "Did you have business here today?"

"Actually, I was just passing by and I stopped to talk with Mrs. McAllister. She's an old family friend."

"Then I'm glad I caught you." A wrinkle appeared on his brow. "I'm afraid I may have offended you the other day at the soda fountain. I didn't handle things very well." He took off his hat and clasped it in his hands, the sunshine catching the golden strands in his hair. "It was wrong to ask you to help with my work." He glanced down at the ground then lifted his eyes back to hers as if seeking permission to continue.

Her breath caught in her chest, his boyish look softening her heart.

He blew out his breath. "I'm getting this all wrong."

"You don't need to apologize, Mr. Brown." A smile pulled at her lips. Perhaps she'd misjudged him.

The intensity in his gaze increased. "Please—call me Samuel."

"Samuel, then. You don't need to apologize."

"I do. I want to be able to spend time with you and I'm deeply embarrassed if I made it sound like I had other motives behind our meeting."

Warmth rushed through Laurie. Her pulse increased. "I—I'd like that. I'm sorry I rushed out so quickly."

A smile spread across his face and he replaced his hat. "Maybe we can start over? May I call you Laurie?"

"Of course."

"How about I buy you some lunch? It would be a treat to take 'Laurie from Laurel Street' to the Laurel Street Café."

Laurie bit her lip, the plan resurfacing in her mind. "That sounds nice, but I've already eaten. How about dessert?" Her confidence grew with each word. "If we really wanted to try again, I think we should go back to Larson's soda fountain."

"Sounds perfect." Samuel held out his arm. "Shall we?"

She looped her hand through his arm. *Okay, Daniel Shepherd. Go tell your boss about this.*

11

Not again.

Daniel ground the pestle against the quinine sulphate, trying not to look at the couple perched on the two stools closest to the pharmacy counter. He leaned into the work, pushing with his shoulder.

"Hey Daniel, take it easy." Granddad peered around the corner. "I've had that mortar for fifty years. I'd like them to survive the summer."

Laurie's head tilted toward Brown, a smile flitting across her face. The man's voice carried across the store, grinding against Daniel's nerves like the pestle. *What does she see in him? She's from a family of rumrunners; he's an overzealous Prohibition agent.*

And why do I care?

Daniel measured out the powder and poured it into a small bottle. Adding the label, his eyes wandered back to the Romeo and Juliet story playing out in front of him.

"Looks like you waited too long." His grandfather spoke in a hushed tone, just behind Daniel's shoulder.

Daniel turned. "Mr. McCurry won't pick this up for an hour, yet."

Crinkles appeared around his granddad's eyes as he smiled. "That's not what I'm talking about." He tipped his head in Laurie's direction. "Time to change that show globe to a new color, I'm thinking. Looks like blue might be taken."

He turned back toward his work rather than rise to his grandfather's teasing. The image of Laurie standing in the rain haunted him. *Oysters.* He shook his head. Rumrunner or no, something about this woman had captured him since he first laid eyes on her.

Granddad was right. He'd moved too slowly.

He braced himself on the counter, trying to ignore Laurie and her date as they laughed and talked over ice cream sodas, the pressure growing in his chest like the carbonation in the soda water. If he didn't get out of here, he might just bubble over.

Unbuttoning his white coat, Daniel strode to the back room, ignoring the amused look on his grandfather's face.

⚬═╪═⚬

Laurie laughed again. "And what happened when you got to the warehouse?"

It hadn't taken much effort to keep Samuel talking. But keeping her focus locked on him instead of the attractive man at the pharmacy counter—that took concentration.

Samuel wrapped his hand around the tall frost-lined glass, lifting the last spoonful of ice cream to his mouth before answering her question. "By that time, they knew we were coming. They had the entire place cleaned out, top to bottom. We didn't find as much as a cork to sniff. The entire operation had been moved in a matter of hours." He wiped his mouth with a napkin.

Keep your eyes on him.

"We were just getting ready to leave when one of their guys comes waltzing in. His eyes were as round as pie pans when he saw us." He laughed. "Apparently, he'd been sick that morning and hadn't gotten the tip we were coming. Lucky thing for us, though, because he squealed like a pig on the way to the butcher shop. Told us all about their other cold house locations, and we were able to get the stash after all." He sat back, smug.

Laurie ran a finger along her jaw, fascinated by how Samuel's eyes followed her hands. "So you got them after all? That's remarkable."

"Sure did. But, man, it was a long day."

Laurie pulled her soda close to the edge of the counter and peered down into the recesses in an attempt to hide a discreet glance over her shoulder.

Mr. Shepherd had disappeared. *Probably off to report to Big Jerry.*

She returned her focus to Samuel, noting his arm draped casually along the counter, mere inches from her hand. He'd spent the last hour regaling her with tales of busting up bootlegging gangs in Seattle and smashing backwater stills—each story more thrilling than the last—but her attention remained divided.

Now that her distraction had left, a hollow ache took up residence in her chest. If only the men in her family could be on the right side of the law.

Samuel reached over and placed a hand on her knee. "Penny for your thoughts."

His touch burned against her leg. She swiveled to the side, out of his reach. "I—I was just thinking how much I was enjoying this."

A grin crossed his face. "Well, that's a relief. You looked a million miles away. I thought perhaps I was boring you. Or you were thinking of some other fellow."

She stifled a laugh. "No, there's no one else."

He slid a few coins onto the counter to pay for their drinks. "Can I drive you home?"

The amusement of the moment vanished. And meet her father?

A familiar voice cut in over her shoulder. "That won't be necessary." Johnny stood behind her, his feet planted and his eyes like steel. "I'll be taking her home."

Samuel stood. "I don't believe we've met."

Laurie swallowed. "Samuel, this is my brother—"

Johnny crossed both arms over his chest. "We're leaving. Now."

Samuel's shoulders rose a few inches. "Laurie, is there a problem?"

Laurie slid off the stool and put what she hoped would be a calming hand on her brother's arm, shooting him a pleading glance. "Johnny, give us minute. I'll meet you out front, directly."

Johnny stood like a scowling soldier for a moment longer before stalking out the door.

A moment of silence followed as Samuel turned to her with a questioning look.

Laurie took a deep breath. "I apologize for my brother. He's very"—she fought to keep the edge out of her voice—"very protective. Ever since my mother passed away, he's turned into a guard dog of sorts."

Samuel touched her arm, his fingers stroking her sleeve. "I'm sorry to hear about your mother. I lost mine also, about a year ago."

An unexpected rush of compassion trickled through her. "That must have been difficult. Mine was many years ago. I barely remember her."

He walked over to retrieve her sweater and his hat. "I hope I can make a better impression on your brother the next time we meet." He held the garment for Laurie as she slipped her arms into it.

She took her time fastening the buttons while she searched for a response. "I think you need to give him time." She cocked her head and offered him what she hoped was an alluring smile. "*Lots* of time. And space."

Samuel leaned closer. "Time, eh? I have time." He put on his hat and grinned at Laurie. "I'm a patient man. I believe I can wait him out—as long as I still get to see you in the meantime."

12

Laurie stepped out of the drugstore and into the heat of her brother's glare.

"Just what do you think you're doing?" Johnny's voice shook.

"Can we discuss this as we walk? I'd rather not have it out with you in the doorway."

A shudder worked its way through her brother's lean frame, like a rubber band stretched too tight. Best to be out of sight of the Prohibition agent before he snapped.

Grabbing his arm, she steered him down the sidewalk. "Before you begin yelling, hear me out." Laurie moistened her lips. "You've already said you won't give up your—your evening runs. By keeping an eye on the federal agent, I can help keep you safe. I can find out what he knows and maybe even feed him some bad information to throw him off your track."

"I told you to stay out of it." Johnny jerked his arm free, but kept walking. "I don't want you involved in this."

"I'm already involved. It's too late for that."

A string of foul words spilled out of his mouth. "I don't need my little sister to protect me."

Laurie squeezed her hands into fists and jammed them into her pockets. "You don't know what you need. You need to quit running booze, and Dad needs to quit drinking it—but we both know neither of those things is going to happen, so I guess it's up to me to protect you both." She took a deep breath and reined in her resentment. "It seems to be my job to protect our family's reputation. Samuel already knows rumrunners are landing on the beaches here, it's only a matter of time before he figures out who is behind it."

Johnny's head whipped around. "Samuel, is it? Geez, Laurie, how long have you been sneaking around with this guy?" He ripped the cap from his head and slapped it against his leg. "I can't believe I had to hear about it from Daniel."

Laurie halted. "Daniel Shepherd?"

"He's an old buddy of mine. He told me you'd been seeing that G-man." His lip curled.

Her stomach twisted. She knew Shepherd had been spying on her, but some little corner of her had hoped—or wished—she was mistaken.

"Tell Daniel Shepherd he can watch his own back." She blinked away tears. "I'm doing this to keep an eye on yours."

Daniel got back from his walk in time to see Laurie and Johnny disappearing down the street. Their stiff postures suggested that all was not well between the siblings. Acid crawled up the back of his throat.

He ducked into the alley behind the store. He had no desire to hear their argument. Going to Johnny behind her back had been a coward's move. But that Brown fellow was up to no good and there was no way he wanted his friend's sister mixed up with him.

She deserved better. A woman like Laurie Burke deserved a man she could rely on. A man she could trust. A man with principles.

A man like me.

His mouth grew dry. The shadows of the brick buildings pressed in against him.

A delivery truck idled at the rear entrance. The driver hopped out and held out paperwork for Daniel. "You work here, right? I still got to see your license before I can unload the crates."

Daniel pulled out his wallet and retrieved his pharmacy license, a new pang of disquiet added to the cluster jostling around in his chest. Only a few shipments demanded that level of protocol.

"Looks good. Shall I bring in the merchandise?" The young man handed the card back to Daniel and pushed his tweed cap up on his forehead.

"Sure. Let me give you a hand." Daniel shoved the wallet back into his pocket, his fingers brushing the temperance coin. His stomach churned as the driver threw open the rear door.

"It looks like we've brought you two cases of sherry and four cases of scotch whiskey. Man, what a party you could have with that." The young man winked as he wrapped his arms around one of the wooden crates.

The bitter taste rising in Daniel's mouth stifled any humor. He reached for the second crate, the bottles rattling against each other.

13

"LAURIE, WHERE IS THAT WORTHLESS FLASHLIGHT?" HER FATHER'S VOICE echoed from the far end of the house.

She dropped her pencil and sketchbook on the kitchen table and pushed back her chair, the imaginary world crumbling. The flashlight stood on the table by the back door—the same place he always kept it. She scooped it up and carried it to her father's room.

Dad's lower legs and feet protruded from the closet, surrounded by dusty boxes and wooden packing crates.

Laurie frowned. "Are you looking for something, Dad?"

"Just give me the light, will you?"

His clipped tone made her heart skip. She shoved the light into his hand and backed away. A few small boxes tumbled out of the closet and one crashed at her feet, spilling its contents. She crouched down fingering the small pieces of jewelry, scarves, and hatpins. Her hands trembled as she gathered the glittering ornaments. *Why must everything of Mother's be kept hidden away?* She scooped the items back into the box and clutched it to her chest.

As her father continued his search, Laurie stole down the hall, hurrying to her room. She shoved the small box under her bed. She'd return it later, after she'd looked through it.

"Laurie!" her father bellowed.

She jumped back to her feet and hurried back. "Yes?"

Here." He thrust the flashlight into her hands. "Point it over here." He gestured with his hand.

Laurie tried to hold the light steady as her father searched through a barrel of clothes, yanking through the taffeta gowns and lace-covered petticoats. She blinked away tears. She had no idea her father had even kept these things and now he pawed through them like they were meaningless. Her fingers ached to touch the beautiful fabrics.

"Can't you hold that fool thing steady?"

She turned her eyes away, keeping the light pointed at her father's hands. "What are you looking for?"

"None of your business."

His harsh tone bit into her. He only talked that way when he was drunk—or when he wanted to be.

"There it is." He laughed, an odd twisted sound. "You can scoot now." Dad balanced on his knees, hands hidden from view.

Laurie switched off the light. *He's got early shift tomorrow.*

"I said, get out. I want to be alone."

She stumbled backward before turning and marching down the hall toward the kitchen. Her picture world waited.

The bedroom door slammed.

⟨⟡⟩

Laurie's eyes glazed as she stared at the panel of jacks and cords. "Number, please." She repeated the words, her earpiece silent. Laurie scanned the board and sighed—she hadn't switched on her connection. "I'm sorry for the wait. Number, please." Laurie struggled to keep her voice low and melodious as she had been taught.

"Oh, sweetie." A thin reedy voice twittered into her ear. "I'm afraid I don't know the number. I never seem to be able to remember."

Laurie smiled, lifting the volume control. "Yes, Mrs. Creswell. I know. Who are you trying to call?"

"Mrs. Johnson down at the Fir Creek Crossing. Do you know Mrs. Johnson? Her son has never been the same since that awful logging accident. I like to check in on them every few days, just to see how they're doing. I thought I might stop by, but I wasn't sure if this was a good day or not."

The back of Laurie's neck itched, as if she could feel Mr. Quinn's eyes on her. *Four seconds.* "Yes, Mrs. Creswell. I'll connect you directly. Thank you."

"That's a good girl. Now make sure to get Mrs. Johnson on Fir Creek, not Mrs. Johnson on Cherry Hill. One of you girls made that mistake last time and I was so embarrassed."

"Yes, ma'am, Mrs. Johnson on Fir Creek Crossing. I will connect you now." She stifled a sigh. "Thank you." She repeated the words drilled into her by her supervisor.

"Is this Millie, by the way?"

Laurie held the cord suspended, just an inch away from its connection. "No, ma'am. It's Laurie Burke. I am going to connect you to Mrs. Johnson, now."

"Oh, yes, Laurie. I was going to ask you about attending the library fundraiser next week. I thought you and your little friend Amelia might like to help with the punch bowl." Another call light flashed and the fragrance of Mr. Quinn's hair tonic hung in the air, always arriving a second before he did.

"I'd be happy to, Mrs. Creswell. I'll come by later to discuss the details. All right? I'm going to connect your call." Her voice rose in pitch with each word. She took a quick breath to relax her vocal chords. *Low and melodious.* "Thank you."

"That would be fine, Laurie. I'll look forward to it. Bye-bye, now." A click sounded on the line.

Laurie pressed her knuckles to her forehead. Mrs. Creswell had hung up. She must have forgotten her call to Mrs. Johnson of Fir Creek. *Should I ring her back?*

The odor of Mr. Quinn's hair tonic nearly choked her. "Is there a problem, Miss Burke?"

She lowered the cord back to the desk. "No, sir."

"We are not to be carrying on private conversations from the switchboard. Do I need to remind you of that?" His nasal tone grated at her nerves.

"No, sir."

"Very well." He backed off a few paces, but his presence lingered.

One of the other girls had already picked up her other call. Laurie hesitated. She hated to ring Mrs. Creswell with Mr. Quinn on the alert, but she had little choice. She switched the cords and rang the Creswell line.

"Yes . . . hello?" Mrs. Creswell's quavering voice crackled in Laurie's ear.

"I'm standing by to connect you to Mrs. Johnson. Would you still like to complete that call?"

The old woman gasped, the sound hissing in Laurie's earpiece. "Oh, my—I completely forgot. Yes, please, dear. I was also thinking—"

"I will connect your call now. Thank you." Laurie jammed the cord in the jack. Hopefully Mrs. Creswell would just think she hadn't heard.

Mr. Quinn eased away down the line of boards, honing in on another operator whose posture needed correction.

Susan, sitting at the next seat, tipped her head and winked at Laurie. "Mrs. Creswell?" she mouthed.

Laurie nodded and rolled her eyes before taking her next call. "Number, please."

"Federal building, PA-2015, please." A familiar baritone echoed in her ear, tickling the hairs on the back of her neck.

She took two quick breaths. "One moment, please." Laurie scanned the board. She located the federal building's connection and tapped the cord against the jack to test for an open line. A series of clicks sounded. *Busy.*

Laurie glanced down the row. Mr. Quinn leaned over a woman's shoulder at the far end of the room. She checked the line a second time, now open. "I will connect you now. Thank you."

"Thank you," Samuel's voice echoed.

Laurie made the connection to the switchboard at the federal building. Her hand hesitated over the switch that would disconnect her earpiece from the conversation. She glanced at the operator sitting to her left. "Susan," she whispered, "I'm going to run a systems check. Can you cover my calls?"

Susan nodded, her gaze never leaving the board.

Pressing her palm over the earpiece, Laurie ran fingers across the board, going through the motions of checking the voltage meters and line connections.

Samuel's voice sounded in her ear. "Yes, sir. I believe we may have some action on the area around Crescent Beach. Let's keep a Coast Guard cutter in that area and watch for boats. I'll take a drive out and survey from the beachhead. Some of the residents reported hearing squealing tires and grinding engines, like folks getting out in a hurry. I'm going to keep a few men on surveillance for a few nights and see what's going on."

A gruff sounding voice replied. "Keep me updated. Let's give these clowns a good scare. Got it? How many men you need?"

Laurie bit her lip, her pulse quickening.

Samuel's rich voice took over. "I've already talked to a few on this end. I think we've got it covered for now. If we see action, I'll give you a call. But if you could make the arrangements with Gallagher over at the Coast Guard, I'd appreciate the backup."

"I'm on it. Good work, Brown."

"Thank you, sir."

The lines went dead. Laurie returned the cords to their original positions, her fingers slick with sweat. The scent of hair tonic brought her back to the moment. She made a note in her log.

"Is everything all right, Miss Burke?"

She lifted her chin and smiled at the narrow-faced man reading over her shoulder. "Yes, Mr. Quinn. I thought I detected some crackling on the line, but I just ran a check and everything seems fine now."

He adjusted his glasses. "You weren't due for a check for another forty-five minutes. But I suppose that shows initiative, Miss Burke. Good work." He wandered on down the line.

"I've got it now, Susan. Thank you."

A line pinched between Susan's brows. "Are you sure everything is all right?"

Laurie placed her hand over her mouthpiece. "It will be."

❦

Daniel maneuvered the broom around the edges of the doorway, guiding the road dust back to the street where it belonged. It had been a tougher job when he was a kid, before the roads and sidewalks were paved.

A dog sniffed its way down the sidewalk, its tongue lolling out to one side. Two doors away, the animal flopped on its haunches outside the grocery store.

It had been a busy afternoon, but now that Marcie had arrived, Daniel relished the quiet moment. That, and sweeping made it easier to keep an eye on the switchboard exchange door. On the tick of 5:30, it swung open. Laurie wore a yellow polka-dotted dress, short enough that he could almost see her knees under the hemline.

She kept her eyes to the sidewalk as she hurried down the street, not stopping to look into store windows.

Daniel leaned on the broom, clearing his throat to catch her attention before she ran over him.

Her eyes looked surprised. "Oh, Mr. Shepherd. I didn't see you."

"I noticed."

She blushed. "Well, if you can excuse me, I—"

Daniel stood firm. "I have something for you." He reached into his pocket and pulled out a small package.

She cocked her head to one side. "What's this?"

Daniel smiled. "A new headache remedy. I've made some adjustments to the formula. That old one you keep requesting is quite outdated. I think you'll find this one is much more effective."

"That's very kind of you, but I don't have any money on me to pay you for it and our account—well, it's . . ."

He pressed it into her hand. "It's a free sample. If it works, you can come back and buy more."

Her fingers closed around the packet, but jerked back from his touch. "I hear you spent some time with my brother."

Daniel sucked in a deep breath, the pained expression on her face cutting into his heart. "We were classmates. I hadn't seen him in years. It was good to get reacquainted." He backed a step from the heat of her stare. "Look, Miss Burke." He lowered his voice. "I expect you're concerned I might tell someone about our first meeting. I don't intend to embarrass you in any way."

"Embarrass me?" Her voice hissed. She clamped a hand on her hip. "You don't care about embarrassing me. If you did, you wouldn't have rushed off to report to my brother about me spending time with Samuel."

Coldness spread through Daniel. "I was concerned for you. I don't think Mr. Brown is who you think he is."

Her lips drew back from her teeth. "I know exactly who and what Mr. Brown is. You're only concerned about yourself." She thrust the package back at Daniel. "Take this back. I don't want anything from you. I don't want anything to do with people like you."

Daniel took the package, bewildered. "People like me?"

She pulled off her hat, her short hair ruffling in the breeze. "And I will spend as much time with Samuel Brown as I like. At least he's on the right side of the law." She pushed past Daniel and took several steps down the sidewalk before turning and pointing her finger back toward his face.

"And just so you understand, I'm doing it for Johnny. The rest of you can rot in jail, for all I care." She spun on her heel and marched off down the road, her hat clenched in her fist, her hair bouncing as she walked.

He stared after her, as lost as a boat drifting in the fog.

⌦────✦────⌫

Laurie hurried toward home, climbing the steep hill on Cherry Lane. Somehow she would need to cook dinner for her father and still find enough time to slip out and warn Johnny before he left for the evening. As she approached Amelia's house, she spotted Johnny's car. She sucked in a quick breath, her steps growing lighter.

Amelia sat under the cherry tree in her parent's front yard—Johnny stretched out on his back, snoring. She jumped to her feet as Laurie approached. Rolling her eyes at Johnny, Amelia paced across the yard to her friend. "Laurie, I'm so glad you're here." Her lip trembled as she spoke. "We were supposed to go on a picnic over at Lincoln Park, but then he called and said he didn't have enough time. Mother suggested I invite him here, and now look!" She turned back to glare at the sleeping figure.

Laurie's heart went out to her friend. "He's been working late."

"I know. I know." She sighed. "And he told me that he's been pulling double shifts, too." She ran her hand along the whitewashed fence. "I don't understand why he has to work so hard. Other men at the mill don't put in nearly so many hours."

She beckoned to Laurie. "Come join us. I'm sick of sitting here watching him sleep. I've already eaten most of the cookies."

Laurie sank down onto the shady ground under the wide, spreading branches of the old tree. Clumps of green cherries stood out among the leaves, waiting for a few more weeks of sunshine to make them rosy red. As Amelia accosted her with a steady stream of chatter, Laurie let the anxieties of the day ease from her back and shoulders. Amelia's home and yard had always been her haven, even as a child.

Her thoughts traveled to the image of Samuel Brown, smiling at her from the stool at Larson's, his knee brushing against hers under the counter. Unbidden, the image of Daniel Shepherd standing on the sidewalk offering her the headache remedy, rose to her mind. *"I was concerned for you. I don't think Mr. Brown is who you think he is."*

"So tell me about him." Amelia popped a strawberry into her mouth.

"What? Who?" Amelia's question dragged her back into the conversation.

Her friend's eyebrows puckered. "Honestly, Laurie, you and Johnny are cut from the same cloth. Haven't you heard a word I said?"

Laurie scrambled to remember what her friend had been saying, the words escaping like smoke dissipating in the fresh air. "I'm sorry. I had a rough day at work. Tell me again."

Amelia frowned. "Everyone's working but me. Daddy won't let me work and so I'm trapped all day with no one to talk to. Then when you all get home, you're too tired to carry on a decent conversation." She hugged her knees. "I was talking about Samuel Brown. Marcie says she's seen you at the soda fountain *twice* with him and that you were quite friendly with him the second time. I guess my prayers are paying off." She drew her lips down. "So, when were you going to tell me?"

Laurie shrugged out of her sweater, the air suddenly feeling uncomfortably warm. "There's not much to tell. We ran into each other there one afternoon and he offered to buy me a soda. It seemed impolite to refuse."

Amelia's face brightened. She scooted closer. "And then?"

Laurie glanced over at Johnny to make sure he was still sleeping. "I saw him over by the courthouse and he asked to see me again." A smile tugged at her mouth. She couldn't deny that the agent's interest was flattering.

"I knew it." Amelia clasped her hands over her heart. "He's such a good looking fellow." She shot a guilty look at Johnny. "Well, not nearly as good looking as your brother, of course."

"Of course," Laurie echoed. Both women held hands over their mouths to quell their giggles.

"What's he like?"

Laurie folded her sweater on her lap and fiddled with its buttons. "He's very nice. He tells the most exciting stories about his job. And he likes being outdoors. That's why he asked to be transferred up here from Seattle." She avoided any mention of his roving hand.

Amelia scrunched her nose. "Imagine, someone wanting to come to Port Angeles." She took another berry from the glass dish at her side. "But that's perfect for you, Laurie. You always did like to be out in the woods and down at the beach and such." Her eyes brightened. "You should take *him* on a picnic." She sniffed, casting a glance at Johnny. "I bet he wouldn't fall asleep."

Another giggle tickled at Laurie's chest. "No, I suppose he wouldn't. That's a good idea."

Amelia sat up taller. "We could all go! Let's plan it for a time when Johnny's not working. We'll go out to the beach. The weather is getting so nice. Just think how much fun it would be!"

Laurie's stomach tightened. A double date with her brother—fun? Unlikely. "Not yet. I barely know Samuel. I need more time before I introduce him to my family. Johnny can be so protective."

Amelia slid back down to the blanket. "Of course. You're right." Her face fell. "But before the summer is out, okay?"

Laurie nodded, but her heart sunk low in her chest. Lying to Samuel Brown was one thing. Lying to her best friend was completely different.

When Amelia excused herself, Laurie poked Johnny in the shoulder.

"Uh, wha'?" he mumbled, squinting at the dappled light coming through the leaves.

"Wake up. I need to talk to you before Amelia gets back." Laurie jabbed him a second time.

Johnny didn't bother to rise, just cupped a hand over his eyes to block the sun. "What is it?"

"Don't go to Canada tonight."

He pushed up to his elbows, his gaze skirting the yard. "Why?"

"They're going to be watching the beach and a Coast Guard ship will be waiting in the bay."

Lines appeared on his forehead. "I thought I told you—"

"If you go to tonight, they're going to catch you and put you in jail. I know what I'm talking about."

Johnny sat all the way up and rubbed his face. "How do you know? Did *Samuel* tell you that?"

"I overheard him talking on the phone while I was at the switchboard."

He grabbed his cap and twisted it in his hands. "I thought you said you could get fired for that."

She glanced back at the house to double-check that Amelia hadn't reappeared. "I thought it might be important."

He blew out a large breath, the air whistling between his teeth. "I don't like you taking those kinds of risks."

Heat scorched through her veins. "Like you're anyone to talk."

He ran his hand through his hair. "All right, all right." He sat silent for a long moment before dropping his cap on the blanket. "Did Brown say which beach he was watching?"

"Crescent Beach."

A slow smile spread across his face. "Gotcha."

Cold fingers tickled at her spine. "Johnny—"

"I won't be anywhere near Crescent Beach. You got my word on that."

14

DANIEL FUMED AS HE MOPPED THE FLOOR BEHIND THE SODA COUNTER. *I don't want anything to do with people like you.* The packet bumped against his leg as he worked. It was ridiculous for her to keep using those old headache powders when the new formulation worked so much better.

Hadn't he seen another prescription in the back room with the Burke name on it?

Daniel stowed the mop and closed the store for the evening. He walked to the back room, unlocked the cabinet and looked over the prescriptions waiting for pickup.

Burke, Raymond. 154 Laurel Street.

Daniel lifted the flask-shaped bottle and rolled it between his fingers. The dark glass obscured the liquid within. "*For now we see through a glass, darkly; but then face to face . . .*" The verse floated from the murky depths of his memories.

Daniel ran a thumb across the cap, a cold sweat washing over him. His throat clenched. *Doesn't this ever go away, God?* He slipped the bottle and the headache remedy in a bag and dropped them in his pocket.

Maybe some answers could be found on Laurel Street.

Twenty minutes later, Daniel maneuvered his Buick out of the alley to Front Street, remembering his days of playing cops and robbers in the old tunnels below the sidewalks. The passages remained a testimony to the city's forgotten past, before the downtown was raised to prevent flooding

The automobile's engine labored up the steep hill. Newer homes lined the best view locations on Cherry Hill, quite a difference from the Hollywood Beach neighborhood where Johnny lived. He turned onto Laurel Street, where a dense grove of oak trees obscured a line of tiny houses.

Daniel pulled the brown bottle from its paper wrapper and checked the house number. The Burke house sat back from the muddy road, in the shade of a spreading maple tree. Only weeds grew in the dim shadows under the giant tree. An old screen door hung crooked on its hinges. The aging Model T sat parked beside the small home.

Daniel shut off the engine as sweat broke out between his shoulders. Taking a deep breath, he got out of the car and closed the door behind him. *It's just a delivery.* Hopefully she wouldn't throw it in his face, again. He swallowed hard and walked up the steps to the front door, clutching the package in front of him.

A short, stocky man with a two-day growth of whiskers answered the door. "We don't want any."

Daniel took a step back. "Any what?"

"Whatever it is that you're selling."

"Actually"—Daniel lifted the package—"I have a delivery for you from Larson's Drugs."

The man's eyes lit up. "Oh, that's a different story, then." He opened the door wider. "You ain't Larson."

"I'm Daniel Shepherd—his grandson. Are you Mr. Raymond Burke?"

The man stuck out his hand. "Yeah, yeah. Call me Ray. No one calls me Mister. Never took to it."

Daniel grasped Ray's hand and shook it. The man's eyes were red, like he'd been sleeping, and his hand left a hint of moisture on Daniel's palm. "I've met your son and daughter, Mr. Burke. But I haven't seen you around town."

Ray took the bag that Daniel offered him. "Well, I work over at the Crown Z Mill. I don't make it into town much otherwise. Laurie works downtown, so she usually picks up what we need."

"I've seen several of these prescriptions come through for you lately. I hope there's nothing seriously wrong." Daniel chose his words carefully.

Laurie's father shifted his weight from foot to foot. "Well, I hurt my shoulder awhile back at the mill. This eases the muscles and helps me sleep."

Daniel nodded. "We have some other options, you know. I could have a chat with your doctor. Pierce, isn't it?"

The man wiped a quick hand across his nose. "I've tried some of those other 'options' as you call them. This works fine. I'm careful, though. Wouldn't want to drink too much of it, you know." A wry grin lifted the corners of his mouth.

"I understand." *Too well.* "Your daughter mentioned she's been having headaches. I put in a sample of a headache remedy I think she ought to try. No charge."

Ray's brows pulled together. "Laurie? Headaches? First I've heard of it." He ran a hand over his bristly chin. "Yeah, well her mother always used to have those, too. I guess it makes sense." He nodded to Daniel. "Free sample you say? Well, I'll give it to Laurie when she gets home."

Daniel edged backward, balancing on the edge of the stoop. "I'd better be going. Have a nice evening, Mr. Burke."

"Thank you. It's mighty kind of you to run this out to me. It will save Laurie a trip to town in the morning." The older man clutched the package to his belly.

Daniel turned and headed down the steps.

Laurie Burke stood at the gate, her eyes like giant blue sapphires in the center of a ghost-white face.

15

"W H-WHAT ARE YOU DOING HERE?" THE WOMAN'S PASTY-WHITE complexion caused a lump to form in Daniel's throat.

Daniel pasted on a smile. "Miss Burke, it's good to see you again so soon. I'm just making a delivery. You rushed off so quickly this afternoon, you didn't pick up your prescription." He gestured toward the door. "I thought your father might be in need of it."

Ray Burke stood watching, framed in the doorway.

"You can go now." She pushed through the gate and held it for him.

Laurie"—her father stepped out onto the porch—"what are you being so rude for? Mr. Shepherd drove all this way to deliver my medicine and threw in something extra for you, too."

"Something extra?" Her eyes locked on Daniel. "I thought I said . . . " She glanced up at her father, her words faltering. She looked back at Daniel. "I apologize, Mr. Shepherd. It's been a long day. I must have left my manners back at the switchboard office." She cleared her throat. "Thank you for the delivery, unnecessary though it was. I planned on returning in the morning."

Daniel felt his temperature rising. Was there no way to impress this woman? He stepped past her through the gate. Turning, he lowered his voice for her ears. "Well, if you do decide to still come to town in the morning, you'll be pleased to know that I have the day off. I'm going to do a little fishing."

She raised a brow. "Is that what they call it now?"

Ray Burke left the porch and came toward them. "Laurie was just gonna warm up some stew for supper. There's plenty, if you'd like to join us, Mr. Shepherd."

Laurie gasped, her hand fluttering to her chest. "Dad, I'm sure Mr. Shepherd has better things to do."

Her father turned toward him. "Do you?"

Laurie's blue eyes rounded, her lips drawing back from even, white teeth.

For a moment he considered walking away, just to ease her apprehension. He steeled himself. "No, I really don't have anything else to do. Thank you, Mr. Burke. I'd be honored."

***

No, no, no, no, no. This couldn't be happening. Laurie followed her father and Daniel Shepherd through the front door into their dilapidated house. She hadn't even invited Amelia over in the past four years, always finding some excuse to meet her elsewhere. She didn't want anyone in her house—or close to her father.

And Daniel Shepherd, of all people?

She glanced around their bare walls, seeing cobwebs she'd left undisturbed and the afghan lying crumpled on the floor next to her father's chair. A stack of papers, including her sketchbook, cluttered the kitchen table and the breakfast dishes still soaked in the sink. Her stomach churned.

She pushed past the two men and retrieved the blanket from the floor, shaking it gently and draping it across the back of the sofa. "Please, sit down, Mr. Shepherd."

"Only if you call me Daniel." He smiled, a dimple showing in his left cheek.

For a brief moment, she was back on that windswept bluff. That smile could make a girl forget the man was a rumrunner.

She nodded. "Laurie. You can call me Laurie."

Her father sank into his chair with a grunt. "I'm Ray. As I said before, I never liked being called 'Mister' anything. Never took much to those kinds of manners. We're plain, simple folk, Daniel. That's how the Good Lord made us and that's how we're going to stay."

Laurie's gaze swept across the untidy kitchen. *Simple is right. That's exactly how we must look, too.*

The springs of the sofa squeaked as Daniel sat down. He and Dad chatted while she gathered her sketchbook and the other papers from the table and moved them to a nearby footstool. After setting the stew to bubbling on the stove, Laurie snatched up a dishcloth and made quick work of the tabletop and counter.

She retrieved the bread from the breadbox and popped it into the oven to warm. Opening the cupboard, Laurie frowned at the odd collection of mismatched plates and bowls. She located three that almost matched and arranged them on the table. Pulling open the bottom drawer, she considered their stash of stained napkins, digging to the back for the ones her mother had reserved for special occasions. They hadn't strayed from the drawer for years—not since Laurie last used them as tablecloths for her dolls.

Laurie's attention kept darting back to her father, bitterness simmering in her stomach like the stew on the stovetop. He appeared comfortable and relaxed, chuckling at something their guest said. She ran a hand over the waves in her hair, wishing she had time to go to her room and check them.

Instead, she turned back to the pot. The stew bubbled merrily, filling the small kitchen with a rich fragrance. She wetted a second dishcloth and discreetly pressed it against her face and neck to calm her frazzled nerves.

By the time she finally called the men to dinner, she had filled the table with good food. Besides the stew and bread, she had butter and some of Mrs. White's homemade jam and applesauce, candied carrots, and salad greens from the garden. She silently thanked Amelia for sending home half of the strawberry pie from her failed picnic with Johnny.

As Daniel walked toward the table, he stopped and stared at the footstool where her sketchbook still lay open to the drawing of the bluff over Crescent Beach. He glanced at Laurie with questions in his eyes.

Dad noticed his interest. "Laurie's quite an artist, isn't she? She must have picked that up from her mother. She certainly didn't get it from me." He pulled out his chair and waited as Daniel joined them.

The two men set down while Laurie added the last dishes to the table. She slipped into her seat just as her father bowed his head.

"For what we are about to receive, may the Lord make us truly thankful. Amen."

"Amen," Laurie and Daniel echoed softly, in unison.

She looked up at Daniel, his smile warming her heart for a brief moment before she pulled her eyes away.

Laurie ladled the stew into bowls and passed them around the table.

Daniel leaned over his bowl and took a deep whiff. "This smells amazing. I can't wait to try it."

"Don't wait, man. Dig in." Her father buttered his bread and took a big mouthful.

Daniel lifted his spoon, taking a small sip of the stew, a smile spreading across his face. "Wonderful."

Laurie's heart quickened, her cheeks warming. Her stomach had been growling on the walk home, but now it took all her strength to manage a small sip of iced tea.

Her father dipped his bread into the stew, wiping it along the lip of the bowl before bringing it up to his mouth. "My girl's a good cook, isn't she?"

"Yes, sir. The stew is delicious."

"So, you're helping Miles with the store?"

Daniel nodded. "I used to work for him back in high school, but I left for the University and haven't been back much since."

Laurie spun the spoon around the bowl, watching the carrots pirouette in the dark broth. "What brings you back?"

"I hadn't really planned on coming back. I was working at a pharmacy in Seattle. But when I got Granddad's letter . . ." A tiny crease formed between his brows. "I knew I couldn't just tell him, 'Thanks, but no thanks.' I owe him so much. My mother and I came to live with him and Gran after my father died. If it weren't for them . . ." Daniel shrugged his shoulders. "Not sure where I'd be now."

Her father helped himself to a second slice of bread. "Families got to stick together. That's what folks up here do. We look out for each other. Right, Laurie?"

Laurie choked down a mouthful of stew, her fingers wringing the napkin hidden in her lap.

"Even though I hadn't planned on coming back to Port Angeles, I'm enjoying it more than I did as a boy." His eyes met Laurie's. "I didn't appreciate its beauty back then." Daniel's words hung in the air like the steam drifting from the stewpot.

Her gaze lingered on his chin—clean-shaven, but still a hint of shadow along the jaw. Her fingers itched for a pencil. And the dimples. She hadn't seen them since the night on the bluff.

"It is beautiful, that's a certainty. Though I don't get out to see it as much as I used to." Dad rubbed his hand through his thinning hair. "I used to take the kids fishing and hunting, back when they were little tykes. But they're too busy for that sort of stuff now, I suppose. It's a shame really."

Laurie pushed away the troubling sensation that she was listening to someone else's father.

Daniel wiped his chin with the napkin. "I was thinking of heading out for Lake Sutherland tomorrow. I haven't seen it in years."

Laurie set her spoon back into her bowl. "Hasn't it been a little cold the last few days for that? There could even be snow up there."

Daniel's eyes gleamed. "I was kind of hoping there would be. I thought it would be fun to see it all frosty and white."

Her father bobbed his head. "It's nice in the snow, but the road'll be muddy. You shouldn't go by yourself."

Daniel's eyebrows rose. "Maybe you two would like to join me?"

Laurie's heart caught in her chest. "No, we couldn't possibly. Dad works at the mill, tomorrow."

Dad grunted. "Yeah, too bad." He chewed his mouthful of bread and gave the napkin a sideways glance before mopping his face with it. "But, Laurie's probably free."

She struggled for breath, a flush climbing her neck. "Daddy—"

Daniel leaned forward. "I'd love it if you could come, Laurie."

She clenched the napkin between her fingers. "No."

His face fell. "Are you sure? It's going to be a lovely day."

"I don't think it would be a good idea."

Footsteps on the back porch brought the discussion to an abrupt end. Johnny burst through the door, "Laurie, why's there a car . . ." He came to a quick stop, his eyes widening.

"Daniel, what are you doing here?" He crossed the kitchen in a few strides, a rare smile lighting his face.

Laurie sat back in her chair. Why did this man receive such uncommon welcome in her house? First her father and now her brother.

Daniel stood and pumped Johnny's hand. "I just dropped some prescriptions by, and your father invited me to supper."

Johnny's brows lifted. "He did?"

Laurie gathered another plate and bowl. Thankfully, she had only dished herself a half a bowl of the stew, leaving enough for all of the men. She could grab a snack later.

"You two know each other?" Dad cocked his head.

Johnny nodded as he sat down and picked up a spoon. "Daniel and I went to school together, Dad. I was glad to see him back in town. We went fishing together a few days ago."

Laurie tucked her skirt under her as she sat. *So, they do call it fishing.*

"Well, that's perfect," Dad chuckled. "Daniel here was just looking for company for a trip out to Lake Sutherland tomorrow. Johnny's got the day off tomorrow, too."

Johnny reached for a chunk of bread. "Yep. First day off in a while, in fact. I've been pulling double shifts the last couple of weeks."

Laurie set her spoon down, trying not to think about Johnny's other activities.

Daniel smiled. "I was just trying to talk your sister into coming along. Maybe if you come, she'll relent and join us."

Johnny took a bite and chewed. "Sounds like fun. We'll swing by and pick up Amelia, too. She's been on me to take her somewhere."

Laurie sat back in her chair. "Don't I get a say in this?"

Johnny and her father turned and stared, as if they had just noticed her presence. The corner of Daniel's mouth turned up in a bemused smile.

I thought Johnny wanted me to stay away from the rumrunners. Then again, she had pestered him to spend more time with Amelia. The dimple in Daniel's cheek made her heart jump. *It's only one afternoon. What could it hurt?*

She dropped her napkin into her lap with a resigned sigh. "Fine."

16

THE NEXT MORNING DAWNED UNSEASONABLY WARM, AS IF GOD HAD purposely designed the day for an outing. Laurie stood on the White's front porch, swinging her picnic basket rhythmically as Johnny and Daniel made some adjustments to the automobile.

Amelia squeezed her arm and whispered, "You schemer—what happened to Samuel?"

Laurie rolled her eyes. "This is all Johnny's doing."

Her friend smiled, sparkles rising in her brown eyes. "Daniel's a good looking man, though. Not quite as knock-you-over handsome as Samuel, sure, but he's attractive. He's got a winner of a smile."

Laurie followed Amelia's gaze and watched as Daniel opened the automobile's hood. "Yes, he does have a nice smile."

The two men bent their heads together, looking down into the mysterious mechanisms inside the automobile's innards. Johnny rolled his sleeves and reached both hands into the recesses of the engine. Her brother had yet to meet an engine he couldn't master.

She turned to Amelia. "And to think, he wanted to drive me to Lake Sutherland alone. What if we'd had engine trouble on the road?"

Amelia's trilling laugh drew smiles from both men. She winked at Laurie. "Well, you might have had a lot of time to get to know each other, if you know what I mean "

Laurie's stomach knotted.

"Johnny and I were out driving one time and the car broke down, over by Miller's pond. He had the thing fixed and running in about ten minutes." Amelia huffed. "Not even enough time for a peck on the cheek."

"Amelia!"

"Well?" The woman tipped her head. "Don't play all coy with me, Laurie Burke. It's not like you've never been kissed."

Laurie sighed. "Never by the right man."

Amelia nudged Laurie's arm with her elbow. "Daniel seems the respectable sort."

Laurie bit her lip. She couldn't tell what she knew about Daniel without exposing her brother's involvement. "He's not my type." *I prefer men who aren't crooks.*

"Then Samuel is?" Her cherry-red lips turned up into a teasing smile. "This little adventure might just make him jealous."

Laurie reached for the doorknob. "This was a mistake. You go with them, I'm going home."

Amelia grabbed her arm. "Come on, I was only teasing." She pulled Laurie's hand from the door. "You know I just want to see you as happy as Johnny and me."

Her words broke into the recesses of Laurie's heart. She turned and looked into her friend's pleading eyes. "Fine, I'll go. But no more of that kind of talk. I'm not interested in Daniel Shepherd. I'm doing this as a favor to you and Johnny."

Johnny covered a yawn with a grease-stained hand and gestured at Daniel to give the motor another crank. Apparently one night's sleep wasn't enough to make up for so many late nights on the water. As the car engine revved to life, he whooped in triumph.

Daniel strolled up the front walk with an easy grin. "We're in business, ladies. I need to get Johnny to teach me a few of those tricks." He reached for the basket, his fingers brushing against Laurie's.

A rush of warmth shot through her at the touch. Laurie released the handle, rubbing both palms down her sleeves to chase away the tickling sensation. She turned her gaze away, a flutter rising in her stomach.

Daniel's pulse quickened as he gazed at the lovely young woman on the porch, the breeze sending the hemline of Laurie's yellow polka-dotted dress dancing around her knees. Her downcast eyes seemed to hide a hundred secrets and his heart ached to know them all.

Daniel strapped the baskets to the back of his Buick, Johnny holding the rear door open for Amelia. Laurie's bottom lip puckered as Johnny moved to follow Amelia into the back seat. Daniel leaned against the rear of the car. "Johnny, it's been years since I've been to Sutherland. How about you sit up front and help navigate?"

Johnny paused, one foot already in the rear compartment. "Sure. I can do that." He stepped back onto the dirt and gestured for Laurie to take his place.

The beaming smile on her face almost made up for sitting beside her on the drive. *Please God, no more car trouble.* Daniel retrieved his jacket from the hood of the car and jammed his arms into it before sliding behind the wheel. "The engine has never sounded this good. Where did you learn that?"

His friend wiped his hands on an old cloth. "I tinker. They all basically work the same way. It's real helpful at the mill. They always need a fellow who can fix things." Johnny covered a yawn with the back of his hand before folding his long frame into the front seat.

Daniel drove out onto the main road and stopped, waiting as a few other automobiles hurried past. He sneaked a glance back at the girls. Laurie stared out at the scenery, her hands clutching the edge of the seat.

Daniel cleared his throat. "What about you, Laurie? What types of things do you like to do?"

Her gaze swung forward, her eyes guarded. "I don't know, really. I take care of my father. I work."

Amelia's voice carried through the car. "She's an artist."

He remembered the drawing he had seen at her house—a rendering of a familiar moonlit beach, if he wasn't mistaken. "What types of art?"

"Just sketches, mostly." Her voice barely rose over the engine noise. "People, animals, scenery. Whatever catches my imagination."

"Did you bring your book with you?"

She nibbled her lip. "Yes. It's in the basket."

He smiled. "Good. Maybe we'll find something to catch your imagination today."

When Johnny yawned again, Daniel turned toward him. "We get you up too early this morning?"

Johnny rubbed a hand across his eyes. "Nah, I was just out late last night helping some friends with a job."

Laurie's hands twisted her pearl necklace as if it were a noose. She pressed her bright red lips into a firm line.

17

Y*OU WENT OUT LAST NIGHT? I THOUGHT I TOLD YOU NOT TO!"* L*AURIE* dragged her brother down the muddy trail on the pretense of retrieving her sweater, leaving Daniel and Amelia waiting on the lakeshore.

"And since when do I answer to you?" He leaned against Daniel's Buick.

"You promised." Her throat ached from swallowing so hard. She wanted nothing more than to dig her hands into Johnny's shirtsleeves and shake some sense into the man.

"I did no such thing. I said I wouldn't go to Crescent Beach."

She stopped and caught her breath. "Then, how—"

He grinned. "We landed at Freshwater Bay. It's a nicer cove there, really. It's quiet and closer to town. We may switch permanently, in fact."

"What about the Coast Guard?"

He tipped the tweed cap back on his head. "Never saw us. They were anchored further west. We just stayed out of their way and no one was the wiser."

The air leaked from her chest. When she had told Johnny about Samuel's plans, she assumed he'd see the folly of his ways, not use the information to his own advantage. She grabbed his sleeve. "You need to be straight with me, Johnny. Why are you doing this?"

She could see the emotions playing around the corners of his eyes. He opened his mouth for a brief moment but snapped it shut and turned away. "You don't need to know, so stop asking. Just trust me." He paced back toward the lake.

Laurie stood in the middle of the muddy trail, fighting the urge to stamp her feet and wave her fists like a toddler. With a sigh, she followed, walking on the weeds along the side of the trail to avoid the worst of the mud.

As she stepped out into the sunshine around the lakefront, she spotted Amelia's blue cloth spread across a damp picnic table near the shore. Laurie hurried to her friend's side and helped her lay out the food as the two men made appreciative comments.

"It's Amelia's doing, mostly. You didn't give us much preparation time, so you get what you get." Laurie unwrapped the cornbread.

Daniel grinned. "We're bachelors, remember? This looks like a royal feast."

His pleased expression sent an unexpected tingle through Laurie. She shrugged it off. There was nothing wrong with feeding the man—even if he was a common criminal. Gazing around the full table, she had to admit the meal had come together well. Amelia had brought along most of the leftover food from her failed picnic with Johnny the day before—cold fried chicken, potato salad flavored with mustard and crumbled bacon, homemade biscuits, and snickerdoodles. Laurie had stayed up late to prepare some buttery cornbread and her favorite peach apple crisp to add to her sweet pickles and candied carrots.

She breathed a sigh of relief when Daniel seated himself next to Johnny, directly across from her. The food-covered table provided a comfortable barrier between them.

As she and Amelia took their seats, pulling their coats under them to protect their skirts from the damp wood, Daniel reached his hand across the table to her. Her heart jumped until she noticed that he had also reached out to her brother.

"Shall I say grace?" A playful smile toyed at the corner of his lips, his open hand still extended.

She dried her palm against her skirt under the table before lifting it to touch his. His fingers curled around hers, sending shivers down her arm.

Amelia took her other hand and squeezed it. Laurie pressed back, thankful to have her best friend at her side in this awkward moment.

As Daniel bowed his head, Laurie stared at their entwined fingers. His fingers were long and his nails well trimmed—not at all like she pictured a bootlegger's hands. *He's also a pharmacist—remember?* His skin had a slight olive cast and it made his hand look very tan against her fair skin.

She swallowed hard and forced her eyes shut.

"Father, we thank you for the beauty of your creation." He tightened his grip. "I thank you for good friends and for good food. Please bless both this meal and our time together. We are truly grateful for all your gifts. Amen."

"Amen," Laurie whispered.

Daniel held her hand a moment longer than necessary before releasing it. The warmth clung to her fingers as she drew them back to her lap.

Amelia gave her palm two quick squeezes and flashed Laurie a brief, but knowing, smile.

The foursome dug into the food, talking and laughing together as they ate their fill. Laurie marveled at how comfortable it felt to have Daniel along, as if he had always been a part of their circle of friends.

Johnny groaned at the end of the meal. "What is it about eating outdoors that makes everything taste so good?"

Amelia giggled. "Everything always tastes good to you. I've never once heard you complain about food."

"That's just because you cook so well. I used to complain about Laurie's cooking all the time."

"That's true," Laurie nodded.

He clutched his midsection. "I think I'm going to have to roll back to the car after that meal."

"It all tastes mighty fine to me." Daniel lifted his plate. "I think I need another piece of that fruit crisp. It's amazing."

Laurie smiled and dished him up a generous helping. "It's my Dad's favorite. My mother used to make it every summer."

Johnny took another bite. "I remember."

Everyone fell silent, listening to the sounds of the water lapping against the shore and the birds twittering in the nearby trees. Laurie gazed at the lake, the beauty of the scenery filling her spirit. Lake Sutherland was nestled deep in the evergreens, like a jewel hidden away in a box and only brought out for special occasions. She glanced down at the ring on her finger—a silver ring with a tiny turquoise stone that she had discovered in her mother's belonging. She should return it to the closet before her father noticed.

"The colors here are so brilliant. They're almost too intense to believe." She gestured toward the lake. "It's like a hand-oiled photograph. Look how the lake reflects the sky. It's perfect."

Daniel swallowed his last bite and set down his fork. "You have an artist's eye, Laurie. How about we take a walk along the shore and you can find a good spot to sketch the lake?"

Laurie glanced at the table. "We should clean up first."

Amelia hopped up from the bench. "Johnny and I will do that. You two run along."

Daniel stood. "You heard the lady."

She hesitated for a moment. "All right. Just a quick sketch, though."

Johnny snorted. "I've heard that one before."

Amelia swatted him on the shoulder. "I can't wait to see it when it's done. Your drawings are always exquisite."

Laurie retrieved her sketchbook and followed Daniel to the trail that circled the lakeshore. For a time they walked in silence, Laurie's thoughts and emotions battling for her full attention. She clutched her sketchbook to her middle, half-fearful Daniel might reach for her hand. The memory of his touch lingered, like the ripples on the lake kicked up by the wind. She needed to stand firm. She couldn't allow her feelings to get away from her.

She pushed aside her unnerving thoughts and hunted around for a safe conversation topic. "There's no snow after all."

His lips turned upward in a rueful smile. "Nope. That's too bad. I guess we'll have to try again in the fall."

His words stole any safe thought from her mind. *Try again?*

"But I like it this way. The sun sparkling off the water, the green of the trees, the birds singing . . ." He sucked in a deep breath. "It's how I picture heaven."

She stared down at her feet. She hadn't thought much about heaven lately.

"I'm glad you decided to come." His words were like a gentle touch.

The long grass beside the trail quivered and a garter snake slithered in front of Daniel's foot. Laurie jumped, grabbing for Daniel's arm to stop his motion, a tiny squeal bursting from her mouth.

He chuckled. "Don't tell me you're afraid of a harmless little snake?"

A barb of irritation stuck in her chest. "I was afraid you might step on it."

His smile widened. "Uh-huh. Sure."

She pressed her sketchbook into his hands and took three quick steps off the trail, dug her hands into the grass and came up with the escaping reptile firmly in her grasp, her fingers clutching the slender body directly behind its tiny head. "You think I'm afraid of this little thing?"

Daniel's eyes widened. "You—you just—"

She lifted it up and looked it straight in its beady eyes. "I'm not afraid of scaly reptiles." Bending down, she released it back into the grass. "It's people who act like snakes . . . that's what scares me."

As Laurie wiped her hands on her skirt and turned and walked away from him, Daniel felt a seed of wonder growing in the center of his chest. He hurried to catch up. "I've never seen a woman pick up a snake."

"There are a lot of things about me that might surprise you."

The feeling in his chest kept growing until he thought he was going to burst. This woman had been nothing but surprises since the moment he spotted her on the bluff. "I like surprises."

She shot him a dirty look. "I don't. I like people and things that I can count on."

He stepped around a particularly muddy bit of trail. "Have you found many of those?"

She sighed, adjusting her hat. "I'm afraid not. I guess I'm just doomed to be disappointed by people. Maybe I expect too much."

The smooth cover of her sketchbook felt good in his fingers. It helped him resist the urge to take her hand as they walked. He wondered what treasures it held in its pages. "Maybe you just need some new people in your life."

She glanced up at him. Her blue eyes almost matched the tranquil shade of the lake, but they seemed to have taken on a stormy gray cast. "Maybe."

His heart turned in his chest. He'd accept a 'maybe.'

She came to a sudden stop, her eyes scanning the lake and her lips parting slightly.

Daniel turned and surveyed the scene. The view didn't seem much different than that which they had been passing. "What?"

"This is it!" She rose on her tiptoes. "The perfect spot."

He followed her down to a large rock resting on the lakeshore. She settled onto it and lifted her hand toward him. His breath caught in his chest. He reached for her fingers, but she yanked them away with a frown. "My book, please."

Heat rushed his face. "Of course." He pulled it out from under his arm and handed it to her.

She flipped it open, a tiny smirk playing at the corner of her lips. She turned to an empty page and lifted her head to gaze around at the view, pencil hovering over the paper.

He stood back and surveyed the scene: a beautiful woman, open book balanced on her knees, a glorious stretch of lake and trees behind her. She was right—it was the perfect spot. He pulled the hat from his head and enjoyed the sun's rays, letting it warm his outsides to match the warmth within.

"You probably should have brought a fishing pole or something. Johnny's right. I might be here awhile." She gazed up at him from her perch. "If you get bored, you can go back to the others. I'll understand."

He shook his head. "I could stay here all day."

He was rewarded with a smile that once again sent the blood pumping through his veins at a breakneck pace. Admiring her beauty, he watched her sketch for several minutes. "Why draw instead of paint?"

She tapped her pencil on her chin as she stared out across the lake. "I used to paint. But the supplies are too expensive." She lowered her pencil to the paper. "Pencils are cheap. I like charcoal, too."

Daniel let his gaze wander around the lake. A scene like this deserved all the colors of God's creation, and the way she laid it down on the paper, you could almost envision the shades of green, blue, and brown. He wanted nothing more than to watch every stroke of her pencil.

Probably best not to make a pest of myself. He paced the clearing before settling on the end of a half-submerged log. He pulled off his shoes and socks and dipped his feet in the chilly water.

"That's got to be cold." Her soft voice hung in the air.

"Invigorating."

Laurie set her book in her lap and kicked off her shoes. "Turn around, please. I want to slip out of these stockings, but I won't do it with you staring at me."

He did as ordered, fearing that if he were to get even a glimpse of her garters, he'd lose all control over his senses. A splash, followed by a whimper, drew his attention. He couldn't resist turning his head to take in the shocked expression on her face.

She stood in the shallow water. "That's f-freezing."

"Yep."

A pained smile crossed her face. She caught the hem of her skirt with one hand and sent a small spray of icy water his direction with her foot.

"Hey!" He reached down for a handful of water.

"No—my book!"

"You should have thought of that before." He chuckled, making sure that the droplets fell far short of their mark.

Laurie perched beside him on the log and drew up her knees so only her toes dangled in the water. She tossed her hat into the nearby grass and ran her fingertips through her hair.

Daniel leaned close to get a peek at the sketch resting on her lap. "Beautiful. I like the little cottage you added on the far shore."

"I didn't add it, it's over there." She pointed.

"Really?" He squinted, the far side of the lake a haze of green vegetation.

She giggled. "Maybe you need spectacles like your grandfather."

Her laughter melted some of the frost seeping into his feet. "You might be right. I don't see it."

"It's more of a fishing shack than a cottage. It blends with the trees." She tucked the pencil over her ear. "But I like it better the way I drew it. We'll just call it artistic license."

"I like your drawing better, too." Daniel grinned. "But of course, I can see yours."

She pulled out the pencil, adding a little extra shading. "I always dreamed of having a cozy little cottage next to a lake."

Daniel remained motionless, relishing the way her arm bumped his as she added details to the picture's foreground. "That does sound nice. A little lonely, perhaps, but nice."

She shot him a sideways glance, a gentle smile on her lips. "I never said I'd be alone."

Daniel took a deep breath, filling his lungs with the mountain air mixed with a hint of lavender—Laurie's soap, perhaps? The image of he and Laurie sitting on the porch of a lakeside cottage pulled at his heart. The bones of his feet ached with cold, but he found absolutely no desire to move.

Laurie's pencil scratched against the paper, adding them into the picture. In the sketch, she leaned back against his shoulder, one of her legs stretched out the length of the log.

"That's nice."

"Just some more artistic license."

He nodded and turned his gaze to the water, still scanning the distant shore for the fishing shack and relaxing to the sound of her pencil gliding against the paper.

After a time, her hand stilled. Daniel held his breath as she scooted closer. He anchored himself so as not to move a muscle.

Laurie leaned against his shoulder. She lifted her toes from the water, the droplets sparkling like diamonds on her skin. Stretching out both legs, she draped them along the sun-warmed log.

Daniel closed his eyes, the tension in his stomach and chest melting. Good thing she'd captured the scene in her sketch. This was one moment he never wanted to slip away.

18

LAURIE LEANED AGAINST DANIEL'S SHOULDER, WILLING AWAY THE DOUBTS coursing through her mind. For the moment, everything in the world felt perfect.

The lake, the forest, and the skies—the ideal world with no drunk father, no bootlegging brother, no menacing federal agents. She could even imagine the man beside her was a good-looking pharmacist and nothing more. She took a deep breath and let Daniel's shoulder support her. The sunshine tickled her skin and she rubbed one warm toe along the arch of her other foot. *If only life could always be like this.*

Daniel shifted his weight, jarring her out of her daydream for the third time in the past few minutes.

"Is something wrong?" She hated breaking the easy silence that surrounded this moment.

"No." He fidgeted again, bumping her shoulder.

She sat up, the tips of her ears burning. "If I am getting too heavy for you, you could just say something."

"It's not that . . ." He grimaced.

She frowned. "What, then?"

"I can't feel my feet."

She glanced down at his feet, still dangling in the water, the skin all red and blotchy. She scrambled up. "Daniel, get them out of there!"

His face contorted. "I'd like nothing better, but I'm not so sure I can." He reached his hands under his knees. Swiveling on the log, he hoisted his dripping legs over the side of the log and onto the rocky shore with a slow groan.

Laurie dropped to her knees. "Why didn't you say something?" She dried them with her skirt and began rubbing them with her warm hands.

He shook his head. "I didn't—ow—I didn't want to—ow!" His face twisted. "I'm so stupid."

The color of his skin looked better already. She kept rubbing them at a slower pace, but let her eyes wander up to meet his. "That was pretty foolish." *But romantic.*

"Please stop." He grabbed her arm. "It hurts too much." A wry smile touched his mouth. "I'm sure I'd like it under better circumstances."

She laughed and scooted backward, releasing his feet. "At least you're getting some feeling back." She glanced up at the sky. "We should go. Johnny and Amelia will be wondering what happened to us. I take a long time on pictures, but not usually *this* long." She reached for her stockings. "Assuming you can walk, that is. I'm not going to carry you."

Daniel wriggled his toes and made a face. "I think I can manage."

Laurie slipped on her stockings, but left them rolled down at her knees rather than ask Daniel to turn his back again. Her brother might think the worst, but why should she care? He had his secrets; she could have hers.

She retrieved Daniel's shoes and socks and handed them to him. "Do you need help?"

"No." His brows clenched as he forced his feet into the shoes.

She stepped back as he pushed up to a standing position. She clucked her tongue as he managed a few limping steps. "You really should have said something."

"I know," he grunted. "Next time, you soak your feet and I'll soak up sun."

A tiny spark grew in her chest. Maybe there could be a next time. She slipped her shoulder under his arm. "Here, lean on me."

"Gladly."

The pair stumbled, laughing, back to the picnic table twenty minutes later. Amelia jumped up from her seat next to Johnny. "What happened to you? We were getting worried."

Johnny shrugged one shoulder. "You were worried. I said Laurie was probably just working on a masterpiece. Plus, she had Daniel to look out for her."

Laurie glanced up at Daniel, tickled by his smile. She was glad that he didn't seem sensitive over the turn of events. She tucked a wisp of hair behind her ear and turned to her brother and Amelia. "Yes, it's always nice to have a strong shoulder to lean on."

Amelia's brows rose, a thousand questions dancing behind her eyes.

She's going to have to wait for answers, because right now I don't have any. Laurie followed in Daniel's wake as he and Johnny hauled the baskets back to the automobile.

Amelia grabbed Laurie's hand and pulled her to the side. "You look happy. Your walk went well, I take it?"

Laurie smiled, squeezing Amelia's hand. "Very well."

"Better than Samuel Brown?" Amelia giggled. "Here I thought Mr. Brown was the answer to my prayer. I guess God had other ideas."

Laurie's throat tightened. "Stop it. They'll hear you." She shook her head as Amelia dissolved into peals of laughter. Anyone would think they were thirteen instead of twenty.

Amelia lowered her voice. "So, what does this mean for Mr. Brown?"

What *did* it mean? Daniel was still a rumrunner. Just because he could act like a gentleman when he wanted to, didn't change who he was at heart. "I don't know."

Amelia touched her arm and smiled. "Well, they're both good prospects, anyway."

Laurie turned her eyes skyward as she walked. *God, you know my heart's desire. Please, help me know what to do.*

As they reached the end of the trail, the two men were still strapping the picnic baskets to the rear fender. Daniel looked over at her and smiled. He walked stiff-legged to the far side of the car, opening the door for her.

A sweet sadness crept into her heart. *God, why couldn't he be the one?*

19

Number, please." Laurie wiggled her toes inside her shoes, striving to keep her feet from falling asleep as she sat at the switchboard. "Thank you. I'll connect you now." She flicked the switch, lifted the cord, and plunged it into the proper jack, moving the switch again.

The soothing murmur of women's voices throughout the room created a lulling hum. Those, combined with so many restless nights, begged Laurie to drop her head down on the desk and take a nap. She blinked her gritty eyes and chewed on her cheek to keep alert. "Number please. Yes, thank you. I will connect you now."

Laurie rolled her shoulders. A few deep breaths helped to further clear her mind. "Number please. Long-distance? I will transfer you to that operator. Thank you."

She glanced at the clock. Five minutes. She could hold out for five minutes. "Number please." Her earpiece remained silent. "Number please."

"Laurie?" A male voice whispered.

She hesitated, risking a quick glance around the room for her supervisor. She lowered her voice. "Yes? Who is this, please?"

"It's Samuel Brown."

Her palms grew clammy. Had he discovered she'd listened to his call the other day? Her fingers trembled as they gripped the cord. "Samuel, I'm not allowed to take calls at work."

"I know. One of the other girls informed me of such when I asked her to transfer me to your desk."

She looked to her right and noticed Susan's knowing smile.

His voice spoke in her ear, soft and urgent. "I need to talk to you. What time do you get off?"

She swallowed. "In about five minutes."

"Great. Meet me at Larson's."

Laurie's stomach churned. Mr. Quinn crossed the floor, heading in her direction. *The soda fountain?* She moistened her lips, her thoughts racing. "N-Number please."

"I'm still here—oh, I see. So, will you meet me?"

She pressed her toes against the floor. "Yes. I will connect you now."

"Aha. I heard a 'yes.' I'll see you there in say, ten minutes."

"Thank you." Laurie fought to keep her voice steady.

"No," he paused. "Thank you."

She flipped the switch and lifted the cord to the panel. *Which one?* She glanced over her shoulder.

Mr. Quinn leaned over Anne-Marie's board, lecturing the girl on proper intonation and posture.

Releasing the breath trapped in her chest, Laurie lowered the cord and returned it to the open call position.

Susan winked, brandishing a smug smirk.

Laurie ran a hand over her tense neck muscles. How could she face Daniel? She had never said that she wouldn't be spending time with Samuel. But to meet him right under Daniel's nose?

She glanced at the clock. Two more minutes. Maybe she could catch up to the agent before he arrived at the drugstore.

She continued answering calls, her shaking fingers making it difficult to achieve the four-second goal, but at least she didn't accidentally transfer someone to Timbuktu. When the clock struck the hour, she sat back in her chair and disentangled the headset from her hair.

Georgia O'Neal stood nearby, waiting to take her place at the station.

Laurie stood, her backside aching. "Have a nice day, Georgia."

"You too, Laurie."

Mr. Quinn stood five paces behind Georgia, a predatory gleam in his eyes. "Miss Burke, a word?" He spoke in clipped tones. No wonder he could connect a call in four seconds.

"Yes, Mr. Quinn?" She maintained her smooth, melodic operator's voice even as her stomach churned.

"You sent two calls over to long distance in the past thirteen minutes."

Her mind retraced her calls. "Did I?"

"Both of those calls were local. You realize that you need to clarify the numbers if the caller seems the least bit uncertain. We had to reverse charges on both calls." His bushy eyebrows dropped low over his eyes, like a disgruntled owl. Reversed charges meant extra paperwork.

"I'm sorry, sir. I'll be more careful." Her heart rate picked up speed. Every word spent on four-second Quinn meant less of a chance of catching Samuel before he walked into Larson's without her.

"From now on any extra charges will be docked from your check, Miss Burke." His lips popped as he enunciated her name. "And don't forget, too many infractions could mean termination."

His voice felt like a needle pricking her skin. Repeatedly. "I understand."

As he turned away, Laurie bolted for the door like the building was on fire. She dashed out into the street only to realize she'd left her hat and coat behind.

Samuel Brown disappeared through the door at Larson's Drugs.

⚬━✦━⚬

Daniel wiped the mortar and pestle with a soft rag before returning it to its place of honor. Probably best not to have heavy objects in his hand when greeting this particular customer.

The tall, broad-shouldered man took off his gray fedora and glanced around the store as if searching for someone.

"Can I help you?" Daniel stepped out from behind the pharmacy counter.

Samuel Brown greeted him with a cool smile and an equally cold handshake. "I'm meeting a young lady friend here—Miss Laurie Burke. I believe you two are acquainted?"

Daniel released Brown's hand and wiped his fingers across his lab coat. "Yes, we've met. On more than one occasion, in fact."

"She must be running a little late. I'll just grab a stool." Brown's light-colored brows lifted. "I hear you got a new shipment in this week."

Daniel's shoulders tensed. "You're tracking our deliveries?"

"I keep an eye on things." Brown straightened the knot on his green paisley tie.

Daniel's eyes narrowed. "Even on legitimate businesses?"

"When I feel it's necessary." He gestured toward the fountain. "It's quite a simple matter for an establishment such as yours to serve more than 'soft' drinks. You must know that." He met Daniel's eye with a firm stare.

Daniel felt a surge building in his gut. No one had ever accused his family of working outside the law. "Are you accusing us of serving alcohol at the fountain? That's ludicrous."

Brown raised his hands. "I said no such thing. I was merely explaining my interest in your store." He lowered his voice. "Of course, there are always ways to avoid such close scrutiny."

An icy trickle seeped down his spine. "What are you suggesting?"

Brown glanced around the store. Several customers sat at the fountain and another perused the few rows of merchandise that Daniel's grandfather carried. "We can discuss it another time, perhaps, when you're not so busy. Now, if you'll excuse me, I think I will go secure a seat for my date and myself."

Daniel folded both arms across his chest as the federal agent sauntered to the soda counter, other customers visibly angling away from him. Distrust of government men ran deep in this small community. In the case of this one man, he trusted their instincts.

Good thing Marcie's working the counter today. I'd be tempted to put a few extra drops of phosphate in the man's drink just to see a pucker on that ugly mug.

The door jingled, catching Daniel's attention. Laurie stood in the entrance, her face blotchy, her chest rapidly rising and falling. She stared at him with round eyes.

Every other time she'd appeared at the store, a spark jolted through him. This time it fizzled—like a match dropped in a bucket of cold water. He forced a brusque nod, a cold weight settling in his stomach. "Miss Burke, I believe your *date* is waiting for you."

"Daniel . . ." She stood as if her feet were frozen to the tile floor, her eyes locked on his.

He turned away.

The hurt in Daniel's eyes cut through her and she fought the urge to chase him down and explain. Instead, she pasted on a smile and walked to meet Samuel.

The agent jumped to his feet. "Laurie, I'm so glad you could meet me on such short notice." He beamed at her, his smile wide and welcoming. He patted the stool by his side. "Please join me."

Knowing full well she had no choice, she sat down and cleared her throat. "It was pleasant to hear from you, Samuel, but we're not allowed personal calls at the switchboard."

He perched on the edge of his seat, swiveling his stool toward her. "I apologize, again. I didn't mean to cause you any difficulty." He cocked his head to one side. "Did I get you into trouble with the boss?"

"Not this time."

He patted her fingers, his thumb stroking the back of her hand. "I won't do it again."

She pulled her hand into her lap, resisting the urge to glance toward the pharmacy counter.

Samuel leaned closer, touching her shoulder and letting his fingers trail down her back. "Next time, I'll just stand outside the door and sweep you off your feet when you emerge."

She ducked her head, her mouth dry. Last time she'd been pleased with his attentions. Today, it felt awkward and uncomfortable. "What is so urgent?"

He leaned back. "Maybe I just missed the pleasure of your company."

His teasing, combined with the few inches of extra space, eased the tautness in her stomach muscles. "I think it was more than that."

"Let's order first." He turned to the menu, prominently displayed along the back wall. "An egg cream, perhaps? Or are you in the mood for something else this evening?"

While he was distracted with the menu, Laurie glanced toward the pharmacy section. A gray-haired gentleman stood at the counter, shoulders rounded.

"You only need *two* spoonfuls every day, Mr. Morgan." Daniel's voice carried a note of tension.

"Two every morning?" The man's loud voice suggested he was hard of hearing.

The pharmacist held up one finger. "No, that's one in the morning and one at bedtime."

"One spoonful a day?"

Laurie smiled. When she turned back, Samuel was staring at her with a questioning look in his eyes. She moistened her lips. "I'm sorry, did you ask me something?"

He cocked an eyebrow. "I asked what you would like to order. You seem distracted. Perhaps you'd like coffee instead?"

"Coffee sounds wonderful, actually. And a dish of vanilla ice cream."

He waved to Marcie. "We're ready."

After ordering coffee and ice cream for them both, Samuel turned to her, his face growing serious. "Now, Laurie. I know I said before that I wouldn't pressure you to help me, but I'm getting desperate. I thought I had the guys behind this rum-running operation trapped the other night, but somehow they slipped through my fingers."

Laurie clenched her fingers, pressing them against the smooth counter.

He sat forward and looked deep into her eyes.

She struggled to maintain eye contact, but his long pause made her heart pound. *Lord, he doesn't know about Johnny, does he?*

Reaching over, Samuel placed a hand on top of hers. "You've lived here your whole life. Between the switchboard and the church, you know everybody. You must have some inkling who might be involved in this." He shook his head, glancing around the store. "Once people find out I work for the government, they clam up on me. I can't make any inroads with these folks."

The warmth of his fingers melted into her skin, his earnest green eyes awakening a hunger in her. *How did I end up on the wrong side of this battle?* She took a deep breath, energy coursing through her limbs. "What do you want me to do?"

A smile spread across his face crinkling the skin around his eyes. He sat back as Marcie arrived with their coffee.

Laurie reveled in the easy manner he used with the young waitress. Samuel had a gift for putting people at ease. Marcie's face brightened in response as she set the dishes in front of them and turned back to her other customers.

Samuel took a sip of the coffee and smiled. "Mmm. Just like I like it."

He set the cup down. "Give me some names, if you have any. If not, then ask around. Someone has to know who's behind this."

She poured cream into her coffee and watched as the color lightened. "I don't pay attention to rumors and gossip."

He frowned. "Rumors and gossip are my bread and butter. I just need a place to start." He took another sip and reached for her hand, again. "Please. Just think about it. Ask around. Keep your ears open."

Daniel's voice in the background lured her attention.

Heat climbed the back of her neck, Samuel's hand like a lead weight. Laurie lowered her voice, keeping it barely above a whisper. "I'll try."

"That's my girl." He squeezed her hand and lifted it to his lips. "I knew you would want to help."

Her stomach clenched. Samuel Brown was a good man—perhaps the first worthy man she'd met. Why couldn't she relax and allow herself to enjoy this?

She cast one last glance over her shoulder. Her eyes met Daniel's. *That's why.*

20

DANIEL TOSSED OFF THE BEDCOVERS AND SAT UP, SWITCHING ON THE LIGHT. Brown's nothing but a cunning fraud. Why can't she see that?

The cold floor stung his bare feet as he strode to the kitchen, reaching for the icebox. Pulling out a plate of leftovers, he banged it onto the counter, the harsh sound echoing through the nearly empty rooms. Jamming the leftover meatloaf between two slices of bread—a bachelor sandwich—he carried it to the table he'd set against the front windows. The downtown street echoed with the sounds of folks searching for a good time. From his vantage point, he could see light spilling from the wide-open doors of the card room down the street. Several other storefronts stood open, bawdy music pouring out into the evening air.

Daniel leaned against the cool glass and gazed out. He raised the window sash and listened to the sounds of their celebrations. Drunken singing wafted upwards.

In his isolation, the walls started closing in on him, his skin crawling with desire. He shuddered with the knowledge that he wouldn't have to go far to find relief. He wouldn't even have to leave the building. His storeroom key lay conspicuous on the counter.

"I don't want that life anymore." Out of habit, he reached for the temperance coin, forgetting he wore only pajama pants. His eyes strayed back to the street.

Samuel Brown wouldn't have to search long for his underground speakeasies. Why bother Larson's Drugs when anyone with two eyes could spot the culprits without even trying? Daniel shoved his fingers through his hair. The police and Prohibition agents in Seattle were notoriously corrupt. He hadn't expected to find the same here in Port Angeles.

He took a bite, the chewing motion breaking his concentration. After a few bites, he stopped cold. Perhaps Brown was shaking the Burkes down for a bribe, as well. He dropped the sandwich to the plate as the thought washed over him. *Maybe Brown knows about Johnny's involvement with the rumrunners and is using that information against Laurie.*

Daniel blew out a long breath, the weariness of the day pulling on his shoulders. *Or maybe I'm just jealous.*

❦

The sound of breaking glass yanked Laurie from a sound sleep. Her heart beat a deafening rhythm as she clutched at the bedcovers. A final few clinking noises followed as she sat up in her bed and swung her feet over the side. Tiptoeing across the floor, she opened her bedroom door a crack.

Muffled sobs wafted through the house.

"Daddy?"

Light glowed from the crack under the bathroom door. The sobs stilled, but she could hear his ragged breathing.

She padded through the hall. "Are you hurt? Open the door."

When there was no answer, Laurie turned the knob. Jagged pieces of the shattered mirror lay in the sink and on the floor, mixed with pieces of a busted whiskey bottle. Her father sat cross-legged in the mess, his head tipped back against the wall, tears running down his ruddy cheeks. "Laurie, I—" He drew his shaking hands, smeared with blood, close to his chest. "Just go away."

She sank against the doorframe, her stomach a bubbling cauldron. Closing her eyes, she shut down her emotions. She learned years ago that no good came of engaging with him in his pain. The only thing to do was to clean up the mess and go back to bed. He'd forget by morning. She wouldn't. Laurie picked up the whiskey bottle from the sink. Broken and empty—like so many other things in her life.

Dad's hands dropped to the floor, streaking blood across the dirty tiles. "Leave it be."

Laurie waited until her father staggered off to bed, his bloodied hand resting on top of the quilt. It shouldn't prevent him from working, assuming he was sober by morning.

With a sigh, she hurried to the bathroom to clean up the latest mess. Laurie trembled as she lifted the large shards of glass and placed them into the wastebasket. The broken bottle lay on the floor. She picked it up and turned it in her hands. It wasn't from the pharmacy.

A sick feeling gripped her stomach. *Johnny wouldn't bring him liquor. Would he?*

She brushed away the ridiculous thought. Her father could have bought it from anyone. Even with the Prohibition laws, booze could be obtained without much difficulty. There was no reason to believe that the bottle she held in her hands came from Johnny's late night trips to Canada.

One by one she relaxed her fingers, her grip on the bottle loosening until it dropped, smashing down into the wastebasket full of broken pieces. She picked up the basket and gazed down into the mess. A thousand broken splinters, just like her family.

And here she stood—cleaning up the pieces.

21

DANIEL STROLLED DOWN THE RAUCOUS STREET, HIS HANDS JAMMED INTO his pockets, soaking in the jazz piano strains wafting out into the night. As long as he stayed outside, he'd be fine.

Dark blinds obscured the view into some of the establishments, but light poured out of the windows of one and Daniel identified some of the soda fountain regulars circling the gambling tables.

A woman in a low-cut flapper dress leaned out a second story window and called to him. "Hey there, handsome!" Her fingers twisted a long string of jet beads, accentuating the milky white skin of her bare shoulders. "Why don't you come in and have some fun?"

He pushed back his hat. "It's a nice evening for a walk."

She stuck out her lower lip in a childlike pout. "I think it feels a little nippy out there." She wrapped claw-like fingers around her lanky arms, the ornate dress sparkling in the low light. "Why don't you let me warm you up a bit, first? It's a great night for dancing, if you got a mind to. Or I can deal out some cards. Anything you'd like!"

He chuckled and shook his head.

She sat down on the edge of the sill, dangling one long leg over the edge. "I'm sure we could find something you'd enjoy."

He waved off her siren song and walked away down the street. If she'd leaned any further, she would have fallen into his arms. He wouldn't mind having a beautiful woman fall for him, but he'd rather it happened the old-fashioned way.

And he'd rather it be someone like Laurie.

He could hear the woman calling out to someone else as he wandered away.

A man's voice echoed back, "Hey, Rapunzel, let down your hair!"

Daniel's gloom returned. *Maybe that is the old-fashioned way.*

A shadowy figure barreled out of the alley, ducking around the side of the building. Daniel dodged, his shoulder colliding with the brick wall. Walking downtown at night was always risky—too much temptation and too many drunks.

"Daniel?" Johnny Burke clutched a slack burlap bag, his chest heaving.

Daniel grunted, rubbing his shoulder. "I thought you were working tonight,"

Johnny grasped Daniel's good arm and tugged him down the street. "I am—well, sort of. You live over the store, right? Do you mind if I hole up at your place for a bit?" Johnny fidgeted like a hunted rabbit.

Daniel tried to follow his gaze, but Johnny jerked his arm. "Don't look back." Johnny set off toward the drugstore.

"What's going on?" Daniel hurried to catch up.

"I'll tell you when we get there." Johnny pressed the bag into Daniel's hand. "Here. Take this, would you?"

Daniel thrust the empty bag under his coat, a sick feeling washing over him.

The pair reached the drugstore and Daniel followed his friend up the cement stairs—Johnny hungrily taking them two at a time. When they got inside, Johnny shoved the door closed and leaned against it, his chest heaving. Dark circles shadowed his eyes and creases lined his brow.

Daniel dropped the bag on the table. "So what is this? What's going on?"

Johnny's eyes shifted. "I was making a delivery."

Daniel put the kettle on the stove, knowing his friend would open up in time.

Johnny closed the window blinds. "I saw that Brown fellow skulking around and it made me a little jumpy."

Daniel leaned back against the kitchen counter. "I thought you were just running booze, not selling it."

The color drained from Johnny's face. "But I'm not—"

"You're a rotten liar."

Johnny paced the room. "I told Laurie to keep quiet. When I get my hands on that girl—"

Daniel raised his hand. "Don't bother. I put it together when I saw her out by Crescent Beach that first night."

"You—" Johnny's stopped in his tracks. "You saw her at the beach?" He slumped into a chair. "Nothing goes without notice in this town."

Daniel's chest tightened. "I can understand you getting messed up in this business. You've always had some sort of scheme going. But why would you get Laurie involved in it?"

Johnny lifted his head, eyes narrowed. "I didn't. She wasn't supposed to know." He balled his fist. "She always does this to me. She sticks her nose in where it doesn't belong and then I'm stuck babysitting her."

Reaching in to the cupboard, Daniel pulled out mugs and a canister of tea. "So now you're selling it, too?"

Johnny sank lower in the chair. "I was just supposed to help with the boats. But one of our guys weaseled out, so I had to make the drop tonight, too." He ran a hand through his hair.

"It's a good thing I spotted Brown, or I'd be sitting in county lockup." He shook his head, the corner of his lip twitching into a faint smile. "Remember when we used to play cops and robbers in the tunnels under downtown? I never imagined I'd ever use them to actually duck the law."

Daniel filled his cup, the scent of chamomile filling the kitchen. "What's Laurie's part in all this?"

His friend's face grew dark. "She ain't got a part. I told you that."

Daniel frowned. "It doesn't look that way to me. When I met her on the bluff that night, she said she was helping friends—presumably you and your buddies. And now she's conveniently 'seeing' Samuel Brown. Did you put her up to that?"

Johnny jumped to his feet, his face turning red. "I told her to stay away from him."

Daniel took a sip, letting the hot liquid roll around on his tongue. "Apparently she's not listening." He set the cup down on the table, the image of Agent Brown and Laurie together gnawing at his gut. "You don't suppose she's actually falling for him?"

"Nah, Laurie's got more sense than that. She thinks she can throw him off our trail or something. It's too risky, though. I don't like it."

"That makes two of us."

Jazz music drifted up through Daniel's open window, dancing across his thoughts. How easy it would be to fall back into that lifestyle.

His friend hunched forward over his teacup, clenched brow shadowing his eyes.

A prickle of suspicion drifted through Daniel's heart. "Why are you doing this?"

Johnny started, as if Daniel's voice had awakened him from a dream. "I need the money. I didn't get your fancy education."

"You've got a decent-paying job. What's so desperate you're risking your neck—and your sister's?"

Johnny sneered and pushed his hand through his hair a second time, making it stand up in blond spikes. "You don't know nothing."

Daniel leaned forward in his chair. He'd known Johnny long enough to recognize his junkyard dog routine. Growl, bark—anything to scare you away from the truth. "So, educate me. What's so important? Gambling debts?"

His friend pushed to his feet, jutting out his chin. "Just because I stayed here, doesn't make me stupid, Daniel. I know better than that."

The music outside kicked up a notch, as if keeping pace with their conversation. "Are you in some sort of trouble?" He lowered his voice. "Is it—is it Amelia?"

Johnny turned on him, his face clenched. "Don't you ever say anything like that about Amelia." He grabbed his jacket and strode to the door.

Daniel blocked his path. "No way. You can't ask for my help and then rush out without a word. I have a right to know what's going on."

Johnny sidestepped and yanked at the knob, but Daniel threw his shoulder against the door.

Johnny turned on him, his fists clenched. "I don't want to knock you down, Daniel. But I will. You know I can take you."

Daniel pushed away the childhood memory. "I remember. But I also remember that after you were done blowing off your steam, we were better friends." He clenched his jaw. "So let's get it over with, so we can get to the truth. I can't help you or Laurie until I know what's really going on."

"Get out of the way." Johnny's voice shook.

"I can understand you running booze. I can get that you're selling it to that card shark next door. But letting your sister sacrifice herself to that loser Brown? Are you going to let her move into that brothel next? Is that what you want?"

Daniel didn't even see the fist coming.

<hr/>

The sun crept upward in the sky as Laurie finished cleaning and bandaging her father's hand in silence. The morning oatmeal bubbled in the cook pot.

"I'll stop at the glass shop on my way home from work."

She filled their bowls and brought them to the table. "Don't bother. I have a mirror in my room." With her father's current inclination for glass breaking, it seemed pointless.

"You never said anything about your trip to Lake Sutherland. How was it?"

She shrugged. "Beautiful. As always, I guess."

Dad bobbed his head as he chewed, his face hanging low over his bowl. "We should go out there and do some fishing. You and me and Johnny."

The cereal sank into a deep pocket of her stomach.

"No, wait . . ." His eyes brightened. He raised his bandaged hand, the spoon dangling between his thumb and forefinger. "Let's go up to Hurricane Ridge. Maybe we could stay a few days."

"Sure. Why not?" The sarcasm tasted as bland as the oatmeal. She reached for more brown sugar.

He brought his hand down hard on the table making the silverware jump. "I'm trying here, Laurie. Don't give me lip."

Laurie grabbed her bowl and coffee cup and marched to the back door. Using her shoe, she pushed open the screen door and let it bang shut behind her. The fresh morning air lifted the edges of her hair and cooled her face. She settled into the wicker bench and propped her feet up against the porch railing, knocking flecks of white paint to the ground. She shoveled the cold oatmeal into her mouth where it sat on her tongue like a wad of glue.

The screen squeaked. She closed her eyes and took a deep breath, counting her father's slow shuffling steps. Opening her eyes, Laurie gazed across the lawn at the big maple tree.

He faced her, lowering himself to sit on the porch rail. The old wood creaked.

Acid rose in her throat. She didn't need another mess this morning.

Her father grimaced and pushed back to his feet. "I should get out here and repair that, I suppose."

Fire erupted in Laurie's chest. "You won't. You should, but you won't." The words hissed from her mouth, like steam escaping the teakettle. "Just like you won't go to Hurricane Ridge or Lake Sutherland or anywhere else. You'll go to work and you'll come home and drink. It's all you do. It's all you ever do." She pitched the bowl at the railing.

Laurie pushed herself to her feet. "I cleaned everything up. It's what I always do." Tears sprang to her eyes, but she threw up her fist to brush them away. "It's what *we* always do."

His shoulders slumped, hands hanging limp. "I'm sorry. I can do better. I'll quit." The long-desired words fell flat. "I'm done. No more drinking." He repeated the words, as if saying them again would somehow make them true.

Laurie swallowed. "I have to get ready for work." She pushed through the door, leaving behind her broken bowl. *Let him clean up something for a change.*

22

DANIEL PRESSED ANOTHER TOWEL-WRAPPED CHUNK OF ICE AGAINST HIS EYE.
He had hoped to get the swelling down before showing up at
the store, but the shiner refused to be hidden. How would he
explain it to his grandfather, not to mention to every nosy customer that walked through the door? He stared into the mirror
with his good eye. *It would be less noticeable if I strapped on an
eye patch and talked like a pirate all day.*

Daniel dropped the ice into the basin and reached for his tie
and jacket. He knew Johnny's temper—he just hadn't ducked
in time. He grabbed a last bite of breakfast before hurrying out
the door.

His grandfather pulled the broom across the floor in a
steady rhythm.

Daniel reached for his white coat. "I thought Marcie did
that before she left."

"I dropped a glass. Getting clumsy in my old age."

"You're not old, Granddad." Daniel skirted past him and
headed for the back room. "I'll put the coffee on."

"It's already done. You're late, you know. Were you out
carousing last night?" His grandfather's teasing voice followed
him.

Better get this over with.

As Daniel turned to face him, Granddad's broomstick hit the floor. "What in blazes happened to you?"

"I helped a friend." Daniel turned back to the coffeepot.

His grandfather chuckled. "Well, you know what they say, 'With friends like these, who needs enemies?'"

Daniel filled his cup, the brown liquid sloshing over the rim and scalding his fingers. Reaching for a towel, he mopped up the mess.

His grandfather approached. "Let me take a look at that eye."

"It's fine."

"You look more like a prizefighter than a pharmacist. You're going to wreck our image as outstanding pillars of society." Granddad accepted the cup Daniel extended to him. "But then again, maybe the young ladies will like your dangerous new look."

Daniel took a gulp of the dark brew. "More likely, they'll run for the hills."

The bell on the door jingled and Johnny peeked in before skulking up the aisle toward him.

"Hmm. Our first customer is a friend of yours. Isn't he?" Granddad's eyebrows lifted. "I'll be in the back room if you need anything."

Johnny stood like a penitent child waiting at the door to the principal's office.

"You forget something last night?" Daniel knew his voice sounded sour, but something about waking up on the floor would do that to a person.

Johnny shuffled his feet as he approached. "Daniel—" His voice cracked. He glanced up and then away, as if he couldn't stand to see his handiwork. "Look, I'm sorry. You'll never know how sorry I am. I know that doesn't mean much to you right now, but . . ."

Daniel turned and reached for the coffeepot. "How about some coffee?"

Johnny didn't answer, so Daniel just poured it and set it on the counter. He grabbed his own cup and settled on one of the fountain stools.

After a tense moment, Johnny sat down next to him. "Thanks."

"For the coffee? Or for saving your hide last night?"

Johnny stared into the cup. "Both."

"You're welcome." He lifted the glass dome off of a platter filled with donuts and scooped up two, handing one to Johnny. "I'm sorry for what I said, too. I took it too far."

Johnny grunted and took a bite. "I owe you an explanation. But it's just between us. Laurie doesn't need to know."

Daniel nodded.

"You remember when my mom died, right?" Johnny turned toward Daniel, bags under his eyes.

"Yes. We were what . . . about fourth grade?"

"Fifth." Johnny took a sip of his coffee. "Well, she was hospitalized in Port Townsend for eight months before that."

Daniel set down his cup. "I didn't know that."

"We didn't really talk about it much." He turned toward the window. "My father—he was so broken after Mom died. He couldn't handle being around us kids. He handed us off to an elderly aunt and enlisted." Johnny set the donut on the counter as if he couldn't bear its sweetness.

"When he came back, he was even worse off. He had always been a drinker, but . . . he got mean, violent. And . . ." He shook his head. "Well, it don't matter much now. I left home a few years ago, for all our sakes."

A hole opened in Daniel's chest. "What about Laurie?"

"He never really bothered her. She reminds him of Mom, I think. She knows how to stay out of his way. I was never very good at that."

Daniel touched his bruised cheekbone. "I can imagine."

A wry smile graced Johnny's lips. "Yeah."

"So what has this got to do with everything else?"

Johnny wrapped his fingers around the coffee cup. "A few months ago, I was at home helping Laurie fix a broken screen. I try to visit when he's not around." He turned to face Daniel. "I found a stack of bills in the desk drawer. Hospital bills."

Daniel frowned. "From your mom's illness? But that was ages ago."

Johnny ran his hand over his chin. "Yes. But he stopped paying years ago. He drank every paycheck."

Daniel whistled. "So, what did you do?"

"I contacted the bank." Johnny's knuckles whitened around the coffee cup. "They were getting ready to take the house."

The pain thickened in Daniel's chest.

"I don't care about the old man, but this would kill Laurie. She tries so hard to pretend everything is normal. How would we explain losing the house?"

"You've been paying the bills yourself?"

"What other choice do I have?" Johnny shoved the last bite of donut into his mouth, talking through the crumbs. "I didn't make enough at the mill to even pay the interest. So when the guys at work offered me this chance to make a few bucks—I leapt at it. I thought I could pay off the bills and maybe set some aside for the future, without anyone being the wiser. No one would have to know—about my dad, about my mom—nothing."

Daniel ran a finger around the cup's rim. He knew a few things about hiding the truth.

A tentative smile grew on Johnny's face. "I've even got my dad paying part of the bills, now."

"How did you manage that?" Daniel cocked a brow.

"Where do you think he's buying the whiskey?"

Laurie sucked in her breath, her heart jumping to her throat. Samuel leaned against a creamy-white Studebaker coupe outside the telephone exchange. He held his hat in one hand and a bouquet of lilies in the other. With his head tipped back, he appeared to be watching the clouds.

Anne-Marie sidled up beside her. "He's so sweet, waiting for you like that." She sighed. "I wish I had a handsome fellow to drive me home."

A chill swept over Laurie. She couldn't let Samuel take her home. She pushed through the door, the warmth of the summer day washing away the tension of work.

Samuel straightened and beamed in her direction. "There you are. I didn't call this time." He stretched his arms wide in a "ta-da" gesture. "I learn quickly. I hope I'm not making a pest of myself."

Laurie's spirits lifted. The man could be so sweet. "Not at all."

"I know so few people in town, and all. It gets lonely." He ducked his head, his smile turning sheepish. "Who am I kidding? I just can't stop thinking about you."

Her pulse accelerated. "I can't imagine why, I'm not that memorable."

He cupped his hand under her chin and lifted her gaze to meet his own. "How could you say that? The loveliest face in all of Port Angeles? Not to mention how you listen to all my boring stories without complaining."

She laughed, but didn't pull away. "Boring? Gangsters, hidden stills, and shootouts? If that's boring, then I'm a monkey's uncle."

He lowered his hand, leaving her chin with a faint tingle. "Well, that would have to be one lovely monkey." His brow furrowed. "No, I mean—okay, I don't know how to turn that one into a compliment."

"Don't bother." She laughed and glanced at his Studebaker. Even the mayor didn't drive such a nice automobile. "So, where are we headed?"

He swept his hand through the air. "The world is our oyster, my dear. And you are the pearl. I would be honored to treat you to an evening on the town—dinner, dancing, or a show, perhaps? What would be your deepest desire?"

A shiver ran across her skin. Being in his presence muddled her thinking. "My father is working late tonight, so I do have the evening free." She nestled her hand in the crook of his arm. "But the choices are pretty limited here. It's nothing like Seattle, I'm afraid."

His eyes lit up. "It so happens that I found a lovely place last night. Great music, dancing . . ." He reached for the car's door handle. "Unfortunately, when I showed up, everybody went home."

A giggle rose in her chest. "I wonder why?" She stepped into the fine car, tucking her skirt under her knees.

His eyes retained their teasing glint. "I seem to have that effect on people." He walked around to the other side.

She rested an elbow on the edge of the door. "I guess we can cross that place off our list."

"Unless I can wrangle some sort of disguise. What do you think? A cowboy hat and boots?"

She narrowed her eyes and imagined Samuel in cowboy duds. *Nice.*

He reached a hand through his hair. "Maybe with some shoe polish and a dark mustache, I could be Charlie Chaplin." He climbed into the driver's seat, patting the spot beside him with a welcoming smile.

Laurie took the invitation, sliding closer to him. "It wouldn't matter what you wore. You have a face that is not easily forgotten."

The corner of his mouth rose. "Why, thank you—I think. Or are you still thinking along the lines of monkeys?"

She smiled and glanced at her feet again, allowing for a tiny shake of her head.

He put a hand on the steering wheel. "In that case, how about we leave the kind folks of Port Angeles to their clandestine activities for one evening? We could just grab some fish and chips and head for the spit. It's a lovely evening for a picnic, and I'm dying to see the waters of the harbor reflected in those blue eyes of yours." He settled his other arm around her shoulders.

Forgetting the charade momentarily, she risked a glance up at his smiling face, her heart leaping.

Daniel picked up the pestle and glanced at the compounding book lying open on the counter. It had been a while since he mixed digitalis. The words wavered on the page as he squinted at them with his one good eye. Maybe Laurie was right. He should be thinking about getting some glasses.

Or a monocle.

Granddad leaned over his shoulder. "Be careful with that one."

"Would you like to do it?" Daniel set his jaw.

He pulled back. "No, of course not. I trust you."

His grandfather's words sent a jab through Daniel's chest. Should he be trusted? He reached for the blue jar and tipped a small pile of the dried leaves onto the scale. Not much to fear when it came to these items, but he avoided the supply room when he worked by himself.

Even with one eye closed, he could sense the old man hovering near his shoulder. Irritation crept in and snaked around his growing headache.

His grandfather cleared his throat. "I hear that federal agent was in here yesterday. Was he meeting the Burke girl again?"

Daniel didn't answer. He squinted at the tiny numbers on the scale.

Granddad clucked his tongue and moved away.

Daniel straightened and pushed his hand against his temple. The room drifted off-kilter for a moment before settling back into place. Maybe Johnny's blow did more damage than he thought. He gripped the edge of the counter.

Daniel glanced at his granddad, mixing another prescription nearby. "Brown had the gall to suggest we might be running a speakeasy on the side."

His grandfather huffed. "No one would believe him. That's ludicrous."

"I know, but I think he's going to be a problem."

"How so?"

Daniel returned the digitalis bottle to its place. "I've dealt with his type, in Seattle. I think he was fishing for a bribe."

Granddad's face remained neutral, but his hands stopped and hovered over the mixture. "Did you give him one?"

"Of course not."

His grandfather reached for an empty jar. "Next time he comes by, go ahead and pay him."

The room seemed to tip again as Daniel processed his grandfather's words. "You're joking."

Granddad removed his glasses and wiped them. "Let's just get him off our backs."

A wave of heat climbed up under Daniel's collar. "We haven't done anything wrong. He has no business demanding anything from us. Let him search the place if he wants."

"I don't want some crooked agent pawing through our merchandise and our files. He'll find what he wants to find, and we'll have a devil of a time proving our innocence."

Daniel released his grip on the counter. "I'm not giving that crook anything. If you want to pay him off, you'll have to do it yourself."

His grandfather remained silent, measuring white powder into the jar.

"We don't have anything to hide—right?"

His grandfather's face hardened. "I'm just trying to protect the business. It's your future I'm concerned about."

Daniel pushed his fingers against his eyes again. "I'm sorry, Granddad. I'm not feeling like myself today."

"It's little wonder. Why don't you take the rest of the day off? Marcie should be here any minute. We can handle things fine."

The digitalis waited on the scale. The numbers swam in front of Daniel's eyes. He closed his eye and the motion stilled. "I think I'll take you up on that. You mind finishing this one?"

"Sure. Go on, get some rest."

Retrieving his hat, Daniel dragged himself through the front door of the shop, heading for the narrow stairwell that led to his upstairs apartment. A laugh from down the street caught his attention. A light-colored Studebaker with an ornate grill breezed past. Samuel Brown sat behind the wheel, one arm draped lazily out the window. Laurie sat beside him, a graceful hand holding her blue hat in place as she smiled at him.

Daniel turned and plodded up the stairs, Johnny's story pulling at his feet like a lead weight.

23

THE LIGHTHOUSE STOOD LIKE A SENTRY, GUARDING THE ENTRANCE TO THE harbor. Laurie sank her teeth into the last chunk of fish, dabbing at the grease dribbling from her chin. The wind lifted her hair, blowing it back from her face.

Samuel leaned back against the upholstered seat, stretching his arms upward. "That was amazing. I haven't had fish that good in years." He turned in the seat, his gaze traveling over Laurie. "You are being very quiet."

She stared out at the water, mesmerized. "The water is so rhythmic. I always find myself drifting away when I watch it."

"Drifting where?"

"Nowhere. Everywhere."

He reached for her hand. "How can I bring you back here?"

His touch sent a shiver up her skin. She drew her hand away. "I think you just did."

"So, have you thought about our conversation the other day?"

She rubbed a finger along the side seam of her dress. *As if I could think about anything else.* "Yes, but I don't know that I have anything new to tell you."

He slid his hand up and down along the white leather seat, mere inches from her leg. "I've been wondering about some of the men at the mill where your father works."

Her throat tightened. "My father doesn't talk about work much. And he doesn't usually spend time with them after hours."

Samuel tipped his head, tapping his left hand on the steering wheel. "He doesn't go play cards with the boys or anything?"

"What are you implying?"

"Nothing unseemly. I just thought maybe he would have an idea of who is behind the bootlegging. I could come by and talk to him—"

"No." Laurie twisted in her seat to face Samuel. "You don't need to do that." She slowed her breathing, forcing her knees to stop bouncing. "It would be better if I spoke to him about it."

Samuel lifted his fingers from the seat and placed them on top of her hand. "If you think it's best."

She laced her fingers between his and maneuvered their hands to a safer location away from her knee. "I—I do. He's very private."

He rubbed a finger along her palm, sliding a few inches closer. "Does that trait run in your family?"

"I suppose." His presence sent jolts of current across her skin. She shifted in her seat. "Tell me more about your evening. Did you see any likely suspects?"

He leaned back, creating a bubble of comfortable space between them. "Pretty typical stuff. Men playing cards, couples dancing, women serving drinks and food."

"Drinks? Like hard liquor?"

"Those disappeared quickly after I arrived. Probably replaced by soft drinks and water."

Laurie smiled as she imagined the frantic rearranging that must have taken place.

"I think I saw your brother there."

His words were like a bucket of cold water. She opened her mouth and closed it again. "Johnny?" She retrieved her calm operator voice. "He sometimes likes to play cards, I suppose."

A tiny twitch in Samuel's forehead made her stomach churn. She'd revealed part of her hand.

"I only saw him briefly. He slipped out the back as soon as he spotted me." Samuel lifted her hand and placed it on his leg, as if to draw her closer.

Sweat broke out on her skin.

"He didn't seem to care for me when I met him that first time. Do you think he'd approve of us sitting here like this?" He ran his other hand up her arm.

Her thoughts raced. "No, I'm certain he wouldn't approve." She lifted her chin and forced herself not to pull away. "But that's his problem."

"Glad to hear it." His hand continued up her arm until it reached her shoulder. He leaned close and nuzzled his nose along the side of her face. "You hair smells wonderful. Lavender."

She held her breath. As his hand traveled up her neck and snaked into her hair, it felt like a real snake coiled in her belly. When his lips touched her ear, she jerked back, feeling his hand pull through the strands of her hair. "Samuel, don't."

A grim shadow flashed in his eyes. He released his grip, retreating to his own side of the seat.

She shivered with the tension of the moment, awaiting his angry outburst. "I'm sorry, it's just—"

He held up his hand. "Don't apologize, please." He sat in silence for a long moment, his gaze fixed on the reddening sky.

She scooted closer and touched his arm with her fingertips. "Samuel . . ."

"I'll take you home."

An oppressive silence and chill loomed in the automobile as they approached her house. He opened her door, his green eyes glittering with some unspoken emotion that she couldn't decipher. She stopped him from following her to the door by placing a hand on his chest. "Let's say good-night here."

"If that's what you want." Samuel placed a hand over hers, pressing it to his chest.

Her mouth grew dry as she focused on the sensation of warmth radiating through his shirt, her feet suddenly unwilling to move.

Samuel locked his other hand behind her waist and hauled her close. Lowering his face, he pressed his lips to hers, a lingering kiss. His hand caressed the curve of her back. "That's all I wanted," he whispered.

She kept her eyes closed until his arm released her. She stepped back, her chest aching from holding her breath, her lips tingling.

"Can I see you again tomorrow?"

A moment passed before she trusted her voice. "Let's make it Saturday."

He smiled, touching a finger to the brim of his fedora. "Saturday, then. I'll be counting the days."

Laurie walked up the steps on rubbery knees, clinging to the doorpost for stability until Samuel got back into his automobile and drove away, a cloud of dust rising in the dim light. Her body trembled, whether from fear or attraction, she wasn't certain. Laurie reached for the screen door, eager to collapse on her bed and hide under the covers.

"Have a nice evening?" The voice floated from shadows lingering in the far corner of the porch.

24

Her stomach lurched as Johnny rose from the high-backed chair at the far end of the long porch and sauntered toward her.

"Well?" His voice thickened. "Did you have a good time?"

Her fingers fell from the doorknob. *How much had he seen?* "Yes."

He grabbed her wrist. "I thought I told you to stay away from him."

Her heart jumped. "What was I supposed to say when I found him waiting outside the exchange? 'I'm sorry but my brother, the rumrunner, doesn't allow me to date G-men?'"

His stormy eyes bulged, like a bull on a rampage. "I don't care what you tell him, but I won't have you seeing him. And certainly not—" His lip curled away from his teeth. "You were *kissing* him. It took everything I had not to march down there and tear his head from his shoulders." His fingers dug into her wrist.

"I've kissed other men and you haven't gone after them." Laurie lifted her chin. "Now that I find a decent man, you're just scared for your own hide."

He shoved her back against the porch rail. The rotted wood cracked under her weight and for a dizzying moment Laurie teetered, but Johnny's hand yanked her back.

"Blast it, Laurie. Why do you have to keep pushing? Why won't you listen to reason? I'm trying to keep you safe, but you just blow right through and do whatever comes into your head."

A geyser sprang up inside her, pushing its way from deep within. "You're trying to keep me safe? That's comical—because as I see it, you're the one hurting me." She lifted her reddened wrist in front of his face. "All because I'm trying to keep *you* safe."

He released her, pushing her toward the door. He raised a finger and jabbed it toward her face. "I'm doing this for you." His face had turned purple in the dim light. "You stay away from Brown."

"I'm not a child and you're not my father."

"I wish I were—you'd be a lot better off."

"I'm not so sure about that," she snapped. The evening air grew hushed and still, with even the crickets falling silent.

Johnny pushed his hand up through his hair. "If I ever catch him touching my little sister like that again"—He dropped his hand and glared at her—"I'll kill him."

She forced herself to breathe slowly as she rubbed her bruised wrist. There was no point in throwing more gasoline on the flames. "He's not like that. He treats me with respect."

"Is that what he calls it?"

"You wouldn't understand." She turned toward the door and reached for the knob. "There's no use talking to you about this."

He pushed his hand against the door. "Laurie, please." Softening his voice, he continued. "I understand better than you think." He blew out a long breath. "Look, I only have a few more runs to make and I'll be done. I know you think you're protecting me, but I won't let you to do something that you'll regret."

She refused to meet his eyes, keeping her gaze locked on the door. *I'll do what I have to do.*

❦

Daniel woke late the next morning, relieved as the ceiling came into focus. He touched his puffy eyelid. The swelling had lessened and he could now see with both eyes. He raised his head from the pillow, noting how the sun spilled in through the tall window and extended across the bedroom floor. Stretching his arms upward, he felt the muscles in his back unwind.

His mind flashed to the memory of Laurie driving away in Brown's car. Daniel crashed back against the mattress, glaring at the cracks in the ceiling.

That afternoon at the lake had been so idyllic. He could still feel her leaning against him—gentle and trusting.

He balled his hands into fists and drove them into the bedcovers. She deserved better than Samuel Brown. He had to find a way to convince her of that.

Daniel pushed up from the bed and padded down the hall to the bathroom he shared with the other two apartments. He splashed cold water onto his face, relishing the startling effect on his senses.

The droplets cascaded from his face into the sink as he examined his reflection in the mirror. The effects of Johnny's blow were fading, but he still looked like he'd been in a barroom brawl.

It didn't matter. He had to see Laurie and find some way to convince her that Brown wasn't worth her time. And even if she was only seeing Samuel Brown to protect her brother, someone had to step forward to protect her. That someone might as well be him.

The whole next day passed in a blur. Laurie sat perfectly erect at the switchboard, her hands and voice doing all the work, while her mind wandered elsewhere.

What was I thinking? He's a federal agent; my brother is a rumrunner.

She fiddled with the cord between her fingers, lifting it from one hole and jabbing it into the next, pressing on her earpiece with a single finger hoping that it would help her concentrate. She imagined Samuel's fingers running through her hair and she closed her eyes for a second and shivered, the hair on the back of her neck standing up in response.

And then there was Daniel. She sighed. How foolish to pine after a man so utterly unsuitable. She ran a hand across her face, trying to push away the battling images.

"Are you feeling okay?" Anne-Marie leaned close to her and whispered.

Laurie completed her call and nodded to her friend. "Just a draft." She ran a quick hand over her finger waves. She'd spent extra time on them this morning, dawdling in front of the mirror far longer than usual. Her father, working the night shift this week, had gotten home, given her a bleary-eyed grunt, and headed straight to bed.

Laurie handled another call before allowing her mind to wander back to Samuel. She still marveled at how he reacted when she pulled away. She was accustomed to men with fiery tempers. His quiet response completely disarmed her. "He respects me," she had told Johnny. *Then why the stolen kiss?*

Her life had been shaped by her father's drunken rages and Johnny's sober ones. What did she know of respect? Samuel's lingering touches left her reeling.

Laurie closed her eyes between calls. She had to make the images and sensations fade so she could focus on her work.

⊙━✦━⊙

Amelia answered the door even before Laurie had finished knocking. Seizing Laurie's hand, Amelia pulled her inside, light dancing in her eyes. "I'm so glad you've come!"

Laurie let Amelia take her sweater, hat, and pocketbook before settling on the sofa.

"Your hair looks wonderful." She reached up and touched the gentle waves clinging to the sides of Laurie's face. "I knew you'd get the hang of it."

A wan smile lifted Laurie's lips, though she felt like collapsing on her friend's shoulder and weeping. The tensions of the past weeks made her head spin.

Amelia cocked her head to the side. "What's going on?" Her lips pressed into a line. "Is it Daniel? Samuel?" She grabbed onto Laurie's hands and squeezed.

When Laurie winced, her friend looked down and gasped. Pulling back her sleeve, she stared at the marks on her wrist. "What's this?"

Laurie yanked her sleeve back down. She hadn't come to tattle on Johnny. She wanted her friend's sunshiny outlook to blow some warmth back into her day.

"Who did that to you?" Amelia's eyes rounded.

Laurie pulled away and stood. "It's nothing. I banged it against the doorframe on my way out this morning."

Amelia's face dissolved into a frown. "I'm not stupid."

Laurie's heart plummeted. She sank down next to her friend on the sofa.

"It wasn't Daniel, was it?"

"No, of course not."

"Good." Amelia folded her hands in her lap. "He looked kind enough, but sometimes looks can be deceiving." She sat back and eyed Laurie. "Your father?"

Laurie swallowed and glanced at her hands. "No."

Amelia sprang up and paced around the room. "I know your father has hit you before. Not that you'd ever confide in me about it."

A stabbing pain pierced Laurie's heart. "What makes you think that?"

Her friend stopped midstride and settled her fists on her hips. "Johnny."

Laurie's jaw dropped. "He—he said that?"

"Not in so many words. But I've heard enough to realize that your father is a violent man."

Laurie pushed to her feet, her knees trembling. "You take that back, Amelia White."

"Then tell me the truth."

A silent cry rose in Laurie's throat. *No one can know.* She covered her face with her hands.

Amelia walked to Laurie's side and tugged her hands downward. "Enough secrets. We're best friends. You understand I'll love you regardless, right?"

A tear slipped from Laurie's eye and she lifted one hand free to brush it away. "My father doesn't hit me. But he used to hit Johnny." She gulped back her tears.

"That's why he left home?" Amelia's shoulders sank as if she were the one who had been beaten down.

"Yes." Laurie bobbed her head, not trusting her voice.

Amelia's mouth turned downward. "Did it happen often? I spent so much time with you two. I never saw any signs."

"No, only . . ."—Laurie pushed her fingers against her eyes, trying to use pressure to stop the tears—". . . Only when . . ."

Footsteps sounded in the hall. Both women jumped to their feet.

Johnny stood in the entrance to the room, his face haggard. "The door was open." The air fell silent but for the sound of breathing. "You going to finish that statement, Laurie?"

Laurie ran the back of her hand under her eyelids to catch the moisture.

He turned to Amelia, his chin firm. "She means to say, he only hit me when he was drunk." He faced his sister, his expression dark and unreadable. "But that's not completely true. He hit me worse when he wanted to *be* drunk."

"Johnny . . ." Amelia's voice broke. She dropped Laurie's hands and moved toward him.

He raised a hand to keep her at arm's length. "Wait." He turned to Laurie. "I never told her anything. You've got to know that."

Laurie felt their pain merge, like three vines clinging together on the same tree.

Amelia stood between the two of them, glancing back and forth. "How did I not know any of this?" A tiny crease formed between her brows. "You were both like family to me, but you kept me in the dark." She clamped her hands into fists. "You two are like locked rooms. You don't let anyone inside. Not even me." Tears appeared in her eyes.

Johnny's face contorted. "Amelia."

Amelia pulled at her dress collar as if in sudden need of air. "You were willing to marry me but not tell me anything about this?"

Johnny took a step toward her, but she pushed him away and took several steps back.

"You've heard the wedding vows before, haven't you, Johnny?" Her voice rose. "Good times and bad? If we're going to be family, I don't want to be sheltered and protected like some child." She took another step back, away from the two of them, a new shadow crossing her face. "The marks on your wrist, Laurie—if it wasn't your father, then who?" A tear trailed down her cheek, as if she already knew the answer to her own question.

Laurie sank onto the edge of the sofa, unable to speak. The truth would hurt Amelia worse than simple bruises.

Johnny took his cap in his hand, his shoulders sagging. "It was me."

25

LAURIE CROSSED HER LEGS AND JIGGLED THE TOE OF HER SHOE UNDER the cover of the soda fountain counter. The fragrance of fresh coffee had pulled her in from the sidewalk like a honeybee to an apple blossom. Since her father was still on nightshift, she hadn't bothered to brew any this morning and had sneaked out early so as not to wake him. She'd had enough family drama for a few days.

She couldn't deny the undeniable urge to see Daniel, again. And yet, since she'd walked through the door, she'd had difficulty meeting his eye.

Now, watching Daniel's back as he poured cream into the pitcher, she felt a fresh shiver race through her.

What am I doing here? Last night all she could think of was Samuel. Now she sat pondering Daniel's back.

He straightened, turned, and passed the pitcher over to her with a hesitant smile. "You're my first customer this morning."

She tipped a small stream into her cup, careful not to let it run over the top. "I thought you had turned the soda fountain over to Marcie."

"She doesn't come in for a few hours yet. We don't get many customers this early."

She sipped the coffee, careful to keep her eyes on the cup and not let them drift back to Daniel. Every time she looked at him, she felt a needle jab her heart. They'd had such a wonderful time at the lake, but she'd barely spoken to him since. And that had been when she was here with Samuel.

He leaned on the counter. "How are those headaches?"

She glanced up at him from under her lashes, holding the cup in front of her lips. "I haven't had any trouble with them lately." She noticed the bruise on his face and nearly reached to touch it before she caught herself. "What happened to you?"

"A little late-night brawl. No big deal."

The glint in his eye told her he was teasing, but she decided not to pursue it. Instead, she glanced over his shoulder at the clock. Twenty minutes until her shift. "You must have things to be doing. Don't let me stop you." She fingered the cup, half hoping he'd stay.

He did.

They spent the time talking about her work at the exchange and the customers at the pharmacy. Laurie marveled at how easy it was to talk with the man—no tension in the air, like the time she spent with Samuel.

Maybe I'm just more comfortable around gangsters. She gazed at his long fingers as he tapped them on the counter, overcome with a sudden longing to touch his hands.

She finished her coffee and laid a coin on the counter. "I should be getting to work, I suppose."

He pushed the coin back to her. "Keep it. I've missed talking to you. I'm sorry I was rude when you came in the last time."

"It was awkward. I shouldn't have come."

"No." He shook his head. "It was unprofessional of me. I need to apologize." He paused, gazing at her. "I'd like to make it up to you."

The hair prickled on Laurie's arms.

"Let me take you to dinner tonight."

She swallowed, words failing her. *Dinner with a federal agent one night and a rumrunner the next?*

He leaned forward, palms against the marble counter. "Unless you had other plans?"

Her breath quickened as she gazed into his eyes. "No, I don't. Not tonight, anyway."

A smile spread across his face. "Is that a yes?"

Have I gone completely insane? "Yes."

☙——◆——❧

Daniel hurried through his day and rushed out a few minutes early to change his clothes. After spilling some sulfur powder on his sleeve, he decided it would be best to not arrive smelling like brimstone.

He hurried down to the exchange, his heart swinging between joy and dread. Somehow, he needed to convince Laurie of Brown's true nature without sounding the jealous suitor that he was.

Brown stood at the corner, reclining against his pretentious Studebaker. The government man's fedora slanted to the side, his hands hidden in the pockets of his wool slacks.

Daniel set his jaw. Brown may look like a gentleman out for a jaunt, but he'd already convinced Daniel that inside the well-dressed man lurked the soul of a snake.

Brown straightened as Daniel approached, a smirk creasing his face. "Ah, Mr. Shepherd. Are you here to meet one of the girls?"

His words were like sandpaper to Daniel's nerves. "As a matter of fact, I am."

Brown turned and gazed at the squat brick building. "It's a wonderful place"—a smile twisted the corner of his lip—"filled wall to wall with lovely young ladies. No better hunting ground for a man on the prowl." He turned and faced Daniel, a dark look settling in his eyes. "Except perhaps a nursing college."

Daniel's throat tightened. *Brown couldn't know about that.*

"You went to the University of Washington, right?" Brown brushed lint from the hem of his jacket, his voice as slick as oil. "You must have spent some time around the nursing school."

Daniel's mind raced. What possible reason would Brown have for digging into his past? His palms grew damp and he slipped them into his pockets to discreetly dry them. "Yes."

"And you worked in a Seattle pharmacy, too?"

"Yes." The hair on his neck prickled. "How did you know that?"

Brown folded his arms across his chest and smiled. "People talk. I listen. It's amazing what you can learn."

At that moment, the door to the exchange opened and several young women exited the building, Laurie at the rear. She stood still while the others departed, her gaze flicking between the two men.

Daniel, still reeling from Brown's revelations, held his tongue.

Laurie approached, her lips opening and closing like a fish struggling for a breath. "Samuel. Daniel. This is a surprise."

Brown raised his eyebrow at Daniel. "Could it be that we are here to meet the same young lady? Now that makes things uncomfortable, doesn't it?"

Laurie fingered her skirt. "Samuel, I thought our plans were for tomorrow night."

"So they are." He took his hat in his hands. "I just thought I'd come by and see if you'd like a ride home from work. But I see now that you already have that covered. I'm glad you are in such capable"—he cast a pointed glance at Daniel—"and *experienced* hands."

Daniel had misjudged the federal agent. Brown didn't have the soul of a snake—he didn't have a soul at all.

Brown nodded to Laurie and Daniel. "You two have fun tonight." He inclined his head toward Daniel. "Treat her right. She deserves it." A momentary smirk lifted his mouth as he turned back toward Laurie. "I have plans of my own tonight. I thought I'd take a long drive—see if I can find any excitement brewing."

He took her hands and leaned down, brushing a kiss against her cheek. "I'll see you tomorrow, beautiful."

She blushed and stepped back, but her eyes lingered on Brown as he made his way to his automobile.

Daniel's stomach soured. The silence grew bulky between them.

A flurry of emotions played out in Laurie's eyes. "I'm sorry," she said, finally. "I didn't know he would be here."

Daniel shrugged one shoulder. "It doesn't matter." He struggled to sort out the conflicting sensations in his gut. Seeing her reaction to Brown's attention made him want to turn on his heel and head for home.

And yet, the luminous blue eyes pulled at him. Daniel set his jaw, determined to wipe every thought of Samuel Brown from her mind and heart. Offering an elbow, Daniel forced a smile. "Shall we?"

Her cherry-red lips pressed together and she slid her hand into the crook of his arm. "I'm ready, if you are."

He escorted her down the street, his gut still churning from Brown's artful insinuations. How much did he know, and whom had he told? A cold chill swept over Daniel. This dinner with Laurie might be his last.

Laurie struggled to maintain her composure as she strolled down the street, her hand on Daniel's arm. All day she had been thinking of this moment, but seeing Samuel waiting at the door had thrown her heart into a whirlwind.

She cast a quick glance up at Daniel's face, the bruise on his cheekbone drawing her eyes. *I am going to dinner with a rum-running gangster. So much for turning over a new leaf.*

One thing was certain. She wouldn't be kissing those lips goodnight.

⚮

The candles flickered, casting a warm radiance on Laurie's beautiful face. Their conversation—stilted at first—dissolved into easy banter. Daniel took a sip of his water as Laurie spoke of summertime visits to relatives who lived on Orcas Island in the San Juans. He regaled her with stories about how he, Johnny, and the other boys snuck through the downtown tunnels, pretending to search for lost pirate treasure or rescue Chinese slaves.

By the time they finished dessert, Laurie's face sported a ruddy glow that warmed Daniel's heart. He dared to take her hand as they walked down the street to his Buick. A thin crescent moon swung low in the sky over the water, like a fishing hook angling for a big catch.

Daniel hated for the evening to end, plus he still hadn't broached the unpleasant subject of Brown. "Would you care to go for a drive?"

Her fingers stiffened in his grip.

He cleared his throat. "It's a beautiful evening. We could drive down the spit."

"I don't think so." She hesitated and squeezed his hand. "But I had a wonderful time tonight."

A cloud dropped over him. "I'll drive you home."

After pulling up to her house, Daniel cut the engine and the sputtering motor fell silent. The wind had picked up and a chilly breeze flowed through the car. "Before I walk you to the door, Laurie—"

"That's not necessary."

He raised his hand to bid her to wait. "I need to tell you something. Please, just give me one more minute of your evening."

Laurie adjusted her hat before turning to give him her full attention.

He swallowed and pushed the words out. "You're seeing Samuel Brown tomorrow."

A shadow crossed her face and she pulled her hands into her lap.

"I think you need to know the truth." He took another deep breath and blew it out. "He's not what he seems. He's a crooked agent."

Her brow furrowed and she wove her fingers together in a tight nest. "What do you mean?"

"He's been in the drugstore looking for a bribe."

"He asked you for a bribe—for what?" She cocked a brow. "Why would you need to bribe a federal agent?"

Daniel brushed a hand across his face. "We don't—I mean, we're not hiding anything."

She pursed her lips. "But he asked you for a bribe?"

"Well, not in so many words. But he was hinting."

She rolled her eyes skyward.

He reached for her arm. "Listen, Laurie, I've talked to Johnny. He told me why you are seeing Brown. But I agree with him, you're taking too big of a chance. The man's—"

"I'm not listening to this." Laurie grabbed for the door handle and pushed it open.

He grasped for her hand, but she bolted from the car. Pushing open his own door, he raced after her. "Laurie—"

She rounded on him, face flushed. "You and Johnny are two of a kind, aren't you? You think you can control me. *Protect* me." She stuck her finger in his face. "But you're only protecting yourselves." She sputtered. "Crooked? Look who's talking. I can't believe I agreed to go out with you. I've had enough of men who make promises with one side of their mouth and lies with the other."

Her fiery glare sent a jolt through his system. Daniel scrambled for words that wouldn't worsen the moment.

"I deserve better." She twisted her pearl necklace like a noose. "Samuel Brown is respectful. And respectable, for that matter. What do you or Johnny know about that?" She jabbed her finger against Daniel's chest. "You can tell Johnny I'm done protecting him. You two deserve what you get." Laurie turned and bolted into the house, slamming the door behind her.

Daniel pulled off his hat and ran his fingers through his hair. He stared at the ramshackle house as the porch light clicked off, plunging him into semi-darkness. A thick layer of clouds drifted in from the water, blotting out the moon.

26

LAURIE DIDN'T BOTHER PUTTING IN THE WAVE COMBS BEFORE FALLING INTO bed and pulling the covers over her head. *What is it with men?* They can't all be drunks and crooks. She sighed, rubbing her toes together to warm them. Wind rattled her window and the first drops of rain tapped on the roof.

She rolled over and curled up on her side, drawing Mama's afghan close under her chin. The soft yarn brought its own peace. As she closed her eyes, she pictured Samuel Brown's pleasant smile and wide green eyes. *At least he's one of the good guys.*

She longed to confide in Amelia and get her advice about this situation, but her friend still didn't know about the rum-running. And Laurie didn't want to be the one to tell her.

She tossed and turned, the sheets tangling about her legs. Clicking on the lamp, Laurie climbed out of bed and padded over to her desk. Sliding open the drawer, she fingered her mother's jewelry box. *So many secrets, hidden away.*

She pushed it aside and retrieved her sketchbook. Hurrying back to the warmth of her bed, Laurie tucked her feet back under the covers. Propping a pillow behind her back, she gripped the pencil and turned to a blank page.

Laurie slid the pencil across the paper, sketching Samuel's profile, the hymnbook open in his hands, sunlight streaming through the stained glass window behind him. Her pencil wandered to the far side of the paper and she sketched Daniel Shepherd, leaning over his mortar and pestle, dark brows knit together in concentration. She frowned, unable to get the line of his jaw exactly right.

Laurie tapped the pencil against her mouth as she listened to the rain pattering on the roof. Was Johnny out on the water tonight? Pulling her drawing of Crescent Beach and a fresh sheet of paper, she sketched the image from the perspective of the water, the boat in the foreground and the beach and the dark bluff beyond, adding streaks of falling rain. Several shadowy figures hunched in the boat, rows extended.

A few more shipments—that's what he'd said. Laurie shivered and pulled the afghan higher around her middle. She added details on the shoreline and shaded the bluff, a dark mass against the sky. An automobile at the top with its headlights aglow, showing the sailors where to land.

There must be some way to help Samuel and still keep Johnny safe. Her eyes wandered back to the sketch of Samuel singing in church. Would he show her brother any mercy?

The expanding sketch now consumed most of the page. She used the edge of the pencil, deepening the shadows on the dark bluff, leaving white streaks where the automobile's headlamps glared through the murky night.

The beach itself looked so empty and flat. She penciled in a few logs, but they created little depth for the picture. With a grimace, she added a lone figure, waiting for the boat to arrive. Daniel perhaps, acting as lookout. But as her pencil scratched along the beach section of the image, she glanced back at the drawings of Mr. Shepherd and Mr. Brown, a cold finger reaching into her heart.

Samuel had mentioned a long drive tonight. Her heart skipped a beat.

Throwing back the covers, she swung her feet over the edge, the sketchbook falling to the floor in her haste. With a kick of her foot, she sent it sliding under the bed. Laurie hurried to her closet, stripped off her nightgown, and dressed in warm clothes. Grabbing her raincoat and hat in one hand, she scooped up her shoes in the other.

She glanced at the clock—fifteen minutes past midnight. She sank down on the edge of her bed, her breathing ragged. If the men were going to Canada, they would have left by now. There was no way to get word to them.

What do I do, God?

Rain thrummed on the roof. She squeezed her coat to her chest. She could go to Johnny's house and look for him there. Or to the dock. *But what if they've already gone?*

Samuel's face loomed up in her mind. He rented the old Smythe place on Maple Street.

Laurie crept across her bedroom and eased open the door. She peered down the dark hall, relieved to hear her father's snores. Stealing through the house, Laurie paused to gather up her father's flashlight from the drawer in the kitchen.

She opened the door and slipped out to the back porch without a sound. Barely breathing, she inched the door closed behind her. Jamming her bare feet into her shoes, she pushed her arms into the sleeves of her coat.

Laurie's heart pounded as she pattered down the dark steps and raced across the wet grass. The flashlight bounced in her pocket. She vowed not to use it unless absolutely necessary. The last thing she needed was for a neighbor to spot her sneaking out after midnight. Her family already gave the town enough material for their gossip chains.

Laurie hurried to the Smythe house, just five blocks away, splashing through mud puddles and soaking her shoes. The shrubs at the side of the road offered minimal protection.

She approached the house, relieved to see the windows completely dark. Samuel's car was nowhere to be seen. Stepping carefully around the corner, she withdrew the flashlight and flicked it on. Laurie wrapped her fingers over the lens to keep the light dim. Inching step by step, she stole around the back of the house and pointed the shaft of light down into the alley.

The Studebaker gleamed in the fragile beam, rain streaming off its hard top.

Hot tears sprang to her eyes. *Such a fool, tromping out here in the rain for nothing.* She tipped her head back, letting the rain splash down on her upturned face. *Thank you, Lord.*

Laurie turned toward home, determined to crumple—no, burn—the sketch that had tricked her imagination and sent her out into another dark, rainy night. She slogged through the wet grass along the side of the house, keeping the light carefully pointed at her feet.

A shadow darted through her circle of light. Laurie shrieked in alarm before clamping her mouth shut. She pointed the light, the white face and glowing eyes of an opossum staring back at her.

A window rattled above her head. Laurie flung herself against the house, her heart jumping into her throat. The curtain parted, light flooding out across the grass. The opossum, caught in the glare, crouched low in the grass, bared its teeth, and hissed.

Laurie pressed herself against the clapboard house and held her breath.

Finally the curtain dropped and after a few more moments, the light clicked off. The opossum ambled off into the shrubs.

She counted to fifty before edging around the corner of the house. She kept the flashlight off and shuffled her feet, feeling carefully with her toe before each step. It took several minutes to retrace her path back to the front of the house.

She rounded the corner, her heartbeat slowing to a normal pace. Five minutes and she would be snuggling back in bed, ready to put this nightmarish evening behind her.

A light erupted in her face. "Hold it!"

Laurie twisted to run, her feet slipping in the wet grass, her heart ready to jump from her chest.

Footsteps banged across the wooden porch and landed next to her. A strong hand grabbed her arm and wrenched her backward. "What do you think you're doing?"

Samuel's face twisted, his lip lifted upward in a snarl, a gun clenched in his hand.

"I—I—" she stammered as she pulled against his grip, words failing.

"Laurie?" He hauled her back, fingers digging into the soft flesh of her upper arm. "What are you doing here?"

"Let me go!"

"Why are you skulking around my house in the middle of the night?"

"I wasn't skulking," Laurie gasped. "I was just out walking."

His grip on her arm tightened. "In the dark? In the rain?" He dragged her toward the porch.

"Where are you taking me?"

"Inside. It's cold out here and I'm not exactly dressed for the weather." He stood on the lawn in nothing but pajama bottoms, his bare feet exposed in the wet grass.

She set her heels and pulled against his hand, averting her eyes from his muscled chest. "No, I can't go in there."

He didn't reply, just hauled her up the porch steps and pressed her through the open door.

Laurie stumbled in, dripping water on the floor.

He released her arm and shut the door behind them, shaking raindrops from his hair. "Sit down and wait for me." His eyes burned, as if daring her to leave. "I'm going to get dressed. And then I'm going to make us something hot to drink. Maybe by that point you'll have an answer for me."

Laurie perched on the corner of the sofa as Samuel stalked from the room. She shivered, whether from shock or cold, she wasn't certain. Her mind jumbled with possible excuses, each more ridiculous than the last.

Samuel re-appeared five minutes later, shirt hanging unbuttoned over a white union suit, and the gun tucked in the waistband of his trousers. He carried two steaming cups. "Tea." He handed her a cup, not bothering to ask about cream or sugar.

Laurie placed it on the end table, trying to still her trembling hands.

He eased into a chair, his eyes locked on her. "Well?"

Laurie took a deep breath. "You—you said that you had plans this evening." She grasped at excuses, even if they weren't good ones. "I was curious." She cleared her throat and reached for the tea. The cup clattered against the saucer as she tried to lift it. "Were you out on a date or searching for bootleggers?"

He cocked an eyebrow. "Are you jealous?"

"That depends on your answer, I suppose."

He leaned back in his seat, eyes gleaming. "How was your date with Shepherd?"

She shrugged, tucking a strand of hair behind her ear. "It was nice enough."

"Hmm." He propped a hand under his chin. "He doesn't seem like your type."

"And what would you know about that?"

Samuel leaned forward, scooting to the edge of his chair. "Mild-mannered pharmacist?" He shook his head. "You strike me as the type of girl who'd like a little more excitement in her life." He reached out a hand and brushed her knee.

Her heart hammered in her chest. "Excitement is over-rated, I think."

"And yet, here you are on my doorstep in the middle of the night." A sly smile lifted one corner of his mouth. "You're not willing to settle for boring."

She pulled back in her seat so his hand dropped from her leg. "I'm afraid I may have given you the wrong impression."

He settled his hands on his knees. "I don't think so. I've heard some stories about your family since I got to town. I'd hate to believe that there's any truth to the rumors about your father and your brother." His eyes narrowed. "Maybe you can convince me of the truth."

A cool prickle ran across her skin. "Don't believe everything you've heard."

"I told you. Rumors are my bread and butter."

She fell silent, biting her lip.

He sat back and tapped his hand against the arm of the chair. "Then maybe you're ready to give me some names. Some others have pointed fingers, but I'm trying to be fair, here. You know more than you're telling me."

Laurie closed her mouth and pressed herself into the sofa's cushioned back.

"I see the fear that crosses your face every time I mention it. Your eyes are fountains of expression. You're hiding something, that's a certainty. Is it your father?"

Laurie's heart raced, her mouth suddenly dry.

Samuel scooted forward until his knee touched hers. "You need to tell me the truth. I can't help you if I don't know what's going on." He stood, coming over to join her on the sofa. "You're not helping anyone by keeping these secrets. If you tell me the truth, I might be able to help the person you're protecting."

Laurie stared at her hands. "I don't know what you're talking about."

"Is it your father? His boss at the mill said that he's been acting a little peculiar."

His boss said that? "No."

He ran his fingers up her arm, his touch like an electric current. "Then it's your brother."

Laurie jumped to her feet, nearly upsetting her teacup. "I've got to go. I shouldn't be here."

Samuel grabbed her hand and pulled her back down beside him, wedging her in the corner of the sofa. "Laurie, either give me some names or show me how wrong I am about you." His warm breath tickled her cheek.

Her stomach lurched. "I don't know what you are suggesting."

"I think you do. You can't be nearly as innocent as you act." He placed his hand under her chin, lifting her face. "Shall I call the sheriff? We can show up at the mill tomorrow with a warrant. Your father or your brother—which one?"

Her world spun. "Neither."

"Laurie . . ."

"I'm telling you," she gasped, "they're not involved."

He squeezed his hand on her shoulder, his fingers pinching into her skin. "Then show me." He lowered his lips to her neck.

Laurie closed her eyes. "No." She pushed against him, wrenching her shoulders free. "I'll give you names."

"I'm listening."

Her mind reeled, latching onto the first name that came to her lips. "Shepherd. He's one of them."

"The pharmacist." Samuel's hands loosened. "The one you've been all cozy with?"

She broke free from his grip and jumped to her feet, her stomach churning. "He's one of the rumrunners."

27

Daniel crouched behind the pharmacy counter, sorting through prescriptions. The door's jingle caught his attention and he pushed up to his feet, unfolding his knees with a grimace.

Samuel Brown strode into the store like he owned the place, Sheriff Martinson and four deputies on his heels.

Daniel ignored the cold sweat breaking out across his skin as he stepped out from behind the counter. "Can I help you gentlemen?"

Brown came to a stop two paces away from him and crossed his arms over his chest, a pleased smile gracing his face. "Daniel Shepherd."

A weight settled in Daniel's stomach. "What can I do for you, Brown?"

Sheriff Martinson stepped forward. "Mr. Shepherd, I'm afraid I have a warrant for your arrest. I'd like you to come in for questioning and I hope"—he cast a quick glance at Brown—"we can clear this up, quickly."

Granddad appeared from the back room, the color draining from his face. "Daniel, what's going on?"

"I'd like to know that, myself."

The sheriff stepped forward. "Miles, we have to take your grandson in for questioning. He's been implicated as a suspect in a rumrunning case." He turned to Daniel. "You are being arrested for activities in violation of the Volstead Act."

Daniel squeezed his fingers into a fist. "What kind of activities?"

"The import, transport, and sale of intoxicating liquor." Sheriff Martinson's gaze flickered between Brown and Shepherd.

"Marty, this is ridiculous." Granddad yanked off his spectacles. "My grandson is as dry as they come."

Brown snorted. "Doesn't matter. We have an eyewitness who fingered Shepherd as a member of the ring. Now, Sheriff"—he gestured with his head—"you said the county would cooperate on this matter. Would you like to have the honor of arresting him, or shall I do it myself?"

Martinson stepped forward and grasped Daniel's arm. "Come on, son. We're going to take you down to the station and ask you a few questions."

Brown slipped a pair of handcuffs from his pocket. "Restrain him. We don't want him running."

Daniel's anger bubbled over. "You are so far out of line, here, Brown. I'm no more a rumrunner than you are an honest lawman."

Brown's eyes darkened. He fastened onto Daniel's coat and rammed him against the counter. "You're going to regret that comment." He turned him around and snapped the cuffs on one wrist.

Daniel gritted his teeth. "Who's this eyewitness, anyway?"

Brown twisted his arm. "How I would love to tell you that. But it's not allowed."

Daniel felt the cuffs click into place behind his back. "Don't I have the right to face my accuser?"

"Soon enough. Now, Sheriff, you can take him. I have a second warrant here giving me the right to search this store from attic to basement and I plan on doing just that."

Daniel's grandfather frowned. "We've got nothing to hide."

"I'll make sure of that. You might want to close up while we do this."

Sheriff Martinson sighed. "I'm sorry about this, Miles. But Revenue has jurisdiction in these cases."

Granddad nodded, face grim. "I understand."

A small crowd gathered around the entrance to the store as the sheriff escorted Daniel to the street. Sheriff Martinson gestured with his arm. "Go on about your day, folks."

Daniel gazed at the sidewalk, oblivious to the stares of the crowd.

⸎

Laurie's stomach curdled as she watched Daniel being led out to a police car by two tommy gun–toting deputies. She pushed away her swirling emotions. She'd only done what was necessary to protect Johnny. Besides, Daniel was guilty, after all. It's not like she had lied to Samuel.

"Laurie, what's going on?"

The sight of her best friend brought hot tears stinging her eyes. "Amelia, Daniel's been arrested."

"What? Why?"

The police car pulled away down the street while the crowd gaped and pointed.

Laurie let the tears fall. "Because of me."

28

DANIEL LOWERED HIS HEAD INTO HIS HANDS AS HE SAT IN THE TINY CELL IN Clallam County Courthouse.

Sheriff Martinson stood outside, gripping the door. "Daniel. You know I'm good friends with your grandfather." He ran his hands down the metal bars and sighed. "I don't like being told what to do by these federal busy-bodies. That Brown fellow has it out for you. I'm not sure what I can do, but if you got anything to confess, you'd best do it to me rather than to that vulture."

Daniel lifted his head and stared dully at the wall. "I've got nothing, Sheriff. This is a mystery to me."

Martinson shook his balding head. "Been to Canada lately?"

"No."

"You selling booze out of the back of your grandfather's shop?"

"Only the legally prescribed stuff and it all goes out the front door."

"I don't know you, son, but I trust your grandfather like my own brother. I'd hate to see him get hurt."

Daniel met the sheriff's eyes. "You and me both."

"Just so we understand each other." The man ran his hands across his paunch. "When Brown gets back, he's going to lead the interrogation. We'll wait on any formal charges until he's done." He shook his head. "Though if he's conducting a thorough search, that may take awhile."

Daniel lowered his head back into his hands. His grandfather's words haunted him. *Next time he comes by, go ahead and pay him. . . . He'll find what he wants to find, and we'll have a devil of a time proving our innocence.*

❦

Amelia walked Laurie to a bench away from the milling crowd. "How can you be to blame for Daniel getting arrested?"

Laurie sniffled, wiping her face with her handkerchief. "Samuel kept pushing me to help him with his investigation and he threatened my father and Johnny—"

Amelia's eyes grew round. "He threatened them? What do you mean by that?"

"Somebody told him Johnny and my father were involved in the rumrunning. He made it sound like he was going after them unless I gave him some other names." Laurie rubbed her palms against her skirt.

Amelia grew silent, her face drawn. "*Is* Johnny involved?"

Laurie sat on her hands and gazed at the grass. "Please, don't ask me that."

Amelia flopped back against the bench with a huff. "He's been working late so often." She closed her eyes. "I should have known." Amelia ran a finger through her blonde curls, her eyes troubled.

Laurie touched her friend's arm. "He did say he was almost finished. He told me he only had a few more runs."

"And Daniel's involved, too?" Amelia blew air out from between her lips as if she'd been holding it for a while. "We'd

199

better go tell Johnny what's happened. If they've arrested Daniel, he can't be far behind."

⌀━╪━⌀

Johnny paced across Amelia's porch. "You did what?" His eyes bulged.

"I told them Daniel was involved. I didn't have a choice." Laurie squeezed her fingers together in her lap, trying to keep her hands from shaking.

"Didn't I tell you to stay away from him? Didn't I tell you something like this would happen?" Johnny dragged a claw-shaped hand through his hair.

Amelia leaned against one of the tall white posts supporting the porch roof. "That's not important now. Now we have to figure out how to keep you out of jail."

"I ain't going to jail."

Amelia placed one hand on her hip. "Just like you 'ain't' a rumrunner?"

He clamped his mouth shut, staring at his work boots.

"That's what I thought."

He turned to Laurie. "Why Daniel?"

Laurie shrugged. "Better him than you. I don't know why I should protect any of you, really. But at least you are my family."

Johnny's face grew red. "But, how could you point a finger at an innocent man?"

Laurie rounded on him. "Innocent? You said he was the lookout at Crescent Beach."

"Where did you get that fool idea?"

"On the beach, you said . . ." She paused, trying to bring back the details of that awful night.

Johnny huffed. "The lookout was Lew Barnes—the same guy you saw me talking with at the boarding house. You must have seen him up on the bluff."

Laurie sank back, feeling the world sway in time with the porch swing. "Lew Barnes? But—but, I thought . . ." She covered her mouth. "Daniel was there on the bluff. I just assumed . . ." Pain gripped her chest. "He was there."

Johnny grabbed the chain on the porch swing and shook it hard. "Laurie, Daniel doesn't even drink."

"Johnny . . ." Amelia walked to his side. She took his arm and ran fingers across his tensed shoulders. "She made a mistake, that's all."

"And look where it's gotten us."

"You're still with us, aren't you?" Amelia pointed out.

"What do we do about Daniel?" Johnny paced the length of the porch.

Laurie's head swam. *Daniel's not a rumrunner.* She walked back through her memories of their time together, viewing it in the light of this new reality. Her heart lifted in her chest like a fledgling bird learning to fly—just before it crashed to the ground. "I sent him to jail."

"You're just now figuring that out?" Johnny snapped. "Now I'm going to have to go turn myself in. I can't let him take the fall for something he didn't do." He wrapped an arm around the pillar, leaning his head against the smooth white paint. "What a disaster."

"No, you won't." Laurie stood. "I'll fix this. I'll tell Samuel I made a mistake."

"Like he's going to believe that?" Johnny paced to the far end of the porch and stared out over the yard.

Amelia frowned. "Laurie, you said that Samuel was already aware of Johnny's involvement. What can you do to change his mind?"

A shiver ran through Laurie's gut. She had to get Daniel out of jail and keep her brother from taking his place. "Anything I have to."

29

SAMUEL'S VOICE ECHOED FROM THE BASEMENT OF THE DRUGSTORE. "I want you to box up all these records, Mack. We're going to need copies of everything."

Laurie edged down the steep stairs, digging her fingernails into the wooden railing. The dank smell of cool underground wafted upwards, giving her an overwhelming sensation of descending into a dungeon.

Halfway down, she paused. "Samuel?" The sound of boxes being dragged and drawers being opened and banged shut made her shiver. *He's going to be furious that I've wasted his time.*

The sounds quieted and footsteps approached. Samuel appeared out of the back room, a quizzical expression on his face. "Laurie? You do show up in the oddest of places."

"I need to talk to you. It's important."

Samuel hesitated for a moment before turning and speaking over his shoulder. "Keep at it. I'll be right back." He followed her up the steep stairway and out the back door into the alley.

She took a deep breath of the fresh air, thankful for the slice of sun peeping through between the brick buildings.

"So, what's this about? We're in a bit of a hurry." Samuel brushed a cobweb off his sleeve.

Laurie forced herself to speak the words that weighed on her heart. "I made a mistake. Daniel's not a rumrunner. I jumped to that conclusion because of some faulty information." She watched as Samuel's face hardened. Her stomach tightened in response. "I'm sorry. I didn't mean to cause so much trouble—but you need to let him go."

"I can't do that."

Fingers of tension inched their way up her neck. "You must. You arrested him because of what I said and I'm telling you, I was wrong."

A smile toyed at the corners of his lips. "I couldn't have arrested him on just your word, Beautiful. You just put the nail in his coffin, so to speak." He turned and faced away from her, staring at the backside of the drugstore. "So what changed your mind? Did someone threaten you?"

"I simply made a mistake."

"You seemed pretty certain last night." He took a step closer to her, reaching a hand out and touching her arm.

She locked her knees, preventing herself from stepping back. "I just realized I was wrong. It couldn't be Daniel. He's an honest man—he doesn't even drink."

"He doesn't?" The corner of his mouth turned upward. "Who told you that? Him?"

"Does it matter?"

He narrowed his eyes. He slid his hand up her arm to her shoulder. "You're going to have to give me more than that."

A shudder passed through her body. *More what?*

"Maybe we need to talk about some other names."

"I'll tell you what"—Laurie hugged her sweater to her chest—"I'll make more of an effort at the switchboard. I think if I'm careful, I might be able to find you the information you want."

A light appeared in Samuel's eyes. "Even if you don't like what you hear?"

Laurie nodded, digging a fingernail into her palm under the cover of the sweater. *As long as I can find some way to keep my brother's name out of it.*

"Good. It's a deal." He pulled his hand from her shoulder and held it out to her. "And we have a date on Friday night."

A flicker of surprise raced through her. "We do?"

"This Friday and every Friday, until I bust this case open." His eyes gleamed.

She set her jaw. "Fine." She shook his hand, holding her breath as he squeezed her fingers and raised them to his lips. "And you'll release Daniel?"

"For now—if you're sure that's what you want."

She let go of her breath. "I do."

⚹

Daniel glanced up as the jail door opened. A grim-faced Sheriff Martinson stood outside. Daniel rose from his seat on the rickety bench, pushing away the sensation of being led to the gallows.

"Brown's here. You ready?"

"Might as well get it over with."

The sheriff escorted him to a small windowless office and gestured to an open chair on the far side of the wooden table. Martinson exited, pulling the door closed behind him.

As soon as Daniel sat, the door opened again. Brown resembled a cat preparing for the kill. "Mr. Shepherd. So good of you to join us." He grasped the back of the chair opposite Daniel and spun it around, straddling the seat and crossing his arms across its high back.

"I had a choice?"

"Well, not really. But I'm trying to be polite, here."

Daniel placed his hands on the table. "Why start now?"

Brown chuckled. "I took you as a smart man the first time I laid eyes on you. Being insolent with a federal agent is not what I'd call a smart move, however."

"And not what I'd call a crime."

Brown dropped his chin against the high back of the chair and gazed at Daniel. "Do you want to know what I found at your shop?"

The man's arrogant stare set him on edge, but Daniel maintained eye contact. "Nothing?"

"Not exactly." Brown gestured to a cardboard box on the floor, crammed with papers. "Long lists of customers, prescription reports, and delivery receipts."

Daniel leaned back against his chair. "Most of that information is confidential."

"Then it's convenient that this badge gives me the right to see it." Brown lifted the box from the floor and dropped it onto the table. "And do you know what else I found, Daniel?" He picked out one of the papers and gazed at him over the top. "May I call you Daniel?"

Can I call you a malevolent snake?

When Daniel didn't answer, Brown shrugged and looked back at the paper. "There seems to a discrepancy between the amount of liquor arriving at your back door and the amount going out the front."

Daniel drummed his fingers against the table. *Granddad was right—they'll find what they want to find. Even when there's nothing there.*

Brown set the paper down on the table and offered a cruel smile. "Do you know why that is?"

"Enlighten me."

The agent slid his hand into his shirt pocket and drew out a pair of reading glasses. "I'm no bookkeeper, but it appears that you're bringing in a lot more money than you should be, according to your prescription logs." He glanced up at Daniel, peering at him over the lenses. "I think you're selling more alcohol than your records claim."

Daniel felt a twinge in his neck. Brown was going to make the records say whatever he wanted. "We're not. If you care to show me the papers, I could explain them to you since, as you say, you're not a bookkeeper."

Brown dropped the papers into the box and closed the lid. "No, I don't think so. I can't have you tampering with the evidence, after all." He leaned his arm on the top and stared at Daniel once more. "I will have our own accountant go over your figures."

He rose, turned the chair, and returned it to its original position. Brown lifted the crate into his arms with a slight grunt and stepped to the doorway. Turning back, he glanced at Daniel. "Oh, yes. You're free to go. For now." He patted the side of the box. "We'll be in touch."

Daniel sat back against the chair, his hands falling slack at his sides. *He's letting me go?*

Sheriff Martinson smiled as he entered the room, his face crinkling into a series of grooved wrinkles. "You heard the man, Shepherd. I'd say that must have gone well. Very well, indeed."

Daniel stood, a lingering discomfort lurking in his chest. This game was far from over.

30

LAURIE SLUMPED ON THE SAME BENCH WHERE SHE HAD WAITED FOR Samuel months before. The fragrance of roses—normally her favorite—pricked at her raw nerves. When the door finally opened and Daniel strode out into the evening air, a wave of exhaustion swept over her. She slumped against the backrest and waited.

He eyed her posture and cocked his head to the side. "You look like you've had nearly as bad a day as I have—though I have difficulty believing it."

"Daniel, I'm so sorry. I can't begin to tell you how foolish I feel." Tears stung her eyes and she blinked to force them back. "I can't expect you to forgive me, but I need to explain."

Daniel's mouth opened and closed with no sound. His face pinched. "You—you did this? You're the eyewitness?"

She picked at her nails as the words rushed from her mouth—everything from the first night until her encounter with Samuel Brown at his home.

Daniel sank onto the bench beside her, rubbing a palm across his face.

She touched his sleeve. "I'm very sorry. I can't believe I thought you were one of them."

He shook his head and laughed ruefully. "Well, I assumed you were part of it, too, at first. You and your 'oyster picking.'"

"I feel horrible about what happened. Was it very bad?"

"Not the best day I've had, but it's over. I'm starving, though." Daniel pressed his hands against his stomach.

"Let me buy you dinner. It's the least I can do after what I've put you through."

He shook his head. "I couldn't possibly sit in a restaurant. How about I make some sandwiches at the store and we take them down to the waterfront? I've been sitting in that cell all day; I could stand some fresh air and exercise."

Warmth rushed through Laurie. "That sounds nice. But if your grandfather doesn't mind me behind the counter, I'd like to make them." She fell in step beside Daniel, casting a quick glance up at his face. Handsome, honest, forgiving . . . his list was growing longer by the moment.

And best of all—not a rumrunner.

❦

Seagulls rose and fell on the breezes drifting inland at the Port Angeles Harbor. Large rafts of timber floated on the water, men jumping from log to log with long poles clutched in their hands, guiding their bounty toward the mills along the shore.

Daniel turned and watched as Laurie balanced on one of the logs washed up on shore, carefully placing one foot in front of the other with her arms spread, like a tight-rope walker at the circus.

Laurie tipped to one side and her arms flailed for a moment before she righted herself. She turned and walked back in his direction, chewing her lower lip in concentration. When she came close, she took his offered hand for extra balance, a smile toying at the corners of her mouth. She tugged his arm. "Come join me."

With a deep breath, he hoisted himself up onto the massive timber, careful not to unsteady her in the process. "What if it rolls? I'm not as light on my feet as those fellows out there."

"It's half-buried, it's not going anywhere." She released his hand, executed a perfect pivot turn, and walked with confidence along the straight trunk.

Daniel stood with his hands outstretched, willing his feet to stop wobbling on the rounded perch. He tried turning his toes forward to walk along the line, spinning his arms to catch himself. Choosing to keep the larger amount of surface area in contact with the log, he edged sideways down the log, arms splayed.

Laurie laughed, the gentle sound trilling through the damp air. Walking backward, she reached her hand for him.

"Show off."

"I've been practicing all my life. It's not a particularly useful talent, but I had a lot of fun doing it when I was little."

"I've always preferred to keep my feet on the ground." He slid his shoes along the log until he could grasp Laurie's steadying hand.

"And here I thought you were a risk taker. I really don't know you at all, do I?" She shook her head, her blue hat curving around to her chin.

He stepped closer, grasping her hand and pulling her close under the guise of support. "A risk taker? Like your brother, you mean?"

She ducked her head. "Yes."

"No. I'm more the make-a-plan-and-stick-to-it type."

She glanced up, her eyes warming. "Steady. Honest."

He wobbled and she placed her other hand in the small of his back. "Steady? Maybe when I'm safe on the ground. Of course, I hope steady isn't just another word for boring."

She cocked her head and examined him. "No. More like . . . responsible, trustworthy."

He locked his knees and gazed at her beauty. Her honey-brown hair curled around her chin and her blue eyes danced. He released her hand and reached to touch a freckle on her cheek, rubbing it with his thumb. He wanted nothing more than to reach down and kiss that lone freckle.

"And trustworthy is hard to come by these days," she sighed.

He hardly dared to breathe as she leaned against him. He put his arm around her back as she rested her head on his shoulder, gazing out across the harbor.

31

THE WARMTH OF DANIEL'S SHOULDER REMAINED ON HER CHEEK DURING the walk home. Daniel had wanted to escort her, but she insisted they part ways at the drugstore. Her father would be home by now and she didn't want him to spoil the evening. Her heart took wings as she walked, swinging her arms as if she might float off at any moment.

And Daniel hadn't even kissed her.

Finding her father hungry and irritable didn't squelch the spark of joy growing inside of her. She pulled together a quick dinner, tidied up, ironed clothes for tomorrow, and packed his lunch without a single moment of resentment.

"What's with you tonight?" Dad gathered the evening paper from the table.

She smiled as she breezed past him with a load of laundry. "The world just seems a brighter place this evening."

He burrowed down into his chair, the paper on his lap. "Yeah, well, that will wear off. Just read some of this news."

Laurie put away the last of the dishes and kissed her father goodnight. "At least that's all far away. Everything and everyone I care about is right here in Port Angeles."

Her father huffed and snapped the paper closed. "I think I'll go out for a bit."

Laurie paused on her way to her room. "Go out? This time of night? What do you need?" She frowned.

He shoved the gray cap down low on his forehead. "None of your business. Get to bed, now."

A few of the sparkles from her day fizzled as she watched him push open the door and disappear into the night. She left the porch light on and sauntered off to bed. Plumping up the pillows, Laurie fetched her book. Summoning Daniel's face, she lowered the pencil to the paper. She sketched him with one foot on the ground and the other propped up against the log, gazing across the harbor toward the curve of the spit and the lighthouse in the distance. No bootleggers, no G-men, no storm. Just strong shoulders. Her pencil shaded the curve of his back.

Strong enough to do the right thing.

⊶✦⊷

Daniel sat at his grandfather's table, his arms resting on the table. "So, how bad is it?"

Granddad leaned against the kitchen counter. "They swept through the records like a tidal wave. The paperwork is in shambles. What they didn't take with them is strewn around the basement."

"Brown claims our numbers don't add up."

His grandfather shook his head. "He just grabbed as much paper as he could and shoved it into boxes, carrying it off. He wasn't crunching any numbers." He scratched his chin. "If you ask me, he wasn't even looking for numbers. He was looking for names."

Daniel's blood chilled. "Names?"

"Who's using prescriptions to drink and who's not."

Daniel leaned back against the chair. "He can't do that. It's supposed to be confidential between doctor, patient, and pharmacist."

Granddad lifted his hands. "I don't understand why he'd even care. When someone comes in with a prescription, the Volstead Act doesn't apply."

A headache simmered behind Daniel's eyes. He pushed fingers against his temples. "I thought he was just trying to lay in a case against me. Why would he care who is buying the liquor? It doesn't make any sense."

His grandfather walked around the table and refilled Daniel's coffee cup. "For the sake of our business, we need to call off his dogs."

"I hate the idea of buying him off."

"What choice do we have? If Brown continues digging, he'll find something that will either shut us down or lock us up. Or both."

"He'd have to fabricate something."

"You think he wouldn't?"

Daniel closed his eyes. "No, you're right. I just wish I knew what he was up to. Why is he targeting me?"

"Other than his obvious interest in Laurie Burke?"

Daniel opened his eyes and stared at his grandfather. "He pressured her into giving him my name."

"So you said. But it's clear that he has his eye on her." Granddad picked up his breakfast plate and walked it to the sink. "And you are the competition."

Daniel looked down at his plate, still full. He couldn't seem to summon an appetite this morning.

"And Daniel, one other thing." He ran some water over the plate and turned to face his grandson. "How come he let you go so quickly?"

"That bothered me, too. He claimed he needed time to go over the paperwork."

"Perhaps a certain young woman intervened?"

Daniel pushed his chair back from the table and stood. "Laurie said she explained her mistake to Brown."

Granddad's forehead creased. "I just hope that's all it was."

Daniel froze, his hand reaching for his plate. "What do you mean?"

"That girl has a heart of gold, Daniel. She's protected her father for years. Now, as you explain it to me, she's protecting her brother." The older man rolled up his shirtsleeves as the sink filled. "She was willing to sacrifice you to protect Johnny, right?"

Daniel scraped his plate into the wastebasket. "Something like that."

"What is she willing to give up to protect you?"

The words sank into Daniel's stomach like a lead weight.

32

THE WARM LUMP ON THE BED SNORED, FACE PLASTERED INTO THE FEATHER pillow.

Laurie shook her father a second time, her jaw aching from gritting her teeth. "Dad, you have to get up. You've got early shift this morning."

She headed for the kitchen. The coffee gurgled in the percolator, but she added some bacon to the frying pan along with the eggs. Maybe the smell would rouse him from his liquor-infused dreams.

She banged the pan against the stovetop and glanced at the clock. He wouldn't make it to work at this rate.

She spotted Johnny walking up to the porch moments before the doorknob rattled. Shadows circled his eyes, but somehow he still managed a grin as he strolled into the kitchen.

"Hey, Sis. Breakfast ready?"

She turned the bacon. "Why are you here? You're not on morning shift today, are you?"

"Nah. But, I thought you might need a hand this morning."

She wiped her hands on her apron, her curiosity nearly as strong as the coffee she poured for him. "You came to help cook breakfast?"

He chuckled as he took the cup. "That would be interesting, wouldn't it?" His smile faded. "No, I saw Dad last night. I figured he was . . . how shall we say . . . *sleeping in* this morning?"

She frowned. "Where did you see him?"

"My house." He took a sip and grimaced.

Laurie sank into one of the kitchen chairs. "Why would he go there?"

Johnny went to the cupboard and got a plate. "You made enough food for me, right?"

He dished up some eggs and a couple of pieces of toast. "Fix up his thermos with some of that oily sludge you call coffee, and I'll go drag him out of bed." Johnny shoveled the eggs up onto the bread and consumed them in a few bites.

"Why was he at your house, Johnny?" Laurie's voice barely registered over the sound of her brother's chewing.

He stared at her across the table a long moment before answering. "Look. I help him get what he needs. I knew you'd be mad—but Laurie, he's going to drink regardless. Better that he gets clean stuff from me than the rotgut stuff other people sell."

The floor seemed to drop away. She shoved her chair back. "Get out." Her voice rattled, low and hoarse, as if her throat were full of sand.

His eyes rounded.

"Get out." She pushed against his shoulder, knocking him slightly off balance. Her chest squeezed until she could barely draw a breath. "I want you out!"

He shook off her arm like she was an irritating child begging for a piggyback ride. "Are you going to haul him to work?" His brow furrowed, giving him a pinched look around the eyes. "Get the coffee."

He stomped off down the hall, leaving Laurie standing in the kitchen alone. Turning around, she banged the pan against the stovetop, appreciating how the loud noise echoed in her empty heart. She bashed it twice more for good measure before daring to pick up the glass-lined thermos. Without bothering to pre-warm it, she dumped in the coffee and shoved the cork into its throat. *Someone needs to invent a cork for the drunken throat.*

"A good daughter would add a slosh of whiskey to that," her father's voice slurred from the hall, where he leaned against Johnny's arm. He turned his head and spoke into Johnny's face. "She don't know nothing, do she?"

Johnny gagged. "Dad, don't do that. Your breath is awful."

Laurie secured the metal cap over the cork and thrust the container at Johnny. "Here. He's all yours. You two deserve each other." She retreated to her room, listening as Johnny dragged their father out the door.

33

DANIEL KEPT AN EYE ON THE WINDOW AS HE ORGANIZED THE MORNING'S prescriptions. When Laurie appeared, his heart jumped. The haunted look around her eyes and the sluggishness in her step tugged at him. He hurried to unlock the door even though ten minutes remained until opening time.

She pointed at the window where the show globe still hung, casting its bluish hue over the floor. "You haven't changed it yet."

He smiled, bowled over by the simple tilt of her head while she spoke. "It's difficult to improve upon perfection—you already said it was your favorite color."

Her yellow dress fluttered in the wind, its blue flowers matching her cloche. She reached out and touched his sleeve with a gloved hand. "You don't have to keep it that way for me. I'd love to see some of your different creations—it's artwork. In a bottle." A shadow passed in front of her face after she said the word.

"For you—anything." It took every bit of restraint to keep from pulling her into his arms right there on the sidewalk in front of the world. "How about some breakfast? Coffee?"

She glanced down at the sidewalk, pulling her toes back from a crack that ran the width of the concrete. "I've already eaten. But coffee sounds nice. I'm early, again, so I have some time to sit and visit." She cast a shy glance up at his face. "If you'd like to, that is."

He reached for the door. "I'd like nothing better. Well, maybe a whole day of visiting . . . but I'll take what I can get."

She laughed in time with the jingling of the door and walked inside, heading straight for the fountain counter.

Granddad, stocking supplies at the pharmacy counter, cast a wide smile at the pair. "Laurie, it's good to see you this morning."

She hurried to him, her face creasing. "Oh, Mr. Larson—how can you say that after what I put you through yesterday?"

Daniel's grandfather waved his hands dismissively. "Daniel explained the whole thing. I'm just relieved to have it cleared up."

"But you lost a whole day's business and then to have those men going through your store—"

"It would take more than a bunch of government turkeys to shut down this store. We've been here practically since the town began." He squeezed her shoulder. "If you want to make it up to us, let's see you in here a little more often. We miss your smiling face."

She blushed and nodded. "I think I can do that."

Daniel guided her to a stool. "Just coffee this morning? Maybe a pastry?"

She nodded. "That sounds wonderful. Thank you."

He filled her cup and another for himself and then leaned on the counter across from her, where he could watch her beautiful face. *I had her in my arms last night—why didn't I kiss her?* Warmth rushed through him at the thought. "You got home all right?"

"Of course." Her lips curved upward. "I've been walking home by myself since I was five."

"But that was before we knew the town was full of dangerous rumrunners."

She lifted her cup and looked at him from under her long lashes. "One fewer than I previously believed."

He touched the fading bruise on his cheekbone. "I guess I'm losing that swashbuckling appearance. My masquerade is finished."

"You never did tell me how you got that."

He lifted his own cup. "You know what they say about these port towns—full of all kinds of shady characters."

"You're not going to tell me, are you?"

He shook his head. "Not yet. Maybe someday." He pushed his cup along the counter until it sat beside hers, gathering the courage to reach for her fingers. "How is your father doing?"

She stiffened. "Why do you ask?"

"You haven't picked up any prescriptions for him lately. Is his shoulder doing better?" Daniel chewed on the inside of his lip. He should have known better than to ask that question.

She locked her gaze on the marble counter. "I don't think he's in much pain." Her jaw twitched.

Daniel topped off her coffee. "I wish he'd talk to his doctor about some of the other options."

"Me, too." She dropped a sugar cube into the cup and swirled it with her spoon. Her voice lowered. "You know—don't you? I can see it in your eyes."

He laid his elbows on the counter, leaning forward so he could keep his voice low. "Yes. Johnny told me about your father's situation." Granddad had retreated from sight. Daniel reached for her hand. "It's nothing to be ashamed of. He is the one with the problem—not you."

She ran a fingertip along the side of his hand. "It's not that easy. If he keeps drinking like this, he's going to lose his job. And then what's going to happen to us?"

"Would it help if I talked to him?"

She shook her head. "No. It would only embarrass and anger him."

He blew air out through his teeth. "I wish there were some magic concoction I could blend up and send home with you that would just take away his longing for booze. But unfortunately . . ."

Laurie's brow furrowed. "Did Johnny tell you where my father is getting his liquor?"

Daniel thought carefully before responding. "Do you know?"

"Johnny's supplying it. Can you believe that?" Laurie pulled her hand back. Her face flushed and tiny lines formed around her mouth. "Why would he do such a thing?"

"Did you ask him?" Daniel reached for a cleaning rag to wipe the counter, uncomfortable with the fact that he knew the answers to her questions.

"Of course." Her eyes flashed. "He said he was afraid Dad would get some of the tainted stuff."

Daniel nodded. "That makes some sense. That's why Granddad carries it in the store."

She squeezed her hands around her coffee cup. "By giving him the booze, Johnny's just encouraging him to drink. We should be trying to keep it away from him. Sober him up and maybe he'll listen to reason."

"Maybe." Daniel took another sip of his coffee, apprehension growing in his stomach. Her father's struggle felt all too familiar to him. "But alcoholics will find a way to feed their desires. He has to want to change, and then if he can get into a hospital program—"

Laurie's eyes grew wide. "Hospital program? What would people say?"

"No one would need to know. You could say he was there for some other reason."

She shook her head. "I don't know. It would be hard to get him to agree." She shifted on her stool. "Of course it might be easier if you and Johnny would let him sober up a bit, first."

"Me?"

"Yes. Your booze is every bit as bad as Johnny's."

"It's not *my* booze." The jab cut deep. "And I don't write the prescriptions."

She stared into her cup. "You fill them."

Daniel stuck his hand in his pocket, reaching for the temperance coin. "It's my grandfather's decision, not mine."

Laurie's shoulders sank and her eyes fixed on her fingers folded in front of her.

Daniel felt like crawling under the counter. He reached for her again, desperate to bring the light back to her face. "I'll speak to my grandfather. Maybe we can come up with some ideas."

She pressed fingers against her lips, eyes glistening. "Thank you."

When the door jingled, Daniel reluctantly drew his hand away. The customers—two older women—smiled and waved before walking in the direction of the pharmacy counter. Granddad appeared from the back room to greet them.

Daniel leaned close. "What time are you off tonight?"

A smile twitched on her lips. "Six o'clock."

"Care for another evening stroll?"

She slid from her stool. "I don't know. I hear there are a lot of dangerous types hanging about."

He puffed out his chest. "I'd keep you safe. I'm quite the brawler, you know."

She laughed. "How could I resist such an offer?"

Daniel watched, in a trance, as she walked to the door and cast a final smile at him over her shoulder.

Port Angeles is looking a little finer every day.

34

AMELIA DROPPED DOWN ONTO THE PORCH SWING. "YOU AGREED TO SEE Samuel again? Why would you do that?"

Laurie pressed her lips into a firm line. "I don't know. I didn't think I had a choice at the time. He insinuated that he wouldn't let Daniel go unless I agreed. Every time I get near Samuel, it's like I'm a puppet, responding to his every whim."

Amelia gripped her arm. "That's exactly why you shouldn't be seeing him."

"I promised."

"Did you tell Daniel or Johnny about this agreement?"

Laurie lifted her head. "Are you kidding?"

Amelia hopped up and paced a quick circle around the porch. "I'll go with you. He didn't say you had to go alone, did he?"

"No, but . . ."

Amelia raised an eyebrow. "Shall we bring Johnny, too? Or Daniel?"

"No. Absolutely not."

She crossed her arms over her chest. "Then it will have to be me."

"Amelia, I don't know." Laurie pushed against the ground with her foot, setting the swing into motion.

Amelia reached out and grasped one of the metal chains, sending the swing lurching sideways. "Why tell me if you don't want my help?"

"I'm tired of keeping secrets. Of doing things my way."

"I'm your friend. It's good to rely on others sometimes. Let me help with this one." Amelia sank down next to her, her leg pressing up against Laurie's. "Besides, if you don't let me come, I'm walking into the house and telephoning Johnny. You're not going out with that man by yourself. I don't trust him any further than I could throw him."

A laugh bubbled up from somewhere deep within Laurie's chest. "Weren't you the one insisting he had a 'delicious smile'?"

Her friend wrinkled her nose. "I've changed my mind. It's more of an oily smile, if you ask me."

Laurie sat back. "I just wish there was one man that I could trust like I do you, Amelia."

Amelia's lips turned upward. "What about Daniel?"

Laurie's heart skipped. "Maybe." She folded her hands in her lap, squeezing her fingers together. "I hope so."

"You're just not used to trusting anyone. Men, especially." Amelia pushed up and stood in front of Laurie. "Now, what does one wear to go to dinner with a G-man?"

A few hours later, the pair sat in Laurie's bedroom. Amelia added a feathered hairpiece to Laurie's bob. "What do you think?" she asked.

Laurie turned her head, looking sideways at the mirror, the ornament swaying with the movement. "It's ridiculous."

"Nonsense." Amelia patted the adornment, tucking a few bobby pins in to secure it. "You'll be the most stylish woman in the room. And with a few more of these, it'll stay put even if you do the Charleston all night long."

Laurie grabbed her arm. "Amelia, I won't be—"

"I'm just kidding. Don't worry, I won't do anything more to you tonight." She reached up and pinched her own finger waves into position as her cranberry-colored lips turned downward. "We shouldn't fuss too much. It's only Samuel Brown, after all." Her chin twitched. "Now, if it were Daniel, I'd really want to work on your look."

Laurie pushed down the misgivings rising in her stomach as the pair made their way to the front room. "I wish it were Daniel."

Amelia peeked out the window. "I don't understand why you're so nervous." Her tapping foot revealed her own emotional status.

Laurie sank down onto the armrest of the sofa. "I know what men can be like when they don't get their way."

The sound of a motor drew both of their eyes back to the window. The highly polished automobile crunched up the gravel driveway. Laurie's heart capered around in her chest as she watched Samuel check his reflection in the car's side mirror before turning toward the house.

Laurie touched Amelia's arm, drawing her away from the window. "Just as we planned, now." She turned the knob and opened the door before Samuel could reach the porch. Laurie stepped outside. "Hello, Samuel."

"Hello, Sunshine." He whistled as he walked toward her. "You are gorgeous."

She was completely over his compliments. "I have a surprise for you."

He pushed his hat back, gazing up at her with a sly smile. "Well, now. Is that right?" He spread his arms. "And I didn't even bring flowers."

She cleared her throat. "My friend Amelia stopped by earlier this evening. My brother—the clod—stood her up tonight.

She was feeling pretty low, so I invited her to join us." Laurie did her best to flutter her eyelashes innocently. "I knew you wouldn't mind."

Samuel's expression faltered as Amelia stepped out, joining Laurie on the porch. "Mr. Brown, I told Laurie how I hated to intrude on your evening."

Laurie hurried down the steps and touched Samuel's sleeve. "It wouldn't be right to leave her alone, Samuel. You understand, don't you?"

Samuel's jaw tightened, making his cheek twitch. "Of course. Miss White, please join us."

Amelia descended the creaky steps. "I hate to be a bother."

Laurie grabbed her arm and squeezed it, casting a bright smile in Samuel's direction. "You could never be a bother."

Samuel stood rigid, but after a few heartbeats a forced smile appeared. "Two lovely ladies in one evening? Who am I to complain?" He held out an arm to each of them and escorted them to the waiting vehicle.

Samuel held open the door and visibly glowered as Amelia slid into the center seat. He grasped Laurie's arm as she headed for the door. "Don't think I can't see what you're doing."

Laurie legs trembled. She stepped into the Studebaker, heart pounding.

◦▬◆▬◦

Daniel's eyes burned as he dug through the wreckage of their files, sorting the papers into piles. He tried not to imagine all the ways he'd like to see Brown suffer for causing this mess.

He lifted a faded slip of paper closer to his face so he could read the name and year. "Burke, Lucinda. 1916." His skin crawled—Laurie's mother? He scanned it, a lengthy list of medications. It stopped abruptly on April 16.

Daniel lowered the paper to the table, rubbing his fingers over his temples. Where was God's hand in all of this? Should one woman's death derail a family forever?

Daniel lifted the paper and dropped it into the appropriate stack before turning and gazing at the cabinet on the opposite wall. He'd already reorganized the current standing prescriptions. One in particular remained in his thoughts.

Could he help a grieving man take the first step toward recovery? *God, I'm going to need your help on this one.*

⊂══✦══⊃

Laurie settled into the chair across the table from Amelia and examined the fine tablecloth, polished silver, and crystal water glasses. Her friend's eyes shimmered as she gazed around at the lush décor.

"I hope you approve," Samuel said, one brow raised. "Tonight is the grand opening. It was a challenge to get a reservation for two, much less three." He shifted his gaze to Amelia.

She bowed her head. "I'm sorry my presence is such a nuisance."

Laurie watched as the waiter poured a cascade of ice water into her glass. "I'm glad you're here. You appreciate this sort of atmosphere much more than me." She turned to Samuel. "I'm really a simple girl at heart. You already know that I'd just as soon walk by the water as dine in a fine restaurant."

He raised his water glass, the facets in the crystal catching the sparkling light from the chandelier. "A woman of your beauty deserves elegance, Laurie. It's time for you to see what you're missing."

Laurie turned her head, admiring the modern artwork hanging on the wall behind her. "It is lovely. I would imagine this sort of restaurant in Paris or London, not Port Angeles."

Samuel scooted his chair closer to the table. "Actually, this is rather a cheap imitation of my favorite restaurant in Seattle."

She choked on her sip of water. "Cheap imitation?"

He gazed around, the light reflecting in his green eyes. "Yes. Sort of like a second-rate wine instead of quality champagne."

"Interesting talk from a Prohibition agent." Amelia raised her eyebrows.

A smile creased his face. "My job pays the bills, Miss White. It doesn't prevent me from enjoying life."

Laurie glanced around at the stylishly dressed men and women at the nearby tables—many in evening gowns and tuxedos. It was difficult to believe Seattle had fancier restaurants than this one. She tucked her hair behind her ear and focused on sitting up straight.

The meal passed in a flurry of courses. The waiters whisked away plates, bringing ever-finer arrangements of fruits, vegetables, meats, and breads.

Samuel and Amelia seemed to understand their role in the elaborate dance—taking only bites and tastes from each dish rather than finishing anything. Laurie marveled as each new flavor exploded on her palate. Concerned for the feelings of the chef, she continued to force food into her mouth far beyond the point of discomfort.

When dessert arrived, Laurie fluttered a hand to her mouth. "There's more? I couldn't possibly—"

"Ah, but wait, *Mademoiselle* . . ." The waiter leaned over the dish with a gleam in his eye.

With the strike of a long wooden match, the syrup-drenched cherries burst into flame. Laurie jumped from her chair, knocking her water glass onto its side.

Samuel laughed, pressing his napkin to his mouth. "Laurie, Laurie . . . it's so much fun seeing all of this through your eyes."

She lowered herself back into her chair as the waiter made quick work of the wet tablecloth. The flames dwindled, their heat taking residence beneath her collar. Once the waiter moved away, she leaned close to Samuel. "Pardon my ignorance, but why did he do that?"

Samuel chuckled. "Purely for the spectacle, my dear. I'm told it adds to the taste, though I have to admit, I've never really noticed."

Amelia spoke in low tones. "Perhaps they just like to watch their customers jump. Such excitement—my heart is still pounding." She fluttered her hand in front of her face.

Samuel smiled. "Then the whole night was worthwhile. I'm pleased to be able to bring a little excitement to your lives, ladies."

Laurie sat back. *I could use a little* less *excitement in my life.* She lifted her fork and made an act of stirring the cherries around on her plate, but her mouth refused to take a bite. Even the sight of the glistening fruit agitated her sour stomach. She held the fork aloft and gazed at the view outside the enormous windows. The city lights reflected off the waves, matched by a few flickers from the distant Victoria harbor. She imagined Johnny and his buddies leaning on their oars, negotiating the treacherous waters and ducking the Coast Guard, all for a few dollars. And here sat Samuel—spending a ridiculous sum on food that none of them could even fathom finishing.

"How does it work?" Amelia frowned. "How come the cherries don't burn?"

Samuel leaned forward, speaking in hushed tones, "They're coated in brandy."

Laurie dropped her fork and it clattered against the china plate. "What?"

Samuel sat up and straightened his ascot. "Just a touch, and it burns off."

KAREN BARNETT

"But, what about—"

He waved a dismissive hand. "It's taken care of. They feed us a wonderful dinner; I look the other way. Everyone wins." He shrugged. "They're not doing any harm."

Laurie pushed the plate away, the taste turning bitter in her mouth.

Everyone wins.

35

"Thank you," Laurie finished her call before turning to Mr. Quinn, fidgeting nearby. The man didn't usually hesitate.

"We have a problem." Mr. Quinn cleared his throat noisily before gesturing toward the door. "Your father."

Sweat broke out between her shoulder blades. She pulled off the headset, yanking at the wire when it wedged on a button on her dress. The other operators kept their faces fixed on their stations.

Dad's voice carried through the hushed room. "I need to see my daughter. Laurie?"

With a few rapid movements, she shut down her station, the tempo of her heart quickening with every lost second. "I'll take care of it, Mr. Quinn."

"See that you do." His lips puckered.

Laurie intercepted her father at the door, steering him away from the entrance and back to the sidewalk. "Dad, what are you doing here? What's wrong?"

He pushed against her hand. "Stop dragging me, girl."

"You can't be here. I'm working. Why aren't you?" Her mind rushed to fill in the possible answers.

Her father shook his head. "The boss-man sent me home. He said I was working too slow." He dragged his hand over his face as if pulling off a mask. "Said to come back tonight and work a double-shift."

Laurie's chest squeezed. "Too slow?"

He shrugged. "I'm dragging. What can I say? I just need to get a drink or two and I'll be fine."

She ground her toe into the sidewalk. *That's the last thing you need.* "So why are you here?"

"I can't find your brother. Do you know where he is?"

She rubbed a hand over her cramping neck muscles, staring up at the clouds in frustration. "Wasn't *he* at work today, either?"

"He's been on late shift. But he's not home right now. I thought you might know where he loafs around."

Laurie crossed her arms and stared at her father. "I don't know where he is. Why don't you go home and get a bite to eat, instead."

He glowered at her. "I don't want a bite. I want a drink."

"I can't help you."

Her father turned and stormed off.

She exhaled, the weight of her day blowing out with her breath. The sun beat down, warming the sidewalk. She turned back to the exchange and braced herself for Mr. Quinn's disapproving stare.

<hr />

Daniel glanced out from the storeroom door when the front door jingled, a jolt of surprise rushing through him. Laurie's father? He didn't remember ever seeing the man in town before. He closed the wooden box and returned it to its spot on the shelf.

Daniel strode toward the front of the store. "Mr. Burke. Such a pleasure to see you. Is there anything I can help you find?"

Ray stood just inside the door, glancing around with wide eyes. "You've changed things."

"Yes sir. My grandfather has made quite a few changes in the past year. You haven't visited the soda fountain since it opened?"

The man took off his cap and ran a hand through his thinning hair. "No. I . . . uh . . . I don't come into town much. I work long hours. Laurie runs most of my errands."

Daniel smiled. "I'm pleased that you stopped by. Why don't you sit down and I'll get Marcie to whip you up something."

Ray ambled forward and frowned at the cherry-red stools. "I ain't never been to a soda fountain."

Daniel stepped behind the counter. "They've grown pretty popular lately—Prohibition's answer to the neighborhood bar, I suppose."

Laurie's dad scuffed a foot on the tiles. "Yeah. I see. So, what you got?"

"We've got all kinds of soft drinks. Ice creams sodas, phosphates, egg creams—just about whatever you could want." Pride crept into Daniel's voice.

"Whatever I could want, eh?" Ray snorted, but lowered himself to a seat. "I don't think so."

Daniel let the comment roll off the counter. "Most anything. What do you fancy?"

Ray's eyes glazed over. "Don't rightly know. What do you suggest?"

"Laurie is particularly fond of egg creams."

Her father rested an elbow on the counter. "Is she now? She comes in here often, then?" His eyes—so like his daughter's—stared directly at Daniel.

"She comes in occasionally." Daniel turned to Marcie, feeling the sudden urge for company. "Marcie, you're more familiar with the fountain drinks than I am. What is your favorite?"

The young woman pushed a lid back onto a jar of chopped nuts. "It's all good, sir. But my favorite is the chocolate malted."

One corner of Ray's mouth lifted. "I'd rather have my malt in other forms."

Daniel placed his hands on the counter, ignoring Marcie's giggle. "How about a soda? A cola, maybe?"

"Yeah, that'll work, I guess." Ray rubbed his eyes. "I hear that's good to perk a person up."

Marcie bobbed her head as she reached for a tall glass. "Oh, yes. I make sure to have one every morning. It wakes me right up." She settled the glass under the tap.

Daniel leaned against the freezer. "I'm more of a coffee man, myself. I guess I never cared for the sugary sweetness."

"Good man. You know what they say about too much sweets." Ray winked at Marcie as she set the tall glass in front of him. "Of course, a little sweetness never hurt a fella. If you know what I mean."

Daniel's stomach churned. "I'd better get back to work. Let me know if there's anything else I can get for you." He started back to the storeroom.

"There might just be one thing, there, Daniel." Laurie's dad trailed after him, the soda glass still gripped in his palm. He glanced behind him before turning his bloodshot eyes back to Daniel. "I need some of my medicine." He rubbed his shoulder and grimaced.

A weight lowered onto Daniel's chest. *I'm going to need some help here, Lord.*

Ray took a swallow of the soda and coughed. "I'm all out at home . . . and . . . and I gotta work tonight. My shoulder's been paining me something fierce."

Daniel set his jaw. "I'm afraid that's the one thing I'm *not* going to be able to help you with."

Burke's eyes narrowed. "What are you talking about? I have a prescription. Just talk to Doc Pierce."

Daniel took a deep breath. "Mr. Burke, I've made a decision. I cannot in good conscience give out alcohol to customers who—um—who . . ."

The man straightened to his full height, his eyes narrowing to a squint. "Who what?"

Daniel placed a hand on the counter for strength. "Who I don't feel are actually in need of it."

"And how do you know what I need? Are you a doctor?"

No, not a doctor. Just a drunk like yourself. Or a former drunk.

Rubbing a hand through his hair, Daniel shook his head. "Look, Mr. Burke. I understand your struggle with alcohol. I can't be a party to that."

The corner of Ray's lip twitched. "A party." He snorted. "I ain't got a problem with alcohol. I got a problem with pain. And I got a problem with a boss who wants me to work two shifts after I was up half the night with that pain." He took a step closer to Daniel. "Right now it seems my biggest problem is you."

Daniel kept silent.

"Miles Larson never had a problem filling my prescription."

A sick feeling twisted in Daniel's gut. He hadn't told his grandfather of his new resolve. He didn't yet have the authority to make those kinds of decisions for the store—only for himself. "I have a problem with it."

The large man leaned against the counter. "She got to you, didn't she?"

"Who?"

His lips drew back from his teeth. "My bossy, good-for-nothing daughter. The one who keeps telling me to quit drinking—like it's a choice." He brought a finger up into Daniel's face. "You want to get in good with her, so you're letting her order you around."

"I make my own choices. I have to stand up for what I believe."

Ray curled his fingers into a fist and slammed it down against the counter. "What kind of man are you, anyway? You—in your starched white shirts with your egg creams and root beer—you've probably never done a real day's work in your life. You don't know nothing about what a real man puts up with." He snarled, spittle forming at the corner of his mouth. "You stay away from my daughter."

Daniel set his jaw. "This has nothing to do with Laurie."

Laurie's father pressed his hands against the counter and leaned in. "Your grandfather's going to hear about this, Shepherd. The whole town is going to hear. Let's see what that does for business."

Ray strode to the front door. As he reached the front, he turned, face twisted. He lifted the half-filled glass and heaved it across the room. It smashed against the tile floor, shards of glass and sugary syrup spraying across the store.

He stomped out, slamming the drugstore door behind him, vibrations rippling through the blue liquid of the show globe like a storm kicking up waves in the blue sea.

⚓

Laurie gathered her pocketbook, hat, and gloves from the exchange's coatroom, stretching the tension from her shoulders. She dithered for a few moments, folding and refolding her handkerchief as she waited for Mr. Quinn to work his way to the far side of the building. She didn't need another quarrel with him. Her job dangled by a thread already.

When he fixed his attention on Susan's station, pointing out three misplaced switches, Laurie jammed the handkerchief into her pocket and darted for the door. Stepping into the bright sunshine, she lifted her chin, allowing the rays to warm her skin.

"Rough day?" Daniel stood on the corner, a smile lighting his face, a bouquet of pink dahlias in his hand.

Laurie measured her steps, fighting the urge to dash to the man's side. They'd settled into a comfortable routine, sharing a coffee before work and ending the day with a sunset stroll. But tonight, he leaned against his freshly washed Buick. The automobile lacked the allure of Samuel's fancy Studebaker, but she much preferred the owner.

"I thought you might prefer to take a little drive tonight." Daniel swung open the automobile's door.

She abandoned the dignified act and hurried to his side, squeezing his elbow in greeting. "How did you know?"

The low rays of the evening sun emphasized the dimple in Daniel's cheek when he smiled at her. She settled herself on the seat. "We don't have time to make it to the lake, I'm afraid."

He laid the flowers on her lap and made his way around the automobile to climb in beside her. "How about Crescent Beach? I imagine there'll be a lovely sunset this evening."

She laughed. "Where we first met? Perfect."

He glanced down at her thin sweater. "Are you going to be warm enough? You know how breezy it is down there."

"I'll be fine."

"I've got a picnic blanket you could probably wrap around your shoulders."

She scooted closer to him as he guided the car out onto the downtown street. "Or I could just stay close to you." She wove her hand through his arm.

He lifted one hand from the steering wheel and looped it around her shoulders. "I've got to be the luckiest fellow in all of Port Angeles."

"Probably."

The evening sun offered little opposition to the cool wind blowing in off the Strait of Juan de Fuca. Laurie didn't wait for Daniel to open her door, springing from the automobile as soon as it came to a stop on the windswept bluff. She hurried to the overlook, pulling her sweater snug to block the biting wind.

Daniel caught up a few breaths later, wrapping both arms around her waist, leaning his chin against the top of her head, his body radiating warmth. "I want to tell you something."

She held her breath. He couldn't have brought her to such a romantic location to deliver bad news.

"I've decided to stop filling your father's prescriptions."

Laurie relaxed. "You have? That's . . . " She thought about her words. "I'm pleased. Thank you."

He sighed, his breath stirring her hair. "You're not going to be pleased for long."

"What happened?" She tugged his arms tighter around her mid-section, tucking her icy fingers inside the sleeves of his coat.

"He came in this afternoon and—and it wasn't pretty." He nestled his chin into the gap between her neck and shoulder, his stubble tickling her skin. "I'm afraid that he blames you for this decision, even though I assured him that you were not responsible." He took her hand and turned her to face him. "I'm concerned for your safety, Laurie. I saw the look in his eye."

She ran her fingers down his lapel. "My father would never hurt me. He'll be better off without the booze, Daniel. You did the right thing."

He placed a hand over her fingers, stilling their progress. "I'm only a piece of the puzzle. And a small piece, at that. What are you going to do about Johnny?"

"I'll talk to him."

Daniel's brow furrowed. "You cannot make this decision for your father. He has to come to it on his own."

She pulled her hands free, his words pricking her skin like a needle. How could he possibly understand? "I have to do *something*. The men in my family are all throwing their lives away and mine with them."

"So, what will you do?" Daniel pulled off his coat, draping it around her shoulders.

She laid her head on his arm. "I don't know. Protect them. Clean up all this . . ."—she lifted a hand to the sky—"mess. The only trouble is, once I have one mess contained, they go and create another."

Daniel took her hand, cradling it against his shirt front. "It's not your job to protect them. How would you do that, anyway?"

She chewed on her lower lip. How much could she tell him?

"I think the person you need to protect is yourself. Is your father as volatile as he seemed today? Should you really be staying there?"

"Maybe I should let him cool off a little."

He stroked her back. "Maybe I could help you kill some time until he's calmed down."

She smiled. "Maybe you could."

The sun dipped lower in the sky as he leaned toward her. Laurie held her breath as their lips touched. Keeping her face close so she could feel his warm breath against her temple, Laurie reached up with one hand and touched his rough jaw line.

His voice whispered in her ear, "I've wanted to do that since the first night we met."

"Me, too," she sighed.

36

WHY WOULD YOU DO THAT?" RED SPOTS FLARED BEFORE LAURIE'S EYES AS she glared at her brother. "He was supposed to work tonight and you gave him booze?"

Johnny lounged on the back steps of their house. "He's at work, Laurie. If I hadn't of given him enough to take the edge off, he'd have scoured the town until someone else did. Then he'd be dead drunk."

Daniel placed a hand on her shoulder and squeezed. "I told you, you can't make his choices."

She folded her arms, the evening crickets rankling her nerves.

Johnny curled his lip as he stared at Daniel's hand. "So, Amelia was right? You two are officially an item?"

Laurie looked away. She didn't owe him any explanations. "You've got to stop supplying him booze, Johnny."

Johnny ran his hand through his hair. "We've been over this before. If I don't give it to him, someone else will. Plus, when he gets desperate, he gets mean. You know that." He glared at Laurie. "I don't want you to get hurt."

Daniel's grip tightened. She shook it off and stepped forward. "I can watch out for myself, but I'm sick of taking care of his drunken messes. He showed up at the exchange today. How long will I keep my job if he shows up there drunk? How long will he keep his job at the mill?"

Johnny spit on the ground. "How long is he going to keep his job if he's spending all his time searching for booze?"

Daniel took a seat on the steps next to Johnny. "I know of places that could help him, but he needs to be willing. If you and Laurie talk to him together and convince him he needs the help—"

Johnny's eyes flashed. "You mean a hospital? Like my mom? Now I'm the one paying for that, ten years later, just to keep my family afloat."

Laurie's heart jumped. "What do you mean?"

A shadow crossed his face. "Nothing. Forget it."

Daniel cleared his throat. "If he learns how to lick this, you and Laurie can get on with your lives instead of keeping an eye on him all the time."

Laurie lifted her hand. "Wait—Johnny, what did you mean by that?"

"I said, forget it."

Claws ripped at her heart. "No. I won't. Tell me!" She took another step toward him.

Johnny jumped to his feet and stormed up the creaky porch steps.

She turned to Daniel. "Do you know what he's talking about?"

Daniel's eyes closed briefly, his head lowering.

Laurie's heart dropped in her chest. "You do."

"That's his story to tell you, not mine."

Laurie pushed free of Daniel's arm and ran up the stairs, bursting through the door.

Johnny sat at the kitchen table, the newspaper spread in front of him like nothing had been said.

Laurie snatched the paper away. "I want answers. Now."

His eyes blazed. "I was reading that."

She crushed it in her hand and pushed it behind her back as Daniel entered the room behind her.

Johnny blew his breath between his teeth. "There are still bills from Mama's hospital stay."

"That was ten years ago." She sank into a chair across from him.

He rapped the table with his knuckles. "That don't stop the bill collectors from knocking."

"Didn't Daddy . . ."

He looked up at her, his eyes tired. "He's put every extra dime into the whiskey bottle and you know it."

Laurie grabbed the edge of the table. "How much does he—do we—owe?"

Johnny leaned forward. "That's just it. I'm almost done paying it off. With what I'm getting from the weekly runs—and what Dad's donating through his 'purchases,' I'm almost done paying. I'll be able to quit."

Laurie looked between Johnny and Daniel, her heart swamped with emotions and questions. "Why—why didn't you tell me?"

Johnny shrugged. "You already take on more than your share of responsibility. You try to do everything, for everyone. You didn't need one more burden."

"I could have helped."

He smirked. "With what you make as an operator? Not likely."

Daniel spoke softly. "Johnny, I could help. I'll loan you the rest, you can pay me back slowly, from your wages at the mill."

Johnny shook his head. "No more loans. I'm not going to be beholden to anyone ever again."

Laurie pressed her fingers against the bridge of her nose as she struggled to process all that her brother was telling her. "This has all been for hospital bills? You weren't trying to buy a ring for Amelia?"

Johnny laughed. "Is that all you girls think about? No, I wasn't doing this for a ring. Dad gave me Mama's ring for her. I've had it for months."

"Then why haven't you asked her?"

"I figured I'd wait until I was done with the rumrunning. I didn't want to give her a reason to say no to me." He looked at his hands, a shadow crossing his face.

"You dope." Laurie shook her head. "As if she could ever say no to you."

A smile turned the corners of his lips. "Well, maybe it was more about being worthy of her."

Laurie patted her brother's hand, casting a glance at Daniel. "I'm sometimes wonder if any of us are worthy of love."

Daniel reached for her other hand and squeezed it.

Daniel rocked on the back legs of his chair, watching the two siblings dance around the delicate issues without declaring war on each other.

His chest ached with words left unsaid. His story—his recovery—could give Laurie and Johnny reason to hope. He gazed at Laurie, her face pinched in worry for her family. If he spoke up . . .

Several times he opened his mouth only to snap it shut, his stomach churning. How would Laurie react? Would he ever see her again?

Laurie filled her coffee cup from the pot on the stove. "I don't like it."

Johnny straddled his chair and rested his chin on the back rail. "I got two or three more shipments to go and we'll be free and clear."

"Not if Samuel gets a hold of you." Laurie drummed her fingers on the table.

Daniel settled his chair legs back on the floor. "Brown's out for blood, Johnny. He strikes me as the type to shoot first and deal with the consequences later."

Johnny lifted his hands. "Laurie's keeping an eye on him. And we keep switching the landing zones. He's never going to catch us."

A chill washed over Daniel. "Keeping an eye on him?" He sat up in his chair. "You're still seeing him?"

She glanced up at him, her chin tucked low. "It's not like that, exactly."

The force of emotion in his chest surprised him. "Then tell me what it's like."

"I'm just—well—I don't have any feelings for him. . . ."

"And that makes it all right?"

The hurt on her face was unmistakable. "What are you accusing me of?"

Daniel pushed his hands across his eyes, his pulse echoing in his head. "It sounds like you're 'seeing him' socially—leading him on, perhaps—in order to protect your brother and his cronies."

Johnny turned. "Hey—"

Daniel lifted a hand to prevent his interruption. "Does Brown already know about Johnny's activities?"

She bit her lip. "I think he's suspicious."

"If he already knows, then what kind of information are you hoping to get from him?"

Her gaze darted between him and Johnny. "I'm hoping he'll tell me if he plans to go after them."

Daniel leaned across the table. "Did it ever occur to either of you that he may be using *you* to get information on Johnny?"

After a pause, she nodded.

"Then why are you still doing this?"

Johnny's expression darkened. "Laurie?"

Her scarlet-colored lips pressed into a thin line. "After you were arrested and I went to tell him you were innocent..." Her voice quavered. "He said he would let you go, if..."

Daniel's palms grew damp. "If what?"

Johnny's hands closed over the chair back, his nostrils flaring. "You'd better not be saying what I think you're saying." His back tensed, as if he were preparing to leap over the table.

Daniel thrust an arm across Johnny's chest. "Easy." He took a deep breath. "Laurie, what did you ..."—he swallowed, acid crawling up his throat—"what did you promise the man?"

Her skin paled, but she lifted her chin in defiance. "I only said that I'd keep seeing him. Nothing else." She pushed up from her chair.

"I'll kill him," Johnny growled.

Daniel lowered his arm, fire crawling through his chest. Brown had extorted him, arrested him, and trashed his office. And now he had the gall to threaten Laurie? He clenched his jaw. "You might have to beat me to it."

Laurie's blue eyes flashed. "I make my own choices, remember?"

"This wasn't a choice. You were bullied into it." Johnny banged his hand on the table.

She settled a fist onto one hip. "I tell you what. I'll stop seeing him—on one condition."

Johnny's brow furrowed. "Oh, you're going to stop seeing him, all right."

"Listen to me." She glared at them. "I'll stop seeing him, if you two agree to stop selling—or giving—Dad any more booze."

"We're not cutting bargains here, Laurie." Daniel braced one hand on the table. "I don't think you understand the risks you're taking."

"I choose who I see and who I don't." She narrowed her eyes at him.

The implied threat in her words came like a punch to the stomach. He pulled his coat from the back of the chair. "I think it's time for me to leave."

Johnny grabbed his arm. "Hold it. I need you on my side, here, Daniel."

Daniel crushed his coat in his grip. The floor swayed as if he stood in a canoe. He could no longer deny the depths of his feelings for Laurie Burke, but he refused to allow her to trifle with him. *Save those tricks for Brown.*

Daniel's jaw ached. "I've already stopped supplying your dad with liquor. You really expect Johnny to stop providing him whiskey just so you'll stop socializing with Samuel Brown?"

Laurie nodded.

Daniel shook his head. He'd expected more from her. Maybe he didn't know her at all.

Johnny growled, running a hand across his chin and neck. "Done."

37

I AIN'T GOING TO NO HOSPITAL." HER FATHER THREW THE CHAIR BACK from the table.

Laurie kept a safe distance, choosing not to argue. *Plant the seed and give it time to grow.*

"Hospitals are for sick folk. There ain't nothing wrong with me." He grabbed another biscuit from the platter and trudged from the room.

She cleared the table, consumed by thoughts of Daniel. A sharp pain gouged through her heart every time she pictured his distraught face and remembered the door closing behind him.

Lord, you sent me an honest man and I shattered any chance I had with him.

"You've forgotten that your mother died in one of those places. Like I'd ever step foot there, again." Her father's muffled voice echoed from the far end of the house.

Laurie carried the dishes to the sink and stopped to gaze out at the darkening sky. She hadn't dared stop in at the drugstore this morning. And the curb outside the exchange remained empty.

Her lips tingled with the memory of their evening on the bluff. One kiss. That's all she got? She blinked away the tears. No good would come from dwelling on it.

Johnny would be going on his second-to-last shipment tonight and he'd promised not to bring any of the whiskey to their father. She stopped and closed her eyes. *Lord, keep him safe.* A lump formed in her throat. Was it wrong to pray protection over someone who was knowingly committing a sinful act? She opened her eyes and swished a hand through the warm soapy water, tiny waves splashing over the dirty dishes.

"No hospitals!" Her father hollered down the hall.

Maybe she was praying for the wrong family member.

The telephone rang, causing Laurie to jump and splash suds across the floor.

"Aren't you going to answer that? Isn't that what they pay you to do?" Dad's voice floated in between rings.

She grasped the receiver and lifted it to her ear. Out of habit, she straightened her neck and summoned her most melodic voice. "Hello, Burke residence."

"Hello, Miss Operator."

"Johnny?" She sputtered, all pretense vanishing. "What are you doing? I thought you were out—working, tonight."

"Johnny?" Her dad stuck his head into the kitchen. "He ain't working tonight. Is that him on the telephone?"

She covered the mouthpiece. "Just a minute, Dad." She lowered her voice and moved her fingers away. "What's wrong?"

"I can't talk, Sis. But I need help. One of our guys can't make it."

Her heart lurched. "Why are you calling me? What can I do?"

"We need a spotter. I don't know who else to ask."

Laurie leaned against the wall, trying to catch her breath. "I couldn't possibly . . ."

"It's just one night, Laurie."

She tugged on her earlobe. "No. Just call it off for tonight."

She could hear Johnny's breathing through the receiver. "Not possible. We already put in an order; we've got to be there to get it. All you got to do is take Dad's Ford and drive out to the water. When you spot our light, flash the headlamps to show us it's safe. Come on, Laurie, I'm desperate."

She dug her fingernails into her palm. "Johnny—"

"Let me talk to him." Her father stomped into the room, gesturing for the telephone.

Laurie's stomach dropped. "Dad—"

"Give me the telephone, Laurie."

She passed it to him, her fingers trembling.

His large hand closed over the receiver. "Johnny?" He stopped and listened as Laurie stepped backward.

"Yeah, you got more for me?"

She turned and walked back to the sink, the muscles in her neck tightening into a hopeless knot. Her father's voice rose in pitch as he talked.

This was shaping up to be a rough night.

She rinsed the last dish and lifted it from the dripping water just in time to hear her father return the receiver to the telephone with a disgusted grunt.

"Johnny said he'd meet you at 3 o'clock at Freshwater Bay." He turned and scowled at Laurie. "You two got a picnic planned or something?"

Laurie stood mute, water dripping from the plate suspended in her hand.

He rubbed his shoulder and grimaced. "I'm going out. Don't wait up."

Laurie shut her bedroom door, her heart hammering in her chest. She paced to the window and laid her forehead against it. *God, what do I do?*

The half-moon shone its thin light down on the side of the house and across the empty spot normally occupied by the Model T. Now, even if she wanted to help Johnny, she had no automobile.

Laurie pressed her hand against her stomach. She needed to do something, but every choice seemed impossible. As soon as her father had left, she'd tried telephoning Johnny, but the line had gone unanswered.

I can't let him land without a spotter. She pulled away from the window and stumbled back to the bed. She could call Daniel, but he didn't approve of the rumrunning any more than she did. Did she want to admit to him that she was considering helping out with it?

How could she not?

Laurie pulled her sketchbook from under her pillow. It lay open to the portrait she had drawn of Daniel at Crescent Beach. Rather than the shadowy figure of that first night, in this one he stood on the shore, a rock in his hand and arm cocked to skip it along the top of the water. His handsome face shone with a trace of little-boy glee.

She closed the book and pushed it back under her pillow.

Could she now call him and ask him to return to the beach to help with a whiskey delivery?

What choice do I have?

Laurie drove her fist into the pillow. How dare Johnny put her in this position? She hit the pillow a second time, momentarily placated by the lovely "thwump" sound it made. Picking it up, she slammed it hard on the bed, feeling the tightness in her arms easing with the movement.

Casting the pillow aside, she strode to her closet and pulled out an old wool sweater and a scarf to wrap around her head. Somehow, she was going to be on that beach by the time the boats arrived—even if she had to steal a car to do so.

☞——✦——☜

Laurie sprinted toward town, the road flying by under her hurrying feet. Once she decided, she didn't want to give herself a moment to doubt. She clutched a cloth bag against her side, her father's military flashlight nestled cozily with his old army knife. She might as well have pulled on his uniform while she was at it, since she raced toward an impossible battle.

Daniel, I need your automobile. I'll bring it back, I promise. The very idea made her laugh, tears stinging her eyes. *Daniel, think how romantic the beach is by moonlight.*

Maybe she could just borrow the Buick and have it back before he even missed it.

As she approached the edge of Lincoln Park, she slowed to a stop and clutched at her sweater in aggravation. "I can't do this," she whispered. First a liar, then a bootlegger's assistant—now a thief?

Her insides roiled. Wrapping both arms around herself, she rubbed hands up and down her sleeves, shivering in the cool night air. Stars dotted the sky, an example of God's artistry at work. Her heart slowed.

Daniel had said, "People make their own choices. You can't protect them from the consequences."

Just as she'd made her choices and lost him.

She pulled her eyes away from the stars and noticed a Model T parked askew in the shadows of the trees. A man's arm— clad in a familiar twill sleeve—dangled out over the door, his head lolled back on the seat as if asleep.

Or worse.

A prickle raced up her neck. She crept up and peered in at her father's sleeping form, his snores rattling the seat springs. The stench of alcohol was unmistakable, even if she hadn't seen the empty bottle splayed across his lap.

She blew out a hissing breath. As if this night couldn't get more complicated. Laurie prodded his arm. "Dad, wake up."

Her father slumped to the side, the bottle rolling from his lap onto the floor. He mumbled a few unintelligible words into the seat cushion.

She banged a hand against the door and reached for the handle. "Move over, I'll drive you home."

Laurie yanked the door open. "I should leave you here. It would serve you right." With a sigh, she tossed her bag onto the floor and wedged her arms under him. Grunting, she dug her shoes against the earth and heaved. Managing to slide him a few inches, she braced herself against the car door and jostled him a little further before collapsing against his shoulder.

Walking to the far side, she pulled open the passenger door and leaned across the seat. Pushing aside his jacket and vest, she hooked her fingers on his waistband. Jerking hard, she managed to slide him across the seat. His head lolled toward her and landed heavily on her shoulder. Pushing upward, she goaded him back into a sitting position.

Closing the door, she leaned against it, panting. *God, can this night get any worse?* She wiped her hands down her skirt. *Forget I asked that.*

She settled herself in the driver's seat and glanced over at her father, his head lolled to the side and his mouth hanging open. "I'm not responsible for your choices, Dad." She blew a wisp of hair out of her eyes and adjusted her hat with one hand, keeping the other locked on the wheel. "And yet, somehow I'm always the one forced to pick up the pieces."

She gripped the wheel. Now that she had the automobile, Johnny's desperate voice tugged at her heart. How could she just leave him out there without a light to guide him? She wouldn't really be breaking the law, would she? She'd just be flashing the headlamps a few times, bringing some sailors home. Who would know?

God would know.

Laurie pushed her fingers against her eyes. A man of honor—that's what she kept asking from God. She lowered her head against the cold wooden steering wheel. *I'd be breaking the law as surely as if I were holding the oars.*

Her father coughed and shifted in his sleep, making Laurie jump and open her eyes.

A woman of honor, she thought. *I'm sorry, Johnny.* She reached for the ignition and cranked the Ford's engine. Turning on the headlamps, she inched backward onto the road and turned toward home, the twin beams cutting through the murky blackness.

The dark image of an automobile parked a block ahead, caught her eye. As she drove past, her headlights glared off a memorable grill and illuminated the face of the man sitting inside. Laurie's heart lurched. She jerked her gaze back to the road.

Samuel.

38

Daniel sat on the stool, leaning his back against the counter. His eyes wandered across the drugstore to the artwork his grandfather had displayed on the brick wall. Words spun through his head, but none traveled as far as his mouth.

Laurie's spoon clinked against the sides of her coffee cup, the only sound in the quiet store. She lifted her head, her eyes like two round pools glistening in the morning sunlight streaming in through the front window. "I'm sorry, Daniel."

He exhaled, his anger streaming away before he could catch hold of it. "Laurie—"

"I won't see Samuel again." She touched the sleeve of his jacket with her tender fingers. "I just . . ." She bit her lip. "I'm not sure what he'll do when he finds out."

Daniel set his jaw. "Let me take care of that."

"I don't want anything to happen to you." A pinched line formed between her brows.

"I'm glad you didn't go along with Johnny's scheme."

She sighed. "I just hope he's all right. I thought my heart would stop when I saw Samuel parked on the side of the road." She took a sip of coffee. "I could have led him straight to them."

Daniel frowned. "Do you think Brown is following you?"

"Either me or my father." She rubbed her arms. "I'd like to think that information would be enough to make Johnny stop, but he's so obsessed with this debt business, I don't think anything is going to convince him."

"And . . ."

She sighed for a second time. "I'm not responsible for his choices."

"Do you want me to talk to Johnny?" He sat forward and touched her arm.

She placed her fingers over his hand. "I don't think it would do any good."

He laced his fingers through hers and squeezed. "Then can I interest you in another sunset drive tonight?"

A smile crossed her face—the first he'd seen that morning. "I'd love that."

Since the store was still empty, he brushed a kiss across her forehead before she left, breathing in the lavender scent of her hair. That whiff would have to hold him until this evening.

⊙══✦══⊙

Laurie smiled as she walked to the exchange, pushing away thoughts of her family in exchange for anticipation of another evening with Daniel.

The exchange door opened as she arrived, Samuel's wide shoulders filling the doorway. He stepped out onto the sidewalk, a smile lifting one corner of his mouth. "Hello, Beautiful. Fancy meeting you here on this lovely morning."

Her throat suddenly dry, she swallowed hard. "What are you doing here?"

Samuel squinted as the morning sun topped the foothills and scattered out over the town. "Just having a little chat with your boss. Trying to follow up on some possible leads."

Her heart quickened. "My boss?"

Samuel lifted his hat and settled it on his head, running his fingers along the brim. "Rumrunners use telephones, too, don't they?"

Laurie's mind raced. Is that how he'd known last night? Was he listening in on calls? On *her* calls? "I suppose they do. I wouldn't know."

He reached out his hand and ran his fingers up her arm, causing gooseflesh to race across her skin. "Of course not. You are the picture of innocence." He cocked one eyebrow. "So, we have a date tonight?"

She stepped back, squeezing her arms around her midsection. "I'm afraid that's out of the question."

He let his hand drop to his side and then tucked it into his jacket pocket, pulling out his gold watch and checking the time. "I thought we had an understanding."

Laurie moistened her lips and folded her hands in front of her for confidence. "I'm afraid I made that agreement before I had all the facts about you, Mr. Brown. Under duress, shall we say?"

His brows shot upward. "Duress?" He stepped closer, causing her to back up against the brick building. "You showed up at my home in the middle of the night. I didn't see any concern then." He shook his head. "It would be a shame if that little story got around."

Sweat broke out across her skin, bathing her in a clammy chill

His gaze lingered, locking on her face for a long moment before traveling the length of her frame. "I suppose it gives me more time to focus on this case." He stepped back. "I believe I'm getting very close to a breakthrough."

Laurie's throat tightened, like a noose closing. "I need to get to work."

Samuel stepped to the side with a gallant sweep of his hand. "Please, do not let me distract you. I know how important is to focus on one's job."

⚬━┿━⚬

Daniel glanced up from his work just in time to see Johnny saunter past the drugstore window. "Marcie, I'll be right back." He grabbed his hat and headed for the door.

Daniel quickened his pace, calling out to his friend.

Johnny lifted a hand to shield his eyes from the bright sun.

A storm brewed in Daniel's chest. "Laurie told me what you put her up to last night."

Johnny pulled the tweed cap from his head, clenching it in his hand. "That girl talks too much."

"You said you didn't want her involved. Now you're going to drag her into it?"

"She didn't even show up. I guess I should have figured as much. She used to have some spunk, but she's been all 'good girl,' lately."

Daniel struggled against the desire to grab Johnny's shirt collar and shake him. "What kind of brother puts his little sister into that sort of position?"

Johnny's eyes blazed. "The kind of brother who's trying to keep a roof over her head."

"I offered to help with that."

Johnny's face grew mottled. "Yeah, just what she needs, one more man to be beholden to. What kind of demands would you make on her?"

A growl rose in Daniel's throat. Grabbing Johnny's shirt, he yanked him close. "I seem to remember you cold-cocking me for saying something like that. Should I return the favor?"

Johnny's hand flew up, clamping on Daniel's wrist. "I'd like to see you try."

Laurie's face filled Daniel's mind. He shoved Johnny, sending him stumbling backward. "For your sister's sake, I'll restrain myself."

After regaining his balance, Johnny splayed his feet, jaw jutting forward. "We ain't borrowing any more money. Not from you, not from anyone."

"What if I gave it to you?"

Johnny snorted. "No."

"You'd rather break the law—maybe end up in jail—than take money from me?"

"I ain't taking money from anybody."

"Then you're a fool." The words tumbled from his mouth. "You don't really care about protecting Laurie. If you did, you'd find a way to raise the money without turning to rumrunning."

Johnny's brow furrowed. "We don't all have your fortunes, college boy. Some of us got to make our own luck."

"Keep Laurie out of it. You can go to prison if you choose, but leave her be."

With a scowl, Johnny shoved his cap back onto his head and turned away.

Daniel crossed his arms. "Did you know Brown is following her?"

His words had the desired effect. Johnny turned, eyes dark.

"She spotted him last night. Can you imagine how she'd have felt if she'd led him straight to you? Do you think Brown is above arresting her, too?"

"For what?"

Daniel pushed his hat to the back of his head. "You can't be that stupid."

Johnny stalked off.

"Leave her out of it," Daniel called.

Johnny swung his hand dismissively.

Daniel glowered at Johnny's retreating form, sickened by the confident swagger in his walk.

⚬════✦════⚬

Daniel rested against his automobile, a storm raging in his heart. He took a deep breath, blowing out the tension as best as he could manage. This evening needed to be an escape for Laurie, a diversion from the tension of the past few days. It would be his gift to her. If he could keep his mouth shut.

Laurie stepped out of the exchange, her blue flowered dress fluttering in the breeze, a smile bringing light to her face.

Daniel swallowed and reached for the Buick's door, a rushing sensation in his chest. If a simple smile from this beautiful girl made him weak, he was a goner.

The door jammed. Frowning, he rattled it and tried a second time. Not exactly the suave moment he'd envisioned.

"Is there a problem, Mr. Shepherd?" Her lilting voice crossed the space between them.

He reached over the door and jiggled the inner handle with a groan. "Just a moment, I'll get it." He put his shoulder into it and yanked. The door remained stuck fast. "My automobile seems to have a mind of its own sometimes."

Laurie hurried around to the driver's door with a gleam in her eye. "If it thinks it can keep me out that easily, it doesn't know me very well." She slipped behind the wheel. "Are you going to join me?" She slid across the seat, bouncing the springs in her child-like enthusiasm.

Daniel walked around the car, the tension easing from his shoulders as he anticipated the evening ahead.

"Is that fish I smell?" She glanced over the back of the seat.

"I stopped at McCurry's and picked us up some dinner. It'll be cold by the time we get there, I hope you don't mind."

She breathed deeply, inhaling the scent of the greasy fried fish. "My hero."

They pulled up at Crescent Beach just as the sun dipped on the horizon. Laurie grabbed the basket from the back seat.

Daniel stepped out of the Buick and held out his hand to her.

Laurie grasped his fingers, sliding across the seat toward the driver's door. As she stepped out, an odd sensation rushed through her. *This is good.* It had been a long road, from that first night on the bluff to now. A shiver raced through her gut. *Too good.*

They walked down the trail, fingers laced together. Daniel carried the basket while Laurie kept a hand planted on her hat to keep it from loosening in the breeze. Her heart jumped around in her chest. She didn't deserve such a good man. How long would it be until he figured that out?

The beach was edged with massive logs. Daniel gestured toward a large one. "Is that a good spot?"

Laurie surveyed the colossal tree and laughed. "I don't think I could get up there."

"Allow me." His eyes gleamed as he handed her the basket and scrambled up the sand-encrusted log. Crouching, he reached for the hamper.

She handed it up to him, looking around for an easier approach.

"Here." He bent down on one knee and stretched out his arm to her.

She took his hand, her stomach fluttering. "I don't think—"

"Grasp my arm up higher."

She stretched higher and gripped his forearm, his strong fingers circling her wrist in return. She placed her other hand on top of the log and dug a toe in a large crevice. "All right. If you're sure."

His grin was her answer. With a firm pull, he hoisted her upward.

The next thing she knew, she sat on her backside gazing at the waves crashing against the jagged stone outcropping just off-shore. "This is amazing!"

"I thought you'd like it." He crouched, pressing a palm to the salt-washed timber for balance before kicking his leg out and plopping down beside her.

She brushed the sand from her hands and enjoyed the warmth of his thigh next to hers in the cool evening air.

Daniel reached into the basket, a boyish smile lighting his face. He laid a wrapped gift on her lap.

"What's this?"

"Open it."

She untied the ribbon and gazed in wonder at the set of watercolor paints and brushes of various sizes. Her heart skipped, her fingers stroking one of the wooden handles.

"I just wanted to add a little color to your life."

A lump formed in Laurie's throat. "I can't wait to use them. I'll paint something for you, first thing."

After eating, the two sat in silence, watching the waves darken and the sky streak with red and purple. A tickle ran up Laurie's arm every time Daniel's thumb rubbed across her wrist. She licked her lips, growing dry and salty in the marine breeze. "You can see some lights over in Canada." She pointed toward Victoria. "I can't believe Johnny and those men row all that distance in the dark. How frightening." After a pause, she added, "I promised myself I wouldn't talk about him tonight."

Daniel turned toward her, the last glow of the sunset reflecting across his face, accentuating the curve of his jaw. "Let's not." He pulled her hand under his arm. "Let's have one evening where it's just us. No family. No federal agents. No rum-runners. No drugstore." He slid his arm behind her and settled it around her waist. "Just us."

She felt the warmth and security of his arm and smiled. "I'd like that."

The intensity in his gaze sent a shiver of anticipation through her. As he leaned in, she closed her eyes. Their lips met, his mouth warm against hers. After the gentle kiss, Daniel kept his face close, brushing his chin against her cheek.

Her breathing quickened and she lifted her lips back to his, wanting nothing more than to fall into their softness and not let the moment pass. *Too good.*

He pulled her closer, his lips traveling across her cheek and temple. His fingers wound through the hair at the nape of her neck.

She pulled off her hat, enjoying the contrast between the cold wind and the warmth of his hand. She slipped her hands under his jacket, her cold fingers sinking into the warmth between his coat and his shirt. She slid her palm up the smooth fabric until she touched his shirt collar.

Daniel's breath moved the hair just behind her ear and she closed her eyes, a tremor racing through her. His lips kissed her neck and she slid her hands around his back, pulling him closer.

Daniel paused, as if holding his breath, drawing back a few inches.

The cool air rushed into the space between them. Laurie's pulse fluttered. "What's wrong?"

He pulled back, his eyes unreadable in the growing darkness. "I—I think we should go."

Laurie took a deep breath, releasing her hold on his waist, even as her heart cried for more. "Of course."

39

LAURIE SNUGGLED DEEPER UNDER THE COVERS, TRYING TO PRESERVE THE remnant of the dream before it slipped away.

"Laurie!" Her father's shout came a second time, startling her awake.

She flung back the covers and grabbed her robe from the chair beside her bed. "Just a minute," she called back. Morning light filtered through the curtains, illuminating the motes of dust suspended in the air.

As the heavy footsteps approached, she pushed her arms into the sleeves of her robe and pulled the belt snug.

Her father stood framed in the doorway, shoulders hunched. "Where's breakfast?"

She ran fingers through her tousled hair. "I overslept. I was out late."

His brows rose. "Yes. I noticed you didn't get home before I had to leave for work." When she didn't respond, he took a step forward. "You been gone a lot. Is it that Shepherd fellow?"

Laurie spotted her slippers hiding under the nightstand. She jammed her toes into them. "Yes, well, I have been spending some time with Daniel." She felt a flush climbing up her cheeks. "I can make you breakfast now, if you'd like."

He stepped aside and let her pass. "I was a little harsh with him the other day."

She padded into the kitchen and reached for the breadbox. "I had heard something of the sort."

He followed her, his voice gruff. "I'm your father. It's my duty to look after you."

Laurie cracked an egg into the frying pan. "Of course." *When it's convenient.*

"Yeah, well. I'll go wash up for breakfast." He paused. "And if you see your brother today—tell him I need another couple of bottles, will you?"

She braced her hands against the counter. "He's not bringing any more."

Her father's eyes narrowed. "He'll bring it if he knows what's good for him."

Laurie gripped the robe's belt, the corners of her vision fogging. "He won't be bringing more because he knows what's good for *you.* You need help. Daniel knows of a hospital where they can teach people to stop drinking."

Dad wrapped his fingers around the back of the kitchen chair. "Oh, Daniel does? So he's behind this sudden mutiny?"

Laurie crossed her arms. "No. I am. I'm sick of your drinking. I'm sick of cleaning up your messes and putting up with your tirades. Johnny's not bringing you any more booze and I'm not waiting on you hand and foot—not until you agree to get help." She plowed forward before her courage failed. "You can cook your own breakfast." Laurie snatched the pan from the stovetop and dropped it into the sink, the hot cast iron protesting with an angry hiss. The half-cooked egg smeared into a streak of yellow slime. She hurried past her father, darting into her room and slamming the door.

Her dad pounded on the door. "Where do you get off talking to me like that? I've been working all night to keep this roof over your head. Get out here."

The door rattled, but she kept a firm grip on the knob, tremors racing up and down her body. His footsteps tramped down the hall.

The silence sent a chill through her heart. She dashed to the closet and pulled on the first dress she found, her trembling fingers fumbling with the buttons.

When her father's hand banged against the glass window, she shrieked. Dashing from the room, she pulled on a shoe as she hopped down the hall on one foot.

Hearing the glass break, Laurie sprinted for the door. When she arrived at Amelia's home, her friend pulled her inside, eyes wide. "Laurie, why are you here so early?"

Laurie adjusted the belt on her dress. "My father's in a rage. I didn't know where else to go."

"You said he never hits you."

Laurie shook her head. "No, but . . ." She chewed on her lower lip. "I told him I wouldn't stand his drinking anymore. And I convinced Johnny and Daniel to both stop supplying him with whiskey."

Amelia took Laurie's hand and led her over to the sofa.

Laurie perched on the very edge, digging her fingers against her knees to keep them from trembling. "I've never seen him so angry. I wasn't sure what to do."

Her friend sat down beside her. "You did the right thing, coming here. You can stay with us until this blows over. I'm sure Mama and Daddy won't mind."

Laurie's throat squeezed. "What will they think of me?"

Amelia laid her hand on Laurie's back. "They won't ask. We'll just say your father is working night shift and you don't want to stay alone. That much is true—isn't it?"

Laurie sniffled. "Yes. He'll be working nights for two more weeks, at least."

"Perfect. And with him working nights and you working days—you'll hardly see him anyway. It'll give him time to cool off. Maybe sober up."

Laurie leaned back against the soft, cushioned back, her knotted stomach muscles unwinding. "Maybe."

⚓

Daniel pulled open the back door as an angry voice cut through the store. "I've had a standing prescription here for years, Larson!"

Daniel leaned against the frame and listened. No need to rush in and stir the pot.

His grandfather's calm, soothing voice answered, "Yes, Mr. Burke. I know that. But our files are still a jumbled mess, thanks to that federal agent and his colleagues. Your prescription is missing, it seems. I'll put a call in to Dr. Pierce and have him issue you a new one."

"And how long is that going to take?"

"I'll send a message over to him this morning. If he's in the office and gets right back to me—perhaps by this afternoon. I could telephone you as soon as we have it filled. Perhaps your daughter could pick it up on her way home from work. We've been seeing quite a bit of her around here. She's a good girl, your Laurie."

Daniel held his breath, but he couldn't make out Mr. Burke's response. From where he stood, it sounded like a guttural growl.

His grandfather's voice remained even. "That's fine. I'm sure we'll get this figured out quickly, Mr. Burke."

Daniel edged down the stairs to the basement, running his hand along the cold metal handrail. The cabinets and cupboards stood in neat order, all reorganized and cleaned since Brown's visit. What had seemed a disaster at the time had actually proven to be a benefit. Daniel and his granddad had gone through every paper, discarding the old, filing the important, and doing a thorough reorganization.

Granddad's voice echoed down the stairs. "You hiding out down there?"

Daniel chuckled. "Is the coast clear?"

"For now, but I think your young lady's father is on the warpath and you're on his 'most wanted' list. Now get up here. We need to talk. And I've got a stack of prescriptions for you to compound."

Daniel took the steps two at a time, retrieved his white coat from the storeroom peg, and joined his grandfather at the pharmacy counter. "At your service."

Granddad snorted. "And in my debt, I believe." He handed Daniel the first slip and gestured toward the supply shelves. "Now while I've got you as a captive audience, would you care to tell me what's going on?"

Daniel glanced over the prescription before meeting his grandfather's eyes. "Ray Burke is a lush."

"Tell me something I don't already know."

"He's a mean drunk. He's hurtful to his family. I can't condone that. I refuse to contribute to it."

Granddad leaned back against the counter and crossed his arms. "Is he hitting Laurie?"

Daniel gathered the list of ingredients and began making measurements. "She says he isn't. But I know he used to knock Johnny around when we were kids. And I've witnessed his temper. We shouldn't be handing him more ammunition."

"I've told you, that's not our decision to make."

"We don't have to sell it to him. There are other options folks could use."

His grandfather pulled another slip off the stack. "And many of those options are worse than liquor—you know that. Not everyone who buys alcohol is a drunk.

Daniel reached for the pestle. "But we do choose what items to carry in the store. And we can choose not to serve certain customers."

"Not if we want to stay in business for long."

Daniel brought the pestle down with a bang. "Granddad, Burke is a miserable drunk and I refuse to sell him his poison of choice."

His grandfather narrowed his eyes. "Raymond Burke is the father of the woman you love. Don't you think you're a bit too close to this for a rational decision?"

Turning to face his grandfather, Daniel pushed down the emotions threatening to overwhelm him. "It's because I'm so close to this that I understand Ray Burke's problem." His chest ached. "Granddad, I've been there."

His grandfather set down the jar he was holding and pulled off his glasses.

Daniel pressed his hands against the pharmacy counter for strength. "It's time you knew the truth."

40

"I DON'T UNDERSTAND IT," JOHNNY SAID. "HE'S BEEN TOO QUIET."

Laurie pushed open Amelia's screen door with her hip, balancing a tray filled with a pitcher of lemonade and four glasses. "Can't we just be thankful for that? Maybe he's realized booze isn't the answer." She set the drinks on a small wrought-iron table.

Daniel took a glass. "It's too soon for that. And I agree with Johnny. It was too easy."

Johnny accepted the glass from Amelia's hand. "He hasn't called to ask for more whiskey in over a week now."

Daniel nodded. "And he never questioned my grandfather when he told him that Dr. Pierce revoked his prescription."

Breathing in the heady fragrance of the roses climbing the trellis beside the porch, Laurie sank down onto the bench swing, wishing she could enjoy the newfound peace in her life. But the peace felt artificial—like the eerie stillness before the first jagged bolt of lightning. "I haven't even seen him since the morning I left."

Amelia lifted her glass to her lips. "I think Laurie's leaving may have been the incentive he needed. Maybe he's decided to dry out on his own."

Johnny curled his lip. "It's going to take more than that to make him give up the bottle. He's been drinking since before the war. If I had a dime for every bottle he downed, I'd be a rich man."

Laurie's heart wrenched at his bitterness. She had to believe there was still hope for their father. "So what do you think is going on?"

Johnny took a long swig of the lemonade. "I think he's got a new supplier. I just can't figure out who it'd be—the boys and I are pretty much the only game in town and they swore they weren't selling none to him."

Daniel leaned back and stretched his arm along the back of the porch swing. "And you believe them?"

"They got no reason to lie to me."

Laurie tried to focus on the conversation, only slightly distracted by Daniel's arm mere inches from her shoulder. Apparently he wasn't brazen enough to put his arm around her in front of her brother. The thought brought a smile in spite of her somber mood.

Daniel cleared his throat. "What about moonshine? Sheriff Martinson came by yesterday and said that they'd broken up a still over on the west side last weekend and another out at the old Westerfield barn."

Amelia frowned. "Do you think he'd go that far?"

A chill swept over Laurie. The papers were full of stories of people sickened or blinded by drinking bad moonshine.

"Sure he would." Johnny leaned against the porch rail. "In a heartbeat."

<hr />

Laurie moved the cords and switches in a trance. The voices blurred together, her hands working without much help from her head. Sleeping on a makeshift pallet in Amelia's room,

Laurie missed the comfort of her own bed, but at least she slept without fear.

Except for the nightmares. She kept seeing Johnny floating face down in the water, his limp body rising and falling with the gentle lapping of the waves. She pushed the image away. "What number, please?"

"Laurie—it's me." Johnny's voice spoke into her earpiece.

She gasped, the cord trembling in her fingers. Glancing around, she lowered her voice to a whisper. "Why are you calling here? You know I can't—"

"Laurie, Dad never showed up for his shift last night. I'm at the house—you need to come."

Sweat broke out under her collar. "Now? I can't—I—"

"Bring Daniel, if you can."

Her stomach rolled at the quaver in his voice. The connection went dead, sending Laurie surging to her feet. She ripped off her headset.

All the women in the room turned, eyes wide. Mr. Quinn's head jerked up, his perpetually pinched face widening into a gaping stare.

"I'm sorry." She dashed across the floor, the sounds of her hurried steps echoing through the quiet room.

Laurie bolted out of the switchboard exchange and sprinted for the pharmacy. The bell pealed as she burst through the door. Marcie gasped and juggled a glass in her hand. At the pharmacy counter, Mr. Larson lifted his head, brows raised.

"Daniel?" Laurie yelped, blinking to keep the tears at bay.

He poked his head from the storeroom, mouth open. "Laurie?"

"My father."

⊙━◆━⊙

Not now. Please, not now. Daniel threw open the Buick's hood as he clenched his jaw. Recalling Johnny's mechanics lesson before their lake trip, he peered into the motor, located the wires, and gave them a quick jiggle. Sure enough, one was disconnected. He pulled it up between his finger and thumb. "Now, where does it go?"

He eyed the machine, wishing he had spent more time learning how it functioned. He fastened the wire back into a likely looking spot, he leaned away from the hood and nodded to Laurie. She reached for the ignition. With a loud backfire, the engine jerked to a start.

Daniel closed the hood with a sigh of relief and climbed into the driver's seat. "Your brother might just make a mechanic out of me yet." Laurie's pale, tear-stained face made it difficult for him to breathe. "Johnny didn't say anything else?"

She lifted her hands, chin trembling. "Just 'come.'"

He reached for the throttle. "No time to waste, then."

✧

Laurie's knees weakened as she stared at the metal drums, containers, and copper tubing strewn across her living room. The sour smell burned her sinuses, sending her eyes watering. Even with the window standing open, the house was hot and steamy—worse than when she and Amelia spent all weekend canning peaches and pears.

"What . . ." She didn't need to finish the question. She already knew the answer. Tears sprang to her eyes.

Sweat dripped down Johnny's face and stained his shirt. "I got here an hour ago and found it. There are different barrels in the bedroom—looks like wood alcohol from the mill."

Daniel appeared in the doorway, his eyes wide.

Johnny turned and faced the still. "I thought he'd find someone else making moon. I never dreamed he'd try it himself."

The mixture of emotions in Laurie's heart simmered, a burning sensation exploding in her chest. "What is wrong with the men in this family?" She kicked the door shut. She started toward the contraption, determined to tear it apart with her bare hands.

Daniel caught her wrist and dragged her back. "Can't you feel the heat coming off it? And who knows what kind of nasty compounds are bubbling around in there?"

Johnny stood between her and the still. "I've already shut it down, Laurie. Drinking is one thing, but I ain't going to let him burn the house down trying to make his own rotgut whiskey. I'd rather give him the real thing."

"No!" Laurie yanked her arm against Daniel's firm grip. "You promised."

Johnny glowered. "You'd rather have him distilling wood alcohol in the living room?"

Some kind of horrid concoction boiled in her own gut. "Those barrels from the mill. How did he get them?"

"Probably stole them." Johnny pushed open another window. "Maybe that's why he didn't show last night. Anyway, I'm getting rid of them and taking this blasted thing apart—piece-by-piece. Hopefully I can get done before he gets back."

"Where is he?" Daniel asked.

"Don't know. Don't care."

Daniel pulled off his jacket and rolled up his own sleeves. "I'll give you a hand."

Laurie remained motionless, staring at the ramshackle piece of machinery in the heart of her family's home.

As Johnny took a wrench and began pulling the pipes apart, dark amber liquid dribbled from a thin copper pipe and pooled on the floor.

Daniel snatched a towel from the kitchen counter. "If he's drinking this stuff, he's going to have worse problems than the sheriff on his back."

Laurie strode for the back door, propping it open and taking deep gulps of the fresh air.

The Ford stood ajar in the yard, the driver's door hanging open. She stood frozen for a long moment before stumbling forward and running down the steps. Her father's prone shape lay sprawled in the dirt.

Laurie fell to her knees at his side, her hands fluttering across his back and arms, unsure what to do first. He felt cold to the touch. Her own wheezing, whimpering breaths filled her ears. "Dad . . . Dad—"

Footsteps sounded on the porch. "Laurie?" Daniel's alarmed voice rang out.

She rolled her father to his back, his head lolling against her lap.

Daniel pounded down the steps and knelt at Laurie's side.

A whirlpool formed around her, sucking away her breath, her life, her emotions. "Just tell me he's not dead," she whispered.

Daniel touched his face. "He's still breathing, but he's been out here a while."

Johnny appeared at Daniel's side, face ashen. He reached for his father's arm. "His skin is as cold as ice."

"Let's get him inside." Daniel shoved his hands under her dad's back and hooked his wrists under his arms. Johnny seized his legs and lifted, grunting.

Laurie scrambled to her feet and followed as the men hauled her father up the wooden steps. Daniel and Johnny carted him to the bedroom and lowered him to the mattress.

"Shouldn't we take him to the hospital?" Laurie grabbed blankets and tucked them around her father's cold frame.

"And tell them what, Laurie?" Johnny snarled. "You want him to go to jail for this still? And do you think they're going to believe I wasn't involved?"

Her throat closed. "Better in jail than dead!"

"Be quiet, both of you. Let me take a look at him." Daniel leaned over her father, pressing back one of his eyelids.

Laurie pressed her hand against her mouth, biting back the sobs that threatened to climb up her throat.

"Can you tell?" Johnny hovered on the far side of the bed. "Is he dying?"

Daniel stood upright, his fingers splayed on Dad's brow. "It doesn't look good to me, but I'm not a doctor—"

Her father choked, his eyelids parting, eyes rolling in their sockets.

Laurie jumped forward and grabbed his legs, as if to hold him on the bed.

"Quick—roll him on his side." Daniel jammed his hands under Dad's shoulder and shoved him toward Johnny.

Johnny caught and steadied him just as he choked and vomited a stream of vile-smelling liquid across the bedding.

"What's happening?" Laurie grabbed a sheet and mopped her father's face.

Daniel grimaced. "His body's trying to clear the toxins."

Her dad's movements slowed and stopped. Daniel rolled him to his back.

"That's good, then. It should help, right?" Laurie leaned forward and touched her father's ashen skin, fear expanding in her chest until there was no room for her lungs. "Could we call Dr. Pierce? He wouldn't say anything."

Daniel's hand settled on her shoulder. "I think we're past that. He needs to go to the hospital—no matter the consequences. We don't know how much of that poison he's ingested."

"It's just a little moon." Johnny's face paled.

Daniel's eyes flashed. "Methyl alcohol—wood alcohol—is not easy to distill. Who knows what else was floating around in there? Formaldehyde? Lead? Turpentine?" He scowled. "If we do nothing, he might die. You want to gamble with his life?"

Laurie headed for the bedroom door. "I'm telephoning for help."

Johnny's arm reached out and caught her by the hand. "Just get the door, Laurie. We'll take him ourselves."

41

DANIEL SAT HELPLESS, WATCHING LAURIE GRAPPLE WITH HER EMOTIONS IN the hospital waiting room. He wanted to pull her into his arms, but she resembled an agitated porcupine.

Johnny paced the floor, apparently ready to bolt if someone so much as looked at him wrong.

Daniel blew a long stream of air between his lips. If only they could have gotten to Ray before he'd sampled his wares. He dropped his head into his hands, suddenly understanding his grandfather's philosophy.

Laurie's luminous gaze remained locked on the door through which her father had disappeared, her hands clenching and unclenching in her lap.

"I'm going back to the house to finish cleaning up the . . . the mess," Johnny scowled. "Just in case."

Laurie glared at him, crimson lips curling back from her teeth. "Is that all you can think about? Saving your skin?"

Johnny took a step forward, lines forming around his eyes. "I can't stay here. I'm going crazy."

"We all are."

Daniel stood, hesitant to step between the battling siblings. "Your place is here, Johnny. What if the worst happens?"

"Then there ain't much I can do, is there?"

"Just let him leave, Daniel," Laurie said, dropping back into her seat. "It's what he does. He runs away and leaves me to pick up the pieces."

Johnny squeezed his fingers into a fist. "And I'm the one who does all the dirty work to keep the family intact."

Laurie breathed out. "Dirty work is right. That's all you know how to do."

Daniel saw Johnny surge forward and stepped to intercept him. Their shoulders collided with a crunch. Gripping Johnny's elbows, he steered him toward the door. "That's enough. Go home. Do what you have to do."

Johnny shook himself free and jabbed a finger in Laurie's direction. "If he dies, this'll be your fault. You're the one who made me stop bringing him the clean stuff." His eyes showed red around the edges. "Your fault—you hear me?"

Fire scorched through Daniel. Grabbing Johnny's shirt, he yanked him through the doorway and out onto the sidewalk, sending Johnny stumbling backward. "Don't say something you're going to regret."

Johnny spit on the ground. "Regret's my middle name."

<hr />

Hot tears spilled down Laurie's face as the truth of Johnny's words echoed in her head. The room spun and she lowered her face into her hands. Ten years without a mother and soon she'd be fatherless, too, all because she wanted him to be more than he was. Why was she so selfish? *God, I know he's a hopeless drunk, but he's my dad.* She pressed a handkerchief against her lips.

A gentle hand touched her knee. Daniel crouched on his heels in front of her. She fell against his chest.

He rocked back slightly, adjusting for her weight. "You didn't do this."

"Yes," she gulped, "I did. I wanted him to quit drinking, but he couldn't. I wanted him to be like everyone else's fathers. Why couldn't I just love him as he was?"

Daniel slipped his hand under her chin and lifted it. His brow furrowed. "You wanted the best for him. He's an adult, so he makes his own choices. You didn't pour that stuff down his throat."

She pushed down the surge of sorrow boiling up from her gut. "I might as well have."

He sighed and got to his feet. Sitting in the next chair, he pulled her close.

A nurse entered the room, silver hair glistening under her white cap, her cheeks wrinkled pouches that sagged over her jaw. She tapped a pen against her clipboard. "Burke?"

Daniel stood, gripping Laurie's hand. "Over here."

The nurse frowned, a crease pinching between her eyes, and walked over to them. She glanced down at her paper. "You the son?"

Laurie lifted her head. "I'm his daughter."

The nurse shot a disinterested glance at Laurie before turning to address Daniel. "Mr. Burke is stable for now. There's nothing else we can do but wait. If he makes it through the night, you can see him in the morning."

Laurie sagged against Daniel's arm.

"Can we speak to the doctor?" Daniel asked.

The woman shot him a dark look. "In the morning."

42

JOHNNY JAMMED A LAST ARMFUL OF PIPES INTO THE FORD AS DANIEL leaned over the main boiler with a hacksaw. They had dragged the metal apparatus into the backyard and worked on it by lantern light. Daniel resolved to whittle it into the smallest pieces possible.

He stopped and brushed the sweat away from his eyes. "What are you going to do with this stuff, anyway?"

Johnny shrugged. "Dump it in the bay, probably. Or out in the woods. Somewhere no one will find it."

"What about the barrels, the wood alcohol?"

Turning back to face him, Johnny sighed. "Not sure. I hate the idea of dumping that stuff in the Straits. It can't be any better for the fish than it was for the old man."

"Can you return it to the mill?"

"Maybe I can leave them by the back delivery gate. Someone will spot them in the morning."

Daniel braced his foot against a log bench and lifted the saw. It made a horrible rasping sound as it slashed through the metal sides of the still. He glanced up at Laurie's window. The noise could wake the dead, but he hoped she might get some rest, anyway.

Johnny picked up a few of the pieces that had fallen at Daniel's feet. "One more secret for Laurie to try and cover up."

"The still?"

Johnny scoffed. "You—spending the night at her house."

The strain of the day left Daniel little patience for humor. "You really need to watch your mouth. I've been within an inch of clobbering you tonight."

Johnny threw the metal into the back of the Ford. "What's stopping you? You owe me one, if I'm not mistaken." He hooked his thumbs through his suspenders. "Unless you just figure you're a better man than me."

Daniel grunted as he pushed the saw.

"That's it, ain't it? You're the high-and-mighty saint and I'm the miserable sinner. It's no wonder Laurie's fallen for you. She's always wanted a hero."

Daniel threw down the tool and jammed a hand through his sweat-dampened hair. "You don't know anything about me, Johnny, so why don't you just can it?"

"Come make me, college boy."

Daniel rounded on him. "What is it with you? Why are you itching for a fight?"

Johnny stepped forward. "I need to know you're willing to stand up for her. That you're not going to turn and run out on her when things get tough."

Heat rushing up his neck, Daniel stood tall. "I'm here now, aren't I? You think things are going to get worse than this?"

Johnny chuckled, retrieved the saw and picked up the sheet of metal. "I think you don't got a clue."

 ◦══✦══◦

Laurie twisted in bed, the sheets winding around her legs. She hadn't bothered to undress. Somehow, knowing that

Daniel and Johnny were working in the backyard, it didn't feel right.

She rolled to her side and stared at the shadowed wall. Her muscles ached with the tension and her ears hurt from listening for the telephone. The only sounds that reached her room were the banging and sawing in the backyard. *The neighbors must be livid. And dying of curiosity.*

Laurie closed her eyes, her mind racing through the images from the day: her father lying face down in the grass, choking in the bed, disappearing through the hospital doors. She lifted her hands and pushed them against her forehead.

A hot tear squeezed between her eyelids and rolled down her temple and into her hair. At least Daniel stayed at her side. *My one honest man.*

43

LAURIE BLINKED OPEN SCRATCHY EYES, SQUINTING AT THE YELLOW LIGHT spilling in her window. She rolled onto her back and stretched, the muscles in her limbs stiff, as if she'd spent the entire night in one position rather than the hours of tossing and turning. She reached for the bedside clock and squinted at the numbers. At least she'd gotten an hour of sleep.

Climbing out of bed, Laurie pulled on fresh clothes, frowned at her reflection, and stole through the silent house. The sour smell lingered in the morning air, but the floor had been scrubbed clean, the furniture arranged as if nothing unusual had taken place.

After checking each room, Laurie peeked out the window, scanning the yard for signs of life. Daniel's Buick sat in the place of the Ford. She draped a sweater over her shoulders and hurried outside.

Daniel slept slumped over in the back seat, wrapped in the red-and-white-checkered picnic blanket. A lock of dark hair draped across his forehead, one arm pillowing his head.

After his long night, the man deserved a decent breakfast. Laurie tiptoed through the damp grass until she reached the back steps. What would the neighbors think of Laurie having a man over for breakfast? She tossed her head. Why should she care?

When the telephone jangled, Laurie scooped it up, pressing the receiver to her ear with a shaking hand.

"Miss Burke—your father is awake."

⊙══╬══⊙

Laurie pressed her fingers against her lips, forcing herself to stay silent while Dr. Pierce finished his examination. Her father's yellowed eyes focused somewhere over the doctor's left shoulder, his face the color of cold fireplace ashes.

Doctor Pierce loomed over the bed like a vulture. "Mr. Burke, I believe I was right to revoke your prescription."

He turned and directed his words at Laurie. "Your father's situation is precarious." He glanced down at the clipboard in his hand. "It's going to be a difficult few days as the poison works its way out of his system. *If* his liver and kidneys hold up, he just might get through." He lowered his glasses peering over their top edge. "This time. But there's going to be lasting damage. Another episode would be fatal."

Laurie pressed a knuckle against her lip, hoping her father understood the doctor's message.

Doctor Pierce turned back to her father, gesturing with his pen. "You need to give up the bottle, Mr. Burke. Your liver won't stand any more. And there's absolutely no question about the moonshine."

Laurie cleared her throat. "Thank you, Dr. Pierce. I'll keep an eye on him."

"You're a lucky man to have a daughter who loves you. Listen to her."

Dad turned his face to the wall.

⊙══╬══⊙

Daniel dragged himself up the steep stairs leading to his second-story apartment over the drugstore, the long day and night finally behind him. The morning rays drifted through the tall windows, gleaming across the polished hardwood floors.

The clammy night air clung to Daniel's skin even as he fell into bed, drawing the covers up to his chin. The muscles of his back ached from the hour-long catnap curled up in the backseat of the automobile. The petty complaints paled in comparison to the nightmarish images haunting his dream, images that refused to be forgotten.

Daniel rolled to his side, balling the pillow under his ear and clamping his eyes shut, hoping to chase away the flashes of dreams. The taste of gin lingered in his mouth, as real as if he had actually tipped a bottle, the booze burning down the back of his throat and pooling in his gut.

He rolled out of the bed and fell to the floor, sweat glazing his skin. Pulling up to his knees, Daniel laid his hands and face against the mattress.

I can't take the chance of doing that to her, God. I can't.

44

Laurie smoothed a hand across her wrinkled skirt and took a deep breath before stepping into the switchboard office.

Mr. Quinn's glare raked across her raw nerves.

Straightening her shoulders, Laurie strolled to the coatroom. The reek of her boss's hair tonic accosted her before she had even shrugged out of her sweater. "Miss Burke—a word."

She closed her eyes for a heartbeat, willing her heart to beat at a normal pace. "Mr. Quinn, I apologize for my abrupt departure yesterday. I received a call that my father had been taken ill. He's in the hospital."

"Yes, well . . ." His frown lessened. "Come with me, please."

Laurie pressed a palm against her midsection as she trailed Mr. Quinn to the small office. He gestured to a straight back chair before edging behind the imposing desk consuming the bulk of the floor space. As he settled into a swivel chair, the diminutive man resembled a child daring to sit at the teacher's desk.

"Miss Burke, I've spoken to you several times lately about business protocol—receiving private calls, not meeting time quotas, family members loitering outside . . ."—he cleared his throat—"not to mention gentlemen visitors."

A flash of heat crawled up Laurie's neck.

"Even if I were to excuse the incident yesterday, today you showed up late and noticeably disheveled. You are aware that we insist that our operators be respectable young ladies from our community and we expect your behavior and dress to reflect that policy."

She ran her hand over her skirt, tugging it to cover her knees. "I must apologize, Mr. Quinn. I came straight from the hospital. If you will excuse me, I'll go to the ladies room and try to improve my appearance."

He lifted a hand. "I only wished to say that your employment here is on shaky ground, Miss Burke. I will need to see a marked improvement in your conduct if you expect to remain working for Port Angeles Telephone." He drew out the company name as if it were a badge of honor.

Laurie gritted her teeth and faked a smile. "Yes, sir. I understand."

He spread his arms, flattening his palms against the vast, glossy desktop. "You may see to your appearance."

She nodded and pressed her fingers against her burning cheeks before hurrying to the powder room. Leaning toward the mirror, she eyed her complexion. Other than the flush and the dark circles under her eyes, she didn't look so bad.

"That man is just a bully," she whispered to her reflection.

She splashed some water over her fingers and ran it through her hair, smoothing the random fly-aways and tucking a few loose strands behind her ears. Laurie touched up her lipstick before glancing down at her clothes.

A loose thread caught her eye. Laurie traced the offender to the exposed seam at her side. Fingers shaking, she fumbled with the buttons, pulled off the garment and tugged it right side out. No wonder Mr. Quinn was so appalled.

Laurie fastened her leather belt, giving the skirt one final tug. *If only my legs weren't so long.* Women in magazines wore far shorter hems than this, but likely they didn't work for Mr. Quinn.

After a last few adjustments, Laurie hurried to the board and took her seat. Slipping the headset over her hair, Laurie attempted to push aside her exhaustion. Best not to give the boss more ammunition by slouching.

Laurie's eyes glazed as she struggled to keep them focused on the board through the day, her stomach tightening with each silly mistake. Thankfully, the other operators covered for her, catching her errors and redirecting them before they came to Mr. Quinn's attention. She maintained the expected rod-straight posture as she perched on the high chair, but her heart sagged. She needed to get through today without being fired.

Other patients lined the hospital ward, but Laurie's gaze skipped over them as she raced back to her father's bedside.

Johnny leaned over the bed, his cap clutched against his midsection as he muttered quiet words to his father.

Acid crawled up Laurie's throat. "What are you doing here?"

Johnny's eyebrows lifted. "Hello to you, too. What's gotten you in such a foul mood this evening?"

She bit her tongue and turned her eyes away, pushing down the storm of bitter words threatening to erupt from her mouth. "It's been a long day."

Johnny turned back to face the bed. "I'll come see you tomorrow, Dad. Okay?"

Dad grunted, shifting under the sheet. "I want something to drink."

"Laurie will get you some water. I've got to go." Johnny tipped his head toward her and smirked. "The man's thirsty."

Laurie clamped hands on her hips. "I'll take care of it. Goodness knows he shouldn't have anything you'd offer him."

His eyes narrowed. "Just what are you accusing me of?"

"I know you, Johnny. You think this little episode proves that you were right." Heat surged up Laurie's spine.

Johnny lifted his chin. "You said it, not me. But I warned you. He's not going to change. He'll drink himself to the grave."

Red spots danced before her eyes. "If he didn't have access to booze, he'd have no choice but to quit."

"What are you going to do? Stand over him day and night to make sure he ain't brewing his own beer or mixing gin in the bathtub? Shut down every speakeasy? Are you going to single-handedly chase all the bootleggers out of Port Angeles?" Johnny sneered at her. "You are so naive, Laurie. It's time you grew up."

"You're as bad as he is." A hard lump grew in her throat.

"Bring me a bottle." Dad groaned, twisting under the sheet.

Johnny pulled the cap over his hair. "You heard the man." He bent over the bed. "I'll see what I can do, Dad. There's a fresh shipment coming in the day after tomorrow." He turned back to Laurie. "And don't worry—I won't be going along this time. I've got an extra shift at the mill."

Laurie gripped the iron rails of the hospital bed, throat closing. "I'm finished worrying about you, Johnny Burke. Whatever happens to you now is on your head."

⊙━━◆━━⊙

Daniel's palms dampened as Laurie walked into the drugstore late in the evening. The vivid memories rushed back.

Her feet shuffled over the tile floor as if she no longer had energy to lift them. Laurie dropped onto one of the stools, forehead etched with lines.

"I don't know what to do anymore, Daniel. My dad can't wait to get his hands on another bottle of booze. Johnny's threatening to bring him one. My entire world has tilted on its axis. One wrong move and I might fall clean off of it." She pulled off her hat and ran her hands through her rumpled hair. "You and Amelia are the only ones I can trust."

Daniel's mouth grew as dry as desert sands. He took a damp cloth and wiped down the counter, scrubbing at a stubborn spot of unidentified stickiness.

Laurie leaned forward, catching his eye. "You haven't asked me about a walk this evening."

"It's been a long day, following an even longer night. Don't you think you should get some rest?" His chest ached, a gaping hole opening deep inside.

She folded her hands, an impish smile touching her red lips. "I think it might clear my head a little. Maybe help me sleep."

Daniel lifted his head and gazed at her. The dark circles under her eyes only accentuated the intensity of the blue color. "I wish I had some magic pill to make all life's problems go away."

She reached for his hand. "I thought you pharmacists had every cure-all under the sun."

Daniel stepped back, pushing his hands into his pockets, the tightness in his chest intensifying. "I'm starting to discover that we can actually cure very little, unfortunately."

Laurie's eyes rounded as she withdrew her hand. A crease formed in her brow. She sat silent for a moment, gazing at him. "What's wrong?"

Daniel turned his eyes away. It hurt too much to look at her. "Nothing. I just think you ought to get home. You can get started on that good night's sleep." He turned and walked away, refusing to give in to the longing to pull her into his arms.

Longings are what got him in trouble in the first place.

⚬━◆━⚬

I knew it would eventually come to this. Laurie pressed her fingers against the pounding in her temples, the silence in the house failing to bring peace to her heart. Remembering the emptiness on Daniel's face brought a lump to her throat. She'd bared her heart, and he turned away.

She filled a glass and pulled the headache powders from the kitchen cupboard. Grasping one of the small packets, she unfolded the paper and let the bitter powder slide down onto her tongue. Trying not to gag, Laurie quickly gulped down the water.

Laurie filled the glass a second time. *I can't let Johnny start bringing Dad bottles again.* The cool liquid eased the bitter taste in her mouth but did little for what lingered in her heart. *I can't watch my father all day and night, Lord.* She wandered to her room and crawled under the covers. *God, you have to take this one. I'm out of answers.*

Hours later, she jerked awake in the darkness. Rain pattered against the window. She turned over in the bed, drawing her pillow down beside her. Accustomed to listening for her father, even the sound of the rain roused her easily.

Tomorrow she'd speak to Dad once more about the in-hospital treatment Daniel had suggested. How long would it take to dry a man out and convince him to stay that way?

It would never happen if Johnny started bringing him booze.

She dug her fingers into the blanket and pulled it tight against her chin as if it could somehow screen out the worrisome thoughts. Drawing her pillow to her chest, Laurie curved her body around it. She visualized Daniel's sleeping face and reached out to touch the smooth pillowcase.

The only way to fix everything would be to rid Port Angeles of liquor entirely. Johnny's words floated back to her mind. *"Are you going to single-handedly chase all the bootleggers out of Port Angeles?"*

Laurie bit her lip. Could she?

45

Samuel's chair squeaked as he leaned back, tapping the large oak desk with a fountain pen. "You're sure about this?"

Laurie nodded, taking a deep breath to slow her pounding heart. After tonight, Port Angeles would be a dry town. "Yes."

"I believed you before when you pointed your finger at Shepherd. Look how that turned out."

Laurie dug a fingernail into the tip of her thumb. "Yes, well, I wasn't really sure that time. Now I am. I heard them on the telephone connection. The man said that they would be hauling whiskey and gin."

Samuel wrote down the information on a notepad. "What else did they say? Any names?"

A chill washed over her. Names? "No ... wait—Jerry."

"Jerry who?" Samuel raised one eyebrow. "What number?"

"I don't remember. I'm sorry." She fidgeted, avoiding his moss-green eyes. "He said that the drop point would be Freshwater Cove."

He sat up. "Freshwater Cove—not Crescent?" He tapped the pen a few more times before scratching the name down on the pad. "Anything else?"

She searched her memory for useful facts that would not incriminate her brother. "Two boats."

"Fishing boats? Speed boats?"

"Row boats."

The swivel chair squeaked as he pushed to his feet. "Row boats? You're kidding."

"One of them mentioned using oars."

"Who would be crazy enough to row across the Straits at night?"

Laurie shrugged. "Maybe I misunderstood."

Samuel wandered the room, rubbing the pen against his chin. "It would be quiet that way. And if you've got plenty of muscle, it could be done." He perched on the edge of the desk in front of Laurie, propping his shoe on the corner of her chair.

His eyes gleamed. "Thanks to you, I'm going to bust this operation wide open. We'll catch those rumrunners with their pants down. There will be no more smuggling whiskey into Port Angeles right under our noses."

Laurie ran a finger along the edge of Samuel's desk, fighting to steady her resolve. "That's what I've wanted all along."

His gaze lingered on her. "I've missed you, Laurie. I thought you were spending all your time with that pharmacist fellow." He lowered his two-toned shoe to the floor, brushing her ankle in the process.

Jumping to her feet, Laurie paced to the window, staring out across Fourth Street toward the front window of Larson's Drugs. A blue glint flashed, as if a glimmer of sunlight hit the show globe. "Yes, well. Things change."

"I thought after our first evening together, maybe I had a chance with you." Samuel's milky voice carried across the confined space. "I thought you were looking for a trustworthy man. A man you could respect."

Her shoulders stiffened. "What are you implying?"

Samuel drew close behind her. "Daniel Shepherd isn't the man you think he is."

She turned, matching his gaze. "That's odd, because he said the same about you." Laurie locked eyes with Samuel. "So, what are you suggesting?"

The corner of his mouth twitched before lifting into a grim smile. "You don't know? He hasn't told you about his past?"

Her stomach twisted. "He grew up in Port Angeles. He went to Seattle for college and to work. Now he's back. What's so startling about that?"

Samuel stepped closer, settling one hand on the windowsill behind her back and leaning in. "College and work—is that what he said? Did he mention what he did in his free time?"

Laurie ears began to buzz, weakness spreading through her body.

He bent his head close, as if to hide his words from listening ears. "He's no saint, Laurie."

Her words came out in a strangled whisper. "I wouldn't expect him to be."

"I asked around at the University of Washington. Shepherd was put on probation twice for drunkenness. And once . . ."—he paused, searching her face—"for assault."

❦

Laurie stumbled out of Samuel's office and onto the sidewalk, tears blinding her eyes. Larson's Drugs stood at the far end of the street. She spun and trod down the hill toward the water. She shoved her hands deep into her coat pockets, lifting her face toward the gray sky. Misty raindrops fell, cooling her burning cheeks.

Lifting her hands, she gripped the edges of her hat and pulled it further downward, hiding her from the world. She let gravity hurry her feet until she was nearly running—pressing past people as they did business in the downtown establishments. She aimed for the spit and the clarity the water always provided. The horizon seemed to dip and sway, as if she were riding the ferry over storm-tossed waters. She lurched off the street and onto the rocky shoreline.

"No," she choked the word out into the wind that brushed past her. "No, God. It can't be true."

Laurie tore off her hat and cast it onto the ground at her feet. She unbuttoned her coat and let the wind lift its edges, cleansing her hurt with its damp crispness. Breathless, she bent over to clutch at one of the massive logs lining the water. Daniel was different—truthful. Or so she'd believed.

She remembered sitting next to Samuel Brown the day Pastor Yoder had preached on forgiveness. A single verse whispered in her memory: *"There is none righteous, no, not one."* The truth echoed in her heart, sinking to the very depths of her being.

She collapsed against the log, dropping to her knees in the wet gravel and spreading her arms over the tree's wet, gritty bark. Laurie let her face fall forward, pressing her forehead against the fallen tree. "Lord, please let Samuel be wrong. I can't love a dishonest man."

Her heart pounded as the ache burrowed in, nestling against her ribs. Daniel's face hovered in her thoughts—reaching his hand out to lift her up on the log at the beach, holding her as she wept in the hospital, smiling that first night on the bluff. She needed to know the truth.

❦

Daniel lifted the globe from the window, balancing it carefully so the blue fluid lapped against the glass. The sapphire liquid reminded him too much of Laurie's eyes. It needed to go. A nice, gloomy forest-green, perhaps.

Marcie maintained a brisk pace at the fountain, but few wandered over to the pharmacy counter. Maybe he'd spend some time carefully mixing the chemicals so to create a layered rainbow effect. He'd seen it done, but had never attempted it.

He'd keep a little of the blue at the bottom and layer the other colors above. A rainbow above the sea.

Daniel carefully tipped the yellow fluid, sending it through a glass tube. The color glided along the side of the show globe, spilling over the blue layer. He held his breath, careful to keep the glass motionless as the color slid across the top of the liquid without intermingling.

A smile played at the corners of his mouth. It might not be life-saving medicine, but it sidetracked his thoughts—a medicine, in itself.

He reached for the next beaker, filled with a blood-red ferric chloride solution. Daniel held it up and swirled it in the light. He balanced the show globe in his palm, holding his breath while he tipped the beaker, the red mixture sliding down the smooth glass.

Daniel held his breath, concentrating on tipping the beaker at a gentle angle. When the bell sounded from the door, he didn't pay attention. Marcie could take care of it.

"Daniel?" a voice quavered.

Daniel glanced up, his hand jerking.

Laurie stood facing him, her arms wrapped around her middle, fingers gripping her elbows.

An icy chill swept across his skin—just like when he woke from his liquor-flavored dreams. He lost his grip on the glass sphere and it thumped against the counter, wetting his fingers. The ferric acid invaded the other layers, claiming each of the colors until the whole globe turned dark.

His body went weak. Daniel swallowed, gripping the counter for stability. *She knows.*

46

Daniel pressed one hand against the cold cement wall in the basement storeroom, head down.

"Is it true?" Laurie's voice barely stirred the musty air.

He swallowed against the lump growing in his throat and nodded.

The slump spread through her shoulders and spine. Laurie lowered her forehead to the table. "Why did you hide this from me?"

Daniel balled his fingers into a fist and pressed it against the wall. He pulled out a chair. "Laurie, I realize any excuse won't be worth a plugged nickel to you—but I hope you'll listen, anyway."

She remained motionless, head down.

Daniel braced himself against the chair back, pushing one foot behind him for strength. "I'm not the same person I was then."

Her shoulders convulsed and her head lifted. Tears stained both cheeks. "Johnny said you were a teetotaler."

"I am"—he pushed fingers through his hair—"I was." Daniel turned and pressed a hand against his forehead.

"Which is it?"

Daniel sat next to her, his heart pounding. Reaching a hand into his pocket, he withdrew the temperance coin and ran a thumb across its face before setting it in front of her. "I have carried this since I was a boy. They handed them out at school to anyone who would sign the temperance pledge."

"What happened?"

Daniel pushed up from the chair and walked across the floor, returning to his place by the wall. "In college, I was terrified of presenting in front of my professors and my classmates. My roommate—an older student—told me to take a swig of whiskey to calm my nerves. At first that's all it was. I told myself it was fine, since I was using it medicinally. I even measured it precisely."

He cleared his throat. "Other students were using opium and heroin—all sorts of things. As pharmacy students, we had access to countless medications."

Laurie traced a circle on the tabletop with her fingernail. "You should have known better."

He sighed. "I did. But sometimes it's just easier to lie to yourself."

The room grew still, except for the sound of Laurie's ragged breaths, each one pulling at Daniel's soul.

"It's a long stretch from a *swig* of whiskey to drunkenness and assault."

"Not as far as you'd think." The long-hidden memories burned in his mind. "Once I started, it was a quick slide into drinking with my buddies after classes. First it was just Friday nights—a reward for surviving the week. It rapidly became an every night thing. I was already drinking in the morning before class to ease my nerves. Pretty soon it was all around the clock."

"You're a liar like the rest." Laurie squeezed her fingers together. "You made me think you were a decent man."

"I never *made* you think anything." Daniel's heart recoiled at his own words. He dropped his head. "No, you're right. I pretended to be something I wasn't." He pushed his hands against his face. "You'll never know how much I regret that. How much I regret everything in my life." He cleared his throat. "I wanted you to think well of me. I wanted to be the kind of man you deserve."

Her gaze faltered and she looked downward. "I don't deserve anything."

Her words ruined any hope of staying away. "You do." He reached for Laurie's hands, but she pulled free.

"Tell me about the girl." Her words stung like alcohol on an open wound.

Daniel turned toward the table, not able to face the tears glittering on the edges of Laurie's downcast eyes. *No more secrets.*

"My roommate had been dating a nursing student—Molly. When we'd head out to the jazz clubs in downtown Seattle, she'd bring along some girlfriends." The memories pulled him along like a riptide.

"One night, he spent most of the evening dancing with one of the other girls and, well, Molly made it clear that—that she was more interested in me." Daniel dug in his pocket for a handkerchief and mopped it across his brow.

Laurie leaned back against the basement wall, her face dark and unreadable. Her arms clenched around her midsection, as if the story made her ill. "What happened?"

"I walked her home and she invited me in." Daniel shook his head, the memory refusing to fade with time. "I never should have gone. It was foolish. Molly insisted she was in love with me—claimed she had been for some time but was too afraid to tell me. It was flattering. Heady stuff, really. I got carried away." He cleared his throat. "She seemed to welcome my attentions, but then—wisely—she began to push me away. I didn't want to leave. I was hopelessly drunk—and she probably was, too. I didn't know what I was doing. I got frustrated, angry even. My roommate had boasted about his conquests; I just assumed . . ."

Laurie turned her face away.

Daniel plowed forward, determined to finish the story out before he lost his nerve. "I called her some names, I think. Tried to steal another kiss—that sort of thing. I'm sure it was quite frightening for her. And heartbreaking. This man that she thought she'd loved . . . " Daniel's throat constricted. "I'd never done anything like that before. I didn't go to classes the next day. I went straight over to apologize, but her roommates wouldn't even let me through the front gate. I never saw Molly again."

Laurie frowned. "What about the assault charge?"

Daniel shook his head. "I think my former roommate was behind that. Maybe that's the story she told him, I don't know. I'm certain I never struck her or threatened her in any way—not that it excuses anything."

"But they put you on probation?"

"I didn't contest it." Daniel pressed his lips together, the silence broken only by footsteps from the store above. "I swore I'd never drink again."

Several more moments passed before Laurie spoke. "Did you?"

"Yes."

Her eyes filled.

"The guilt ate at me until I walked away from school, entirely. I sank deeper into the bottle. My life spiraled downward. I might have ended up on Skid Road with the other drunks if it hadn't been for a couple of my classmates. Apparently they'd been praying for me, even before the incident with Molly. Their minister told me about the hospital program."

Laurie's head jerked upward. "Like the one you were telling me about?"

"Yes." He lifted the temperance coin from the table and rolled it between his fingers. "It was the hardest thing I'd ever done. But, even better than giving up drink, it's where I really came to understand God. I'd never really grasped the depth of His forgiveness, the love my gran had always tried to teach me." He lifted the coin and held it between his finger and thumb. "This coin means more to me now than it did to me as a child. It's more than a simple pledge. It's a reminder of how easily I can fail unless I rely on God's strength."

Laurie pressed her hands against her chest, a shadow crossing her face.

He pushed the coin back into his pocket and laid his hands on the table, leaning forward and meeting Laurie's eye. "I don't expect you to trust me again. I'm not even sure that I want you to."

Her brows pulled down and her lips tightened.

His throat grew raw. "I still deal with the desire to drink. Every day I have to choose." Pushing to his feet, he tore his gaze away, the sight of her blue eyes threatening to render him mute. "It's better that you know the truth about me and walk away now." Daniel's throat closed until he had to choke out the words. "Because I can't bear the idea that I might fail you."

⌖

After spending a long, miserable day at home, Laurie pulled on her coat and headed for Amelia's house. She took off her hat and let the blustery wind muss her short locks. She hadn't even bothered to put any waves in it the past few days—just let it fall where it wished. Why not? It matched her life.

Every time she built her house of cards, the men in her life reached in and snatched her supports, sending it crashing down again. Laurie balled her hands and shoved them into her coat pockets.

I don't expect you to trust me again. I'm not even sure I want you to.

Amelia remained the one constant in her life, and at this moment, Laurie wanted to fall into her embrace. Her friend opened the door before Laurie's hand reached the knocker. "I saw you coming up the walk. How is your father?"

"He's doing better. His recovery astounded the doctors." She let her friend guide her inside. "He might be coming home by the end of the week."

A tiny crease appeared between Amelia's eyes. "So soon?"

Laurie sank down on a kitchen chair. "I don't know what will happen. The doctor says he shouldn't drink at all, but how am I supposed to prevent it?"

Amelia pulled out the chair across from Laurie and perched on the very edge. "Something else is bothering you. I can see it in your face."

Laurie spilled the whole gruesome story. "I don't know who to trust anymore. It seems like everyone has some horrible secret just waiting to jump out and pounce on me."

Amelia walked to the stove and poured two cups of tea from the pot simmering on the stove. "You can't expect people to be perfect. Remember what Pastor Yoder always says—that we all sin and fall short of the glory of God?" She brought the cups to the table and set one in front of Laurie.

Laurie traced the pattern of the tablecloth with one finger. "I don't expect perfection. But I would like to be able to trust someone." She pulled her cup close, watching the steam form above the cup like morning mist over the water. "I wanted to talk to Johnny about this hospital program that Daniel suggested. Do you know where he is today?"

"Well, that's actually a bit of good news." Amelia sipped her tea. "He told me he was going out on his final run tonight."

"Johnny's going tonight?" With all the agony over Daniel, Laurie had forgotten about Samuel's plans. Her cup clattered down onto the saucer. "He said he was on graveyard shift."

"I think he traded with someone." Amelia's head tilted to the side. "Laurie, you've known about the rumrunning longer than I have. Why are you so shocked?"

Pushing up to her feet, Laurie's heart quickened. "He wasn't supposed to go *tonight*." She hurried to the door, grabbing her jacket and hat from the coat tree.

Amelia followed. "Why? What's happening tonight?"

Laurie jammed the hat down over her hair and reached for the door handle.

Amelia grabbed her elbow. "Tell me!"

"Samuel's going to be waiting for them."

47

Laurie jammed her foot against the reverse pedal and yanked the Model T's steering wheel to the right, the tires flinging loose gravel.

Amelia clutched the dashboard. "Laurie, be careful!"

"I have to stop him." She lifted her foot off the pedal and twisted the throttle. The automobile jerked forward, its engine backfiring in complaint.

"You don't have to get us killed in the process." Amelia braced one hand against the door.

The Ford careened down the road toward the boarding house. "I think they've probably already left." Laurie stiffened her legs as the car bounced down the bumpy road. "What if he's not there?"

"Go down to the boat dock?"

Laurie banged a hand against the wheel. "He said he wouldn't be going this time. I thought this was the perfect opportunity to close down the rumrunning shenanigans."

Her friend didn't answer, apparently focused on keeping herself from sliding off the seat.

"I can't let him get arrested. Daddy's probably already lost his job at the mill. If Johnny goes to jail, we'll be finished for sure."

They hurtled down the hill on Vine Street, eating up the distance between their neighborhood and Johnny's as a yellow-mopped mongrel chased them, barking. After two more corners and at least twenty bone-jostling potholes, Laurie pulled up beside the boarding house. Not waiting for Amelia, she shoved open her door and darted down the walk. No one answered when she pounded on the door. Stepping back, she searched the upper-story windows, locating his room. The window stood open, a checkered curtain flapping in the wind. Laurie cupped her hands around her mouth. "Johnny!"

Amelia came up behind her, clutching the fur-lined collar of her coat up around her trembling chin. "Laurie, there are no lights. He's not here."

Laurie grabbed Amelia's arm, tugging her back toward the car. "Let's go to the docks."

Amelia had barely found her seat when Laurie shifted the Ford into gear and headed off down the street. They careened down the hill to the docks.

Johnny's slip stood empty.

Laurie's lifted both hands to her cheeks. *What have I done?*

⊙══╬══⊙

Laurie shivered on Samuel's front walk, the light in his window oddly inviting on this cold blustery evening. And yet her skin crawled at the thought of what lay ahead. She couldn't even bring herself to pray.

No options remained except one—throwing herself on Samuel's mercy.

Which means throwing myself at his feet.

She counted the steps to the front door. A strange calm descended on her as she lifted her hand to knock on the black-painted door. For a long moment, nothing happened. Her breathing quickened. *Do I want him to answer or not?*

Pushing down her fear, she rapped a second time. Footfalls inside made her heart race. She ran a hand across her skirt, tugging it down to cover her knees. Then she jerked it back again.

Samuel opened the door, surprise lighting his features. "Laurie, what are you doing here? I was just getting ready to leave."

She moistened her lips. "I need to speak with you."

He stepped back and gestured for her to enter. "Don't bother telling me you made another mistake. I've already got police and Coast Guard on the way." Samuel led the way to two cushioned chairs in the parlor and waited for her to sit.

Laurie pulled off her hat and rested it on her lap, leaving her coat in place.

"Can I take that for you?"

She shook her head, squeezing the brim between her fingers. "This won't take long, I hope." She glanced around the luxurious room, not wanting to meet his eyes. *Odd that a single man, working a government job, should have such nice belongings.* "Samuel, you don't have all the facts. I've been keeping some information to myself."

He dropped into the seat across from her and settled his hands on his lap. "I'm listening."

Words scrambled through her mind, but they were so mixed with emotions that none of them made it to her mouth. She licked her lips and opened her mouth to speak, but her tongue grew thick and wouldn't cooperate.

Samuel scooted forward and reached for her hands. His touch sent a wave of panic shooting up her arms. She tried to pull away, but he captured her wrists and held her in place. Her breath caught in her chest. *I can't.*

The words refused to come, but a knot grew in her stomach. "I . . . I . . ."

He squeezed her hands. "Just say it."

She shook her head, dizziness clouding her senses. Her skin grew clammy in his grip. She twisted her hands free and stood, pacing across the room to the window. The night had grown dark.

Laurie squeezed her eyes shut, picturing Johnny wrenching the oars through the stormy waves on the Straits. *I must do this for him.*

She exhaled, all her choices vanishing into the night. "My brother is one of the rumrunners."

Samuel sat back and the corners of his lips rose into a smile. "I knew that long before I met you."

Laurie's hands went cold. She backed up against the windowsill, tucking her fingers under her arms. "So, why did you need me?"

He shrugged, rising from his seat. Walking to her side, he reached for her coat. "I think it's plenty warm in here."

She forced herself to stand still as he unfastened the knot on her belt and let it fall open. He stepped closer and slid his hands under her coat, around her waist.

Her heart pounded. "Samuel. Please. My father is in the hospital. My brother can't go to jail. It'll ruin us."

"I know that, too."

She lifted her face to meet his callous gaze. "What don't you know?"

"I don't know why you're telling me this right now." His cheek twitched as he smiled. "But I like it. Keep going."

She tried to take a step back, but his hands locked behind the small of her back. She gripped his arms. "Johnny wasn't supposed to be on the run tonight. I thought you would just catch the others."

He smirked. "Even better."

"You could let him escape."

"Maybe. What's in it for me?"

Her stomach tightened. "What do you want?"

"You know the answer to that." He gripped her waist, his face lowering until she could feel his breath ruffling her hair. His lips brushed against her ear and her neck.

Laurie closed her eyes, holding her breath as he pushed the coat off her shoulders, his hand traveling up her back.

∘⊶✦⊷∘

Daniel glared out the dark window of his apartment. Rather than seeing the dark sky or the lights of the city, he saw the hurt swimming in Laurie's eyes. *I put it there.*

The storeroom key clung to his sweaty palm. How simple it would be to sneak downstairs, pocket one of the bottles, and drown the murkiness that surrounded his soul. Altering the records would be a simple matter.

He pressed his forehead against the dark window, the cold glass a shock to his damp skin. Beyond the buildings, the glow from the Ediz Hook light blasted out across the dark water.

Hadn't the minister at the hospital warned him about these black thoughts—these lies? Daniel set the key on the windowsill and reached for his Bible, sitting open on the table. He flipped to the Psalms, fingering through the pages until he reached the 139th chapter. He had memorized the words during his hospital stay, but right now he needed to fix his eyes on the words.

> Whither shall I go from thy spirit? Or
> whither shall I flee from thy presence?

If I ascend up into heaven, thou art there: if I
make my bed in hell, behold, thou art there.
If I take the wings of the morning, and
dwell in the uttermost parts of the sea;
even there shall thy hand lead me, and thy right
hand shall hold me.
If I say, surely the darkness shall cover me; even
the night shall be light about me.
Yea, the darkness hideth not from thee; but the
night shineth as the day: the darkness and
the light are both alike to thee.

Daniel took a deep breath, pulling the words into his soul like oxygen to his lungs. He understood what it meant to make his bed in hell. His heart hammered in his chest. He could lie to his grandfather, to Laurie, to anyone—but there were no secrets with God.

He pressed his face into his hands. "God, I can't do this without you. You know the longings of my heart—my fears, my desires. Show me how to make this right."

Pounding on the door startled him out of his chair, the Bible falling to the floor. He took two steps and paused. "Who is it?"

The pounding came a second time, followed by a muffled sob. He crossed the floor in a heartbeat and wrenched the door open.

Amelia stood in the dark stairwell, tears staining her face. "Daniel, help . . . Laurie's gone to Samuel."

⚭

Laurie twisted in Samuel's grip. Her plans to seek mercy for her brother at any cost crumbled to dust. *I can't do it.*

With an amused grunt, Samuel twined his fingers through her hair, smashing her lips against his.

Bile burned in her throat. Stifling a cry, she shoved her hands against his chest, jerking her face away. "Stop."

He chuckled, breath hot against her ear. "Why did you come here, Laurie?" His words curled around her soul. "No money, no connections. You've got nothing to offer me." His arm, as hard as an iron rod, crushed against the small of her back. "You want my help? Give me something I can use. We'll see—if you're good enough maybe we can do something about your brother." He tugged at her skirt.

Laurie dug her fingers into his arm. "Let me go."

"It's your last chance. Do you want me to stay here with you, or you want me to go bust up some rumrunners?"

Laurie jabbed her fingers into the flesh under his ribs. Samuel released his grip enough for Laurie to wrench free. She stepped back, breathless.

Samuel crossed his arms over his chest, the corner of his mouth tipping up. "Made your choice?"

She smoothed her dress and retrieved her coat from the floor. "I deserve better." She turned toward the door.

"Walk out and you'll see your brother rot in prison. That is" —his voice lowered—"if he makes it there." Samuel stood with legs spread, a sneer on his lips.

If she gave herself to this man, it wouldn't change a thing— except her. "You have nothing to offer me, Samuel. Nothing."

48

Daniel jammed on the brakes as he spotted Laurie climbing into her father's automobile. He leaped from his car and splashed through the puddles until he reached her window. "Please, tell me you're all right."

She drew a ragged breath. "Get in, will you? You're getting soaked."

He rounded the car and clambered into the passenger seat, slamming the door behind him.

Laurie jammed the car into gear and steered out onto the road without even checking for traffic. "Can you come back for your car later?"

Daniel twisted in his seat to face her. "Forget the car. What's happening?"

"Let's just say, I don't want Samuel's kind of help."

Daniel sagged against the seat back, heart returning to an almost normal rhythm.

He glanced out the windscreen as they bumped down the road. "Where are we going?"

Laurie pressed one wrist against her mouth, but it didn't stifle the hiccupping sob. "I don't know. I just needed to get away from that house." The Ford rattled down the road, lurching side to side over the ruts in the road.

He reached over and grabbed her wrist. "Pull over."

She yanked the wheel to the side and let the wheels roll to a stop, covering her face with her fingers.

Daniel heaved a sigh as the motion ceased. He pushed open the door and stood, letting the rain wash over him. He walked around the car and opened her door.

Laurie hunched over the wheel, her face in her hands.

"Slide over."

She shifted, giving him room to slide in before falling against his shoulder. "I've made such a mess. I don't know what to do anymore."

He shifted, turning so he could wrap his arms around her. "What's the worst that could happen? Rumrunning convictions are mild. He shouldn't see much time for that."

She lifted her tear-stained face. "Samuel said he might not make it to jail."

Daniel's chest tightened. "What?" He reached for the ignition. "We'll go back. Let's hear him say that to me."

Laurie grabbed his sleeve. "No. He's already got other agents and police gathering out at Freshwater Cove. It won't fix anything."

The coldness of her fingers soaked through his sleeve. Reaching over, he covered his hand with hers. They sat in silence as the rain pattered down on the canvas top.

The seed of an idea coiled in the corner of his mind. Laurie had closed her eyes, resting her head against his shoulder. He gazed down at her face, feeling her warmth pressed against his side. *What if?*

He reached for the throttle.

She lifted her head. "Where are we going?"

Daniel glanced over his shoulder and guided the Model T out onto the dark road. "I was just thinking . . ." He lifted his right arm away from her shoulder to settle both hands on the steering wheel. "I think it's a nice night to do some fishing."

49

Clutching at the hood of the oilskin slicker with her frozen fingers, Laurie used her other hand to grip the boat's railing. Spray blew into her face, stinging her cheeks. She pulled the hood over her hair but immediately shoved it off, scanning the inky blackness. She hurried back into the boat's wheelhouse.

"It's going to be pretty tough." Daniel lifted his voice against the sound of the wind. "I'm not certain we can find them in the dark."

As he steered the boat into another swell, Laurie's stomach rolled. The wave lifted them and sent them sliding down the opposite side. She swallowed hard, pushing down the nausea. "They're out here, somewhere."

She stared out into the night but saw only the foam on the whitecaps.

Daniel's brow creased. "Do you swim?"

"Of course. Don't you?"

"Not well. Granddad's got a life ring strapped on the back, just in case."

She wrapped her fingers around his arm. "No one could swim long in these conditions, anyway. Let's focus on staying out of the water."

Daniel nodded and faced the front, the strength of his jaw even more pronounced in the shadows. "Sounds good to me."

Laurie stepped closer and weaved her arm around his waist as he gripped the controls. She struggled to connect the man standing next to her with the drunken college student from his past.

"There's the Race Rocks light." Daniel pointed into the distance.

She leaned forward as if the signal had a magnetic pull. "We're near Victoria. Shouldn't they be on the return journey by now? Did we miss them?"

"They're like a needle in a haystack." He yanked on the wheel, bringing them about while keeping a good angle on the swells. "I'll take us a bit further west on the return. Maybe with the tidal currents, they've been pushed off course."

"Johnny says if you don't time the currents just right, you could end up rowing twice as far to get the same distance." Laurie leaned down and plucked at her wet stockings. They clung to her skin, doing little to protect her knees from the icy chill.

"It's a moonless night, too. They could be anywhere."

God, please. Laurie paced to the back of the boat. Out in the spray, she lifted her arm over her head, pushing her hair from her eyes. Her brother was out there in the darkness—heading into a disaster of her making.

A swell lifted them, nearly jostling Laurie off her feet.

You can calm the storm, God. You find lost lambs and bring them home. Johnny was no lamb, but he did need divine intervention.

A flicker of light—like a candle in the darkness—caught her eye for a second before vanishing in the gloom. She clutched the side of the boat, willing the light to reappear. Would Johnny's boat even have a light?

"Daniel!" The wind sucked the sound away. She slid across the deck, surging into the wheelhouse with the wind. "I saw something."

"Point."

She raised a hand and gestured in the direction of the phantom light.

He spun the wheel, the waves buffeting them as the boat bounced like a cork bobber on a fishing line.

She kept drawing quick breaths as the wind snatched the air from her lungs. "It was a light."

He leaned against the wheel, trying to keep them facing the direction Laurie had indicated. "I sure hope it's not the Coast Guard."

She tucked her fingers under her arms, but little warmth remained.

"How far away?" Daniel lifted his voice over the storm.

"I couldn't tell. It was just a flicker and then it vanished." Laurie chewed on her lip, scanning the darkness. The wind even seemed to hold its breath, the air growing calmer as they bobbed along with the surges.

The flash blinked again, like a firefly in the night air. "There!" She grabbed Daniel's shoulder.

"I see it, hold on."

He gunned the motor for a few seconds, sending them surging toward the faint speck as it rose and fell in the darkness.

Laurie grabbed the flashlight and aimed it out across the water, illuminating the rain-pocked waves. She swung it from side to side, willing the longboats to appear from the darkness.

The beam lit up a craft struggling in the waves. Six men huddled in the boat, arms spread across the oars, faces twisted against the glare.

"There!" She fought to keep the circle of glow locked on the longboat refusing to let it disappear back into the storm.

Daniel guided them alongside. The men ceased straining against the oars, apparently resigned to not outrunning the more powerful vessel.

"Johnny!" Laurie threw back her hood and leaned over the side.

Johnny stared up at the larger vessel, his mouth a circle of slack-jawed surprise. "What—what do you think you're doing?"

Daniel threw him a rope and pulled the boat in close. Johnny clambered aboard, followed by Big Jerry. The other men stayed huddled in the long boat, their collars turned up against the weather.

Jerry's eyes bulged, his face mottled red and white. "What's going on, Johnny?"

Laurie grabbed her brother's arm and pulled him into the wheelhouse. "Samuel knows about the shipment. He's waiting for you at Freshwater Bay."

Johnny pushed back his hood. "What? How do you know that?"

Daniel spoke up. "That doesn't matter right now. What matters is that you and your men don't sail right into his clutches."

Big Jerry snorted. "What are we supposed to do? Row back to Canada?"

Johnny wiped the sea spray from his face. "We could land at Crescent Beach, but we got no vehicles there."

"She don't know nothing. We ain't changing plans now." Jerry pulled his hood low over his head, his eyes shadowed.

A red-hot flare shot through Laurie. "Do you think I came out here for pleasure? Samuel Brown told me himself."

Daniel gripped the rail as the boat rocked over a large swell. "Johnny, just dump the cargo and go in. If you've got nothing in your boat, they've got nothing to pin on you."

Big Jerry's balled his fists. "Do you have a clue how much money you're talking about pouring down the drain?"

"But if Brown's just going to take it, anyway . . . " Johnny rubbed a hand over the stubble on his chin. "I think Daniel's right. If we got nothing, he can't book us."

The icy rain trickled down Laurie's face. "He could still shoot you, though."

Big Jerry lifted his arms. "This is insane. I'm the boss and I say we land as normal. That's why we got a spotter. Lew will signal if G-men are on the beach."

Johnny shook his head. "We could really dig in with the oars and see how far down the beach we can get by morning. Maybe put in at Port Townsend or LaPush."

The portly man growled. "I tell you, we ain't changing nothing."

Laurie threw back her hood, battling the urge to shove Jerry over the side. "Then give us the whiskey." The words spilled from her lips.

Daniel's mouth dropped open.

Laurie's stomach tensed. If Daniel objected to whiskey on his grandfather's boat, her plan wouldn't hold water.

Johnny and Jerry exchanged glances. Big Jerry hooked his fingers through his belt loops. "How do we know that you won't just chuck it overboard as soon as we're out of sight?"

Laurie clamped a hand on her hip. "You don't."

"No deal. That booze ain't leaving my sight and I sure ain't gonna trust Little Miss Temperance here." Jerry hooked a thumb at Laurie.

Daniel stepped forward, grabbing Johnny's elbow. "Then I'll buy it from you."

Laurie gasped, her heart jumping. "You shouldn't have to do that."

Johnny turned, locking gazes with his friend. "What are you talking about?"

Daniel squinted through the driving rain. "Sell it to me, right here. You'll make your profit and still get home in one piece." He reached a hand inside his slicker. "What's the price?"

Big Jerry laughed. "More than you got on you, Mr. Druggist. There's twenty-five hundred dollars of liquor in this boat."

"Twenty-five hundred?" Laurie stumbled, a swell knocking her off balance.

"No way." Johnny shook his head. "Don't do this, Daniel."

Daniel opened his wallet and peeled out several large bills. "Here."

Laurie dropped his arm. "Why are you carrying that sort of money around?"

Daniel leaned close and spoke into her ear. "When Amelia came to me, I knew I might have to take matters into my own hands. Cash is one of the few things that men like Brown understand."

A tremor traveled down Laurie's back, tears stinging her eyes. After how she had treated him?

Johnny gestured to the long boat bobbing in the waves. "Can you sell this lot at the pharmacy?"

"Let me worry about that. Just get yourself home in one piece."

Big Jerry swiped the money from Daniel's hand, an unholy gleam in his smile. "Pleasure doing business with you, Shepherd. I guess there's more cash in ice cream sodas than I thought."

He turned to the men waiting in the other boat. "Transfer the load, boys."

Johnny lifted his hands, his skin raw and cracked. "I hope you know what you're doing, Daniel."

❦

Daniel' fingers stiffened in the cold as he jostled the heavy bags across the slippery boards and lashed them together. "Didn't you have two boats tonight?"

Johnny grunted. "We could only get enough men together for one. That's why the loads's so heavy and we're so far behind. Kind of makes me wonder if some of the boys aren't on the take for Brown. I should have known we were pushing our luck."

Daniel turned away, securing the knots holding the bags in place. The sight of the bulky cargo brought a sour taste to his mouth.

Johnny placed a hand on his sister's shoulder, his voice carrying on the wind. "I never wanted to involve you in this, you know."

Laurie tipped her head. "Why don't you come with us? I don't trust Samuel. He might just kill you all, anyway."

Johnny leaned forward, resting his forehead against the top of her head. "How many times have I got to tell you? I can take care of myself."

Johnny turned and reached his hand out toward Daniel.

Daniel grasped it, a lump rising in his throat.

"I'm trusting you, Daniel." Johnny glanced down at his sister and tightened his grip. "Get her safely back to shore."

Daniel released his friend's hand, an ache lodging in his chest. He cleared his throat and leaned in to speak into Johnny's ear. "Last trip?"

"One way or the other." Johnny pressed a hand to his heart before lowering himself over the edge and landing two-footed in the rocking longboat. The other men sat huddled against the wind, blowing on their hands and rubbing them together. Johnny gripped the oars. "You're a good man, Daniel." He shouted against the wind.

Daniel lifted a hand in farewell.

Big Jerry cupped his hands around his mouth and shouted. "Smooth sailing, Shepherd!" The man's small snake-like eyes glittered in the near-darkness.

Laurie's fingers touched his hand in the darkness, sending a shiver through Daniel. He squeezed them in his palm as he stared down at Johnny, already straining at the oars. *Protect him, Lord. He may be a sinner and a lawbreaker, God, but so am I.* Daniel turned and surveyed the row of bags lashed to the rocking deck. *So am I.*

༺══✦══༻

The wind died down as Daniel gripped the wheel and guided them along the dark coastline. His arms ached after hours of battling the controls and the waves. The beam from the Ediz Hook lighthouse pierced the night, escorting them through the murky water.

Laurie stood silent at his side, casting anxious, uncomfortable glances over her shoulder at the cargo hidden in the back.

Daniel didn't need to look back. It called to him, taunting him in the depths of his chest—over two thousand dollars of illegal liquor. *I'm sorry, Lord. But what else could I do?*

The boat negotiated the swells, the motor pushing them through the night toward their destination. Daniel tipped his hat further back on his hat and glanced down at the young woman leaning against his side. Her tremors seemed to have eased. Perhaps she had accepted that Johnny's fate lay in God's hands. She stared off into the distance, clutching at her hood.

Lights dotted the edges of the bay beyond the spit where the smokestacks of the mills rose into the darkness.

"They'll be okay." Daniel mustered his most confident tone. "When they show up empty-handed, Brown will have no choice but to release them all."

Laurie blinked. "I know."

His arms ached to hold her, but he kept his hands firm on the wheel. "Then what is it?"

"I keep thinking about how I always try to pull the strings on everyone's lives and make them do what I want."

"You're trying to protect them."

Laurie shook her head, sodden hair slapping against her cheeks. "That's just it. I'm not. I'm protecting myself." A shadow crossed her face. "I've spent my life searching for one man worthy of my trust. Unfortunately, I seem to be a magnet for rogues and miscreants."

Daniel fought back a chuckle. "Well, I guess that explains it."

Laurie jerked her head back, blinking. "What?"

He reached for her hand, this time pulling her close to his side. "How you ended up with a loser like me."

Laurie smiled and pinched his arm. "I suppose we do deserve each other." She sighed, the smile withering as the moment passed. "But maybe my goal is all wrong. What if God wants me to trust Him?"

The muscles around his spine tightened. "I understand you not trusting me—but you don't trust God?"

"I'm trying. But since everyone always breaks my heart . . ."

Daniel frowned. "I don't ever want to do anything to hurt you, Laurie. I love you. You must know that."

Tears glistened in her eyes. She looped her hands around his arm, settling her chin against his shoulder. "I—I know. I think." She shook her head, as if shaking off an insect. "I find it hard to believe, I guess." She cleared her throat. "And that's the thing—instead of searching for someone to trust, perhaps I should be praying for someone to love."

"Have you found anyone?"

She smiled. "Though I tried to avoid it, I think I may have loved you practically from the moment we met."

"Was that the moment you cracked me across the face with a flashlight?"

Laurie laughed. "Well, maybe not that moment, exactly."

He pulled his arm close, squeezing her hand between his elbow and his side. "Can you forgive me for not telling you about my past?"

"I can understand why you didn't. I hadn't exactly been a fountain of information either." She turned and gazed up at him, her eyes peeping out under her wet hair. "I will forgive you, but I have a condition."

"Name it."

"You can't push me away because you're afraid of what *might* happen." Laurie took a deep breath. "If I decide to trust God on this, you'd better trust Him, too."

Laurie had never looked more beautiful than she did at that moment: her face pale, eyes somber, and a tiny droplet of rain lingering on the tip of her nose. A lump formed in his throat. "I can't believe you're willing to trust me after what I told you."

Her soft laugh took him by surprise. "I said I was trusting God. I was right about you all along—you *are* a rumrunner."

He laughed, too, glancing back at their cargo. "Not for long."

She tipped her head to the side. "What do you mean?"

Daniel cut the engine and grinned at her. "Let's get rid of that lot."

Her eyes widened. "You paid a lot of money for it."

"I paid for Johnny's life, not for the liquor. I swore to myself years ago that I'd never buy another drink." He took her hand and kissed it before striding to the rear of the boat. "Give me a hand, will you?"

"Gladly."

The first light of dawn began to spill over the mountaintops as Daniel gripped the first bag and hoisted it to the railing. "Do you want to do the honor?"

Laurie grinned. She rubbed her hands together and blew on them. Pressing her palms against the burlap, she gave it a shove.

The bundle splashed in the water. It floated for a brief moment before sinking beneath the waves, bubbles trickling to the surface.

Moving faster now, Daniel hefted one bag after another while Laurie shoved them off the side, until the last bag disappeared into the depths.

She came up behind him and wrapped both arms around his waist. "You're full of surprises, Daniel Shepherd."

He pulled her arms tighter, staring out into the brightening sky, a lump growing in his throat for a second time that morning. "You deserve some pleasant surprises, Laurie." He stepped free and turned to take her hands in his. "I hope you will let me keep surprising you."

Her eyes shone, the sunrise casting a glow on her face. "What do you mean?"

Daniel's pulse quickened. "I want to marry you, Laurie. I want to spend every day with you—not just crazy nights at sea, stolen moments on the bluff, and coffee breaks at the fountain. I want to wake up and see those gorgeous blue eyes every morning. And I want your face to be the last thing I see at night."

Her eyes widened, her lips parting and closing, a flurry of emotions scurrying across her features. Her eyes glazed, as if she stared somewhere past his left shoulder.

Daniel squeezed her hands. "Laurie? Will you marry me?" His heart pounded.

Her face paled, hands tightening on his until his knuckles ached. "Daniel . . ."

"Yes?"

"Another boat."

He spun, breath catching in his chest as he identified the approaching craft. "Coast Guard." He glanced around the deck to make sure that no bags remained. "We've got nothing to worry about. The liquor's all gone. We're just out on an early-morning sail."

The flash of gunfire made them both jump. He yanked Laurie down to the deck. "Then again . . ."

The cutter loomed ever closer. Daniel scrambled to the wheelhouse, Laurie on his heels.

"Was that a warning shot?" Laurie's voice wavered.

"I hope so." Daniel hurried to the hatch. "Granddad has a set of bunks below. I'll grab a sheet. We'll show them we're not fighting back."

He climbed down the ladder, searching in the darkness for the berth. His hand closed on a box of matches. The flash of bluish-orange flame lit up a small area crammed with wooden crates before fizzling in his fingers. Daniel struck a second match and held it steady while he leaned forward to read the labels.

Pure Rye Whiskey. Bottled in Bond.

The lit match fell to his feet and Daniel smashed it with his damp shoe. Lunging forward, he lifted the lid on the nearest crate and thrust his hands inside, his fingers closing around smooth glass.

Stumbling back, Daniel cracked his head against the ladder. He scrabbled up to the deck, heart threatening to pound its way out of his chest.

Laurie crouched on the wooden boards, her eyes round.

Daniel pushed past, leaping for the controls. Gunning the engine, he wrenched the wheel to the side.

Laurie pushed to her feet, stumbling as the boat lurched. "Where are we going?"

Daniel glanced over his shoulder, his stomach churning as the cutter approached. He pointed the boat toward the bay entrance and accelerated, sending a spray of water in their wake.

"Daniel, what's going on?" She gripped the rail with both hands, splaying her feet to keep her balance.

"I need you to trust me." After their recent conversation, the words tasted bitter in his mouth.

"But, we look guilty." She staggered as the boat bounced over the swells. "They're going to think we're running."

"We *are* running, Laurie."

The rocky point of Ediz Hook rose from the water ahead.

Laurie's pressed both hands over her temples. "You're almost to the lighthouse—why are we heading for shore?"

"Because I made a promise to your brother!" He slowed the boat and sent them into a gentle curve.

Grabbing Laurie's arm, he yanked her out from the cab and into the open air at the rear of the boat. "There's no time to explain. You sure you can swim?"

She pulled against his hold, like a donkey on a line, her lids opening until the whites of her eyes were visible.

Without waiting for her answer, Daniel thrust arms under her back and knees and flung her up on the rail, like one more burlap bag. Only this time, he was the one who pushed.

50

THE ICY WATER CLOSED OVER HER HEAD AS HER SKIRT AND ARMS FLEW upward, slowing her descent into the dark. She flailed as the salt water rushed into her mouth and nose. Bursting through the surface, spluttering and choking, Laurie rose and fell with the swells. Her vision blurry, she glimpsed Daniel's boat moving away as a white life ring spun through the air and splashed down a few feet from her.

Laurie's chest ached and her limbs grew heavy as the chill soaked through her body. She paddled toward the floating object as the waves drew it further out. *God, help.*

She pushed again, commanding her shaking legs to plow through the freezing water. The rollers from the boat's wake hit her in the face, sending more water into her nose and mouth. It also pushed the life preserver toward her. Laurie gulped air as she lunged, her numb fingers barely closing around a rope dragging alongside it.

Locking her arms around the floating ring, Laurie panted as the swells lifted her. The rocky shore loomed nearby. She kicked with her feet, her shoes dragging against the water.

Treading with her legs and flailing with one arm, she pressed herself toward the shore, the waves alternately pushing her forward and sucking her back. Her feet scraped against the rocks and she forced herself up onto her knees, the wind cutting through her wet clothes.

⊶✦⊷

Daniel hovered at the railing, heart racing, until Laurie reached for the life ring. With a lump in his throat, he dashed back into the wheelhouse and gunned the engine. He gripped the controls to steady himself, his legs threatening to give way. *I don't care what happens to me, God, but help Laurie get away.*

Daniel dragged a hand over his face. *My own grandfather?* A hole opened in Daniel's chest, threatening to consume him. Granddad had never once given him reason to doubt, but the evidence lay under Daniel's feet.

He steered for the bay, entering the gentler waters of the harbor, the cutter growing steadily closer. He sucked in a deep breath and cut the engine. As the boat drifted, Daniel stepped from the wheelhouse, his gaze skirting the harbor. The sun sat perched atop the foothills, sending its radiance over the town he'd spent so many years avoiding. Daniel's shoulders sagged, a numbing cold creeping through his body. He'd arrived in Port Angeles with every intent of returning to Seattle. Now the idea settled in his gut like a stone.

The ship finished its approach, crew at the ready. Three sheriff's deputies stood ready, tommy guns at attention.

Daniel lifted his hands, his chest squeezing until he could scarcely take a breath. "I'm unarmed."

A familiar figure joined the others on the deck, equipped with a handgun and a self-satisfied smile. "Daniel Shepherd, fancy meeting you out here." Samuel Brown shoved back his hat until Daniel could see his glittering cat-like eyes. "And to think, Laurie Burke *assured* me you weren't a rumrunner. She does seem to have a blind spot when it comes to you."

Daniel kept his hands in the air, his eyes trained on the deputies and their rifles.

As the ship pulled alongside, Brown and the deputies boarded, faces grim. Samuel gestured to the men with the barrel of his gun. "Go take a look below."

Daniel scowled as the men went down the ladder. "Why bother? You think you already know what's down there."

Samuel smirked. "Maybe I just wanted a minute alone with my suspect. Give you a chance to plead for mercy."

Daniel gritted his teeth. "Unlikely."

Brown pressed the gun against the Daniel's side. "Laurie Burke showed up at my house today. Such a pleasant evening . . . I like to hear women beg, don't you, Shepherd?"

Daniel squeezed his fingers into a fist. "I think you'd better watch what you say."

"Unfortunately, that's all she would do. Too bad. You might have gotten a pass otherwise." He shrugged. "But probably not."

"Laurie would never be interested in a degenerate slimesucker like you," Daniel growled.

Brown's arm shot upward, striking Daniel in the face with the barrel of the gun.

Daniel staggered backward, instinctively grabbing for the agent's arm. An ear-splitting pop sounded in his ear as searing pain tore through his shoulder. Daniel crashed against the rail, sliding onto the deck.

Brown stood over him, a grin snaking its way across his face. "Attacking a federal agent? Not a smart move."

⌐━━╍○

Laurie pulled herself from the water, teeth chattering so hard her jaw ached. Wrapping her arms around her body, she stumbled across the rocks, traversing the spit on rubbery legs. Topping the berm, she scanned the harbor.

The Coast Guard vessel bobbed alongside Daniel's boat, men with guns roaming the decks. One individual stood out from the others, the familiar gray fedora sending a shudder through Laurie's body.

Tears stung her eyes as she stumbled down the spit and straight into the arms of two fishermen.

⚓

"Agent Brown, I think you ought to see this." The deputy's voice wafted up from the hatch.

Daniel lay still, his hand clamped against the oozing wound in his shoulder. Fingers of pain spread through his arms and chest until even drawing a full breath became a challenge.

A calculating smile spread across Brown's face as the uniformed man began hoisting crates onto the deck. "Not a rumrunner, eh? I suppose you're going to claim that those bottles don't belong to you. Maybe they just found their way into your hold by accident."

Daniel gripped his shoulder, laying his head on the wet boards. *What will this do to Laurie?*

"Talk to me, Shepherd. Who's the brains of this operation, because it obviously isn't you?" Samuel chuckled as he crouched down beside him. "My colleagues at Freshwater Cove said the boat there came in clean. What do you know about that? Are you working with those hooligans?"

"No." Daniel's thoughts jumbled, images of his grandfather, Laurie, and Johnny swimming in the foggy haze of his mind. He struggled up to a sitting position, wiping the sweat from his face with his forearm. "No, I work alone. I've been bringing whiskey into Port Angeles for months—ever since I arrived here. I'm the one you want."

Brown raised his gun, pointing it at Daniel's face. "And that's exactly what I had hoped you would say."

⊙━━◆━━⊙

Laurie huddled in a blanket, in front of Amelia's fireplace. "I don't understand it. Why would they arrest Daniel? We threw the liquor overboard."

Amelia poured a second steaming mug of tea and forced it into Laurie's hand.

Johnny shook his head. "Mr. Simon from the grocery store said Brown found cases of liquor on board. He saw them unloading the crates onto the dock."

"I'm telling you—we threw them over the side." Laurie shivered, tea sloshing onto her fingertips.

Johnny sat down in the rocking chair, kicking his lanky legs out in front of him. "It couldn't have been our stuff, anyhow. We always dump the boxes—we wrap the bottles in newspaper and stick them in bags."

Amelia stood over her friend and gestured to Laurie's cup. "Drink!" She turned to Johnny. "Could Daniel be running booze, too?"

"No way." Johnny bounced his knee, the corners of his mouth pulling toward his chin. "But . . . " He chewed on his lower lip. "The boat belongs to his grandfather."

Laurie stopped mid-sip, the hot liquid scalding down her tongue as his words took hold. "Mr. Larson? Do you think they could be his?"

"I suppose, but it doesn't seem likely." Johnny situated another log on the fire. "Likely or no, it sounds like Daniel is in a boat-load of trouble."

⊙━━◆━━⊙

The cot squeaked as Daniel collapsed across it, his shoulder bandaged and throbbing. The day dragged at him like an anchor. Sitting in jail was the least of his troubles. He laid his head back and covered his face with his good arm, trying not to think about Laurie.

Brown stood outside the bars as the metal door slid shut. He hooked his thumbs in the pockets of his pinstriped trousers. "Won't Laurie Burke be pleased? She saved her brother and freed herself of a villainous wretch, all in one fell swoop. I guess maybe she is worthy of my affections after all."

Daniel mentally recited the periodic table to keep himself from rising to Brown's taunts, but he doubted the chemical reaction churning in his gut would be contained for long.

"In fact, I think I'll go over and see her. Rumor has it she took an early swim in the harbor this morning. Seems like an odd choice of activities. Maybe I'll ask her about it over dinner."

Daniel tried to struggle upright but slumped back against the bed, his stomach threatening to turn against him as well. He dug his fingers into the thin mattress. He hadn't stepped in Brown's trap; he'd jumped in with both feet. "Leave her out of this. I told you, I work alone. I'm the one you want."

Brown laughed, the sound echoing through the cellblock. "Oh, Daniel, that's rich. Haven't you figured it out yet?" He lowered his voice until it seemed to float like a dark fog through the room. "*She's* the one I want."

⚓

Laurie tucked the ends of her hair under her cloche as she followed Johnny into the drugstore. Her heart pounded so loud, it threatened to draw the attention of the customers. Marcie buzzed around the soda fountain likely filling orders for both drinks and gossip.

Laurie scanned the store for Mr. Larson. She caught Marcie scampering between the coffeepot and the icebox. "Where is Mr. Larson? We need to speak to him."

Marcie looked up, eyes red and teary. "Oh, Laurie. I wish I knew. I have no idea what's going on. And what I do know, I don't understand."

Laurie touched her brother's arm. "Maybe he's gone to see Daniel."

Johnny's brows furrowed. "Maybe he's skipped town."

Laurie pulled off her hat and darted a quick glance at Marcie. The girl balanced a soda in each hand, hurrying to the far end of the marble counter.

Laurie leaned close to her brother's ear. "Follow me."

She ducked behind the pharmacy counter and through the back storeroom, Johnny on her heels. Laurie tiptoed partway down the stairs to the cellar, her heart sinking at the inky blackness. "He's not here."

Johnny gripped the stair rail. "Let's try Daniel's apartment." He continued out the back door into the alley, climbing the steps to the upper-story apartments.

Laurie rushed after him, stopping on the landing. The door to Daniel's apartment stood ajar.

Mr. Larson glanced up from Daniel's sofa. Craggy lines crossed his face, his hair sticking out from under his cap, rumpled and spiky. "Thank God, it's you, Laurie. You've got to tell me what's happening. Marty—Sheriff Martinson—says that Daniel's been arrested." The old man pressed his hand to his forehead as he spoke. "He said the boat was full of booze and Daniel attacked the federal agent. Do you know anything about this?"

Laurie swallowed against the lump growing in her throat. "I was on the boat with him, Mr. Larson. He wasn't hauling whiskey—" She caught herself, casting an anxious glance at

Johnny. "Well, it's a long story. But he didn't know about those crates, I'm sure of it." She shoved her hands deep in her coat pockets. "Mr. Larson, you need to tell me the truth—are *you* running liquor?"

His jaw dropped. "You can't be serious. I haven't taken that boat out in over a year. The only time it's been out was when Daniel and Johnny went fishing a few months back." He glared at Johnny. "I could be asking you the same question, young man. I heard some interesting rumors about you this morning, too. And I know you're the one who blackened my grandson's eye."

A ripple of surprise shot through Laurie.

Johnny held up his hands. "I didn't put the whiskey on that boat." He pulled off his cap and ran his hand through his hair. "Well, like Laurie said, not *that* whiskey."

Mr. Larson's mouth pinched. "I think you two had better start at the beginning."

The three of them moved to Daniel's table by the front window and Laurie and Johnny filled Mr. Larson in on the night's activities. As they came to a close, Daniel's grandfather stroked his gray moustache in stunned silence.

Laurie sat on her hands to keep herself from picking at her fingernails. "So, you can see why we thought the whiskey might be yours."

Mr. Larson shook his head, a ragged sigh escaping his lips. "If it wasn't mine and it wasn't Daniel's—who in blazes put it there?"

Laurie paced to the window, staring out across the downtown streets and to the water beyond. "And why was Samuel on the Coast Guard ship instead of waiting at Freshwater Bay like he'd planned?"

Johnny sat up. "When we rowed up to the beach, Jerry said something about Brown having bigger fish to fry."

Laurie turned and faced him, a tremor running through her heart. "Bigger fish—like Daniel?"

⌐━━━✦━━━⌐

Laurie perched on the wooden chair, staring across Sherriff Martinson's large desk.

"Miles, your grandson is a fool." Sheriff Martinson leaned back in his swivel chair, kicking one foot up on his desk.

Mr. Larson paced the floor, running his hand across his whiskery chin. "It's a misunderstanding. He must have thought the booze was mine, Marty. He's not involved."

"I'm sorry, but that just isn't good enough. The first time I sympathized. Twice?" Martinson shook his head.

Laurie clutched her pocketbook. "Samuel Brown arranged this in some way. He's been aiming for Daniel since the beginning. I wouldn't put it past him to plant that whiskey as a way of framing him."

Martinson frowned. "Those are pretty big accusations, Miss Burke."

Daniel's grandfather laid his hands on the table, palms up. "Marty, you know I wouldn't waste your time if we weren't serious."

"Miles, I'd like to help you—that Brown is a cad. But Daniel signed a written confession. My hands are tied."

Laurie shifted in her chair. "What would it take to untie them?"

Martinson's brows arched. "I don't work that way."

"No, I don't mean . . ." She shook her head. "I mean, what if Brown confessed to planting the evidence?"

"Well, obviously, that would change things. But that hardly seems likely, does it?"

A rush of cold swept over Laurie, almost as if she had plunged back into the icy water of the Strait. Could she finagle a confession from Samuel?

She clamped her fingers on the edge of the desk and stood. "If that's what it will take—I will get it."

51

THE LATE AFTERNOON SUN GLINTED THROUGH SAMUEL BROWN'S OFFICE window, spilling across his littered desk. Laurie clutched her pocketbook, forcing her hands to remain still. "I can't believe this. Daniel really is a rumrunner?"

Samuel leaned back in his seat, balancing on its two spindly wooden legs. Shirtsleeves rolled up to the elbows and vest hanging unbuttoned, the agent twisted a fountain pen between his fingers. "It's my duty to get reprobates like Shepherd off the street. I'm just sorry you had to get mixed up with him. I tried to warn you."

The handgun resting on the desk turned Laurie's stomach. In the hours since Daniel's arrest, she'd heard stories of Daniel's so-called attack on Brown and how the agent had subdued him. She sidled closer, laying her pocketbook next to the weapon. Laurie hooked a finger through her long jet bead necklace and twisted it. "So, you suspected Daniel all along. This never was about Johnny, was it?"

Samuel set his chair down on all four legs and stood. He gathered the stacks of papers on his desk and shuffled them into a folder. "With the information I gathered from the pharmacy records, and the convenient capture of his cargo, we'll see him behind bars for quite some time."

Laurie took off her cloche hat and placed it next to her pocketbook. "What about the rumrunners at Freshwater Bay?"

He laughed, a deep mocking sound. "Small-timers. I knew a handful of them. I figured you'd be *appreciative* if we let them off the hook." The corner of his mouth lifted.

Her skin crawled. Some of the men were on the take—maybe even Big Jerry, himself. She forced a smile. "You've no idea how grateful I am." She stripped off her gloves and dropped them next to the other items.

Daniel had said that cash was one language Samuel Brown understood. Fortunately, she spoke the other language fluently. Laurie perched on the corner of the desk, crossing her knees.

Samuel took the bait, dropping the folder into a packing crate and stepping closer, his leg brushing up against hers. The corners of his lips inched upward. "That's my girl."

Laurie pressed a palm against her stomach to quell its flutters. "I owe you a lot, Samuel. You protected both my brother . . ."—she stretched out her hand and fingered the silver buttons on his vest—" . . . And me. It looks like I misjudged you." She tipped her head to the side and looked up from under her lashes. "I had no idea Daniel was a common criminal."

He captured her hand and twined his fingers with hers. "I told you the kind of man he was."

Heart pounding, Laurie lowered her voice, summoning the sugary-sweet voice she used at work. "You said he was a drunkard. And that he assaulted some poor woman in Seattle. It all sounded like so long ago. But rumrunning—right here under our noses?"

"You should be glad that I saved you from him. Men like that don't change overnight—no matter what kind of story he told you." He smiled, as if their last altercation was forgotten.

"But Mr. Larson's boat rarely leaves the dock." She leaned forward, tightening her grip on Samuel's hand. "It's never really been to Canada, has it?"

Furrows appeared in his brow, but he inched closer, wrapping his hand around her back. "I don't give away my secrets that easily, no matter what kind of games you're playing."

She sighed and released his hand. "That's too bad. I thought maybe I could help you with more of your busts. I love the excitement." She glanced up at him and shrugged. "I imagine with my connections at the exchange, I could probably locate every still and speakeasy in the county. People talk, you know." Laurie pushed away his hand, walking across the room to stand behind his empty desk chair. Placing her hands on its high back, she gazed at him, breathing a silent prayer. "But since you don't trust me—what's the use?"

Samuel cocked his head and reached down to button his vest. "You'd do that?"

"I want to clean up this town. For my father's sake." She sat down in Samuel's chair. "I didn't have much confidence in your abilities before. I had no idea the lengths to which you would go to get your man."

His lips turned upward. "Or my woman."

Laurie's throat tightened. "But I want to know how you got Daniel to confess. How'd you get the booze on his boat?"

Samuel sat directly in front of her, on the edge of the desk, one foot propped on her seat. "Someone has to look out for women like you, Laurie."

Her heart pounding, Laurie reached a hand out to touch his leg. "So, where did you get the liquor?"

He smiled. "Simple enough. I just pulled in a favor from my boss from Seattle."

She frowned. "Your boss with the Treasury Department?"

"Well, he's pretty useless, actually." Samuel chuckled. "I'm talking about someone else, Sunshine." He lifted his chin, puffing out his chest. "Your brother's bootlegging connections are small-time thugs. I'm connected with one of the biggest rumrunners in the Northwest—a former police officer from Seattle."

A wave of confusion descended on Laurie. Her mouth grew dry as her façade dropped away. She yanked her hand back. "You—you work for a rumrunner? But, you're—"

"Don't be so naive, Laurie. Government men make squat." Samuel chuckled. He took her hands, pulling until she rose to her feet and closed the space between them. "There's much more cash on the other side of the fence. Besides, this way, I get the best of both worlds."

"But you arrest rumrunners."

"Small-time players, troublesome middle-men, ones who refuse to play by our rules. I know which side my bread is buttered on." He placed both hands behind the small of her back

A noise at the door made Samuel turn.

Sheriff Martinson loomed in the doorway. "Apparently your bread is buttered on both sides, Brown."

"Sheriff"—Samuel's face flushed—"Let me explain—"

"I think I've heard enough." The sheriff stepped into the room, flanked by Johnny and several deputies.

Samuel's attention darted from the sheriff to the gun lying on the desk.

Laurie twisted in his grasp, thrusting her pocketbook across the desk and knocking the gun to the floor.

Johnny lunged forward, scooped it up, and pointed it at Samuel. "Get out of there, Laurie," he ordered.

Samuel kept his arm firm on her waist. "This is all a misunderstanding, Sheriff—a story to impress the lady. You know me."

"Yeah, I do. That's the problem." Martinson waved the barrel of his gun. "Let her go."

Samuel eyed her as he removed his hands. "You planned this." His lip curled back from his teeth.

Laurie lifted her chin. "Thanks for your help. Now that we know who the real criminals are, maybe we can clean up this town."

52

Daniel lay on the narrow cot, staring at the ceiling. In his mind he saw the ferric acid solution cascading down the side of the show globe, piercing the layers of beautiful color, and poisoning everything in its path.

He'd been a fool for believing he could start a new life, free from scandal. He deserved this disgrace, but he should have borne it alone.

A rattle at the door piqued his curiosity and Daniel turned his head to see who had entered the cellblock.

Laurie walked down the aisle between the cells, a guard at her back.

He struggled up to a seated position. "Laurie, you shouldn't be here."

"I know," she smiled as she approached the bars. Her face creased as she gazed at the bandages binding his shoulder and arm. She turned her eyes back to his face. "I'd hate to ruin my reputation.

Pushing away the pain, Daniel struggled to his feet, stomach lurching in protest. He walked a few paces and leaned against the bars separating them. "I can explain."

"Samuel's done all the explaining for you."

His stomach twisted. "I'm sure he has."

The guard spoke from the doorway. "We have the release papers, whenever you're ready, Miss Burke."

Laurie squeezed his hand and lifted an eyebrow. "I don't know . . . are you ready?"

Daniel's thoughts scattered. "What?"

"You're not listening. Samuel explained everything. The federal judge has decided to drop your case."

Daniel jerked his head back, sending a jab of pain through his shoulder. "Samuel—the sheriff—but, I confessed. What does a man have to do to get booked around here?"

Laurie laughed, her face a shining beacon in the dim cell. "They're booking Samuel in your place. And I think I'd better run you by the hospital. You seem a little confused. Doctor Pierce is going to want to take a look at that shoulder, maybe give you something for the pain."

Her laugh blew the fog from his mind like a fresh breeze. His pulse quickened. "I know what he usually prescribes for pain. I think I'll pass." Daniel reached out his good arm and gripped one of the bars in disbelief as the guard slid the door open. "I don't know how you did this, Laurie—but thank you."

When she stepped into the cell, Daniel threw his arm around her back and pulled her close. "I figured I'd lost your trust for good."

"Well, I'm not happy about you pushing me overboard, but—as for trust—I've learned a thing or two about that in the past few days." She ran a hand up his back. "There's only one who deserves my trust. I'm going to choose to trust *Him*. I'm choosing to *love* you."

A tremor burst through him, starting in his gut and moving out to his arms and legs. He gripped her even tighter to his chest, the motion making his shoulder throb. "I don't deserve that," he whispered.

"No, you don't. But neither do I."

The imposing stone front on the Port Townsend hospital cast a shadow across the road. Laurie squeezed her father's hand. "Thank you, Dad."

"I should have done this years ago." His face wrinkled. "You sure they can help someone like me?"

Daniel stood to the side, his cap pushed back from his forehead as he gazed up at the large building. "They can give you the tools to help yourself, as long as you're committed."

Dad huffed. "I got every reason to make it work—I want to walk my daughter down the aisle."

Laurie's throat swelled. She lowered her face and burrowed it against his shoulder, like a child.

"Laurie, there's a box in my bedroom closet—it's your mother's things. There's some jewelry in there."

"I know." Laurie squeezed his arm. "I've seen it."

"Well, I already gave your Mama's ring to your brother, but there may be some other things you'll want to keep." Dad cleared his throat, pulling a large, white handkerchief from his pocket and swiping it across his nose. "What you don't want, maybe you can sell . . . help pay the bills until I can work again. I don't want your brother getting any more fool ideas."

Laurie nodded, blinking back tears.

Her father patted her hand. He took a deep breath, hitched up his trousers, and walked through the doors without a backward glance.

Laurie shivered, even as the warm spring breeze sent clusters of white cherry blossoms dancing in the trees. "I hope they can help him."

Daniel stroked her back. "They can't do it for him, but it's good to have a guide. He's got a difficult road ahead."

She turned and looked into Daniel's face, warmed by his presence. "Thank you for encouraging him."

"I've been there. I know what he's going through." He glanced back at the doors. "I just pray I never have to go through it again."

She took Daniel's hand and squeezed it. "It's a long drive back to Port Angeles. Do you think we'll make it before dark?"

He opened the car door and watched her step in. "Assuming we don't have any more engine trouble, we should." Daniel slid behind the wheel. "But we could take our time."

"We could stop at the bluff, for old times' sake."

A playful smile curled around his mouth. "Well, we better get there before dark, then. Someone might mistake me for a rumrunner, otherwise."

She wove her fingers under his arm and scooted close to him on the seat. "We wouldn't want to give anyone the wrong idea."

⁘

Laurie took in a quick breath when she spotted her father's Ford parked at Crescent Beach. "What's that doing here?"

"You'll see." He guided the Buick in beside it.

Amelia bounced out of the black Model T. "I received a note from Johnny saying to take the car and meet him here. Do you know what's going on?"

Laurie shot a quizzical glance at Daniel. "I don't have a clue."

"Come along, ladies, we mustn't be late." He chuckled, stepping between them and offering his arms.

Laurie slipped her hand through his elbow and peered around him at her friend. Amelia's brows drew together, lips puckered as if solving a puzzle.

Daniel escorted them down to the sand where a large picnic basket rested on a red-and-white-checkered cloth.

Laurie smiled, squeezing Daniel's arm. "You planned all this?"

"I had some help."

Amelia glanced around the empty beach. "Isn't Johnny coming, too?"

"In time." He smiled and gestured for them to sit.

Laurie sat on the cloth, tucking her feet under her skirt. Amelia plopped beside her. Daniel opened the basket and retrieved a jar full of pink lemonade, pouring glasses for each of them. They sat back and enjoyed the early stages of sunset, watching as gulls swooped low over the waves.

In time, a dot on the horizon expanded and took the shape of a boat.

Amelia sat up on her knees, gripping her pink felt hat with one hand. "There's Johnny!" She jumped to her feet and rushed to the water's edge. After a moment's hesitation, she scurried back, stripped off her shoes and stockings, and raced toward the water like a child at play.

Laurie grasped Daniel's hand. "This is so sweet."

He planted a kiss on her cheek. "Just wait."

Johnny pulled against the oars until the boat surged into the surf. He reached out his hands for Amelia and she clambered aboard, legs dripping.

Laurie jumped to her feet and tugged Daniel toward the wet sand for a closer view. She couldn't hear her brother's words, but when Johnny pulled their mother's ring from his jacket pocket, her heart leaped.

Amelia flung herself into Johnny's arms, tears glistening on her cheeks.

Laurie grinned. "It's about time Johnny—" Her throat closed as she spotted the silver ring resting on Daniel's palm.

The small sapphire, nestled in a delicate filigree setting, sparkled in the setting sun.

He winked at her, the dimple in his cheek showing. "Yes, I do think it's about time. And I'd love to see this one on your hand. He lifted the ring, holding it between finger and thumb. "Blue—like the Straits on a warm summer day."

Her hand shook as he slipped the ring on her finger. "Daniel Shepherd, I knew you were going to be trouble the minute I laid eyes on you."

Daniel wrapped his arms around her waist.

She laid her head on his shoulder as she watched Johnny carry Amelia across the surf and set her down on the sand. "There's so much to celebrate, it seems like we should have champagne, but in light of recent events—I'm rather glad we don't."

Daniel leaned over and kissed her cheek, "I brought something I thought might be more appropriate."

She turned to face him, hoping the next would land on her lips. "What is that?"

He gave her a soft kiss, leaning down to whisper in her ear. "Oysters."

"You're not serious." She wrinkled her nose.

Daniel laughed, lifting his head. "No, I'm not. How about cake?"

Laurie's chest expanded as if her heart didn't have enough space to contain the joy. She headed back to the picnic blanket, Daniel at her side. She couldn't resist glancing up to the bluff where they had met.

She squeezed his hand. "I think that's absolutely perfect."

Discussion Questions

1. Which characters were your favorites? Did you identify with their struggles? Why or why not?

2. Though Amelia and Laurie joke about listing men based on their looks, Laurie's top priority in romance is finding a man she can trust. What traits top (or topped) your list?

3. Ray Burke is a man broken by grief, war, and addiction. Did you feel sympathy or anger toward him? Did that change throughout the story? What must he do to break the hold alcoholism has on his life?

4. Laurie tells Daniel she loved him from practically the moment they met. Have you ever experienced love at first sight? Do you believe it exists? Why or why not?

5. Daniel hides his past from Laurie, afraid she won't love him if she knows the truth. Have you ever hidden parts of yourself from someone you cared about? Is there one person who knows all of your deep secrets and what led you to trust that person?

6. Laurie says Amelia is the one constant in her life, and yet Laurie still kept secrets from her. Do you have a friend who has been present for all your highs and lows and loved you anyway? It might be the same person from question five, or it

might not. If it's not the same, what makes these two individuals different?

7. Laurie makes several mistaken assumptions about people in the story. Explain a time when you made a snap judgment about someone only to discover you were wrong.

8. Daniel's proposal to Laurie is interrupted when they are forced to flee from the Coast Guard. If you are married, was your proposal a magical moment, or were there some bumps in the road? If you're single, how do you imagine that moment?

9. Daniel keeps a coin in his pocket as a reminder of both his temperance vows and of how easily he can fail without God's help. Do you have any visible reminders of God's work in your life?

10. "In his mind [Daniel] saw the ferric acid solution cascading down the side of the show globe, piercing the layers of beautiful color, and poisoning everything in its path." Think about the imagery in this scene. What does it represent? Has there been a time when you've made a bad choice and it rippled through your life with unexpected consequences?

11. In the end, Laurie chooses to place her trust in God instead of any man. She also chooses to love Daniel. Do you think Laurie made the right choice in the end? Why or why not?

12. Can you separate love and trust? Should you? What are some cases when this would be the wrong decision?

13. Proverbs 3:5-6 reads, "Trust in the LORD with all thine heart; and lead not unto thine own understanding. In all thy ways acknowledge him, and he shall direct thy paths." Think back to each of the characters. How might their stories have been different if they had trusted God to direct their steps? How would your life story change if you remembered to put your trust in God alone?

14. Does trusting in God mean your path will be easy? What's the difference between a straight path and an easy one?

Interview with Karen Barnett

What's the story behind the story? Where did you get the idea for *Mistaken*?

Mistaken was inspired by an amusing anecdote from my family history. Like the character Johnny Burke, my grandfather lived in Port Angeles during Prohibition. In later life, he told stories of how he and a few coworkers from the paper mill would row across to Victoria to buy Canadian whiskey. On one return journey, they were confronted on the beach by G-men and had to flee for their lives. In later years he accused my grandmother of turning them in, but she refused to ever speak of it. We don't even know if the story was true or just family lore, but I thought it was an irresistible premise for a book. I wondered if my grandmother had actually reported them and why she might have chosen to do that. She became the inspiration behind Laurie's character. Everything else in the story is complete imagination.

What part of researching this time period was most interesting to you?

I did most of my study through books, history museums, and the Internet, but I also enjoyed touring the LeMay—America's Car Museum in Tacoma, Washington, which has an unbelievable collection of vintage automobiles, including dozens from the time period. A friend and I had a great time visiting Fairley's Pharmacy in Portland, Oregon, an authentic 1920's-era drugstore and soda fountain. A wonderful soda jerk named Mercedes taught us all about egg creams, phosphates, green rivers, and ice cream sodas. Research can be very fattening.

Your main character, Laurie, learns that first impressions are never what they seem. Can you tell about first impressions— when to trust them and when to question them?
Like Laurie, I often struggle with judging people too quickly. The difficulty with this is that most people have many different layers to their personalities and their characters. We all have layers and we also wear masks to hide our true identities. It takes time and honesty to get down to the heart of who we are.

How much of yourself do you put into your characters? How difficult is it to make historical characters come alive?
Laurie is very much like me: quiet, observant, private, and introspective. In many ways, Laurie is putting on an act so that no one knows the truth about her family. In my case, I often put on a mask of being outgoing and vivacious to conceal the insecure woman hiding within. I don't find it difficult to write historical characters because even though our situations and styles may differ from other times in history, I believe we still have many of the same needs and fears. Deep down, we long to be loved and accepted. We fear rejection and failure. And even more deeply, I think our human souls hunger for an intimate connection to God.

This is your debut novel. Tell us about how this book—and your career as an author—came about.
I've always been a voracious reader. The library is my happy place, and there's nothing I love better than perusing the stacks and finding new treasures. As a child, I dreamed about giving back to my library and filling their shelves with even more books. Over the years I started many stories but, like many aspiring writers, never seemed to finish one. After graduating from college, I spent a few years working as a park ranger before marrying and having a family. When my youngest child started school, I began writing in earnest. I met author Robin Jones Gunn at a Christian camp and she encouraged me to attend

the Mount Hermon Christian Writers Conference, held every year over Palm Sunday weekend near Santa Clara, California. The conference was a life changer for me and helped me turn my writing from a simple hobby to a career. I attended several conferences after that, learning as much as I could about the craft of writing and about the industry. I met my agent at Mount Hermon and my future editor at the Oregon Christian Writers Summer Conference.

What are you working on now?

I am currently writing a three-book series set in 1906 San Francisco, the first of which will be arriving in bookstores next spring. The main character, Abby Fischer, prays for a miracle for her dying sister but doesn't expect the answer to come in the form of the handsome Doctor Robert King. When Robert's innovative treatment fails, Abby's grief is surpassed only by the chaos of the San Francisco earthquake and fires. Will Abby finally find God—and love—in the ruins?

Where can readers find you online?

I love connecting with readers, and I know many people have their own fun Prohibition-era family legends. I'd love to hear them! I have a website located at www.KarenBarnettBooks.com or you can find me on various social media outlets:
Facebook: www.facebook.com/KarenBarnettAuthor
Twitter: https://twitter.com/KarenMBarnett
Pinterest: http://pinterest.com/karenbarnett/